Praise for Barbara Delinsky's

Not My Daughter

"A topical tale that resonates with timeless emotion."
—*People*

"Delinsky has a knack for exploring the battlefields of contemporary life. . . . *Not My Daughter* [is] an emotionally intelligent [book that] offers readers what they want—high drama and realism."   —*Kirkus Reviews*

"Delinsky proves once again a perceptive observer of family relationships. . . . A tautly emotional story about mothers and daughters."   —*The Boston Globe*

"Timely, fresh, and true-to-life. . . . Explores multiple layers of motherhood and tackles tough questions."
—*Publishers Weekly*

"An engaging writer who knows how to interweave several stories about complex relationships and keeps her books interesting to the end. Her special talent for description gives the reader almost visual references to the surroundings she creates."
—*Newark Star-Ledger*

"[She] may be as adept at chronicling contemporary life in New England as any writer this side of John Updike."
—*The Times Union* (Albany)

"Barbara Delinsky knows the human heart and its immense capacity to love and believe."

—*Observer-Reporter* (Washington, PA)

"Delinsky delves deeper into the human heart and spirit with each new novel."   —*The Cincinnati Enquirer*

"Delinsky uses nuance and detail to draw realistic characters and ensure that emotion is genuine."

—*The Providence Journal*

"Delinsky [is] out there with the Anita Shreves and Elizabeth Bergs, perpetually bestselling authors who wrestle with bigger themes."   —*Lexington Herald-Ledger*

"Delinsky treads the same domestic themes as fellow bestseller Jodi Picoult."   —*Entertainment Weekly*

BARBARA DELINSKY

Not My *Daughter*

Barbara Delinsky is a *New York Times* bestselling author with more than thirty million
copies of her books in print. She lives with her
family in New England.

www.barbaradelinsky.com

NOT *MY* DAUGHTER

NOT *MY* DAUGHTER

Barbara Delinsky

ANCHOR BOOKS

A Division of Random House, Inc.

New York

FIRST ANCHOR BOOKS EDITION, MAY 2011

The Library of Congress has cataloged the Doubleday edition as follows:
Delinsky, Barbara.
Not my daughter / Barbara Delinsky.—1st ed.
p. cm.
1. Mothers and daughters—Fiction. 2. Teenage pregnancy—Fiction.
I. Title.
PS3554.E4427 N68 2010
813'.54—dc22
2009031148

Anchor ISBN: 978-0-7679-2896-0

www.anchorbooks.com

Printed in the United States of America
10 9 8 7 6 5 4 3 2 1

To my readers, for their big hearts and their undying loyalty

NOT *MY* DAUGHTER

Chapter 1

SUSAN TATE NEVER SAW IT COMING. SHE ONLY KNEW that her daughter was different. The girl who had always been spontaneous and open had suddenly grown opaque.

Lily was seventeen. Maybe that said it. A senior in high school, she had a loaded course schedule, played field hockey and volleyball, and sang in an a cappella group. And, yes, Susan was spoiled by the close relationship she and Lily had always had. They were a family of two, fully comfortable with that and each other.

Inevitably, Lily had to test her wings. Susan knew that. But she also had a right to worry. Lily was the love of her life, the very best thing that had happened in all of her thirty-five years. As achievements in life went, being a good mother was the one she most prized.

That meant communicating, and with dinner too often interrupted by e-mail or texts, eating out was warranted. At a restaurant Susan would have Lily captive while they waited to order, waited for food, waited to pay—all quality time.

She suggested the Steak Place, definitely a splurge, but lined with quiet oak booths. Lily vetoed it in favor of Carlino's.

Carlino's wasn't even Susan's second choice. Oh, she liked the owners, the menu, and the art, all of which were authentically Tuscan. But the prices were so reasonable for large plates of food that the whole town went there. Susan wanted privacy and quiet; Carlino's was public and loud.

But she wanted to please Lily, so she gave in and, determined to be a good sport, smilingly hustled her daughter out of the November chill into a hive of warmth and sound. When they finally finished greeting friends and were seated, they shared hummus on toasted crostini, and though Lily only nibbled, she insisted it was good. More friends stopped by, and, in fairness, it wasn't only Lily's fault. As principal of the high school, Susan was well known in town. Another time, she would have enjoyed seeing everyone.

But she was on a mission this night. As soon as she was alone with Lily again, she leaned forward and quietly talked about her day at school. With next year's budget due by Thanksgiving and town resources stagnant, there were hard decisions to be made. Most staff issues were too sensitive to be shared with her seventeen-year-old daughter, but when it came to new course offerings and technology, the girl was a worthy sounding board.

Susan's motive actually went deeper, to the very heart of mothering. She believed that sharing adult issues encouraged Lily to think. She also believed that her daughter was insightful, and this night was no exception. Momentarily focused, Lily asked good questions.

No sooner had their entrées come, though—chicken with cannellini beans for Lily, salmon with artichokes for Susan— than a pair of Susan's teachers interrupted to say hello. As soon as they left, Susan asked Lily about the AP chem test she'd had that morning. Though Lily replied volubly, her answers were heavy on irrelevant facts, and her brightness seemed forced. She picked at her food, eating little.

More worried than ever, Susan searched her daughter's face. It was heart shaped, as sweet as always, and was framed by long, shiny sable hair. The hair was a gift from her father, while her eyes—Susan's eyes—were hazel and clear, her skin creamy and smooth.

She didn't look sick, Susan decided. Vulnerable, perhaps. Maybe haunted. But not sick.

Even when Lily crinkled her nose and complained about the restaurant's heavy garlic smell, Susan didn't guess. She was too busy assuring herself that those clear eyes ruled out drug use, and as for alcohol, she had never seen bottles, empty or otherwise, in Lily's room. She didn't actively search, as in checking behind clutter on the highest shelves. But when she returned clean laundry to drawers or hung jeans in the closet, she saw nothing amiss.

Alcohol wouldn't be a lure. Susan drank wine with friends, but rarely stocked up, so it wasn't like Lily had a bar to draw from. Same with prescription drugs, though Susan knew how easy it was for kids to get them online. Rarely did a month go by without a student apprehended for that.

"Mom?"

Susan blinked. "Yes, sweetheart?"

"Look who's distracted. What are you thinking about?"

"You. Are you feeling all right?"

There was a flash of annoyance. "You keep asking me that."

"Because I worry," Susan said and, reaching across, laced her fingers through Lily's. "You haven't been the same since summer. So here I am, loving you to bits, and because you won't say anything, I'm left to wonder whether it's just being seventeen and needing your own space. Do I crowd you?"

Lily sputtered. "No. You're the best mom that way."

"Is it school? You're stressed."

"Yes," the girl said, but her tone implied there was more, and her fingers held Susan's tightly.

"College apps?"

"I'm okay with those."

"Then calculus." The calc teacher was the toughest in the math department, and Susan had worried Lily would be intimidated. But what choice was there? Raymond Dunbar was thirty years Susan's senior and had vocally opposed her ascension to the principalship. If she asked him to ease up, he would accuse her of favoritism.

But Lily said, "Mr. Dunbar isn't so bad."

Susan jiggled Lily's fingers. "If I were to pinpoint it, I'd say the change came this past summer. I've been racking my brain, but from everything you told me, you loved your job. I know, I know, you were at the beach, but watching ten kids under the age of eight is hard, and summer families can be the worst."

Lily scooped back her hair. "I love kids. Besides, I was with Mary Kate, Abby, and Jess." The girls were her three best friends, and the daughters of Susan's best friends. All three girls were responsible. Abby occasionally lacked direction, like her mom, Pam, and Jessica had a touch of the rebel, though her mother, Sunny, did not. But Mary Kate was as steady as her mom, Kate, who was like a sister to Susan. With Mary Kate along, Lily couldn't go wrong.

Not that Lily wasn't steady herself, but Susan knew about peer pressure. If she had learned one thing as a teacher it was that the key to a child's success lay in no small part with the friends she kept.

"And nothing's up with them?" she asked.

Lily grew guarded. "Has Kate said anything?"

Susan gentled. "Nothing negative. She always asks about you, though. You're her sixth child."

"But has she said anything about Mary Kate? Is she worried about her like you're worried about me?"

Susan thought for a minute, then answered honestly. "She's more sad than worried. Mary Kate is her youngest. Kate feels like she's growing away from her, too. But Mary Kate isn't my concern. You are." A burst of laughter came from several tables down. Annoyed by the intrusion, Susan shot the group a glance. When she turned back, Lily's eyes held a frightened look.

Susan had seen that look a lot lately. It terrified her.

Desperate now, she held Lily's hand even tighter and, in a low, frantic voice, said, "What is *wrong*? I'm supposed to know what girls your age are feeling and thinking, but lately with you, I just don't. There are so many times when your mind is somewhere else—somewhere you won't allow me to be. Maybe that's the way it should be at your age," she acknowledged, "and it wouldn't bother me if you were happy, but you don't seem happy. You seem preoccupied. You seem *afraid*."

"I'm pregnant."

Susan gasped. Freeing her hand, she sat straighter. She waited for a teasing smile, but there was none. And of course not. Lily wouldn't joke about something like this.

Her thoughts raced. "But—but that's impossible. I mean, it's not *physically* impossible, but it wouldn't happen." When Lily said nothing, Susan pressed a hand to her chest and whispered, "Would it?"

"I am," Lily whispered back.

"What makes you think it?"

"Six home tests, all positive."

"You're late?"

"Not late. Missed. Three times."

"Three? Omigod, why didn't you *tell* me?" Susan cried, thinking of all the other things a missed period could mean. Being pregnant didn't make sense, not with Lily. But the child didn't lie. If she said she was pregnant, she believed it herself—not that it was true. "Home tests can be totally misleading."

"Nausea, tiredness, bloating?"

"I don't see bloating," Susan said defensively, because if her daughter was three months pregnant, she would have seen it.

"When was the last time you saw me naked?"

"In the hot tub at the spa," she replied without missing a beat.

"That was in June, Mom."

Susan did miss a beat then, but only one. "It must be something else. You don't even have a boyfriend." She caught her breath. "Do you?" Had she *really* missed something? "Who is he?"

"It doesn't matter."

"Doesn't matter? Lily, if you are—" She couldn't say the word aloud. The idea that her daughter was sexually active was totally new. Sure, she knew the statistics. How could she not, given her job? But this was her daughter, *her* daughter. They had agreed—Lily had *promised*—she would tell Susan if she wanted birth control. It was a conversation they'd had too many times to count. "Who is he?" she asked again.

Lily remained silent.

"But if he's involved—"

"I'm not telling him."

"Did he *force* you?"

"No," Lily replied. Her eyes were steady not with fear, now, but something Susan couldn't quite name. "It was the other way around," she said. "I seduced him."

Susan sat back. If she didn't know better, she might have

said Lily looked excited. And suddenly nothing about the discussion was right—not the subject, not that look, certainly not the place. Setting her napkin beside the plate, she gestured for the server. The son of a local family, and once a student of Susan's, he hurried over.

"You haven't finished, Ms. Tate. Is something wrong?"

Something wrong? "No, uh, just time."

"Should I box this up?"

"No, Aidan. If you could just bring the bill."

He had barely left when Lily leaned forward. "I knew you'd be upset. That's why I haven't told you."

"How long were you planning to *wait*?"

"Just a little longer—maybe 'til the end of my first trimester."

"Lily, I'm your *mother*."

"But this is *my* baby," the girl said softly, "so I get to make the decisions, and I wasn't ready to tell you, not even tonight, which is why I chose this place. But even here, it's like you can see inside me."

Susan was beyond hurt. Getting pregnant was everything she had taught Lily not to do. She sat back, let out a breath. "I can't grasp this. Are you *sure*?" Lily's body didn't look different, but what could be seen when she wore the same layered tops that her friends did, and the days when Susan bathed her each night were long gone. "*Three* missed periods?" she whispered. "Then this happened . . . ?"

"Eleven weeks ago."

Susan was beside herself. "When did you do the tests?"

"As soon as I missed my first period."

And not a word spoken? It was definitely a statement, but of what? Defiance? Independence? *Stupidity?* Lily might be gentle, often vulnerable—but she also had a stubborn streak. When she started something, she rarely backed down. Properly channeled, that was a positive thing, like when she set out to win top prize at the science fair, which she did, but only after three false starts. Or when she set out to sing in the girls a cappella group, didn't make the cut as a freshman and worked her tail off that year and the next as the group's manager, until she finally landed a spot.

But this was different. Stubbornness was not a reason for silence when it came to pregnancy, certainly not when the prospective mother was seventeen.

Unable to order her thoughts, Susan grasped at loose threads. "Do the others know?" It went without saying that she meant Mary Kate, Abby, and Jess.

"Yes, but no moms."

"And none of the girls told me?" More hurt there. "But I see them all the time!"

"I swore them to silence."

"Does your dad know?"

Lily looked appalled. "I would never tell him before I told you."

"Well, *that's* something."

"I love babies, Mom," the girl said, excited again.

"And that makes this *okay*?" Susan asked hysterically, but stopped when the server returned. Glancing at the bill, she put down what might have been an appropriate amount, then pushed her chair back. The air in the room was suddenly too warm, the smells too pungent even for someone who wasn't pregnant. As she walked to the door with Lily behind, she imagined that every eye in the room watched. It was a flash from her own past, followed by the echo of her mother's words. *You've shamed us, Susan. What were you thinking?*

Times had changed. Single mothers were commonplace now. The issue for Susan wasn't shame, but the dreams she had for her daughter. Dreams couldn't hold up against a baby. A baby changed *everything*.

The car offered privacy but little comfort, shutting Susan and Lily in too small a space with a huge chasm between them. Fighting panic as the minutes passed without a retraction, Susan fumbled for her keys and started the engine.

Carlino's was in the center of town. Heading out, she passed the bookstore, the drugstore, two Realtors, and a bank. Passing Perry & Cass took longer. Even in the fifteen years Susan had lived in Zaganack, the store had expanded. It occupied three blocks now, two-story buildings with signature crimson-and-cream awnings, and that didn't count the mail-order department and online call center two streets back, the manufacturing complex a mile down the road, or the shipping department farther out in the country.

Zaganack *was* Perry & Cass. Fully three-fourths of the townsfolk worked for the retail icon. The rest provided services for those who did, as well as for the tens of thousands of visitors who came each year to shop.

But Perry & Cass wasn't what had drawn Susan here when she'd been looking for a place to raise her child. Having come from the Great Plains, she had wanted something coastal and green. Zaganack overlooked Maine's Casco Bay, and, with its hemlocks and pines, was green year-round. Its shore was a breathtaking tumble of sea-bound granite; its harbor, home port to a handful of local fishermen, was quaint. With a population that ebbed and flowed, swelling from 18,000 to 28,000 in summer, the town was small enough to be a community, yet large enough to allow for heterogeneity.

Besides, Susan loved the name Zaganack. A derivative of the Penobscot tongue, it was loosely interpreted to mean "people from the place of eternal spring," and though local lore cited Native Americans' reference to the relatively mild weather of coastal towns, Susan took a broader view. Spring meant new beginnings. She had found one in Zaganack.

And now this? History repeating itself?

Unable to think, she drove in silence. Leaving the main road, she passed the grand brick homes of Perrys and Casses, followed by the elegant, if smaller, ones of the families' younger generations. The homes of locals fanned out from there, Colonials yielding to Victorians and, in turn, to homes that were simpler in design and built closer together.

Susan lived in one of the latter. It was a small frame house with six rooms equally spaced over two floors and an open attic on the third. By night, with its tiny front yard and ribbon of driveway, it looked like the rest. By day, painted a cerulean blue, with sea green shutters and an attic gable trimmed in teal, it stood out.

Color was Susan's thing. Growing up, she had loved reds, though her mother said they clashed with her freckles. *Dark green would be better,* Ellen Tate advised. *Or brown.* But Susan's hair was the color of dark sand, so she still adored the pepper of red, orange, and pink.

Then came Lily, and Susan's mother latched onto those colors. *You have a fuchsia heart,* she charged despairingly when she learned of the pregnancy, and though Susan discarded most else of what her mother had said, those words survived. Loath to attract attention, she had worn black through much of those nine months, then a lighter but still-bland beige after Lily was born. Even when she started to teach, neutrals served her well, offsetting the freckles that made her look too young.

But a fuchsia heart doesn't die. It simply bides its time, taking a backseat to pragmatism while leaking helpless drops of color here and there. Hence teal gables, turquoise earrings, and chartreuse or saffron scarves. In the yarns she dyed as a hobby, the colors were even wilder.

Turning into her driveway, Susan parked and climbed from the car. Once up the side steps, she let herself into the kitchen. In the soft light coming from under the cherry cabinets for which she had painstakingly saved for three years and had largely installed herself, she looked back at Lily.

The girl was Susan's height, if slimmer and more fragile, but she stood her ground, hands tucked in her jacket pockets. Pregnant? Susan still didn't believe it was true. Yes, there was picky eating, moodiness, and the morning muzzies, all out of character and new in the last few months, but other ailments had similar symptoms. Like mono.

"It may be just a matter of taking antibiotics," she said sensibly.

Lily looked baffled. "Antibiotics?"

"If you have mono—"

"Mom, I'm *pregnant*. Six tests, all positive."

"Maybe you read them wrong."

"Mary Kate saw two of them and agreed."

"Mary Kate is no expert, either." Susan felt a stab. "How many times have I seen Mary Kate since then? Thirty? *Sixty?*"

"Don't be mad at Mary Kate. It wasn't her place to tell you."

"I am mad at Mary Kate. I'm closer to her than I am to the others, and this is your *health,* Lily. What if something else is going on with your body? Shouldn't Mary Kate be concerned about that?"

Lily pushed her fingers through her hair. "This is beyond bizarre. All this time I've been afraid to tell you because I didn't know how you'd react, but I never thought you wouldn't *believe* me."

Susan didn't want to argue. There was one way to find out

for sure. "Whatever it is, we'll deal. I'll call Dr. Brant first thing tomorrow. She'll squeeze you in."

NEVER A GOOD SLEEPER, SUSAN SPENT THE NIGHT running through all of the reasons why her daughter couldn't be pregnant. Most had to do with being responsible, because if Susan had taught Lily one thing, it was that.

Lily was responsible when it came to school. She studied hard and got good grades. She was responsible when it came to her friends, loyal to a fault. Hadn't she gone out on a limb to campaign for Abby, who had set her heart on being senior class president? When the girl lost the election, Lily had slept at her house for three straight nights.

Lily was responsible when it came to the car, rarely missing a curfew, leaving the gas tank empty, or being late when she had to pick up Susan.

Hardworking. Loyal. Dependable. Responsible. And . . . pregnant? Susan might have bought into it if Lily had a steady boyfriend. Accidents happened.

But there was no boyfriend, and no reason at all to believe that Lily would sleep with someone she barely knew. Was sweet Lily Tate—who wore little makeup, slept in flannel pajamas, and layered camis over camis to keep her tiny cleavage from view—even *capable* of seduction?

Susan thought not. It had to be something else, but the possibilities were frightening. By two in the morning, her imagination was so out of control that she gave up trying to sleep and, crossing the hall, quietly opened Lily's door. In the faint glow of a butterfly nightlight, Lily was a blip under the quilt, only the top of her head showing, dark hair splayed on the pillow. Her jeans and sweaters were on the cushioned chair, her Sherpa boots—one standing, one not—on the floor nearby.

Her dresser was strewn with hairbrushes and clips, beaded bracelets, a sock she was knitting. Her cell phone lay on the nightstand, along with several books and a half-full bottle of water.

In the faintest whisper, Susan called her name, but there was no response, no movement in this still life. *Girl with Butterfly Nightlight* she might have named it. Girl. So young. So vulnerable.

Heart catching, she carefully backed out, crept down the hall to the attic door, and quietly climbed the stairs. There, at an oak table in the small arc of a craft lamp, she turned to a fresh page of her notebook, opened a tin of pastels, and made her first bold stroke. A fuchsia heart? Definitely. If anything could distract her, it was this. She made another stroke, smudged the ends, added yellow to soften a green, then navy to deepen a red.

Typically, she produced her best work when she was stressed—pure sublimation—and this night was no exception. By the time she was done, she had five pages, each with a unique swath of anywhere from two to five hues, undulating from shade to shade. These would be the spring colorways for PC yarns. She even named them: March Madness, Vernal Tide, Spring Eclipse, Robin At Dawn, and, naturally, Creation.

The last was particularly vibrant. Violent? No, she decided. Well, maybe. But wasn't creation an explosive thing? Didn't creation have profound consequences? And what if Lily wasn't growing a child but something darker?

SUSAN RETURNED TO BED, BUT EACH TIME SHE DOZED, she woke up to new fears. By five in the morning, when she finally despaired of sleep and got up, she was convinced that her daughter had a uterine cyst that had been overlooked long enough to jeopardize her chances of ever having a baby. Either that or it was a tumor. Uterine cancer, warranting a hysterectomy, perhaps chemotherapy. Terrifying. No child, ever? *Tragic*.

Keeping her fears to herself, she got Lily up as usual, dropped her at Mary Kate's, and went on to school. The girls would follow later, but this morning, Susan had two early parent meetings, both difficult, before she appeared on the front steps to greet students. It wasn't until eight-thirty that she finally reached the doctor's office.

The only appointment she could get for Lily was in the late afternoon, which gave Susan the rest of the day to worry. That meant she answered e-mail with half a heart, was distracted during a teacher observation, and what little work she put into next year's budget, which was due to the superintendent by Thanksgiving, was a waste.

She could only think of one thing, and any way she looked at it, it wasn't good.

Chapter 2

THE DOCTOR CONFIRMED IT. LILY WAS DEFINITELY
pregnant. Learning that her daughter didn't have a fatal disease, Susan was actually relieved—but only briefly. The reality
of being pregnant at seventeen was something she knew all too
well.

Susan had become pregnant in high school herself. Richard
McKay was the son of her parents' best friends. That summer,
when he was fresh out of college with a journalism degree and
a job offer for fall that he couldn't refuse, something sparked
between them. *Pure lust,* her father decided. And the chem-
istry was certainly right. But Susan and Rick had spent too
many hours that summer only talking for it to be just sex.
They saw eye to eye on so many things, not the least being their
desire to leave Oklahoma, that when Rick dutifully offered to
marry Susan, she flat-out refused.

She never regretted her decision. To this day, she recalled
the look of palpable relief on his face when she had firmly
shaken her head. He had dreams; she admired them. Had

there been times when she missed having him there? Sure. But she couldn't compete with the excitement of his career, and refused to tie him down.

His success reinforced her conviction. Starting out, he had been the assistant to the assistant producer of a national news show. Currently, he was the star, following stories to the ends of the earth as one of the show's leading commentators. He had never married, had never had other children. Only after he became the face in front of the camera rather than the one behind was he able to send money for Lily's support, but his check arrived every month now without fail. He never missed a birthday, and had been known to surprise Lily by showing up for a field hockey tournament. He kept in close touch with her by phone, a good, if physically absent, father.

Rick had always trusted Susan. Rather than micromanage from afar, he left the day-to-day parenting to her. Now, under her watchful gaze, Lily was pregnant.

Stunned, Susan listened quietly while Lily answered the doctor's questions. Yes, she wanted the baby, and yes, she understood what that meant. No, she hadn't discussed it with her mother, because she would do this on her own if she had to. No, she did not want the father involved. No, she did not drink. Yes, she knew not to eat swordfish.

She had questions of her own—like whether she would be able to finish out the field hockey season (yes), whether winter volleyball was possible (maybe), and whether she could take Tylenol for a headache (only as directed)—and she sounded so like the mature, responsible, intelligent child Susan had raised that, if Susan hadn't been numb, she might have laughed.

Silent still when they left the doctor's office, she handed Lily the keys to the car. "I need to walk home." Lily protested, but she insisted, "You go on. I need the air."

It was true, though she did little productive thinking as she walked through the November chill. No longer numb, she was boiling mad. She knew it was wrong—definitely not the way a mother should feel and everything she had resented in her own mother—but how to get a grip?

The cold air helped. She was a little calmer as she neared the house. Then she saw Lily. The girl was sitting on the front steps, a knitted scarf wound around her neck, her quilted jacket—very Perry & Cass—pulled tight round her. When Susan approached, she sat straighter and said in a timid voice, "Don't be angry."

But Susan was. Furious, she stuck her hands in her pockets.

"Please, Mom?"

Susan took a deep breath. She looked off, past neighborhood houses, all the way on down the street until the cordon of old maples seemed to merge. "This isn't what I wanted for you," she finally managed to say.

"But I love children. I was *born* to have children."

Looking back, Susan pressed her aching heart. "I couldn't agree with you more. My problem's with the timing. You're seventeen. You're a senior in high school—and expecting a baby at the end of May, right before exams? Do you have any idea what being nine months pregnant is like? How are you going to study?"

"I'll already have been accepted into college."

"Well, that's another thing. How *can* you go to college? Dorm rooms don't have room for cribs."

"I'm going to Percy State."

"Oh, honey, you can do better."

"You went there, and look where you are."

"I *had* to go there. But times have changed. Getting a job is hard enough now, even with a degree from a top school."

"Exactly. So it won't matter. Anything is doable, Mom. Haven't you taught me that?"

"Sure. I just never thought it would apply to a baby."

Lily's eyes lit up. "But there *is* a baby," she cried, sounding so like a buoyant child that Susan could have wept. Lily didn't have a clue what being a mother entailed. Spending the summer as a mother's helper was a picnic compared to the day-in, day-out demands of motherhood.

"Oh, sweetheart," she said and, suddenly exhausted, sank down on the steps. "Forget doable. What about sensible? What about *responsible*? We've talked about birth control. You could have used it."

"You're missing the point, Mom," Lily said, moving close to hug Susan's arm. "I want this baby. I know I can be a good mother—even better than the moms we worked for this summer, and I have the best role model in you. You always said being a mother was wonderful. You said you loved me from the start. You said I was the best thing that ever happened to you."

Susan wasn't mollified. "I also said that being a single mom was hard and that I never wanted you to have to struggle the way I did. So— So think beyond college. You say you want to be a biologist, but that means grad school. If you want a good research position—"

"I want a baby."

"A baby isn't only for the summer, and it doesn't stay a baby for long. He or she walks and talks and becomes a real person. And what about the father then?"

"I told you. He doesn't know."

"He has a right to."

"Why? He had no say in this."

"And that's fair, Lily?" Susan asked. "What if the baby looks exactly like him? Don't you think people will talk?"

A hint of stubbornness crossed Lily's face. "I don't care if people talk."

"Maybe the father will. What if he comes up to you and asks why this child who was born nine months after the time you had sex has his hair and eyes? And what happens when your child wants to know about his father? You were asking by the time you were two. Some kids do still have daddies, y'know. So now it's your turn to be the mommy. What'll you say?"

Lily frowned. "I'll go there when I have to. Mom, you're making this harder than it needs to be. Right now, the baby's father does not have to know."

"But it's his baby, too," Susan argued. Desperate for someone to blame, she sorted through the possibilities. "Is it Evan?"

"I'm not telling who it is."

Susan wondered if Lily was stonewalling for a reason. "Was *he* the one who wanted the baby?"

Lily pulled her arm free. "Mom," she cried, hazel eyes flashing, "listen to me! He doesn't *know*. We never talked about a baby. He thought I was on the pill. I did this. Me."

Which, of course, was one of the things Susan found so hard to swallow. It was like a slap in the face, a repudiation of everything she had tried to teach her daughter.

Desperate to understand, she said, "Are you sure it wasn't an accident? I mean, it's okay if it was. Accidents happen." Lily shook her head. "You just decided you wanted a baby."

"I've always wanted a baby."

"A sibling," Susan said, because when she was little, Lily had begged for one.

"Now I'm old enough to have my own, and I know you might not have chosen to be pregnant seventeen years ago, but I did. It's my body, my life."

Susan had raised Lily to be independent and strong, but

cavalier? No. Especially not when there were realities to face. "Who'll pay the medical bills?"

"We have insurance."

"With premiums to which I contribute every month," Susan pointed out, "so the answer is me. I'll pay the medical bills. What about diapers? And formula?"

"I'll breast-feed."

"Which is wonderful if it works, but sometimes it doesn't, in which case you'll need formula. And what about solid food and clothes. And *equipment.* They won't let you leave the hospital without an approved car seat, and do you know what a good stroller costs? No, I don't still have your old one, because I sold it years ago to buy you a bike. And what about day care while you're finishing school? I'd love to stay home with the baby myself, but one of us has to work."

"Dad will help," Lily said in a small voice.

Yes. Rick would. But was Susan looking forward to asking? Absolutely not.

Lily's eyes filled with tears. "I really want this baby."

"You can *have* a baby, but there's a better time!" Susan cried.

"I am not having an abortion."

"No one's suggesting one."

"I already heard my baby's heartbeat. You should have listened to it, Mom. It was amazing."

Susan was having trouble accepting that her daughter was *pregnant,* much less that there was an actual baby alive inside.

"It has legs and elbows. It has ears, and this week it's developing vocal cords. I know all this, Mom. I'm doing my homework."

"Then I take it," Susan said in a voice she couldn't control, "that you read how pregnant teens are at greater risk for complications." It was partly her mother's voice. The rest was that of the failed educator whose *crusade* had been keeping young girls from doing what she had done. The educator had failed on her own doorstep.

"I stopped on the way home for the vitamins," Lily said meekly. "Do you think the baby's okay?"

As annoyed as she was—as *disappointed* as she was—a frightened Lily could always reach her. "Yes, it's okay," she said. "I was just making a point."

That easily reassured, Lily smiled. "Think I'll have a girl like you did?" She didn't seem to need an answer, which was good, since Susan didn't have one. "If it's a girl, she's already forming ovaries. And she's this big." She spread her thumb and forefinger several inches apart. "My baby can think. Its brain can give signals to its limbs to move. If I could put my finger exactly where it is, it would react to my touch. It's a real human being. There is no way I could have an abortion."

"Please, Lily. Have I asked you to get one?"

"No, but maybe when you start thinking about it, you will."

"Did I abort you?"

"No, but you're angry."

Susan shot a pleading glance at the near-naked tops of the trees. "Oh, Lily, I'm so many things besides angry that I can't begin to explain. We're at a good place now, but it hasn't come easy. I've had to work twice as hard as most mothers. You, of all people, should know that."

"Because I'm a good daughter? Does my being pregnant make me a bad one?"

"No, sweetheart. No." It had nothing to do with good and bad. Susan had argued this with her own mother.

"But you're disappointed."

Try heartbroken. "Lily, you're seventeen."

"But this is a *baby*," Lily pleaded.

"You *are* a baby," Susan cried.

Lily drew herself up and said quietly, "No, Mom. I'm not."

Susan was actually thinking the same thing. No, Lily wasn't a baby. She would never be a baby again.

The thought brought a sense of loss—loss of childhood? Of innocence? Had her own mother felt that? Susan had no way of knowing. Even in the best of times, they hadn't talked, certainly not the way Susan and Lily did.

"Don't be like Grandma," Lily begged, sensing her thoughts.

"I have *never* been like Grandma."

"I would die if you disowned me."

"I would never do that."

Turning to face her, Lily grabbed her hand and held it to her throat. "I need you with me, Mom," she said fiercely, then softened. "This is our family, and we're making it bigger. You wanted that, too, I know you did. If things had been different, you'd have had five kids like Kate."

"Not five. Three."

"Three, then. But see?" she coaxed. "A baby isn't a bad thing."

No. Not a bad thing, Susan knew. A baby was never bad. Just life changing.

"This is your grandchild," Lily tried.

"Um-hm," Susan hummed. "I'll be a grandmother at thirty-six. That is embarrassing."

"I think it's *great*."

"That's because you're seventeen and starry-eyed—which is good, sweetheart, because if you aren't smiling now, you'll be in trouble down the road. You'll be alone, Lily. In the past, we've had two other pregnant seniors and one pregnant junior. None of them wanted to go to college. Your friends will go to college. They want careers. They won't be able to relate to being pregnant."

Lily's eyes widened with excitement. "But see, Mom, that's not true. That's the *beauty* of this."

Susan made a face. "What does *that* mean?"

Chapter 3

⤙⧉⤚

"I'M PREGNANT."

"Cute," Kate Mello told her youngest and proceeded to pour dry macaroni into a pot of boiling water. *"Lissie?"* she yelled upstairs to her second youngest, *"when are you going? I need that milk."* She stirred the macaroni and said more to herself than to Mary Kate, who stood beside her at the stove, "Why is it that I'm always out of milk lately?"

"I'm serious, Mom. I'm pregnant."

Holding the lid in one hand and a wooden spoon in the other, Kate simply touched her forehead to Mary Kate's and smiled. "We agreed that you had the flu."

"It's not going away."

"Then it's lactose intolerance," Kate said, setting the lid on the pot. "You're the one who's drinking me out of milk. *Lissie? Soon, please?"*

"I'm drinking milk," said Mary Kate, "because that's what pregnant women do."

"You are not a pregnant woman," Kate informed her

daughter and reached for her wallet when Lissie appeared. There wasn't much in it; money disappeared even faster than milk. She found a twenty among the singles and handed it over. "A gallon of milk, a dozen eggs, and two loaves of multigrain bread, please."

"Alex hates multigrain," Lissie reminded her as she pulled on her jacket.

Kate put the car keys in her hand. "Alex is twenty-one. If he hates what I buy, he can get his own apartment and buy what he likes. Oh, and if there's money left over, will you get some apples?" As Lissie left, she handed Mary Kate a stack of plates. "Eight tonight. Mike is bringing a friend."

"I conceived eight weeks ago," Mary Kate said, taking the plates.

Kate studied her daughter. She was pale, but she was always pale. Same with looking frail. The poor thing had the delicate features of an unnamed forebear, but her hair was all Kate—sandy and thick, wild in a way that the child never was. Kate tacked hers up with bamboo knitting needles. Mary Kate tied hers in a ponytail that exploded behind her, making her face look even smaller.

"You're not pregnant, honey," Kate assured her. "You're only seventeen, you're on the pill, and Jacob wants to be a doctor. That's a lot of years before you two can even get married."

"I *know*," Mary Kate said with a spurt of enthusiasm, "but by then I'll be older and getting pregnant will be harder. Now's the time for me to have a baby."

Kate felt the girl's forehead. "No fever. You can't be delirious."

"Mom—"

"Mom, did Lissie leave?" This from Kate's third daughter, who, not seeing her twin, snatched a cell phone from the clutter on the kitchen table.

"That's mine, Sara," Kate protested. "I'm low on minutes."

"This isn't a social call, Mom. I need tampons."

"I don't," Mary Kate said in a small voice, but with Sara calling Lissie and Mike choosing that minute to duck in and ask if he could have *two* friends for dinner, Kate barely heard her.

"It's only mac 'n' cheese," she cautioned him.

"Only?" her twenty-year-old son echoed. "You said it was *lobster* mac 'n' cheese."

"Is that why they're coming?"

"Definitely. Your lobster mac is famous. The guys hit me up every Wednesday morning for an invitation."

"And if your uncle decides to pull his traps on Friday?"

"They'll switch to Friday. So two is okay?"

"Two's okay," Kate said and remarked to Mary Kate when Mike and Sara were both gone, "Lucky the catch is up and the price is down."

"I'm trying to tell you something, Mom. This is important. I stopped taking the pill."

Hearing that, Kate turned. Her daughter looked serious. "Are you and Jacob cooling it?"

"No. I just decided I wanted a baby. Did you know that a woman is more fertile right after she goes off the pill? I haven't even told Jacob yet. I wanted you to be the first to know."

Something about her serious look gave Kate pause. "Mary Kate? You're not joking?"

"No."

"Pregnant?"

"I keep doing tests, and they're all positive."

"For how long?"

"A while. I mean, I would have told you sooner, only I wanted to make sure. But I'm really on top of this, Mom. I bought books, and I'm getting more info online. They have a support group for teens, but I don't really need that. I already have a support group."

Kate frowned. "Who?"

"Well— Well, for starters, my family. I mean, we normally have seven for dinner. Tonight it was eight, and now nine. What's one more?"

Kate would have sent Mary Kate to the back porch for another folding chair, because that was what one more meant in their cramped dining room, if she hadn't been struggling to process what the girl had said. "Is this true?"

"Yes. Anyway, you love kids. Didn't you have five in five years?"

"Not by design," Kate said weakly. "They just started to come and didn't stop." Not until Will had had a vasectomy, though that wasn't something they often discussed with the kids. They would have discussed abstinence, if they believed there was a chance the kids would listen. More realistically, they talked up responsibility. "But wait, back up, I was twenty-one when I had my first child, and I was *married*."

Mary Kate didn't seem to hear. "So now this is the next generation. I like being the first one of us to have kids. I'm always last in everything else."

"The decision to have a child should involve both parents," Kate said. "You need to ask Jacob before you do anything rash."

"Oh, Jacob is just so *serious* sometimes. He would have said no, and he'd have given lots of reasons that made sense, but sometimes you have to just go with your gut. Remember Disney World five years ago? You piled Dad and us in the car and drove us to Florida in the middle of winter, and we didn't have hotel reservations or anything, but your gut told you the trip would be good."

"That was a *trip,* Mary Kate. This is a baby. A baby is for *life*."

"But I'll be a good mother," Mary Kate insisted. "Last summer was *such* an eye-opener—seeing what those moms did? Like, no patience with their kids, wanting to pawn them off on us while they sat way off at the other end of the beach. I'll never do that with my baby. If it's a boy, it'll be a little Jacob. That would be awesome."

Kate was speechless. The quietest of her five, the most passive and deferential, Mary Kate was rarely this effusive. And what had she just said? "A little Jacob?"

Mary Kate nodded. "I won't know the sex for a little while, and I know it could be a girl . . ." Her voice trailed off.

Bewildered, Kate looked around. The kitchen was small. The whole *house* was small. "Where would we *keep* a baby?"

"In my room. Co-sleeping is big right now. By the time my baby outgrows that, Alex will probably be out of the house and maybe Mike, too, so there'll be more room. And then once Jacob graduates from medical school—"

"Jacob hasn't graduated from *high school*," Kate yelped, struck again by the absurdity of the discussion. "Mary Kate, are you telling me the truth?"

"About being pregnant?" The girl quieted. "I wouldn't lie about something like that."

No, she wouldn't. She was an honest girl, a bright girl, perhaps the most gifted of Kate's five kids, and she had a future. She was planning to marry a doctor and be a college professor herself.

"I mean," Mary Kate went on, speaking faster now, clearly sensing her mother's horror, "you always said 'the more the merrier,' that a noisy home makes you happy, that you'd have had more children if we'd been richer."

"Right, but we're not," Kate stated bluntly. "Your father and I barely finished paying off our own college loans in time for your brothers to start college, and now with the twins there and you next year—but you won't be going to college if you have a baby, will you? How can you be an English professor without a college degree—without a *graduate* degree?"

"I'll get one. It just may take a little longer."

Kate couldn't believe what her smart daughter was saying. "May just take a little *longer*?"

"And in the meantime I'll have Jacob's baby."

"Where? How? Jacob's dad drives a PC truck, and his mom teaches first grade. They're as strapped as we are. If Jacob loves you like he says, he's going to want to be with you and the baby, but his parents can't support the three of you."

"I'd never ask them to," Mary Kate said. "Besides, I don't want to marry Jacob yet. I want to stay here."

"So *we* can support you and the baby?"

"Fine," the girl said. "Then I'll move out."

Kate grabbed her daughter's shoulders. "You will not move out, Mary Kate. That isn't an option."

"Neither is abortion."

"I agree, but there are other choices."

"Like adoption? I'm not giving my baby to someone else." She plucked at her sweater. "See this? It was Sara's, and these jeans were Lissie's, but this baby is mine." The hand on her middle was pale but protective.

Yes, Kate acknowledged. Mary Kate often got clothes from the twins—okay, *usually* got clothes from the twins—but didn't large families do that? She was a hand-me-down child in everything but love. Kate had always thought that would make it okay. "Your sisters outgrew those things," she argued. "They were good clothes."

"That's not the point, Mom. This baby's *mine*."

"Just like you and your brothers and sisters are mine," said Kate. "When I was a kid, I dreamed of being a vet. I love animals. But I loved your father more, and then you kids came along really fast, and I loved you all so much that I wanted to be a full-time mom, which was lucky, because there was so much to do for the five of you that our house was chaotic even without my having an outside job. And by the time you all were in school, we didn't have the money for me to train to be a vet. Do you think I work just for kicks?"

Mary Kate was subdued. "You love your work."

"Yes, but I couldn't do it if it didn't pay. We need every extra cent."

"My baby won't cost much," the girl said meekly.

Kate took her daughter's shoulders again, holding on to a dream that was fading fast. "It isn't the money," she pleaded softly. "I want things to be easier for you when you have kids. I want your children to have rooms of their own. I don't want you to have to choose between music lessons or ballet because you can't pay for both."

The door opened and Kate looked up, fully expecting it to be Lissie. But it was Will. Will, who had worked his way from the PC shipping dock to foreman of the department, losing hair and gaining girth, but remaining Kate's rock.

She always felt a weight lift from her shoulders when Will came home, but her relief had never been greater than it was now. "Here's your dad. Will, we have something to discuss."

FIVE BLOCKS AWAY, SUNNY BARROS WAS NOWHERE near as relieved when her husband came home from work. "She's what?" Dan asked her. Their daughter stood nearby, but he was looking at Sunny, who was absolutely beside herself.

"Pregnant," Sunny mouthed. She couldn't say the word again.

"*Jessica?*" he asked and turned to the girl. "Is this true?"

She nodded.

"Who's the boy?"

"You don't know him, Dad."

Dan looked at his wife. "Who is he?"

Sunny shook her head and pressed her mouth shut. It was either that or scream.

"Mom's angry," Jessica said calmly. "I've been telling her that it's fine. People have been having babies since Adam and Eve. She's convinced it's the end of the world."

"Excuse me, Jessica," Sunny cried, but stopped when her ten-year-old daughter skipped into the room. "Darcy." She pointed upstairs. "Violin practice. Ten more minutes."

The child looked wounded. "I'm just saying hi to Daddy. Hi, Dad."

Sunny pointed again, waiting only until the child left before eyeing Jessica. "Tell him what else you told me." She looked at Dan. "Jessica planned this."

"Planned to get pregnant?"

"Decided she wanted a baby," Sunny specified. If the girl had gone looking for the one thing that would dismantle the tidy life Sunny had so carefully crafted, she had found it.

"Is this true, Jessica?" Dan asked.

Jessica eyed him levelly. A tall girl with long brown hair and Dan's verbal skill, she spoke with confidence. "Bringing a child into the world is the most important thing a person can do. I want to leave my mark."

"At seventeen?"

"Age doesn't matter. It's what's inside. I'll be the best mom ever."

"At seventeen," Dan repeated. Looking at Sunny, he scratched his head. "Where did this come from?"

Sunny didn't answer. Folding her arms against the coming storm, she waited. Dan was smart, well beyond the contracts he negotiated for Perry & Cass. He saw cause and effect, and was eminently predictable. Sunny had always loved that about him, but it was about to work against her.

To his credit, he considered other options first. Looking at Jessica again, he said, "Is it school pressure? Fear of college?"

Jessica smiled smugly. "My grades are great. That's one of the reasons I knew I could do this."

She had her father's brains—tenth in her class without much effort—but this had nothing to do with grades, or apparently with brains, Sunny decided. "Do you have *any idea*—" she began, but stopped when Darcy whipped back in.

"My lamp just blew out. It needs a new bulb."

"I'll replace it in a minute," Sunny said and turned her around. "Until then, use the overhead light."

"I don't like the overhead light."

"*Use* it," Sunny ordered and turned back to the others. "And there's *another* problem. What do we tell Darcy so that she doesn't do this herself in seven more years? This is the *worst* kind of example to set."

Dan held up a hand and returned to Jessica. "You talked about going to Georgetown."

"Percy State will do."

"Will *do*?" He lowered his voice. "Is it Adam?"

"Maybe. Maybe not."

"Jessica!" Sunny shouted.

Dan lifted his hand for quiet. "You are dating Adam, are you not?"

"I have been, but he isn't the love of my life."

"He has to marry you if he's the father of this baby," Sunny argued.

"I haven't said he's the father," the girl insisted. "Anyway, the donation of sperm doesn't make a man a father. Involvement does, and the father of this baby won't be involved. I'm raising it myself."

"Raising it yourself?" Dan asked. "That doesn't make sense."

"Maybe not to you and Mom. When everything in your world is as neat as this kitchen—"

"What's wrong with this *kitchen*?" Sunny asked in alarm. Their kitchen—their house—was larger than many in town, reflecting Dan's position as head of the PC legal department and Sunny's as manager of Home Goods. She had decorated every inch of the place herself and took pride in seasonal additions from the store, like the handblown glass bowl of pine cones on the table. Their kitchen reflected everything they had worked so hard to achieve. She hadn't expected an attack on this front.

"Nothing's wrong with the kitchen, Mom," Jessica replied serenely. "That's the problem. Nothing is out of place. Nothing clashes. Our lives are very, very organized." She looked at Dan, who looked at Sunny.

"Where is she getting this?" he asked, sounding mystified.

"Not from me," Sunny vowed, but she knew what was coming.

"From your mother?"

It was the only possible explanation. Sunny didn't have to study Jessica's cell tab to know that she talked with her grandmother often. The girl made no secret of it. She and Delilah had always gotten along, and no warning from Sunny could change that.

Delilah Maranthe was the embodiment of all Sunny had tried to escape. Her parents had been the eccentrics of the neighborhood, bent on doing their own thing. Born Stan and Donna, they went to court to become Samson and Delilah.

They bought a house in suburbia and, under the guise of returning the property to its natural state, refused to mow the lawn. Ever. They spent weeks before Halloween baking cookies and rigging up elaborate electronics, though the local children were forbidden to visit. To Sunny's utter mortification, they appeared at her high school graduation dressed as graduates from the century before.

To this day they remained odd, and though some people found a benign charm in their behavior, Sunny did not. Had her parents ever been benign—had they had an ounce of caring or foresight—they wouldn't have saddled their children with silly names. What kind of mother named her child Sunshine? Sunny would have gone to court to change it herself if she hadn't been adamant against following in a single one of her parents' footsteps. And Buttercup? That was her older sister, who had simply shrugged it off and gone through life as Jane.

Sunny had been more vulnerable, suffering the taunts of schoolmates, and though no one in Zaganack knew her as Sunshine, the fear of discovery haunted her. She had raised Jessica and her sister to be Normal with a capital *N*.

Now Jessica was pregnant, saying that sperm didn't make a man a father and that their lives were too ordinary—and Dan was looking at Sunny like it was her fault. But how could she control Delilah Maranthe? "It's not enough that I had to escape my mother when I was a child, but now she's corrupted my daughter!"

"This has nothing to do with Delilah," Jessica insisted, which irritated Sunny all the more.

"See, Dan? Not Grandma. *Delilah*." She turned on her daughter. "A grandmother shouldn't be called by her first name. Why can't you call her Grandma?"

"Because she forbids me to. She just isn't a grandma."

"There's our problem," Sunny told Dan.

"Why are you always so down on her?" Jessica argued. "Delilah happens to be one of the most exciting people I know. Face it, Mom. We are totally predictable."

"I have a job other people would die for," Sunny reasoned.

"We follow every rule to the letter."

"I'm respected in this town."

Jessica raised her voice. "I want to stand out!"

"Well, you've done it now. What are people going to *think*?"

"They'll think it's fine, Mom, because it isn't just me. It's Lily and Mary Kate, too."

Sunny gasped. "What?"

Chapter 4

SUSAN WAITED ONLY UNTIL LILY HAD GONE UPSTAIRS before opening her cell. Seconds later, without so much as a hello, Kate asked, "Do you know what's going on?"

"Not me. I was hoping you would. You're my guru."

She heard a snort. "I've mothered my kids through broken bones and head lice, not pregnancy. How's Lily?"

"Confident. Naïve."

"Same with Mary Kate."

"How could this *happen*?" Susan asked, bewildered. "We taught them the right things, didn't we?"

Kate interrupted the conversation to say, *"No, Lissie, she is not a loser. There's a solution to this."* Back to Susan, she muttered, "But I haven't a clue what it is. I have to go, Susie. Mary Kate is being crucified here. It's going to be a long night. Can you come to the barn tomorrow morning?"

Susan had a lineup of morning meetings, but would gladly reschedule a few. "Be there at ten."

. . .

THE PROSPECT OF TALKING WITH KATE WAS A COMFORT. Likewise, perversely, the idea that Susan and Lily weren't the only ones with a problem.

But the more Susan thought about it, the more frantic she grew. Three girls pregnant by design? There was a word for that, but the mother in her couldn't say it. And the school principal? She couldn't even *begin* to think it.

One pregnancy could be hidden. Not three.

One might be accidental. Not three.

One would quickly be last week's news. Not three.

"Mom?" Lily's whisper came through the bedroom darkness. "Are you sleeping?"

"If only," Susan said quietly. If only she could close her eyes and make it all go away—find it was just a bad dream, a relic of the panic from her own past—*I can't do this, I'm alone, HELP!* No, she was not sleeping. "But you should be," she said quietly. "You're sleeping for two."

"I'm also peeing for two. Did you talk with Kate?"

Susan glanced at the door where Lily stood backlit, a still-slim silhouette against the frame. "Only for a minute. We're meeting in the morning."

"Mary Kate says her mom's really upset. It's the money issue."

"It's more than that," Susan said. If money ruled the Mellos, Kate and Will would have stopped after the twins. But Kate would be upset, like she was, about the consequences of what their daughters had foolishly done. "Any word from Jess?"

"No. She's not answering my messages. I think she's mad at me. She told Mary Kate that Sunny went berserk. Jess blames me."

"Why you?"

"Because we had agreed not to tell. Only I got pregnant before they did, so I was farther along, and I knew you knew—"

"I didn't know."

"You may not have *known* you knew, but you knew," the girl insisted, "and once I told you, the others had to tell their moms, even though they wanted to wait."

Susan didn't argue about what she had known when. She was already beating herself up about what she should have seen but hadn't. Girls like theirs didn't do things like this.

But they had now. And waiting to tell moms? "Funny thing about being pregnant," she mused, wrapping her arms around her knees. "Before long, it shows."

"But by then, it would be too late to do anything about it," said Lily. "Jess is worried they'll make her have an abortion. If they try, she'll run off to her grandmother. I have no one but you, Mom. If you didn't want me here, I could call your aunt Evie, but she's like, what, eighty now?"

Susan put her chin on her knees. "Sixty, and you're not calling Aunt Evie."

"Well, if I had to, I would—or I'd call Dad's sister. She likes me. I mean, it'd only be for a little while."

"You're not going anywhere."

"I'm sorry if I've messed things up."

Susan wanted to say that she hadn't. Only she had. The fact of Susan sitting in bed, missing Lily's warm body but unable to open the covers for her to snuggle, spoke of a *huge* mess.

"Don't be angry," the girl whispered.

"Why not, Lily?" Susan shot back. "My signature accomplishment last year was the establishment of a school clinic where students can be treated for things they don't want to discuss with their parents. That clinic is staffed by a real nurse, with a real doctor on call, either of whom could have given you birth control if you'd wanted to have sex. Do you realize that I pushed for this specifically to minimize student pregnancies?"

Lily remained silent.

"Mm," Susan concluded softly. "I'm speechless, too."

"You're missing the point. This is not an unplanned pregnancy."

"No, *you're* missing the point," Susan parried with a spike of outrage. "This town lives and breathes responsibility. This *family* lives and breathes responsibility. What you've done is not responsible. You can talk all you want about knowing what you're doing and being a good mother, but you're seventeen, Lily. *Seventeen.*"

"You did it," Lily said meekly.

And that, Susan realized, would haunt her forever. She had worked so hard to get past it, but here it was again. And now she had no idea what to do. She certainly couldn't call Rick. He had trusted her to raise Lily well, and she had failed.

Heartsick, she turned away from the door and curled into a ball. She didn't know how long Lily stood there, only knew that she couldn't reach out to her, and by the time she rolled back to look at the clock, the doorway was empty.

SUSAN RARELY CALLED IN SICK, BUT SHE WOULD HAVE done it the next day if she hadn't planned to meet Kate at the barn. Inevitably someone would see her going there. But Zaganack looked out for its own. If you were sick, people knew. Likewise if you were supposed to be sick and showed up elsewhere.

The prospect of leaving school at ten kept her going, and when she finally ran down the stone steps and climbed into her car, she felt better for the first time that day. She would have walked if she'd had time; the barn wasn't far, and the November air was crisp, still fragrant with the crush of dried leaves. But she didn't want to lose a minute.

No ordinary barn, this one had a past. Originally built on the outskirts of town to house horses, it had also hidden its share of escaped slaves heading to freedom north of the border. For years it had housed nothing but cobwebs and mice, but for Susan, Kate, Sunny, and Pam, who saw PC Wool as their own personal ticket to freedom, it held an appeal. When the last of the Gunn family died and the property went up for sale, the women lobbied for the barn. Envisioning it as a tourist attraction, Tanner Perry, grandson of Herman Perry and husband of Pam, had bought it and moved it closer to the rest of Perry & Cass. The tourist part had never quiet materialized, but the success of PC Wool more than compensated.

Parking beside Kate's van, Susan ran inside, past stalls of raw fiber, shipping cartons, and computers, all the way to the back. There, tubs for soaking fiber and shelves of dye lined the walls. A separate section held newly painted wool, now hung to dry, while ceiling fans whirred softly above. A skeining machine stood nearby.

Had she not been preoccupied, Susan might have admired a mound of finished skeins. A blend of alpaca and mohair, these were the last of the holiday colors she had conceived the summer before. Rich with dozens of shades of cranberry, balsam, and snow, they were the culmination of a year in which sales had doubled. Not only had PC Wool earned its very own section in the Perry & Cass catalogue, but after becoming the darling of the knitting blogs, it had experienced an explosion in online sales.

A large oak table stood at the heart of the work space. Old and scarred, it was the same one on which they had put together their first season of colors ten years before. Back then, the table was in Susan's garage and PC Wool had only been a dream, conjured up during child-free evenings with a bottle of wine and good friends who loved to knit. Even now, a large basket in the center of the table held small knitting projects, while the bulk of its surface was covered with skeins waiting to be twisted.

Dropping her coat on a chair, Susan went to Kate. "Are you okay?"

"Been better," Kate replied. Her eyes were heavy, her hair a riot of ends sticking up around the bamboo double-pointeds at her crown. She opened her arms.

This was why Susan had come. She needed comfort. Petite Kate, with her big heart and can-do approach, had always offered that. "If it had to be anyone," Susan whispered, "I'm glad it's you. What are we going to do?"

Kate held her for another minute. "I do not know."

"That's not the right answer. You're supposed to say that everything will work out, that this is just another one of life's little challenges, and that what happens was meant to be."

"Aha," Kate barked dryly, "at least I've raised *you* well. You can keep telling me that. Right now, I'm not a happy camper."

"What does Will say?"

"Pretty much what you just did. But boy, this came from nowhere. How can smart girls do something so stupid?" Reaching for a hank of yarn, she deftly twisted it until it was tight enough to double back on itself. "My daughter's neck," she murmured as she tucked one end into the other.

"I'll ditto that," Susan said, and the angst of the past thirty-six hours poured out. "I can't get past the anger. I can't ask Lily how she's feeling. I can't hold her. She's been my little girl for so long, but now there's this other . . . other . . . thing between us."

"A baby."

"It's not a baby to me yet. It's something unwanted." She waved a hand. "Bad choice of words. What I meant to say was that this is not what we needed at this stage in our lives. Lily was supposed to have all the choices that I did not. What was she thinking?"

"She wasn't alone."

"Which blows my mind. I've always loved that our girls did things together. They're all good students, good athletes, good *knitters*. I thought they'd keep each other from doing dumb things." She had a new thought. "Where's Abby in all this?"

Kate leveled a gaze at her. "Mary Kate refused to say."

"She's pregnant, *too*?" Four would be even worse than three—though three was surely bad enough.

"Mary Kate just stared at me when I asked."

"Meaning that Abby is either pregnant or still trying."

"All I know," Kate said, "is that Mary Kate begged me not to tell Pam."

"But if Pam can keep this from happening to Abby—"

"That's what I said, but Mary Kate said Abby would do it anyway, and she's probably right. Of the four girls, she's the least anchored."

Like her mom, Susan thought. She didn't have to say it. Kate knew. They had discussed it more than once.

"Besides," Kate said, "it's not like Pam can lock her in a chastity belt."

Susan snorted. "Not many of those around these days, and what do we have instead? The Web. Information enough there to make naïve seventeen-year-olds feel they know everything. What was Mary Kate's excuse for wanting a baby?"

Kate twisted another hank. "She's been a hand-me-down child. She wants something of her own."

"Isn't Jacob that?" Susan was generally skeptical of high

school pairings, but she liked Jacob Senter a lot. He was a kind boy, dedicated to school and devoted to Mary Kate. Lily had no one like that.

"But between school and loans," Kate explained, "it'll be years before they can get married. She wants something now. Something her sisters don't have." She screwed up her face. "Did I miss this?"

"She had love," Susan argued in Kate's defense.

"When I wasn't busy with the others. She has a point, Susie. Her solution may be misguided, but I see where she's coming from. Lily, now, Lily had you all to herself."

"But only me. She wants family."

"She has Rick."

Rick. Susan felt a little tug at her heart. "Rick is like the wind. Try to catch him."

"Have you called him?" Kate asked cautiously.

Susan pressed her lips together and shook her head.

"Do you know where he is?"

"I can find out." Not that it mattered. His cell number was linked to network headquarters in New York. He could be anywhere in the world and her call would go through.

Reaching him was the easy part. Telling him what had happened would be harder.

She practiced on Kate. "When Lily was little, she wanted a brother or sister. That was before she realized her daddy wasn't around. Once she understood that Rick and I weren't together, she turned matchmaker. 'You'd really like Kelsey's daddy, and Kelsey has a sister and two brothers, and they need a mom like you.'" Susan smiled briefly. "It was sweet. Sad. She always wanted a big family, but there's a right way and a wrong way to get it." Grabbing a hank of yarn, she twisted it as she, too, had done hundreds of times. "She keeps reminding me that I was seventeen when I had her, but it's because I was that I *know* how bad this is. They're not ready physically. They're not ready emotionally."

"Neither am I," Kate said tiredly. "For years my life was a blur of diapers, runny noses, and interrupted sleep. I hyperventilate when I think of it. I can't go back."

Susan wasn't as worried about going back as moving ahead. "At least you know it's Jacob. Lily won't tell me who the father is. She says he doesn't know. How crazy is that?"

"You have no idea?"

"None." And it bothered Susan a lot. "She told me when she had a crush on Bobby Grant in second grade. She told me when she got her first kiss. That was Jonah McEllis. She gave me a blow-by-blow of her relationship with Joey Anderson last year. And in each case, I wasn't surprised. A good mother would know if her daughter liked someone, wouldn't she?"

Kate snickered. "Like she would know if her daughter planned to get pregnant?"

"How did I not see something?" Susan asked, baffled. "I look now, and, yes, there's a difference. Her breasts are fuller. Why didn't I notice before?"

"They weren't fuller before," Kate reasoned. "Or her clothes hid it. Or you thought she was just filling out. Susie, I'm asking myself the same thing. My daughter is two months pregnant, has been drinking milk by the gallon, has thrown up lots of mornings, and I thought it was the flu."

Susan actually smiled. Pathetic as the situation was, she felt better. Venting always helped, especially when the person on the other end was in the same boat. Kate would love her regardless of what kind of mother she was.

"Have you and Lily talked about options?" Kate asked.

Susan could only think of three, and abortion was out. She

reached for more yarn. "I mentioned adoption this morning." She twisted the hank and looked up. "Lily threw the question back at me. Could I have done that? We both know the answer."

"What was it like?" came a third voice. Sunny unbuttoned her coat as she approached. "Having a baby at seventeen."

Susan didn't have to pull at memories. She had been reliving the experience in vivid flashes since dinner at Carlino's Tuesday night. "It totally changed my life. My childhood ended—was over, just like that."

Sunny joined them at the table. Clearly on a break from work, she had her hair in a plum bow that matched her sweater and slacks. "I know you're estranged from your parents," she said to Susan. "I don't know the details."

That wasn't something Susan dwelt on. "My parents couldn't deal," she said, "so I went to live with an aunt in Missouri while I had Lily and finished high school. Aunt Evie was great, but she had no kids. She didn't know what I was going through, and I didn't dare complain. It was scary. My doctor was one step removed from my father. He delighted in telling me all the risks of having a baby at seventeen."

"Like?"

"Like a seventeen-year-old's body isn't ready to carry a baby to term. Like I was at risk for anemia, high blood pressure, preterm labor, and my baby could be underweight and have underdeveloped organs."

Kate looked frightened. "Is all that true?"

"I believed it. Now I know that most of these problems arise because teenage moms typically don't take care of themselves. But my doctor didn't say that. I was terrified. There were no classes at the local hospital. I had some books, but they weren't reassuring. I was only seventeen. I dreaded childbirth, and then, if I survived that, I was going to have to take care of a baby who would be totally helpless and who might have developmental issues because I was seventeen."

Sunny scowled. "There must have been someone who could help."

"My pediatrician's nurse. She was an angel. I talked with her every morning during call hours. It was like she had two patients, an infant and a seventeen-year-old—well, eighteen-year-old by then. We still keep in touch."

"Are you in touch with your aunt?"

"Occasionally. But it's awkward. She never wanted to buck my father, either. The deal was that I'd stay with her until I graduated high school, then leave. My dad put enough money in a bank account for me to buy a used car and pay for necessities until I got Lily and me to a place where I could work."

"They disowned you," Sunny concluded, "which is what I may do to my daughter."

"You will not," Kate scolded.

"I *may*. I don't believe she's done this. Do you know how *embarrassing* it is?"

"Not as embarrassing as when I got pregnant," Susan said. "We lived in a small town of which my dad was the mayor—just like his dad before him—so the embarrassment was thoroughly public. My older brother, on the other hand, was a town hero. Great student, football star, heir apparent—you name the stereotype, and Jackson was it. I was the bad egg. Erasing me from the family picture was easy."

Sunny seemed more deliberative than disturbed. "What about Lily? Weren't they curious?"

"My mother, maybe." A fantasy, perhaps, but Susan clung to the belief. "But she was married to my father, and he was tough. Still is. I send cards on every occasion—birthday, anniversary, Thanksgiving, Christmas. I send newspaper articles about Lily or me. I send gifts from Perry and Cass, and yarn to my mom. She sends a formal thank-you every time." Susan held up an untwisted skein. "She thought these colors were very pretty. Very pretty," she repeated in a monotone, startled by how much the blandness of the note still stung.

"I'm trying to decide if Jessica can survive," Sunny said. "How did you make it with an infant and no help?"

"I didn't sleep."

"Seriously."

"Seriously," Susan insisted. She had learned to multitask early on. "I was studying, working, and taking care of a baby. After I graduated from high school, I babysat my way east. Babysitting was the one thing I could do and still have Lily with me, because I sure couldn't afford a sitter. When I got here, I did clerical work at the community college because that got me day care dirt cheap and classes for free. I was halfway through my degree when I met you two." Their girls were in preschool together. "That was a turning point. Friends make the difference."

"Exactly," Sunny cried. "If our girls hadn't been friends, this wouldn't have happened."

Susan was startled. Of the three girls, she saw Jessica as the one most ready to rebel. "If not with our two, then with another two friends," she said quietly.

Sunny calmed a little. "Tell that to my husband."

"Uh-oh." This from Kate, and with cause. Dan Barros was mild-mannered, but there was no doubt who ruled the roost. "He's blaming our girls?"

There was a pause, then a halfhearted "Not exactly."

"What did he say?"

"Oh, he doesn't *say* things. He implies. He infers. I'm telling Jessica that she needs to tell us who the father is, so that they can get married, which would lend at least a *semblance* of decency to this, but Dan keeps grilling *me*. 'How did this happen, where were *you*, didn't *you* see anything?' Bottom line? It's my fault."

"It isn't your fault," said Kate, though she was looking at Susan. "Is it?"

Hadn't Susan asked herself the same question? She picked up a PC Wool tag from a pile that lay beside the skeins. A striking little thing, the tag carried the PC Wool logo, along with the fiber content of the skein, its length and gauge, and washing instructions. "We gave our daughters the know-how to prevent this," she said as she absently fingered the tag. "But they didn't consult us."

"They consulted each other," Sunny charged. "They gave each other strength."

"Bravado," Kate added.

"That, too," Susan said. After touching the tag a moment longer, she looked up at her friends. "I'm forever telling parents that they have to be involved. They have to know what their kids are doing. Kids aren't bad, just young. Their brains are still developing. That's why sixteen-year-olds are lousy drivers. They don't have the judgment—actually, physically, don't have the gray matter to make the right decision in a crisis. They don't fully get it until they're in their early twenties."

"And in the meantime, it *is* our fault?" Sunny asked.

Susan didn't answer. She was suddenly wondering what all those parents to whom she had lectured would say when they learned her daughter was pregnant. Given her age and what some saw as a meteoric rise in her field, she had always been on shaky ground. Now she feared for her credibility.

She must have looked stricken, because Kate took her hand. "What our daughters may have lacked in gray matter, they made up for in parental influence. We taught them right from wrong, Susie. They've never before given us reason to doubt them."

"That's what makes this so *absurd,*" Susan wailed. "I could give you a list of girls at school who are at risk of doing something like this. Our daughters' names would not be on it."

"Now there's a thought," Sunny said, sounding hopeful. "No one expects it from our girls, so no one will know for a while. That gives us time to figure out what to do." She looked from Susan to Kate and back. "Right?"

Susan was thinking that time might not help, when Pam came striding back from the front of the barn. "Hey, guys," she called when she was barely halfway past the stalls. "Were we supposed to meet?" She was unwinding a large scarf as she reached them. "I bumped into Leah and Regina at PC Beans. They said you kicked them out, Kate." Leah and Regina were Kate's assistants that day, two of eight part-timers who helped get PC Wool out in the quantity dictated by recent demand.

"I gave them money for coffee," Kate said after only a second's delay.

But Pam caught it and looked around. "What's up? You all look like someone died."

"No one died," Sunny said brightly. "We were just taking a last look at the holiday yarn. It was a great colorway. People are raving about the freshness of the colors—very holiday, but not totally traditional. I told you that we're giving the spring line a major Mother's Day push in Home Goods, didn't I? Do we have colors, Susan?"

"We do," Susan said, trying to hide the horror that the mere mention of Mother's Day brought. Lily would be in her ninth month then and would be huge. Picturing it, Susan could only think of pink and blue, not PC Wool colors at all.

She couldn't say that, of course. Going along seemed the safest thing. But Pam was a good friend, and her daughter was very possibly pregnant or trying to get pregnant. *Tell her,* cried a little voice in Susan's head.

But no one else spoke up. If Susan did, she would betray the others—and Lily.

So she said, "I'll work out the dye recipes Saturday. Do we have a deadline for the catalogue?"

Pam was their mail-order link. At least, that was what she called herself, though on that front she did little more than pass data to a manager. More crucial to the operation, she was a lobbyist for PC Wool, the women's link to the powers-that-be. If there was a conflict of interest, given that she was a Perry herself, no one cared. PC Wool had shown a higher percentage of growth in the last year than any two other departments combined.

"End of January," she said. "That means we need samples painted and photographed by mid-month." She lit up. "Can we do another spa weekend before Christmas to write copy? I loved that last year."

They had driven an hour inland to Weymouth Farm. The spa there had a reciprocal arrangement whereby Perry & Cass would provide them with PC bath soaps and gels in exchange for free use of vacant rooms.

"I may have trouble with that," Kate hedged. "My Percy State four have finals then. They'll need extra care."

Sunny shook her head. "Dan has every weekend between now and Christmas planned."

Susan was silent. In another month, Lily would be showing. Word might be out. Pam might hate them for not telling her sooner. Worse, Abby herself might be pregnant, in which case Susan would feel *doubly* guilty.

But Pam looked so eager that Susan dredged up her only excuse. "Rick may be coming," she said apologetically. "He's waiting to see how his assignments pan out for December. Until he knows, I don't dare commit."

Pam was crestfallen. "What fun are you guys?" she pouted.

"So I have to settle for Saturdays here? What are we doing this week?"

"Tagging skeins," Kate answered. "And looking at Susan's magic notebook to see the colors she's picked."

"Bring your WIP," Susan told Pam, referring to her work in progress, a cashmere sweater coat that only Pam had the time—or money—to tackle. "How's it coming?"

"The back's almost done. The yarn is exquisite. We need to add cashmere to our line."

"Too expensive," Sunny warned.

"But wouldn't you love to have it in the store?" Pam asked.

"For me? Yes. I just don't know how many people off the tour bus will buy cashmere."

"Maybe not tourists, but diehard yarnies? Online buyers? Bloggers have asked for it." She looked at the others. "A cashmere shrug or a lace-weight scarf would be perfect for spring. Can I research where to buy it undyed?"

"Sure."

"Definitely."

"Great," Pam said. "Let's talk more on Saturday. And on Sunday," she added, turning to Sunny. "What time did you want us?"

Brunch at eleven, Susan thought. It was Dan's birthday.

"Actually, Dan changed his mind," Sunny said, looking pinched. "All he wants is a quiet breakfast. He's feeling old."

Dan was turning forty-three, not old by any standards.

It wasn't age, Susan realized. *He blames us, too.*

SUNNY DIDN'T MAKE IT TO THE BARN ON SATURDAY morning, and, given that she was their ear to the ground when it came to Perry & Cass customers, Susan was hesitant to discuss colors without her. Fortunately, Pam didn't stay long anyway, so they spent the time alternately affixing tags to skeins and admiring the sweater Pam was knitting. The minute she left, though, Susan said guiltily, "That was bad. We have to *tell* her."

"How *can* we?" Kate argued and ran through the arguments about loyalty to the girls.

"But if we can save Pam from facing this—"

"Abby'll do it anyway."

"Maybe not if Pam gets to her first. What if I made her swear not to tell the world?" Susan tried.

"And you trust she wouldn't?"

No. Susan did not. Pam wouldn't tell anyone intentionally, but she was so desperate to be relevant that it might just spill out. "The problem," Susan said, making her final argument, "is that she'll find out sooner or later, and when she does, she'll be hurt."

"She'll understand."

"And in the meanwhile, we have to suffer through Saturday mornings like this one? I don't know if I can do that, Kate. It's bad enough that I'm not calling Rick, but Lily wants to wait. Am I using her as an excuse? I'm such a coward."

Kate put a comforting hand on her arm. "You are not a coward. You're respecting Lily and Mary Kate and Jess by not telling Pam. Besides, there's a reason why Lily wants to wait to tell Rick. The first trimester is crucial. What if she miscarries?"

LILY DIDN'T MISCARRY. SHE PASSED MOST OF THE NEXT week as she had the eleven previous—going to school with no one the wiser, falling asleep at night with her books open and waking later to study, texting often with Mary Kate and Jess, though Jess was at their house more now, escaping her own.

Susan struggled to come to terms with her daughter's condition. She alternately obsessed over Lily's future and refused to think about it, but all the while, there was a pain in her gut. She felt betrayed.

Naturally, Lily sensed it, which perhaps explained why her morning sickness continued. At least, that was what Susan concluded guiltily when she got a call from the school clinic on Thursday morning. Leaving a meeting in the center of town, she quickly headed there.

Chapter 5

THE CLINIC WAS IN THE BASEMENT OF THE SCHOOL. Susan's preference had been for something more open and bright, but with so little available space, the basement was a necessary concession. Its proximity to the locker rooms was a plus; sports injuries were a fact of life in a school that fielded fiercely competitive teams. A direct entrance to the back parking lot also helped when a communicable disease was involved.

Using that back entrance now, Susan passed two students at the nurse's desk and checked the cubicles. She found Lily on a bed in the third cubicle, looking pathetically young. Her knees were bent. One hand lay over her middle, her other arm covered her eyes.

"Sweetie?"

Lily moved her arm and, seeing Susan, immediately teared up. "I'm sorry," she whispered.

One look at her and Susan's heart melted. "What happened?"

The words came in a breathy rush. "I was feeling sick, so I went to my locker for crackers, and Abby was there and announced, I mean, in a big, loud voice, that what did I *expect,* being pregnant. It was a *nightmare,* Mom. There were kids everywhere, and they all stopped walking and stared. I wanted to tell them she was wrong, only I couldn't. I was so upset—I mean, how could Abby do that? I've never actually thrown up before, but I did it then, in front of *everyone.*"

She looked green enough to do it again, but Susan didn't care. Sitting on the edge of the gurney, she pulled her into her arms. Lily was going through what she personally knew was trial by fire. A good mother didn't feel anger toward her child when she was in this kind of pain.

Besides, Susan blamed herself as much as Abby. She had been distant and cool when her daughter needed support. Rocking gently, with her chin on Lily's head, she tried to think.

Just then the nurse opened the curtain. Amy Sheehan was in her mid-thirties, attractive in sweater and jeans, and soft-spoken. Eminently approachable, she had been Susan's first choice for the job, no concessions there. Her voice was gentle now. "Lily told me. She said she saw a doctor."

Susan nodded, but her mind was racing. She had hoped for time. Now what?

Lily looked up. Her eyes were haunted. "I had last lunch. I thought if I got something in my stomach, I'd be able to make it 'til then. I didn't expect to feel so sick. The books said it would stop after twelve weeks."

Susan recalled suffering from nausea well past the magical date. "What do books know? But it is what it is. Time to go to Plan B."

"What's that?"

"Beats me." She eyed the nurse. "Any thoughts?"

Amy was apologetic. "You really can't deny it. Not if Lily's keeping the baby. It'll be obvious soon enough."

She didn't have to go on. Deny the pregnancy now, and when Lily begins to show, the denial itself will be an issue. Especially for the high school principal.

Lily looked at Susan again. "What did you do?"

Susan didn't have to fill in Amy on her history. Her age and Lily's, both, were a matter of record. Besides, Susan had laid it out when she hired Amy to head the school clinic. *I hid my pregnancy for five months. I risked my own health and my baby's because I didn't know where to turn. I want our students to have a place to go when they can't go to their parents. I don't want any sexual problems ignored.*

In answer to Lily now, she smiled sadly. "I was lucky enough not to throw up in public, so I had a little more time. My sport was track. I wore my top loose. But it's hard to hide things in a locker room. My teammates saw it first. They were my Abby."

"Why did she *do* that?" Lily cried, but Susan could only shake her head.

"It's done. There's no going back." She took the car keys from her pocket. "I think you should go home for the day. Let things settle. We'll have more perspective later."

WHAT SHE WAS HOPING, OF COURSE, WAS THAT ABBY'S announcement hadn't actually been heard. It was pure denial on her part, the mother in her. With her emotions seesawing between present and past, a part of her just wanted to hide.

But she had barely returned to her office when the questions began, first from the teacher whose class Lily had just missed, then from another teacher wanting to report what her students were saying. By the time she reached the lunchroom, the looks she received said that word was spreading fast.

Mary Kate and Jess avoided her—but they generally did at school, and with Susan's approval. They had discussed the issue of their relationship when Susan was first named principal. Her closeness to these girls was almost as tricky as her being Lily's mother.

The fact that Mary Kate and Jess were with other friends now—and that none were looking at *them* strangely—told Susan that Lily was the only one who had been outed. For now. Knowing Mary Kate and Jess as she did, she figured they were stressing about that.

Abby never made it to lunch, which wasn't unusual. A student whose schedule was tight often wolfed something down while running between classes. Not that Susan would have been able to talk with her here. What could she have said without making things worse? *How could you do that to a good friend—and knowing about this all along—and trying to get pregnant yourself?*

She couldn't possibly be objective, not with her heart bleeding for her daughter. Lily would be on display, all alone, when she returned to school tomorrow. Susan could only imagine who else would know by then.

IT WAS A LONG DAY. ONLY A FEW OTHER DIRECT questions came, which made Susan nervous. She knew her staff; news like this would fly through the faculty lounge. Friends might be keeping their distance from Susan out of understanding or perhaps respect, but others—her detractors—would be gloating.

She met with two teachers after school. Both, new hires,

were in her office for evaluation conferences. Neither mentioned Lily—but, of course, they were more worried about their jobs than about Susan's pregnant daughter. After the teachers came a pair of parent meetings, one about a drug problem, the other about an alleged plagiarism. They, too, had greater worries.

It did put things in perspective, Susan thought, but by the time she got home, she was discouraged. She wanted to protect her daughter but couldn't, and though she knew that the girl had brought this on herself, her own heart broke.

Lily had been studying, as evidenced by the scatter of books on her bed, but she was sleeping now. Letting her be, Susan went to the den and turned on the TV. She had to wait through stories on the economy, a celebrity murder, and a report on global warming before Rick appeared.

He was covering post-cholera Zimbabwe, in as sobering a report as Susan had heard. Poverty, homelessness, hunger—more perspective here. Lily wasn't poor, homeless, or hungry. But that didn't mean they weren't in crisis.

Remote in hand, she waited until he was into his sign-off before freezing his image on the screen. Then she tossed the remote aside, picked up the cordless, and, with her eyes on his handsome, sunburned face, punched in his number. There was one ring, then another of a slightly different tone as the call was transferred. After five more rings, he picked up.

"Lily?" he asked with endearing hope, his rich voice remarkably clear given how far away he was.

"It's me. That was an amazing piece you just did."

"Sad that someone has to do it," he said, but he sounded pleased to hear her voice. "Hold on a sec, hon." She imagined him pressing the phone to his denim shirt while he spoke to whomever—his producer, a cameraman, the WHO agent he had just interviewed. When he returned, he spoke in an uneven cadence that suggested he was walking, probably looking for privacy. She imagined that he stopped on the far side of the media van.

"We thought things would be better after the cholera epidemic," he said. "It seemed like the world had finally taken notice of what was happening here. But conditions now are worse than ever. Tell me something good, Susie. I need to hear something happy."

Susan had only one thing to tell. "Lily's pregnant."

The silence that followed was so long, she feared they had lost the connection. "Rick?"

"I'm thinking you wouldn't joke about something like that."

"Well, it isn't cholera or poverty. But it is an issue."

There was another pause. Then a frightened "Was she raped?"

"Oh God, no."

"Who's the guy?"

"She won't tell. And no, she hasn't been dating anyone special," Susan rushed on before he could ask. "I see her at school. I see her on the weekends. Usually, if I miss something, I hear it from someone else."

"Why won't she tell?"

Because she's stubborn? Misguided? Loyal? Susan sighed. "Because the guy was only a means to an end." She filled him in as best she could, but even after nine days, the story seemed bizarre. "She and her friends just decided the time was right to have a baby. Mary Kate and Jess are pregnant, too."

She heard a bewildered oath, then an astonished "They made a *pact*?"

There it was, the word she didn't want to hear. "I wouldn't call it that."

"What would you call it?"

She tried to think of a better word. An agreement? A promise? A *deal*? But that was just a way to pretty things up. "A pact," she finally conceded.

"What do we know about pact behavior?" asked Rick the journalist.

"Mostly that Lily isn't your typical candidate," replied Susan the educator. Pact behavior was a school administrator's greatest fear. One kid with a problem was bad enough. But three? "Kids collaborate with one or more friends to do something forbidden. They do it in secret, and it's usually self-destructive."

"But Lily is strong. She's self-confident."

"She's also a teenager with very close friends. They convinced each other that they could be great mothers, better than the ones they worked for last summer."

"They did it because of a *summer job*?"

"No, but that was the catalyst."

"They're only seventeen," he protested. Susan pictured his eyes. They were blue, alternately steely and soft, always mesmerizing. "How far along is she?"

"Twelve weeks. She only told me last week. And no, I didn't see anything. There's still practically nothing to see. I would have called you right away, only she asked me to wait. I don't know if that was out of superstition or fear."

"Fear?"

"That you'd suggest she terminate the pregnancy."

Quietly, he asked, "Is she there? Can I talk with her?"

"She's sleeping." Susan explained what had happened at school.

He swore, echoing Susan's feelings exactly. "It's all over school, then?"

"Not yet. But soon, I'd guess."

He let out a breath, audible over the many miles. "How does she feel about that?"

"Upset. She wanted to wait."

"But she isn't considering abortion."

"No. She's keeping it. She's been firm about that."

"What about you? You think she should?"

That was the question closest to Susan's heart, the dark one, the one she couldn't discuss with anyone else. "Oh, Rick," she said tiredly, "this is where I agonize. You know what I did back then. Once she was inside me, I couldn't bear the thought of not having her, so a part of me understands where she's at now." She paused.

"And the other part?"

"Just wants this to go away," she confessed, feeling like the worst person in the world. "Abortion, adoption—I don't care."

"But you haven't said that to Lily."

"No, and I won't. This is the ugly me speaking. How can I ask my daughter to do something I refused to do? And so what if keeping it changes our lives? We can deal. Who said there was only one way to live a good life?"

There was a longer pause this time, then a quiet "Your dad."

Rick always got it. "Right. So now you're the dad. What do you say?"

"I say *right*'s the word. She has a right to want it, you have a right to want it gone—"

"But I *don't* want it gone," Susan broke in, feeling sinful, "at least, not all the time—only when I think about what a mess this will make of her life, or when I dwell on what an absolutely, incredibly stupid thing this was for her to do. I mean, are *you* proud of what she's done?"

"This minute? No. In five years, I may feel differently."

"Forget five years," Susan cried in frustration. "We're at a crossroads—here, today, now. If she's going to *not* keep this baby, this is the time to decide. *What do I do?*"

"You just said it. How can you ask her to do something you refused to do? She keeps it."

As simply as that, Susan felt a tad lighter. "What do I do about the part of me that resents that?"

"You work on it. You're a good worker."

"Like I'm a good mother?"

"You are. A good mother does her best, even when her own dreams are shot to hell. So, Lily keeps the baby. Does she have a plan?"

"To raise the baby? Well, she says she had a good role model in me." Her voice rose. "Honestly, Rick, I never imagined this. She knows how hard it was for me. She knows what I gave up. I wanted everything to be perfect for her. Maybe I wanted *her* to be perfect."

"No child is perfect."

"Right, so why do I feel betrayed?"

She imagined him considering that, frowning, using a forearm to push dark hair off his face. "That won't help her," he said softly. He was right, of course. This would have to be Susan's mantra. "Think of what you needed back then."

"I do. All the time."

There was a brief silence as the weight of the problem sank in. He might have cursed in the buzz of static that followed, but when he spoke next, there was no mistaking his words. "Will you tell your mother?"

Tell Ellen Tate that the daughter who had disgraced her by getting pregnant at seventeen had let her own daughter do the same? More than at any time in the last week, Susan felt defeated. "This isn't something I imagined sending in a newsy little update, though it might bring a response for once. She'll totally blame me." She pressed the phone to her ear. She had to ask it, bluntly this time. "Do you?"

"Try blame myself," he said, sounding stricken. "I haven't exactly been a hands-on dad. Besides, I've seen you in action. You're the best mother."

"Whose seventeen-year-old daughter is now pregnant and unmarried."

"Like her mom was at seventeen. Maybe Lily's just as stubborn as you were. I offered to marry you, and you refused."

"A decision for which I am grateful every time I see you on TV," Susan told the face on the screen. "You wouldn't have had this career if you'd been saddled with a wife and child."

He made a guttural sound. "Days like today, I'd have preferred the wife and child. What I do can be downright depressing."

"Same *here,*" she cried. "I'm the principal of the high school, where everyone will know my teenage daughter is pregnant. How depressing is that?"

His pause was more thoughtful this time. "Will it cause trouble for you at work?"

Susan rubbed her forehead. "I don't know. We'll see."

"What can I do to help?"

"Strangle the guy who did this to her?" she suggested. "But how foolish is that? She says she seduced him. He didn't know what he was doing."

Rick snorted. "Oh, he did."

"You know what I mean."

"I used to. But this is my daughter, too. Lily has always been innocent."

"Tell me about it," Susan remarked, folding an arm across her middle.

The face on the screen was unchanged. "So what was he thinking? Was he coming on to her for months? Did he just wear her down? Did he ask if she was on the pill? Did he offer to use something *himself*?"

Touched by the spate of questions—loving him for loving her, dark side and all—she actually laughed. "Rick, I don't know. I wasn't there. And no, I didn't ask. If the horse is already out of the barn, what's the point?"

"So here's my next line of attack. Did she pick him for a reason? Like you picked me?"

She smiled. "I didn't pick you. You took me by storm. There was no forethought."

"No." His voice was soft, poignant. "There never is, is there?"

LILY'S CELL RANG AT NINE THAT NIGHT. IT WASN'T the first message she'd received. Mary Kate and Jess had texted to rant about Abby, leaving Lily agitated. Half hoping Abby was calling so that she could rant herself, she tore open the phone. "Yes."

"Lily?" came a cautious male voice.

She knew it well. Its owner was a fixture in her life—never demanding, just there. Her heart raced. "Hi."

"Is it true?"

She didn't have to ask how he knew. Everyone at school must know. Part of her wanted to lie, to make it all go away, to take herself out of the glare. But it would only be worse when she started to show.

Lying back on the pillow, she stared at the front window and said, "It's true."

There was a pause. She imagined him looking puzzled, maybe scratching the top of his head. Finally, unsurely, he asked, "Is it mine?"

The question hit her the wrong way, like he was suggesting she slept with just anyone. "Why would it be you?" she snapped. "You aren't the only guy around."

"I know. But that night . . ."

"Once. We were together once. Nothing happens once. Do you know what the chances are of it happening once? Do you know how *long* some couples have to wait before they get pregnant?"

"You weren't with anyone else."

No unsureness there. Calming a little, she asked, "How do you know?"

"Because I know you. And there was blood."

"Women bleed every month," she said, crawling over the foot of the bed and closing the blind. Easier to fudge things when no one could see. "Really, Robbie. Don't let your imagination go wild."

"It's hard not to," he said, sounding upset. "I was way on the other side of the school when you got sick, but by the time I got out of English, kids were talking about it. They know we're good friends, so they asked me. I didn't know what to say."

"Just say you don't know. That's the truth, isn't it?"

He didn't reply at first. Then he said, "How are you feeling?"

Back on the bed again, Lily stared at the closed blind. She'd been just fine until he called. Remembering the scene at school, she felt sick again.

But everyone would be asking her this. She had to get used to it. "I'm really good. Happy. It's incredible, creating a life." She put a hand on her belly, jiggled it a little to wake the baby up and let her know she was being talked about.

"When are you due?"

"Late May. The timing's perfect," she rushed on. "I'll finish exams, have my baby, do the mom thing over the summer, and be ready to start college in the fall." Mary Kate and Jess were a little behind her and would have less time to recover before classes resumed.

"How can you do college? Who'll take care of the baby?"

"I'll put her in PC KidsCare."

"Her? You know the sex already?"

Lily laughed. "No. It's too soon. I'm just guessing it's a girl." Like she was guessing that Mary Kate and Jess would have girls, too. She wanted her daughter to be best friends with theirs, a third generation of best friends. "Right now, my baby has hands and feet. And *ears*. Doesn't that blow your mind?"

But he was still focusing on the future. "Isn't PC KidsCare only for PC employees?"

"I knit samples for PC Wool trunk shows, so technically, I am one. Besides, I have an in. Mrs. Perry will make it happen." *If* Lily ever spoke with Pam's daughter, Abby, again, which, at that moment, was questionable.

"I still think it's me," Robbie said.

"That's because you're sweet."

"Lily, I have a right to know if it's me."

"So you can drop out of school to support the baby? You're not going to do that, Robbie. Besides, I told you. It isn't you."

"Why do I not believe you?"

"Maybe," she tried, "because it's macho to think you've fathered a baby." *Macho* wasn't a word that she would have used to describe Robbie—but it wasn't totally wrong, she realized. He had grown in the last year and had to be six-two now. Granted, he was still the lightest guy on the wrestling squad, but what he lacked in muscle, he made up for in determination. He definitely knew the moves.

"Forget macho," he said. "It's pure math. If you're due at

the end of May, you conceived at the end of August, and that's when we did it."

"I won't tell you again," she said quietly.

"Then whose is it?" he asked. When she said nothing, he pleaded, "Tell me something, Lily. If you think my questions are hard, just wait'll tomorrow. Whether or not I'm the father, I'm a friend. Let me help."

Lily's eyes filled with tears. The books said she would be emotional. And Robbie *was* a friend. And she was dreading going to school.

But if he helped, people would think he was the father, and she didn't want that. This was her doing alone.

Well, not exactly alone. Mary Kate, Jess, and Abby were in on it, too. But no one knew yet about Mary Kate and Jess, and Abby was sore because she was way behind.

What to tell Robbie? She needed time to think.

"If I told anyone," she finally said, "I'd tell you. Next to Mary Kate and Jess, you're my oldest friend." Since they were six. It was poetic.

No, she had no regrets about Robbie. Abby, yes. But not Robbie. He was loyal. If she did need help, he would be there.

THAT THOUGHT BROUGHT LITTLE COMFORT AS SHE dressed for school the next morning. Mary Kate and Jess would help out if questions got bad, but she felt best when she thought of her mom. Susan had done it, and look at her. She was educated. She was successful. And she had Lily to show for it.

Standing at the mirror, dressed in slim-as-ever jeans, Lily touched the place where she guessed her baby to be and whispered, "You're mine, sweet thing. I'll take care of you. Let people talk. We don't care. We have something special, you and me. And we have my mom and my dad. They're gonna love you to bits. Trust me on that."

AT SCHOOL THERE WERE FEW QUESTIONS, JUST STARES. Her mother wasn't so lucky.

Chapter 6

◦⟨✦⟩◦

SUSAN WAS ON THE PHONE WITH A HEADHUNTER, whom she hoped would locate a replacement for the retiring director of athletics, when Pam showed up at the door and, none too softly, said, "What did I just hear?"

Finger to her lips, Susan waved her in. "Yes, Tom. Male or female. Our current AD coaches football, but that isn't a prerequisite. My priorities are administrative experience and the ability to work well with kids."

"Susan," Pam whispered urgently as she closed the door, "what did I *hear*?"

Susan gestured her to a chair and held up a hand for the minute it took to finish the call.

Pam didn't wait a second longer. The phone was barely in its cradle when she said, "Word's going around that Lily's pregnant. I've had three calls this morning—three moms asking me the same thing—and I couldn't answer, even though I'm your friend, which was one of the reasons they were calling me. I couldn't even call Abby, because *you* don't allow kids to use phones during school. Is it true?"

Pam was a Perry by marriage and, as such, a member of the town's royalty, but she didn't often pull rank. Susan wasn't sure what she heard in Pam's voice—whether it was arrogance, indignation, or hurt—but she felt a quick anger. There would have been no calls, no questions had it not been for Pam's own daughter.

But Lily would still be pregnant. Resigned, Susan nodded.

"How?" Pam asked in dismay. It was a silly question. Susan's expression must have said as much, because her friend hurried on. *"Who?"*

Susan shrugged and shook her head.

Pam was sitting on the edge of the seat, her cardigan open, a paisley scarf knotted artfully about her neck. "You have to know. You're just not saying."

"Pam, I don't know."

"That's impossible. You and Lily are as close as any mother and daughter I know. She must have told you she was sleeping with someone." When Susan shook her head again, Pam said, "How could you not?"

Susan was duly chastised. She had prided herself on being one better than the parent who didn't notice her Vicodin running low long before it should. It was a humbling experience.

"There comes a point," she said in her own defense, "when our children choose not to share some things."

"Some things. This is *major*. When did you find out?"

Unable to lie, Susan said, "Last week." It felt like years ago. She kept flashing back to Lily's conception. Even this morning, reliving her own nightmare of going to school on the day after the whole world suddenly knew, she half expected Lily to show up at her door in tears, looking for a shoulder to cry on.

But either Mary Kate and Jess were walking the halls beside her or Lily was tougher than Susan had been. And perhaps that was for the best. Lily had become pregnant by design— *and* in agreement with friends. She had way more to answer for than Susan had.

Pam Perry didn't know the half of it. Innocently, she exclaimed, "Last week? Omigod, Susan. This is *awful*. What was she thinking?" When Susan simply gave her a look, she said, "What are you going to *do*?"

"I'm trying to figure that out."

"She's keeping the baby? Of course she is. Lily loves kids, and there's no way you'd make her abort it. So the guy has to come forward," Pam decided. "You have to find out who he is." When Susan said nothing, she added, "Well, *some* guy made this happen."

"Obviously," Susan replied, "but does his name matter?"

"Absolutely."

"Wrong. It's a woman's body, a woman's baby."

"You say that because you're a single mom."

"I say it because I'm a realist," Susan insisted. "Even moms in traditional families do the brunt of the child care. The buck stops here."

"Some of us see it differently," Pam argued. "The father has to share the responsibility."

"Maybe in an ideal world," Susan conceded. "You're lucky, Pam. Not only is your husband a gem, but he's from a storied family. Perrys don't divorce, and they don't go broke. But Tanner doesn't change diapers or fold laundry or make school lunches, and that drives you nuts. Remember the time you and Tanner both had the flu? Who was crawling out of bed to take care of Abby?"

There was more to the story, of course. Pam did all of those things without complaint, though she could certainly afford a maid. But with one child and no other full-time job, these chores helped define her.

"So, basically, you're having another child yourself," Pam said. "Isn't that the bottom line?"

Susan considered it, pressed her lips together, nodded.

"You can't do that," Pam argued. "You know the work. You have a whole other job now that is very demanding."

"What would you have me do?" Susan asked. Frustrated, she rubbed her forehead with her fingertips. "She wants the baby, Pam. She's heard the heartbeat. She knows the options. She wants the baby."

"And you'll just let her have it?"

"*What can I do*? Put yourself in my shoes. This has happened—past tense. It's done. Maybe you can do better and talk with *your* daughter about not getting pregnant." There it was, the closest Susan could come to disclosing what she knew.

Pam frowned at the papers on the desk, then at Susan. "This is what you three were talking about at the barn last week. You told them. Why couldn't you tell me?"

Susan felt another stab of anger. At Lily for getting pregnant? At Abby for outing her? At *Pam* for playing the victim? "They already knew," she explained. "Mary Kate had told Kate, and Jess had told Sunny, but clearly Abby hadn't said anything to you, or you would have mentioned it. Has she yet?"

Pam raised her chin. "No, but she considers Lily one of her closest friends. She probably feels it wouldn't be loyal."

"*Loyal*? Abby was the one who shouted it all over school!" Pam looked startled, but Susan couldn't stop. If Pam wanted to be a friend, she had to hear this. "Abby blurted it out yesterday in the hall filled with kids, so maybe you should be talking with her, not with me. But those moms who called you this morning didn't tell you that, did they?"

"No," Pam said, subdued. "They heard rumors. They know

we're friends, and since I'm on the school board, they thought they were killing two birds with one stone."

Susan felt a hitch at mention of the school board. It had seven members. All were elected; most had served for years. At thirty-nine, Pam was the baby of the group, elected largely because of her name. The closest to her in age was the board chair, Hillary Dunn, who was fifty-five. The other five members were men, four of whom were particularly resistant to change. Susan had had to argue for hours, working them individually and as a group, before they gave the school clinic a green light.

They would all be upset when they learned Lily was pregnant. And when they heard about the other two girls?

But first things first. Susan was tempted to ask Pam the names of those who had called, only she could guess. Zaganack was a close community. Its members had a good thing going with Perry & Cass and knew it, and while some were open to innovation, others believed that you didn't tamper with the status quo. Those were the ones who phoned Susan to complain about the slightest curriculum change. They were the ones who would have phoned Pam.

"Were they calling to complain?" Susan asked.

"Mostly to know if it was true."

"And then to complain." When Pam didn't deny it, she asked, "What did you tell them?"

"I said I'd check it out—I tried to make light of it. When all three carried on, I said that if it was true, it was a private matter. Only it isn't, Susan. This could really screw things up. For starters, there's the PC Wool Mother's Day promotion. Boy, does that take on new meaning. Lily will be big as a house."

Susan had thought this herself, but it was offensive coming from Pam. "Were you planning to photograph her in profile for the catalogue cover?"

"You know what I mean."

"No, I don't. Our clients don't have to know about Lily. What she does with her life has nothing to do with PC Wool."

"She knits for us."

"So do Mary Kate, Abby, and Jess."

"They're not pregnant," Pam pointed out.

Tell her, that little voice in Susan cried. Tell her out of friendship and concern. But her loyalty was to Kate and Sunny. Pam was a latecomer to the group and, given her role as a Perry, a sporadic member. That said, when she was with them, she was a devoted friend. The group gave her focus, which she craved. She loved belonging, which added to the guilt Susan felt in keeping silent.

"What should I tell Tanner?" Pam asked. "He'll want to know who the father is."

"Tell him I don't know."

"Hey," she drawled, "if that's hard for *me* to believe, he never will. Same with the school board. They'll be gunning for bear when they hear about this. The principal's daughter? I mean, it really puts me in a bad place. I recused myself when it came to voting on you for this job, but talk about conflict of interest. What am I supposed to do now?"

Wait'll she hears about the others, Susan thought, and her uneasiness grew. "Buy me some time?" she begged. "That's all I ask. A little time."

BUT PAM WAS NO SOONER OUT THE DOOR THAN SUSAN'S assistant, Rebecca, appeared. A capable woman with thick white hair, she was the school's resident grandmother. "Dr. Correlli's on his way over. He asked if you had a few minutes to talk. I tried to tell him you were scheduled to observe sophomore English, but he said it was urgent." She was apologetic. "I'm sorry. Have you told him yet?"

"Not me," Susan murmured and tried to gear up, but there was only one thing she could imagine the superintendent wanted to discuss.

Phillip Correlli was a stocky man who often ran with the cross-country team to try to lose weight. Having risen through the ranks as Susan had, albeit in a different school system, he liked being with kids. Even more, he liked turning life's trials into lessons—the one for the cross-country team being that if you ate badly, you gained weight.

He appeared at her door now with an apology for interrupting, but he didn't sit, and he didn't waste time. "The phone's been ringing. Tell me that what I heard isn't true."

Susan tried to stay calm. "I can't."

"Your Lily? She's the *last* one I'd have expected to be pregnant."

"That makes two of us, Phil."

"How did it happen? Lily is a good girl, and I'd have heard from the police if there was a rape, so it must have been someone she knew. Was she forced?"

"No," Susan said and, leaving the desk, sank into a chair.

He continued to stand. "Careless?"

Even that would have been easier to swallow, Susan knew. But what could she say without betraying her daughter's confidence?

"I'm a friend," Phil reminded her gently. Only it wasn't as simple as that. He was also a colleague, a mentor, and, as superintendent of schools, her boss. He was the one who had pushed her to apply for the principalship, the one who had championed her when the board questioned her youth and lack of experience. He was the one who had shown up in person to offer her the job, and his pride was genuine.

"That's one of the reasons this is so hard," she tried to explain. "I've just learned about it myself. It's still raw."

"I understand, but we don't have much of a window here. You're in a public position. To judge from the calls I'm getting, you won't have the luxury of time." He scowled. "I wish we were talking about someone else's child. We've dealt with pregnancies before. But you're our principal, so the playing field is different. I was caught flat-footed this morning. It would have been better if I'd had a heads-up."

Susan was sorry to have let him down. "In hindsight, you're right. But I've been agonizing over this on a personal level, and I needed more time. I didn't expect word to spread so fast." She explained how it had.

"A friend, huh? That stinks. Did you know Lily was sexually active?"

Either way she answered, Susan was damned. So she said, "Lily and I have discussed sexual responsibility more times than I can count. Right now, we're just trying to plan for the future. She claims she can study and have a baby *and* go to college." Feeling an old shame, Susan added quietly, "Who am I to contradict her?"

"Yup," he murmured. He scratched the back of his head and asked a puzzled, "Is she having trouble in school?"

"No."

"Scared about next year?"

"No. Phil, it just happened."

Leaning against the desk, he asked meekly, "Can I *say* she was forced?"

Susan caught his drift. He needed a story that would sit well with the town. It was about damage control.

He elaborated. "See, I need a reason why this could happen to the daughter of my principal. It'd be best if I could say Lily was forced or even that she's in *love*." He paused. "Otherwise, they'll blame you."

Blame her? After all she'd done with her life in the last seventeen years? And the good will she'd built up in the last two—was it worth *nothing*?

"I had *no say* in this, Phil," Susan argued. "I've been a hands-on mother. I've taught Lily all the right things. But she didn't consult me. She—" *consulted her friends,* Susan nearly said but caught herself. "She *didn't* consult me," she managed to repeat, shaken. She hadn't thought about the others until now, but it was a staggering omission. The idea of a pact made things ten times worse. It might spread the blame around a little, but Susan was still the most prominent of the players. The town would be obsessed with the story. Phil would not be happy.

"But you're her mother."

"She isn't five," Susan cried in a voice heightened by panic. "Would you have me be one of those parents who wait at the curb to whisk their kids off the instant classes are done? Or who e-mail their kids' teachers five times a day? Or stand over their kids' shoulders the whole time they're doing homework to make sure they don't get a texted answer from a friend? That's micromanaging. We've discussed this, Phil. We both hate it. I've talked with parents about it. I've addressed the issue in bulletins. At some level, parents have to trust."

"And when they perceive that the trust is betrayed by someone in a position of authority?" he asked, but quickly relented. "Look. You're a role model for our students. That's one of the reasons I fought to give you this position. You're an example of what a woman can do when life takes a wrong turn. Only it's taking the same turn again, and that won't sit well. Once, okay. Learn from the lesson and move on. Twice?" Lips compressed, he shook his head.

"The situations aren't the same," Susan argued, though if he had asked how they differed, she would have been in trouble. But she was in trouble anyway. There was so much he didn't know.

"You were seventeen," he remarked. "She's seventeen."

What could Susan say to that? He was right.

She must have looked stricken, because his face gentled. Bracing his hands on the edge of the desk, he said, "See, if it had been anyone else getting pregnant, there would be no issue. Because it's Lily, we need a plan. The best we can say is that there was an accident. That'll give us an excuse to talk about the consequences of being irresponsible. We can involve the school clinic, maybe conduct a series of lectures about the downside of teenage pregnancy."

"We already have."

"Well, the circumstances call for more, because here's another flash. With you principal and Lily a model student, there could be copycatting. We don't want that. Get a doctor in to paint the dire consequences of teen pregnancy. It'll be a good use of the clinic, maybe convince a few doubters on that score. We have to hit this hard."

"At my daughter's expense."

"Who told her to get pregnant?" he asked.

He didn't have a clue how loaded the question was.

Chapter 7

THE MINUTE HE WAS GONE, SUSAN OPENED HER CELL. Her hand shook. Even the sound of Kate's *hey* did nothing to soothe her.

"We have a problem—*I* have a problem," she said, head bent over the phone. "Correlli just left. He knows about Lily, but not about the others. He's worried about copycat behavior, when what he really needs to worry about is *pact* behavior. But it doesn't stop there, Kate. This situation is reflecting on me, my character, my *job*." She hadn't imagined this a week ago. Back then, the extent of the problem was Lily's pregnancy. "You'd think there'd be some understanding—everyone knows teenagers act out. Don't I get cut a little slack? School board members who will be the most critical of me are the ones whose kids did God-knows-what behind *their* backs. But forget the board," she hurried on, fingertips to her forehead. "I have to tell Phil about Mary Kate and Jess. He'll find out anyway, and the more he goes ahead with damage control for one pregnancy, the more he'll look like a fool when it turns out there are three. Phil is my boss, Kate. He hires and fires. I need him on my side." She swore softly. "What a mess."

"That's a kind word for it," Kate mused. "All it would have taken was one of them saying, 'No, don't do this, bad idea.' But my daughter went right along. Whose idea was it anyway? Which one of them dreamed it up?"

"I haven't asked Lily that," Susan said. "But the immediate issue is Phil. What am I supposed to do, Kate? He'll learn about Mary Kate and Jess soon enough, and it had better come from my mouth, or his faith in me will be even more shot than it already is. Have you talked with Mary Kate about when she's planning to tell people?"

"She wants to wait."

"And let Lily be strung up alone?"

There was a pause, then a defensive, "It's not easy for us, either."

Susan softened. "I know. But what if I told Phil in confidence? What if I prefaced it by saying that I was sharing this with him because there is *serious* damage control to be done, and he needs to be in the loop? I've shared information on students with him in the past, and he's always been good for his word. He can be trusted." The other end of the line was silent. "Kate?"

"I'm wishing you weren't principal of the high school. I'd have preferred to fly under the radar."

Susan wondered if that was resentment she heard. Unnerved, she said, "Right now, I'm wishing it, too. But don't be angry at me, Kate. *I* didn't dream up this scheme."

"I know."

She waited for Kate to say more—Kate, who could always go with the flow, believing that everything worked out in the end. But that Kate was silent.

"It'd be nice to have a little control over what happens now,"

Susan argued. "That's another reason to share this with Phil. And about Mary Kate—how long can you hide it—maybe two months?"

"No one *cares* if my daughter is pregnant. I never finished college. No one expects great things of my kids."

"Excuse me? Kate, your kids are all at the top of the class."

"But no one's watching us. Alex was pulled over once and ticketed for having open beer in the car, and no one cared. I *like* being anonymous."

"Do you honestly think that if one of your twins had made a pregnancy pact with friends when she was in high school, no one would care? Come on, Kate. It'd be on the front page of the paper!"

"Omigod," Kate shrieked. "Is that where we're heading with this?"

Susan couldn't answer. At every turn, it seemed, there was another layer to the horror. Trying to stay calm, she focused on Phil. "That's another reason to tell Correlli. He has an in with the paper. If he can't keep it out of the press, at least he might be able to control what they print." Tired as she was, *frightened* as she was, she had to convince Kate. "Look, I won't say anything unless Sunny agrees, too. There's no point in telling Phil half the story. It's either all or nothing."

"What if you told him without using our names? Wouldn't that solve your problem?"

"It might solve mine, but it wouldn't solve yours. He'd guess right away it was Mary Kate, and if he didn't, one question to any of Lily's teachers would bring up her name. That teacher might ask another, who might mention it to a third, and before you know it, speculation is rampant. Far better that I tell it all to Phil in confidence. And here's the thing. Phil is really good with kids. He might be a help with our girls."

Kate sputtered. "How can he help? It's not like he has a say in whether Mary Kate keeps her baby, and he sure as hell won't help pay its way. Oh, we can manage, Susie, I know we can. But I wanted my kids to do more than just manage. I keep asking Mary Kate what she was thinking when she took it upon herself to do this, and each time, she goes off on a long discussion of how she's looked at it from every angle and knows it will work. But she hasn't looked at it from my angle or from Will's—or from *Jacob's*. I can't imagine what *he'll* feel when he finds out. Our daughters didn't look past themselves. They didn't consider *us*."

Relieved that they were on the same side about this at least, Susan said, "No. And Phil will know eventually. Let me tell him now."

"I should ask Will. He works for the company. What if the company has a problem with the pregnancies? Will Pam cover?"

Once Susan would have answered in the affirmative, but there was so much yet to play out. "I don't know. She stormed in here earlier, angry that I hadn't told her about Lily. She doesn't know about Mary Kate and Jess, yet, and I couldn't warn her about Abby, for which I will be eternally damned. Believe it or not, Pam isn't as worried about Perry and Cass as she is about the school board. Our being friends puts her in a vise. Honestly? If push comes to shove and she has to take a stand, I'm not sure whose side she'll take."

"She'll take yours. I'd put money on that. She loves you. You represent everything she wishes she could be."

"Unmarried?" Susan asked dryly.

"Your career, your focus. She looks to you for advice. I've seen it even when Sunny and I are right there. She asks you, not us. By the way, what does Sunny say about this?"

"She's my next call. I can wait until you talk this over with Will. Or I can test the waters with Sunny," she said, taking a lighter note. "I can pretend you've given me the okay—you know, take a page from our kids' book—the old '*my* mommy says it's okay' trick. If Sunny agrees, you won't have much of a leg to stand on."

Kate snorted. "Like I have much of a leg to stand on now? I still wish you weren't such a big cheese. But go ahead. I don't have to ask Will. He'll know you're in a bind. Just make sure Phil doesn't blab until we're ready. I'm counting on you, Susie. Don't let us down."

ONE OF THE ADVANTAGES OF BEING PRINCIPAL WAS that Susan's schedule was more forgiving than if, say, there were twenty-five juniors waiting in a classroom for her to discuss *Jane Eyre*. Emergencies were part of her day. She could postpone a teacher meeting or class visit, and the world accepted that she was dealing with something urgent.

So, asking her assistant to reschedule sophomore English observation and ignoring a computer screen filled with pending e-mail, she left school. She walked quickly; it was a cold day. The wind was blowing dried leaves from branches, whipping others up from the ground. When her hair flew, Susan tucked it into her collar and double-wrapped her scarf, leaving a hand in the wool for its warmth. The scarf was of sock yarn from the fall collection—called Last Blaze—and perfectly matched the reds and oranges the leaves had so recently been. They were faded now, but her scarf, knit double-stranded in flamelike chevrons, was as bold as ever.

Head low against the wind, she pushed on to Main Street. She trotted past a tour bus that was pulling up at the curb, crossed diagonally, and continued on another block to Perry & Cass Home Goods. One foot in the door and she was enveloped in the scent of spiced pumpkin. Thanksgiving was coming on fast, with autumnal tableware, wood carving boards, and ceramic serving pieces prominently displayed. Seasonal candles and potpourri were on one side, cookware on another, but it was at the back of the store, where yarn filled huge baskets, that Susan spotted Sunny.

She wore dark green today, coordinating slacks, sweater, and hair bow. Susan immediately recognized the sweater as one Sunny had knit the summer before when the first of the fall colors had been painted and skeined. A rich hunter shot through with tiny wisps of russet and gold, it was one of Susan's favorites. Sunny was an exquisite knitter, the only one of the four who could be trusted doing straight stockinette. Every stitch was precise.

She was talking to a display designer, seemingly engrossed until she saw Susan, at which point she was immediately distracted.

"Um, that might work," she said to the designer, "um, it probably will—but don't line the baskets with anything dark. I want this part of the store to be, um, bright. Excuse me, I'll be right back." Hurrying over, she guided Susan to a nook where mounds of goose down pillows and comforters would be a buffer and, even then, kept her voice down. "What's happened? Does someone else know?"

"No. That's the problem," Susan said and told her about Phil. She hadn't even finished before Sunny was shaking her head.

"Uh-uh. I refuse. This is too humiliating. It'd be one thing if Jessica was in love with someone, like Mary Kate is. She could get married and be part of an adorable young couple who, by the way, is having a baby, but that's not the case at all. Jessica has no intention of getting married and every intention of keeping this baby. I'm so angry with her, I don't know what to do."

"I'm angry at Lily—"

"Not like this. Trust me. I don't want my daughter around, and she knows it. Why do you think she's been at your house so much?"

Susan realized it was true. "I know, but this doesn't solve the problem," she argued. "We need help."

"I can't go public."

"Not public. Just Phil."

"Phil *is* public," Sunny cried in a frantic whisper, gripping the laces that framed her V-neck. "You can't imagine how I feel. I swear, this is in the genes. Jessica called my mother last night—my mother, the queen of quirky—and she's just *fine* with her teenage granddaughter being pregnant, or so Jessica says. I have to take her word for it, because I am *not* about to discuss this with my mother."

"It is not your fault."

"Dan blames me."

"That's because he needs to blame someone, but he's wrong."

"Is he?" Sunny asked. Her V-neck was narrowing as she clenched the laces. "He says I never confronted the issue of my mother head-on, and maybe he's right. I've talked to Jessica until I was blue in the face about the right and wrong way of doing things, but did I ever come out and say my mother is a misfit? Did I ever call her unbalanced or selfish or . . . or evil? Well, she isn't evil, just totally outrageous—but no, I don't call my mother names in front of the kids, because a good person doesn't *do* that. Oh, and Dan blames you and Kate for not controlling *your* daughters, because Jessica would never have done this alone."

Susan felt the same qualm she had earlier with Kate. These friends meant the world to her. With so much happening, she needed them on her side. "Going after each other won't help. Playing the blame game is destructive."

"Tell that to Dan."

"Is he going after Adam, too?"

"No, because Jessica won't confirm that it was Adam, and Dan won't confront anyone on the outside yet. He wants to keep this as quiet as possible. In the meanwhile, he has me to upbraid."

Susan loved Dan for enabling Sunny to create the structured life she needed, but he had strong opinions and was judgmental without ever raising his voice. "Speak up, Sunny. Tell him he's wrong."

"Easier said than done." She continued to tug at her neckline. "You don't know what it's like to have a husband."

Coming from a stranger, it might have been a slap in the face, but Susan knew Sunny wasn't criticizing her; she was simply complaining about Dan.

Susan covered her friend's hand lest she choke herself. "He's being unfair."

"He's my *husband*."

It wasn't anything new. In all the years Susan had known her, Sunny had deferred to Dan on every major issue. There had been times, even during the creation of PC Wool, when he had been an uninvited presence, second-guessing every decision. Much as the others coached her, though—much as Sunny promised not to ask his permission when she wanted, say, to buy a new coat—she always fell back to the default.

But Susan didn't have the strength to argue. "I just think we should get Phil on our side."

"You're worried about your job," Sunny hissed, "but what about mine? What about Dan's? Fine for you to act in *your* own best interest, but what about *ours*? Your daughter may be making waves, but mine is barely seven weeks pregnant. *I* don't need to go public yet. It'll be another three months before anyone even guesses."

"I thought the same thing about Lily, and look what happened," Susan pointed out. Yes, she was acting in her own best interest, but the line between what was best for her and what was best for her friends was fluid. She squeezed Sunny's hand to soften the words. "Who's to say Abby won't blab about Mary Kate and Jessica, too?"

"You need to be talking to her, not to me."

Not a bad idea, Susan realized. But the basic problem remained. "This month, next month, the month after—it doesn't matter, Sunny. You can put it off all you want, but sooner or later the story will break."

"Later is better. At least the holidays will be over. Next week is Thanksgiving, for God's sake. If this comes out now, with us going to Albany to see Dan's family, it'll ruin *everything*."

If it wasn't Thanksgiving, it would be Christmas. There would never be a good time for this, Susan knew. But she could wait a week.

NEWS OF LILY'S PREGNANCY SPREAD. BACK IN HER office, Susan received a call from the middle school principal, who was ostensibly more curious than disapproving, though Susan imagined the latter was there. When she stopped at PC Beans for coffee on her way to a varsity football game, she felt other customers staring. And when she went to the supermarket on her way home, she *knew* the checkout clerk was darting her questioning looks.

The following day, she and Kate were the only ones at the

barn. Sunny was baking pies to take to her in-laws, and Pam was preparing for the Thanksgiving open house the Perrys hosted each year.

They didn't dye yarn, didn't even play with colors. Neither of them had the heart for it. So they knitted. Susan's work in progress was a T-shirt for Lily, Kate's a set of cotton place mats. They admired each other's work and talked about the menu for their own Thanksgiving at Kate's, the rise in postal rates, the weather. Neither of them mentioned that Lily's T-shirt wouldn't fit her for long, or that the place mats might not hold up well spattered with baby food.

ON SUNDAY, SUSAN WORKED ON HER BUDGET, WITH papers spread over the kitchen table beside her laptop and a calculator nearby. She wrote up several teacher evaluations that she had neglected earlier that week. She composed her Monday bulletin, giving a plug for the concert at school Tuesday night, a reminder of the food bank drive that would start after Thanksgiving, and a get-well wish for the school librarian's husband.

Lily's singing group, the Zaganotes, usually practiced Sunday afternoons. With the Thanksgiving concert imminent, the practice today started earlier and ended later. Normally, Susan would have hated the silence of the house and would have either met a friend for coffee or asked someone over.

This week she stayed home. The house was dead quiet and too lonesome for comfort, but she didn't have the strength to go out. She told herself she was tired and, once she had finished her work, burrowed into the den sofa with the Sunday paper. But she couldn't focus on news. The silence of the house was too loud. So she picked up her knitting—not the T-shirt for Lily, but a pair of socks for herself. When she had a split-second thought that she ought to be knitting baby booties, she ignored it.

The problem was, her life seemed to be made up of split seconds now—a split second imagining Lily having sex, a split second hearing the gossips in town spreading the word, a split second wondering what her parents would think—all horrendous thoughts, none of which she could bear to dwell on. Put all those split seconds together, though, and she wasn't thinking about much else.

Except Lily. Always Lily. She missed their closeness, missed the way they could finish each other's sentences, the way they could watch a movie they both loved, the way they could knit together in silence and feel totally at peace.

Lily had ruined all that, which made Susan angry. A good mother loved her daughter no matter what.

She did love Lily. She just didn't *like* her very much right then, and that upset her even more.

BY MONDAY, SHE WAS RECEIVING CALLS FROM RANDOM friends, from a parent of one of her students who had graduated the year before, even from a woman who had worked at PC KidsCare when Lily was first enrolled. As she had done Friday afternoon, Susan imagined each caller hanging up and instantly calling five friends.

Rather than go to the gym after work, Susan went straight home. She had a quiet dinner with Lily. It lasted all of ten minutes. Afterward, she knitted. She had botched shaping her sock's heel gusset the day before, so she ripped out what she'd done and tried again. She had to do it three times before she was finally pleased, but she welcomed the forced concentration.

Still, she heard the shower go on and off, heard Lily come

down for a drink, heard the phone ring. Normally, she would have stopped by Lily's room two or three times before going to bed, but she didn't this night. Nor did Lily come in to see her.

Not that Susan could blame her. Lily clearly felt Susan's disapproval. Having been in her shoes, Susan knew how that was. When she had been pregnant, she had consciously avoided confrontations with her parents.

History was repeating itself.

ON TUESDAY, LILY MADE THE FINAL CUT FOR THE varsity volleyball team. Ebullient, she ran to Susan's office with the news. She saw this as a personal vindication, a *See, I can do this!* moment.

Susan tried to be happy for her, but all the while, part of her was thinking that the coach had no business taking on a pregnant player, that it was sending the wrong message to other students, that Lily had no right to have her cake and eat it, too.

Later that afternoon, when Lily dashed into the house barely twenty minutes before being picked up for the concert, and declined to eat any of the dinner Susan had made, Susan reminded her that her baby needed to eat even if she did not. Moments later, feeling guilty for the sharpness of her tone, she went scrambling to find the black sweater Lily wanted to wear and was in a tizzy trying to find.

After Lily raced out the door, Susan felt abandoned. She sat down to have some of the chicken pot pie that she and Lily both liked, but eating it alone killed her appetite.

Leaving the table, she opened her laptop on the kitchen counter. E-mail was backing up, including a new one from Phil about the budget she had just submitted. She had to address his queries, had to answer urgent parent questions, had to write college recommendations for three students she had taught as freshmen and with whom she remained close. As she stared at the screen, a note arrived from the woman heading the auction that was held every February to raise money for class trips. She was reminding Susan that copy was due for the PC Wool contribution she had offered, which got Susan to thinking that the past few Saturdays had been a bust workwise, that they hadn't begun testing spring colors, much less produced something to photograph for Pam. She wondered if Pam was going to want to go ahead at all once she learned the whole truth—which got Susan into a snit, because she loved PC Wool and couldn't bear the thought that it might be at risk because Lily had decided she needed to have a baby.

Beside herself with dismay, Susan strode into the den, snatched up her knitting, and settled cross-legged on the sofa, but she didn't have the wherewithal to focus on finishing the heel. She needed straight, simple stockinette stitches. Tossing the sock aside, she stomped back into the kitchen, pulled the T-shirt from her knitting bag, and, for a minute, standing there at the table set for a dinner that wasn't to be, she knit feverishly. She was thinking that she was doing a lousy job— lousy knitter, lousy principal, lousy mother—when a loud knock at the door interrupted her.

Startled, she jumped up, dropping a handful of stitches, and, tossing the knitting aside in disgust, went to answer the door.

Chapter 8

RICK McKAY HAD ALWAYS AFFECTED SUSAN. TRUE TO
form, her heart began to race when she saw him on the other
side of the glass. The cause of it this time, though, wasn't
excitement but fury. She continued to glare as he turned the
handle and let himself in, his handsome face lit by a smile.

"Hey," he said. His eyes never left her face, nor did his smile
falter as he leaned against the door to close it. He was clearly
delighted to see her, which infuriated Susan all the more.

"If you're looking for your daughter, she just left. She
breezed through here with no interest in eating the dinner I
took the effort to make—though she did wail for help, child
that she is, when she couldn't find the sweater she wanted to
wear. It's like nothing has changed! She just made the volleyball team, though I can't imagine she'll be able to play the late
games in March, but she's barreling ahead as if everything's
okay. Only it *isn't*. She doesn't seem to see any consequences.
But I'm feeling them already. People are talking—and *they*
don't even know about the *other* two"—she waved the thought

away—"I can't *begin* to go there yet. My boss is furious even without it—at me, not at Lily, at *me*. What did I do wrong, except raise her the best way I know how?" Eyes tearing, she crossed her arms. "Why are you *smiling*? This is serious, Rick."

"Boy, have I missed you," he said in that rich voice of his.

"That is *irrelevant*!" she cried, fighting panic. "We're in a crisis here, only my daughter—*your* daughter—doesn't seem to understand that. Three girls pregnant? Every time I think about it, I start to shake. If she wanted to rebel, couldn't she have dyed her hair pink, or pierced her navel, or gotten a *tattoo*?"

"She says it isn't rebellion."

"No," Susan allowed, "not rebellion. She wants a family. So how does that make *me* feel? I've worked my *tail* off to be her family. If she was that desperate for a bigger one, she should have told me. I could have adopted a baby. I could have gone to a sperm bank."

"You could have asked me."

"Rick, this isn't *funny*. She's pregnant, refuses to identify the guy, and doesn't have a *clue* what her future will be like."

"Would it help if she did?" he asked in a tone so reasonable that Susan's anger ebbed.

"Maybe not." She sighed. "She knows I'll always be there."

"Because you're a good mother."

"I'm a *lousy* mother," Susan cried, quickly restoked. "I'm behaving badly, and I can't seem to help it. I resent her confidence. I resent her cavalier attitude. I'm even feeling jealous—*jealous*—because she's going through the same thing I did, only she'll have it easier. I've *struggled* to get us to this place. People respect me, Rick. I've worked *so hard* to redeem myself for doing what everyone in my life said was irresponsible, and I actually thought I'd made it. Now Lily has taken that away. Negated everything. I feel betrayed. By a seventeen-year-old."

"She's not just any seventeen-year-old."

"No. So maybe some of my anger is justified—but I'm doing exactly what my mother did, everything I swore I would never do, and that's *sick*."

His expression softened. Saying nothing, he reached out and brought her close. And, of course, she was lost. He had that power—could clear her mind of rational thought with a touch—not that she was complaining. This was the first respite from worry that she'd had in two weeks. However briefly, her problems were shared.

She didn't know how long they stood there, but she didn't hurry to leave. Everything about Rick was familiar. For all the different places he'd been and people he'd met, he remained the same man—same warmth, same smell, same heartbeat. Her connection with him was as strong as ever.

The slow breath he took as he held her said that he felt the same. Coming after her outburst, that meant a lot.

Finally, raising her head, she managed a small smile. "You're here for Lily's concert."

His eyes were on her mouth. "I wasn't sure I'd be able to make it. My dad's expecting me for Thanksgiving, so I came in across the Pacific, but I kept thinking that Lily and I needed to talk in person. She won't tell me much on the phone. So I touched down in LA and took right off again. I've been traveling for thirty-six hours. Missed every connection possible."

Susan knew Rick. He was a seasoned traveler who could catnap anywhere. But, yes, his eyes were tired. "You need sleep."

"I need a shower more." He glanced at his watch. "How much time before the concert?"

"Thirty minutes."

"Plenty. First a shower." He shot a covetous look at the chicken pot pie that sat on top of the stove. "Is that what she didn't want to eat?"

"It is."

"I do. Can I?"

SUSAN AND RICK ARRIVED AT THE HIGH SCHOOL WITH minutes to spare. With five different groups performing, the auditorium was packed, so they stood at the rear wall. Rick kept ducking back into the lobby until the very last minute, hoping to catch sight of Lily, but none of the singers appeared.

Susan searched the rows of seats for Mary Kate and Jess but didn't see them. She couldn't imagine they wouldn't be there to support Lily—unless they were simply keeping a low profile, which she could totally understand. Hadn't she been content to arrive at the auditorium at the last minute and not have to mingle with parents herself?

The house lights dimmed, and the concert began with performances by the string quartet and the jazz band, before, finally, the Zaganotes ran down the side aisles and onto the stage singing their trademark "Feelin' Groovy." There were a dozen willowy girls, each with long hair swaying, fingers snapping, their smiles vibrant against black turtlenecks.

Lily wasn't among them.

"Where is she?" Rick whispered.

"I have no idea," Susan whispered back. She took out her phone, but there were no messages. She glanced back at the door, but there were no girls waiting to join the others onstage— and besides, the Zaganotes had a dozen singers, and a dozen were already there. Susan knew who was in the group and who wasn't. One of the girls onstage, Claire DuMont, was new.

"Think Lily got sick?" Rick whispered.

"She'd have called," Susan whispered back.

"What if she couldn't, if it was something serious?" He was thinking about the baby, Susan knew.

"One of the other girls would have come to get me."

The group sang Cyndi Lauper's "Time After Time," then a spectacular arrangement of Seal's "Kiss from a Rose," but Susan's eyes were on her phone. WHERE R U, she texted and waited nervously. When Lily didn't text back, she slipped out of the auditorium and tried phoning, but the voice that came on was the bright, recorded one saying, "Not here, say where." Rick was beside her, looking as worried as she was, when the phone rang.

"Lily's with me," Mary Kate said. "She's fine."

"Why isn't she singing?"

"The Zaganotes asked her to resign."

"*Resign.*" Susan caught Rick's eye.

"Because she's pregnant."

"Wait. Kristen Hannigan picked her up to drive her to the concert."

"Kristen Hannigan picked her up to tell her the news. Lily made her drop her in town, then she called me."

"Where are you now?"

"Your house."

"I'll be right there."

LILY WAS HUDDLED IN THE DEN, EYES RED, TISSUES in her hand. Her bare feet were tucked under her, the black sweater and jeans replaced by purple sweats. Her hair was messed, a sign of the hasty change of clothes. When she saw Susan, her eyes welled, then grew wider when she saw Rick.

"You came all this way to see the *concert*?" she cried, tears spilling. "That is so *bad*!"

"I came to see you," said Rick and, leaning over, gave her a huge hug. "The concert was just an excuse." Drawing back, he brushed at her tears, but they continued to fall.

"How could they do this to me, Mom?" she asked. "I worked for that spot. I *earned* it. I was at practice all day Sunday and no one said a word, but the whole time they must have been talking behind my back." Angrily, she wiped her cheeks with her palms. "I'll bet Emily Pettee started it. Her mom is a bitch."

"Lily."

"She *is*. She acts like she's our censor. She has a thing against any song whose lyrics are at all suggestive, so forget doing Amy Winehouse or even the Dixie Chicks. She's always around before concerts making sure that every little last bra strap is hidden. I *know* she's behind this."

"It doesn't matter—"

"It *does,* Mom. I *love* singing."

Susan knew that, and her heart broke. Kneeling, she took Lily's hand. "It doesn't matter who started it," she finished quietly. "If the girls voted, it's done."

"But how could they do this to me? I've worked with them since freshman year. What about 'esprit de corps'?"

"Babies change things," Susan tried to explain as gently as she could, but Lily wasn't finished.

"I won't be showing until way after the holidays—but no, they thought this would make for a 'smoother' transition. Like they're so pure? They are not, Mom. Jennifer Corbin makes the rounds of the football team, Laura Kirk is with a different guy every month. And Emily? She had an *abortion* last summer, only they called it a *procedure* to correct a gynecological problem."

"Procedure?" Rick asked with a snort. "And her mom's the ringleader? Sounds like self-righteous indignation on the part of someone who's guilty as hell but doesn't want the world to know."

"I should tell the world about Emily," Lily declared.

"And be self-righteously indignant yourself?" Susan asked. "I don't think so."

"Emily did have an abortion."

"She isn't pregnant now, and that's the issue."

Lily pulled her hand free. "So we're back at that—my being pregnant *now* and *your* not wanting this baby. Confess. You don't."

"Want you pregnant now? I don't. But you are. I'm trying to accept it—just like you have to accept that the other girls don't consider pregnancy to be part of the Zaganotes' image. You have reasons for doing what you did, and if this is one of the consequences, you have to accept it."

Lily started crying again. *"Why?"*

"Because that's how it *is*." Susan sighed. "What alternative do you have, sweetheart? Yes, the girls are wrong, but if you tell them that, they'll resent it. Tell people about Emily—or Jen or Laura—and it'll be even worse. Isn't it better to preserve your own dignity?"

"Hey," said Mary Kate from behind them.

Susan had forgotten the other girl was there and looked back to see her edging toward the door.

"Don't leave!" Lily cried. "I need you to help me here!"

But Mary Kate kept going. "Your mom's right. If they don't want you, you shouldn't want them. Your dad wants to visit with you now, and I don't want to hear all this. I hear it all the time at home."

"You're a coward!"

"Actually, yes," said the girl and disappeared in a puff of riotous hair.

Brooding, Lily folded herself into the corner of the sofa. "Why do friends run out on you when you need them the most?"

"Mary Kate isn't running out on you," Rick reasoned. He

was sitting sideways on the sofa with an arm along its back. "She's giving us time." He touched her hair. "I do want to visit with you. You wouldn't say much on the phone. I still don't know the name of the guy."

"Why does it matter?" the girl said with just enough attitude to be mocking Susan. "It's done."

But Rick wasn't. "He's the father of your baby, and that baby is for life. Who he is matters to me because I'm your dad, and I care about you. I want anyone who touches you to be a decent person—okay, I know you were the instigator, but please tell me, at least, that you had real feelings for him."

Her eyes slipped away. "I did."

"Does he live here in town?"

"Yes."

"Is he a classmate?"

She leaned back, eyes on the ceiling. "If I were to tell, what would you do? Hit him up for money?" She turned to look at Rick. "He hasn't got it. Neither do his parents."

"The issue isn't money."

"Then marriage?" She looked at Susan. "You guys didn't marry. Why's this different?"

"Have I mentioned marriage?" Susan asked. She had stepped back, wanting to give Rick time with Lily. But the decision not to marry hadn't been his.

"You're thinking it."

"I am not." She would never want her daughter rushing into a marriage that might be bad. "And your situation is different from ours. I didn't plan to get pregnant. But once I was, Rick was the first person I told."

"And look what happened," Lily argued. "It caused so much trouble that his parents had to leave town."

"That's not why my parents moved," Rick said quietly.

"Then why?"

"Because . . ." He paused, frowned. "Because it was time. My sister was already gone, and I was on my way. There was nothing to keep them around. But at least they knew the score, and that made it easier—which is where I'm heading with this, Lily. You've put your mom in a lousy position. The more she knows, the better she'll be able to deal with it. Besides— trust me—the guy would want to know."

"Did you?"

"I did not want your mother to be pregnant. But given that she was, yes, I wanted to know. You're half mine."

"But you didn't marry her, because Mom didn't want to get married." Her voice rose. "Well, maybe I wanted it. Maybe I wanted a full-time father. Maybe those visits back to your parents were too scary, because I didn't know them, and I really didn't know you, and Mom wasn't there. Maybe it would have been better for me if you *had* married her," she said, building up steam. "But no, Mom wanted you to have a career. Rick wants to be the world traveler everyone knows and admires— and we all want what Rick wants, don't we." It wasn't a question. "Well, what about what *I* want? What's so awful about *my* setting my heart on something? Why can't everyone want what Lily wants for a change?"

Realizing what she'd said, Lily looked shocked. In a flash, she got off the sofa and ran from the room.

When Susan started to follow, Rick said, "Let her go."

"She has no right to criticize you."

"She does." He was sitting forward now, elbows on his knees. "I haven't been here for her. Maybe I didn't think enough about what she wanted."

"She's just upset, Rick. She's never said those things before. I should talk with her. She shouldn't be alone."

"Do you think she is?" Rick asked, and, of course, he was

right. *Alone* was a relative concept. Lily would either be phoning, texting, or Skyping.

Settling beside him on the sofa, Susan took his hand. "You should have told her the truth. Your parents moved away because of my dad."

"They didn't have to. They chose to. My mom's sister was in San Diego. They always wanted to retire there." He laced his fingers through hers.

"Only your father didn't retire. He worked for years afterward. No, Rick, it was my dad's fault. He took his anger out on your dad. They'd been best buddies, and suddenly the friendship was ruined."

"Well, it was an improbable friendship anyway, my dad the mail carrier, yours the mayor." He grew pensive. "When it was good, though, it was good. I was with them on some of those fishing trips. They could talk. It was like they were brothers, totally different from each other but with a really strong bond between them. I never figured out what it was."

"It was the brother thing," Susan said. Rick shot her a puzzled glance. "I had an uncle," she explained. "I never knew him. He died young. But my father adored him. They used to fish."

"No kidding?"

"Big Rick took his place."

"The brother thing?"

"My father's reaction must have been over the top because he had unrealistic expectations of your dad."

Rick considered that. "And here I always thought that was about your father being a public person in a small town and needing to make a statement. But hey"—he tightened his hold of her hand—"either way, my father let him do it. He could have stood up. He could have fought. That's what he should have done."

Susan studied his face. "You think so?"

"Absolutely. He might have talked some sense into your father. Instead, he caved—just walked away, and he lost a helluva lot more than just one friendship. I swear, he's afraid to come here to see Lily because he thinks that John Tate will find out. So his relationship with Lily is limited. She can visit him, but he can't visit her. He wouldn't even when Mom was alive. No, he should have fought. Lily's his only grandchild. He should have been more supportive."

"I never wanted his money."

"Not with money. With time. With attention." He sat back and rested his head on the sofa, his eyes still on hers. "He was on the right side."

"So is Lily when it comes to singing, but I told her not to fight. Should she?"

"Ideally, yes. But you nailed it. If she calls out the girls for voting her out, she alienates them further, in which case being back in the group wouldn't be fun." He closed his eyes.

"So she loses either way?"

He was quiet for a minute. "Maybe she wins either way. She'll have enough on her plate in a few months, and she sure doesn't need those girls."

"Okay. But she did earn her spot—and it was something I wanted her to have. I can't sing, but she has a beautiful voice."

"She didn't get it from me."

"It's from my mom, who has never even heard her sing."

"Her loss," Rick murmured tiredly and kissed her hand.

She settled against him. "Actually, it's ours, Lily's and mine. I thought it was bad when she was little and we had no relationship with my parents, but it gets worse every year. She's grown into such a talented young woman. She deserves to have adoring grandparents."

Rick's breathing was a little too even. Tipping her head

back, Susan saw that he was asleep, and, for a few minutes, she watched. Finally, she closed her own eyes to better enjoy the beat of his heart.

They slept like that for three hours. Susan was the one who finally woke. Nudging him gently, she got him up to the guest bedroom, but he didn't stay there long. She was barely in her own bed when he stole in and closed the door.

There was nothing sleepy about him then. Whispering her name, he stroked her hair, her breasts, her belly. His hunger was contagious. For those precious minutes, she couldn't get enough—couldn't *give* enough—and when her body erupted, she cried aloud at the pleasure of it.

She would have woken Lily, had he not covered her mouth. He had become good at that over the years. He saw to taking care, both of Lily's sensibility and Susan's fertility—particularly gratifying now, Susan thought in the seconds before she fell asleep in his arms. If this mother *and* daughter were pregnant and unmarried?

Susan couldn't begin to imagine the havoc of that.

Chapter 9

RICK OFFERED TO STAY, BUT SUSAN SENT HIM ON TO spend Thanksgiving with his father, who would otherwise have been alone.

Susan and Lily would not be. They were spending the holiday at Kate's, as they had for more than a dozen years. It was one of the few places where their host, at least, knew all their secrets.

KATE LOVED THANKSGIVING — LOVED THE COOKING, the smells, the packed dining room, the noise. She loved inviting holiday orphans who had nowhere else to go. At the last minute there were always an extra two or three guests.

This year there were six, all invited weeks earlier, which should have been fine. Only Kate wasn't wild about the two extra card tables sticking into the hall or the folding chairs that didn't match. She had been awake late the night before setting up with the girls, but she didn't like the way the plates looked—too many different ones—so she was rearranging them again at dawn.

Things just weren't right this year. She ran out of butter making the stuffing, and with everyone else still in bed and the turkey needing to be put in the oven ASAP, she dashed to the convenience store herself, which was all well and good, except that since it was the only shop open, she paid nearly twice what she would have had she bought enough at the supermarket, and that irked her.

Back home again, she drafted Will to help with the turkey, which was huge, and when the kids straggled in and began rummaging for breakfast, she had to reach around them, wait for them to move, or actually move them herself.

"That can wait two minutes," she told Mike as he stretched toward the cereal cabinet over her head. "Lissie, your father's *helping* me here," she complained when her daughter nudged Will aside so that she could get into the fridge. And when Sara weaseled in to peel an orange at the sink, Kate tore off a paper towel with a flourish and pressed it at her. "I'm trying to work here. Can you not see this?"

"Mom needs coffee," said Mike.

"Mom needs a bigger kitchen," said Kate, then yelped, "Not in there!" as her son headed for the dining room. "Everything is *set*."

"I'm just trying to clear out the kitchen. Where do you want me?"

Kate pointed him toward a stool at the counter, though there was barely an inch of free space, what with the bowl of yams that would soon be a casserole, boxes of crackers for the guacamole, and platters of cookies and cakes. "Hold that dish in your hand, Michael Mello, and not another word, please.

Will, this kitchen is too small," she told her husband as he put the turkey in the oven.

He straightened, smiled. "What happened to cozy?"

"I don't know. What did? Cozy is cute. This isn't cute."

He put an arm around her and gave her a squeeze—just enough of a reminder of what she had that was pretty darn good. Then Mary Kate wandered in and reached for the milk, an innocent gesture, but enough to remind Kate that things would be less good with a new baby coming. A new baby would make the kitchen smaller and the dining room more crowded. They were bursting at the seams already. How long before an explosion?

Seams . . . dreams . . . same difference, she thought and, feeling slightly frantic, began rummaging through the papers stuck into cookbooks crammed above the stove for the recipe Sunny had given her for a chocolate pecan pie.

SUNNY KNEW HER MOTHER-IN-LAW'S KITCHEN INSIDE and out, with good reason. She had been the one to set it up when, after years of renting, her in-laws had bought the town house they had dreamed about. Dan helped with the down payment; Sunny helped with the décor. Though in their late sixties, Martha and Hank were still both working and perfectly capable of managing their daily lives, but Sunny liked helping them out. Her mother-in-law had come to count on her for advice on what to wear to local events, where to vacation in March, whether to take vitamin D supplements, and Sunny was flattered. She saw this as a validation that she was worthy of being consulted, proof that she was Normal with that capital *N*.

Normal was definitely the way to go. Immersing herself in what she did best, she had baked every evening that week, then loaded the back of her car with all of the makings for Thanksgiving dinner not only for her own four and Martha and Hank, but for Dan's brother and his family and two elderly aunts. By noon on Thursday, Martha's kitchen was smelling of roasted turkey, mulled cider, and squash bisque. Ceramic bowls were neatly lined on the counter awaiting the soup; matching mugs awaited the cider. Serving dishes, stacked now, would hold the turkey fixings. And the dining room table was a sight to behold.

Everything went off like clockwork. The turkey reached the right temperature at the right time and carved like a dream, while the asparagus, yams, and onions were cooked to perfection. Dan poured the drinks; Hank said the blessing; Sunny ladled bisque from a Perry & Cass tureen. There was a brief silence, followed by a chorus of *yums* and *mmms*.

"You've outdone yourself, Sunny," said Martha. "This is delicious."

Sunny basked in the praise. And it kept coming through the main course, right up to the desserts. That was when Jessica, taking advantage of a lull in the conversation, rapped her knife against her glass and stood.

"I have an announcement to make," she said. Sunny stared at her in horror, but if Jessica felt the stare, she paid no attention. "The family is growing," she announced. "We'll have another member next Thanksgiving."

Martha gasped. "You're engaged?"

Jessica shook her head.

"Well, that's good," her grandmother remarked. "You're far too young." She turned excitedly to Sunny and Dan. "You're having another baby?"

Sunny might have nodded, if Jessica hadn't quickly said, "Not Mom. *Me*."

"*You?*"

"Jessica," Sunny warned. Someone asked if it was true, and she said, "No—"

"Yes," Jessica declared.

"Dan," Sunny pleaded, but anything he might have said was lost in a flurry of questions. Deciding that her daughter was positively hateful, Sunny grabbed an empty pie plate, fled to the kitchen, and began washing pans, but snippets of conversation rose above the clank and splash. She was scrubbing the roaster with a furious force when her mother-in-law joined her at the sink.

"She's only seventeen, Sunny. Do you think she's old enough to have a child?"

"Absolutely not!"

"But you're letting her do it anyway?"

Sunny put down the sponge. "Letting her? She didn't ask my permission. And now it's done. This isn't a dress you can buy and return." Hearing the bite in her voice, she said by way of apology, "This is very upsetting for me. I don't know why she felt she needed to tell you all today." But Sunny did. It was to shame her mother.

"She seems to think it's exciting."

"She is deliberately baiting me, because she knows how angry I am."

"And wanting no part of the boy?" Martha went on sadly. "What is the trouble with children today? They do things our children wouldn't have dared to do. It isn't enough to steal a pencil from the five-and-dime or hide a pack of cigarettes. Well, the difference is, I guess, we were home."

"Home?"

"I didn't start working until the children were grown."

Uneasy with her mother-in-law's inference, Sunny said, "Because back then, women didn't have careers."

"Maybe it was better that way. I'm not sure you can do both well. This is a perfect example."

"Do you think it wouldn't have happened if I'd been at home?" Sunny asked in dismay. "She didn't do this at home, Mom. She isn't allowed to bring boys upstairs. But she's seventeen, she's driving, she's out of the house all day long."

"Now she is. But not always."

No. There had been a period of time when a babysitter had watched Jessica and Darcy after school. "That sitter was in her fifties. She was totally responsible."

"She wasn't you." Martha sighed. "Oh, Sunny. What's done is done. I think you raised your children the best way you knew how."

Not exactly an endorsement. "But it wasn't good enough?"

Martha didn't have to reply. The look she gave Sunny spoke of Disappointment with a capital *D*.

SUSAN HAD A LOVE-HATE RELATIONSHIP WITH THANKS-giving. She loved being with Kate and her family, loved the noise and the warmth. What she hated was coming home afterward and missing her parents. After all, what was Thanksgiving about if not family?

Pam's annual open house was usually a distraction. Held in the early evening and offering light hors d'oeuvres after a large midday meal, it could go on until eleven at night, usually leaving Susan little time to brood.

This year, though, Susan didn't go. Oh, she had quickly accepted when the invitation arrived, but that was before news of Lily's pregnancy leaked out. Since then, Pam hadn't mentioned the open house. When Susan called her Wednesday to bow out, Pam said all the right things—*I don't care what people think, I can certainly understand how you feel, I'll miss you*—but she didn't insist that Susan come.

So, at six that evening, with Lily still at Mary Kate's, Susan found herself home alone. She turned on the television, then turned it off. She opened her work folder, then closed it. She picked up one knitting project after another, but none appealed to her.

Aimless, she wandered through the house. It was a fine house, a testament to how far she had come. When she bought it, she had sent her parents a picture, but that note, like so many before and after, went unanswered.

At the door to Lily's room, she stopped. Lily hadn't apologized for her outburst in front of Rick, but Susan saw small attempts to atone. The bed was made, her clothes were hung, and the desktop litter neatened.

Hadn't Susan done the same? In the months before being sent away, she had been the perfect daughter—helpful and neat, respectful to a fault. She hadn't argued, hadn't tried to get her father to change his mind. His word was gospel, and she the sinner. If she had accused him of being cruel, would anything be different?

At Lily's dresser, Susan fingered the sock her daughter was knitting. Strikingly, it blended seed stitch and cables in a pattern Susan had never knit herself. Feeling a moment's pride, she lifted the sock to admire the back side, which was when she noted the stitches on the working needles. The sheer number puzzled her—way too many for a sock—until she glanced at the handwritten notes nearby and realized that this was no sock. It was a baby sweater being knit cuff to cuff.

Feeling a chill, she left the room, but the image of the sweater stayed with her. The yarn was pink. Lily wanted a girl. There was something shockingly real about that.

Wondering if her mother had had the same trouble accepting Susan's pregnancy, and hoping they might talk about it, she picked up the phone and dialed. Creatures of habit, her parents would have had an afternoon dinner with her brother and his wife's family, and should be home again by now.

The phone rang four times. Seconds before the call would have gone to voice mail, someone answered, only to immediately hang up.

SUSAN WAS IN THE DEN WHEN LILY CAME HOME. THE girl seemed startled to see her. "Are you okay?" she asked from the door.

Susan nodded. "Just felt like sitting."

"You don't usually do that."

"No." She was usually cleaning, knitting, or working out a solution for a student with a problem, a teacher with a problem, a *daughter* with a problem—plotting a solution or, at the very least, an approach to finding a solution. Tonight, she did nothing but sit. "Everything okay with Mary Kate?"

"I guess. She tried to call Abby. We haven't talked with her much since what happened at school, but the open house was still going on, so she couldn't talk. I'm sorry we didn't go this year, Mom."

"Would you have wanted to?" Susan asked in surprise.

"Maybe not. Emily's mom would have been there. I'm still pretty steamed about the Zaganotes." She paused. "But Pam's open house was always a fun time. You liked going."

Susan nodded. "I did."

Lily looked sad. "I'm sorry, Mom. I didn't realize people would react this way. I knew there'd be talk, and I was afraid the coach wouldn't want me on the volleyball team, but being banned from singing? *Voted* out? It's not like pregnancy is an STD."

"Disease, no. Condition, yes—and just as unforgivable in some people's minds."

"But they're *wrong*. It's the oldest condition in the world. Think *Eve*."

"Was Eve in high school? Did she do field hockey or sing? Was her mom a prominent player in town? Times have changed, Lily. Life is complex."

There was no argument, just a troubled look. Hating that—always—Susan patted the sofa.

Lily perched on the edge. "Did Pam say not to come?" she asked.

"No. It was me. I didn't want to have to answer questions."

"All you have to say is that I did this on my own."

"Not that easy," Susan said with a sad smile.

She was thinking that the sober look on her daughter's face meant she might be getting the point, when that look brightened. Putting a hand on her belly, Lily asked excitedly, "Did you talk to me, Mom? You know, when I was a fetus?"

"I did," Susan said. "You were my partner in crime."

"I talk to her all the time."

"Her?"

"It's a her. I know it is."

"I hope you're right. A he might have a tough time wearing that sweater you're knitting. It's a pretty cool sweater, though."

"Isn't it? I'm adapting an adult pattern."

"To infant size? That's quite a reduction."

"Not as much as you'd think. The original pattern calls for light bulky. I'm using DK weight, so it's automatically smaller anyway. I'm doing a hat to match. Infants need hats even in summer."

"They need lots of other things."

"Will you make some?"

"I was thinking of diapers and crib sheets."

"But will you knit for my baby?" Lily asked straight out. "I want her to have things from you. Will you, Mom?"

"Eventually."

"For her to have when she's born? Remember that reversible blanket you made for Mrs. Davidson's baby? I want one of those."

"You could knit it yourself."

"It wouldn't be the same. She'll keep that blanket forever. I want it from *you*."

Susan couldn't commit to knitting for a baby she couldn't yet imagine coming, so she asked, "Are those jeans getting tight?"

Lily slouched back on the sofa and raised her sweater. At first glance, her stomach was flat; at second glance, Susan saw a tiny swell.

Lily stroked the spot. "She is three inches long now. And her intestines are starting to grow. I mean, they've been growing all along, but now they're coming back out of the umbilical cord." Her eyes met Susan's. "Three more weeks, and I'll know the sex for sure. I'll actually be able to see her."

"She won't look like much."

"She will. Four months is significant." She grew cautious again. "I may need a few clothes pretty soon. I mean, like, jeans. The blogs say to get a few pairs in the next size up, not maternity yet." When Susan didn't reply, she said, "I'll pay."

"I pay for your clothes."

"Not Sevens."

"Right, because I don't believe in spending that much for a pair of jeans. If you want Sevens, sweetie, you're on your own."

"I don't need Sevens."

"That's wise. Are Mary Kate or Jess showing yet?"

"Jess no. Mary Kate a drop."

But all three would be visibly pregnant before long. The thought of that gave Susan the willies. "Lily, I have to tell Phil about the other two."

Lily sat up fast. "You can't! Not yet!"

"I told Sunny I'd wait until after Thanksgiving. He's one of the reasons I couldn't go to Pam's. But the longer I wait to tell him, the worse it'll be when I do."

"You can't betray Mary Kate and Jess!"

"It's not a betrayal. It's telling someone who has a right to know. This is going to affect the school."

"Mary Kate will let people know soon. Can't you wait a *little* longer? They'll *hate* me if you tell." She jumped to her feet. "If you were with me in this, you'd understand. But you're still angry because I didn't ask *permission*. When it came to the Zaganotes, you told me to move on. Well, look who can't move on now. Why is it so hard for you to accept this? Why is it so hard to be *excited*? This is *our baby*," she cried and stormed from the room.

SUSAN DIDN'T SEE IT THAT WAY. THE BABY WAS LILY'S, and the situation with Phil was growing acute. She was in a bind, balancing her role as mother against her role as principal.

Later, when Sunny called from Albany weeping, Susan just tried to console her. She didn't discuss telling Phil. It would have only upset her more.

Besides, at some point, the decision was Susan's alone.

AT LEAST, THAT WAS WHAT SHE THOUGHT. SHE WAITED until Monday—why ruin Phil's holiday?—then learned that he was at a conference in Denver. The message on his answering machine referred emergency calls to his assistant, but this wasn't something to share with anyone else, Susan decided. Nor, in a sense, was it an emergency.

It didn't become that until Thursday.

Chapter 10

LILY WAS IN THE LUNCHROOM, AT ONE END OF A LONG
table with Mary Kate and Jess. Other students sat nearby, but
the empty chairs they had left meant they were giving the
three girls space.

"I guess this is how it'll be," Lily said, "but I'm okay with it.
They've always seen me as good little Lily, the principal's
daughter. They don't know what to make of me now." She
thought about it. "I kind of like that."

"I wish my parents weren't so upset," said Mary Kate. "We
may have underestimated their reaction."

"Y'think?" Jess remarked.

Lily knew. "My mom's hurt, like I deliberately disobeyed
her. But I never thought of it that way."

"My mom's *furious*," Jess said.

Lily knew her mother was that, too, and it worried her a lot.
She had hoped that her own control of the situation would
smooth things over. She really had thought this through. Getting pregnant wasn't something you did on a whim.

And in the end, she had to be optimistic. "They'll come around. Once they get over the shock, they'll realize a baby's a baby, and that we have each other, which will make it easier. Look at our moms and PC Wool. No one of them could have created the business on her own."

Mary Kate finally smiled. "Can you imagine our kids taking it over someday? Honestly? I don't think it's a little Jacob in here. It's a girl who'll be best friends with your daughters, just like our moms and us."

Lily thought so, too, but she had pictured a fourth. "Maybe that's why Abby blabbed. She feels left out."

Jess leaned back and peered across the room. "She's still sitting with Theo Walsh. What happened to Michael?"

"Second guy's a charm?" Lily asked, though she knew what Jess was thinking. They had agreed that the fathers wouldn't be involved, but that didn't mean they didn't matter. If you were planning to have a baby, you needed a father with good genes. Theo Walsh was marginal.

"Uh-oh, here she comes," Mary Kate murmured.

"Hey, guys," Abby said, sounding more confident of their welcome than she looked. "How's it going?"

"It's going great," Jess said before Lily could answer. "No thanks to you. What you did to Lily was awful."

Looking contrite, Abby said, "I feel bad, Lily. I didn't plan to tell. It just came out. I'm sorry."

"Being sorry doesn't make it better," Jess said, but Lily pulled out a chair and made Abby sit.

"Do you hate me?" Abby asked her.

Lily couldn't. Hate implied a permanent break, and Lily didn't want that. She felt for Abby. Abby always seemed to be on the outside looking in—like she had a big name and plenty of money, but wasn't comfortable with either.

That said, Lily was hurt. "When we agreed to do this, we

talked about how important it was to keep things secret and stay totally loyal to each other. It may be hard for you right now—"

"That doesn't excuse it," Jess cut in and might have said more if Mary Kate hadn't touched her hand.

Abby stared at Jess. "You don't have a clue."

"I do. It didn't happen right away for me. So maybe you have to work to make it stick. Maybe you have to try *five* guys before it does."

Lily hushed her.

But Abby was glaring. "Maybe I won't try *any* guys. Maybe I'm waking up and realizing what a *stupid* idea this *was*."

"And who came up with this stupid idea?" Jess shouted.

"Shhh."

"No, Mary Kate," Jess argued. "It was *her* idea, and now she's backing out."

Abby stood up. "I was upset, and maybe I said things I shouldn't have that day in the hall, but do you think *you're* any better? I should try five guys? That's *disgusting*. And you think *you're* ready to have a baby? You have *no business* being pregnant! Lily, yes. Mary Kate, yes. But you? I feel *so sorry* for your baby."

She turned and stalked off, leaving a stunned silence in her wake—and no fewer than a dozen riveted eyes on Lily, Mary Kate, and Jess.

"THEY WERE JUNIORS," CAME LILY'S BREATHLESS VOICE, "and they must have heard every word Abby said. I could see it in the way they were looking at us. What do we do, Mom? Should we say it isn't true?"

Susan was walking down Main Street, head low against the wind, phone to her ear. She was coming from a meeting of community service organizations in advance of the holiday food drive. There were serious issues this year relating to new FDA requirements, but they were quickly forgotten.

"No, Lily," she said, trying to stay calm. "Don't lie. But let's not get ahead of ourselves. They may not have heard as much as you thought. Where are you now?"

"Still in the lunchroom. We have five minutes before class."

Susan picked up her pace. "Go ahead to class. Try to act normally until we know for sure that anyone did hear. Tell Mary Kate and Jess to do the same. Are they okay?"

"*No.* Mary Kate is trying to find Jacob. He doesn't even know she's pregnant. What was Abby *thinking?*"

"I don't know, Lily. But Abby is the least of our worries." There were so many other things to consider if word was out. "You all go to class. If you hear people talking about Mary Kate and Jess, let me know. In the meantime, I'll strategize."

Actually, what Susan was thinking was that in the meantime she would pray that those juniors hadn't heard.

But she was barely back at school when she was approached in the lunchroom by a cluster of girls. "We just heard something really weird, Ms. Tate," said one, and the others quickly chimed in.

"Is Mary Kate Mello pregnant?"

"And Jessica Barros?"

"All *three?*"

"Where did you hear this?" Susan asked.

"Kaylee's sister heard it from someone who heard it last lunch. Is it true?"

Susan tried to look unworried. "Well, it's a frightening thought. Let me get back to you, okay?" She lingered for another sixty seconds, casually working her way to the door. Once in the corridor, though, she hurried to her office. Her assistant was just replacing the phone. The look on her face confirmed the problem.

"Who was that?" Susan asked.

"Allison Monroe. She wanted to report what her students are saying."

Allison taught introductory Spanish, mostly to freshmen. Susan considered her a friend, which gave credence to her report.

Knowing she had to act quickly, Susan said, "Would you ask Amy Sheehan to come up here? Tell her it's urgent. Same with Meredith Parker." Meredith was the school counselor. "If my daughter or either of her friends show up, let them in, too."

Entering her office, she closed the door and leaned against it for a minute. This was the calm before the storm. It was time to plan.

But first she had to tell Sunny and Kate. She made the two calls; each was short and upsetting. Amy arrived, with Mary Kate on her heels, and by the time Meredith arrived, Lily and Jess were there, too.

Amy, bless her, relieved Susan of the responsibility of formally spilling the beans by asking a startled, "You're all *three* pregnant?"

The girls stared at each other. Mary Kate was the first to nod.

"How far along?" Amy asked.

"Eleven weeks," said Mary Kate.

"Ten," Jessica said.

"Intentionally?"

There were three nods.

"No one was supposed to know until we were starting to show," Jessica said. "This is all Abby's fault."

Devastated, Susan braced herself against the desk. "Abby was not in that bed, or wherever you were, when each of you had unprotected sex."

"But we wouldn't be sitting here now if it weren't for her."

"You made a *pact?*" Meredith asked, her melodious alto sounding dismayed.

"It wasn't a pact," Lily said. "We just agreed that this would be a good thing to do together."

"That's a pact, sweetheart," Susan said, having learned the lesson from Rick. "You can play with words all you want, but it is what it is."

"*Why?*" Meredith asked the girls.

"Because we love babies," Lily answered.

"So do I," the counselor replied earnestly, "but I don't have a husband or the means to support a baby, so there *is* no baby, and I *am* done with school, and the perfect *age* to have a child." She had been one of Susan's first hires, a spunky African American who seemed perfectly happy mothering high schoolers in lieu of her own kids. She spoke her thoughts freely, and while that upset some parents, it worked for the students. Kids didn't always like what Ms. Parker said, Lily had explained, but they liked knowing where she stood.

So did Susan, particularly since Meredith had brought up husband, money, education, and age, all issues Susan had raised herself.

Subdued, the girls sat on the sofa. Mary Kate, in particular, looked stricken. "Did you find Jacob?" Susan asked.

Eyes tearing up, the girl nodded.

"How was he?"

"Angry. He stared at me, then walked way." Her voice broke. "I ran after him—I mean, he was one of the reasons I *wanted* this baby—but he wouldn't listen."

In different circumstances, Susan would have gone to her, held her, reassured her that Jacob loved her and would come around. But Lily and Jessica were doing just that, now. This, apparently, was the purpose of the pact, to support each other when the going got tough.

Susan wondered what the father of Lily's baby was thinking. She hadn't allowed herself to think about him, was still having trouble visualizing her daughter with any boy. But he would surely know by now. She wondered if other students would guess his identity and whether Susan would learn it that way.

Angry at Lily for this, too, she wandered past the bookshelf that held the summer reading assignments for each grade level. Nearby were pictures of Lily in third grade, sixth grade, ninth grade, looking so innocent that Susan could have cried.

Continuing on to the girls, she took a chair. After a minute, thinking aloud, she said, "We have three planned pregnancies in three seniors who would be the last ones anyone would expect to have done this. The question is how to handle it."

"You can't kick us out of school," Jessica cautioned meekly. "I asked my dad."

Susan sighed. "I wouldn't kick you out, Jess. You need to graduate." She filled in Amy and Meredith on what had happened at lunch. "Word is spreading fast."

"This is Abby's fault," Jessica insisted.

"If you weren't pregnant," Susan said, "she'd have had nothing to say. But it's done, Jess. We have to figure out what to do now."

The door opened. Kate and Sunny slipped in, both looking pale and upset. Kate closed the door, shaking her head when Amy rose to offer her a seat. Sunny stood by the file cabinet, radiating anger. There were glances at the girls, but they were brief.

This is not my daughter, Susan could hear them thinking. She shared the sentiment, but dwelling on the horror of what the girls had done wouldn't help. "It would have been nice to have had a little more time, but the grapevine can be lethal. Everyone will be speculating and exaggerating."

"How do you *exaggerate* this?" Sunny asked in disgust.

Easy, Susan thought. "You say there are ten girls involved, not three. You say that the pact is among the *boys* to impregnate girls. You say that someone is going to parties, slipping Mickeys to sweet little things like you three."

"None of that's true," Jess said.

"Correct, which is why we need to define the story ourselves. Tomorrow's Friday. Students will be heading into the weekend talking—"

"Don't they have anything better to do?" Lily asked.

"That depends on how you define better," Susan said. "Change the parties involved. Think, say, Rachel Bishop, Sara Legere, and Kelsey Hughes. They're your friends, right? What if you suddenly learned that all three were pregnant— three good friends, top students, college-bound kids? Wouldn't you be talking about it? Wouldn't you be calling other friends to find out what they knew? Of course you would. It's human nature."

"Your mother's right," Meredith said. "Kids talk. They text."

"But it's all hearsay," Jess protested.

"Not all," corrected Lily. "What Abby said was firsthand."

"Unfortunately," the counselor said, "it's the classic case of a little knowledge being worse than none. If word is out, we've passed the 'none' stage."

"Fine," Sunny told Susan and folded her arms. "What do you suggest?"

Susan was still trying to decide. One thing was for sure. "I need to tell Dr. Correlli."

"Can you tell him without giving our names?"

"What's the point? He already knows Lily's pregnant. If he doesn't guess that the others are Mary Kate and Jess, a call to any one of Lily's teachers will tell him."

"Teachers can't give out names. What about our right to privacy?"

"It's gone," Susan said, feeling a weight in the pit of her stomach. Her daughter would be named right along with the others. "This is now a public matter. The superintendent is responsible for everything that involves his schools."

"Dan won't agree," Sunny said, but Susan knew the law.

"He'd have a case if a teacher went outside the school system, say to the papers, with a student's name. But Dr. Correlli is within the school system. Especially with my own daughter being part of this, I need him involved. It'd be best if I went to him with a plan." It might even compensate for the incompetence she felt as a mother.

"What do you propose?" Kate asked.

Susan was on shaky ground. She would have given anything to have someone else calling the shots. She was way too emotionally involved for this.

But there was no one else. So she tried to imagine what she would do if she didn't know any of the girls. "We have to contain the story. That means carefully defining it."

"How do you do that?" Sunny asked.

"I'll send an e-mail to my faculty, then one to parents."

Sunny made a strangled sound. "You'd tell everyone?"

"If I don't, someone else will. This is as bad for me as it is for you, Sunny."

"What will you say?" Kate asked, moving on.

"I'll confirm the rumor, say how many students are involved, and that the pact is self-contained." Crossing Abby off the list of potential moms, she stared at the girls. "That is right, isn't it?"

The three nodded.

Susan sat back. "Only three, then. No epidemic."

"For now," said Meredith. "Pregnancy isn't contagious, but

pact behavior can be. That worries me, and it'll worry a lot of parents. Can you imagine if other groups of girls decide to do this?"

"Just because we did it?" Mary Kate asked skeptically.

"Just because you did it," Meredith confirmed. "You girls are respected."

"The whole point," Jess put in, "was to do something different."

"Something for *us,*" Mary Kate added.

"Would you name our daughters in your e-mail?" Sunny asked Susan.

"No. But the names will come out."

"This doesn't feel good."

"Not to me, either," Susan said helplessly, "but can you think of a better plan?"

Chapter 11

⊱❧⊰

THE ZAGANACK TOWN HALL, A WIDE BRICK BUILDING
with white trim, shared the south end of Main Street with the
library, the police station, and the Congregational church. On
its second floor were the offices of the school superintendent.
His windows overlooked the church graveyard, which overlooked the tail end of the harbor. This late in the season, there
were few pleasure boats in the water, but those that
remained—sailboats with masts rising and canvas battened
down, as well as the occasional fishing boat coming or going—
softened the view of the cemetery.

In the past, Susan had stood at the window watching the
water and expressing envy. *How do you get anything done, Phil?
If this was my office, I'd be too distracted to work.* A far cry from
the Great Plains, this view embodied much of what she had
come to Zaganack to find.

Today she barely saw it. From the minute she entered the
office, her eyes were on Phil.

When she was done explaining, he remained silent, elbows

on the desk, chin propped on his fists. Finally, eyes sad, he dropped his hands. "Have you known about the other two all along?"

Susan had expected the question, but that didn't ease her guilt. "At first I thought it was only Lily. When I learned about the others, it was..." Stunning? Infuriating? *Devastating?* Unable to choose the right word, she said, "This is a nightmare. I've been dealing with it on a personal level, and it hasn't been easy. I'd have told you everything before Thanksgiving, but at that point, no one at school knew about Mary Kate and Jess. Their families are my closest friends, and they're going through the same personal trauma I am. I begged them to let me tell you. One of them outright refused."

"That would be Sunny Barros."

Sunny often ran school fund-raisers and was known for discipline. Along with her husband's reputation as a law-and-order guy, stacked against easygoing Kate and Will, it was easy for Phil to guess.

His mouth remained tight. "Well, we can't call it a pact. That's an incendiary word."

"But it is a pact. We have to address it head-on."

"Not using that word, please," he ordered and suddenly lost his temper. "Insecure girls, I can understand. Girls with no future, I can buy. Girls with no *love,* fine. But *these* girls? What is this about?"

"I've asked my daughter that a dozen times," said Susan. "She feels she has valid reasons—they all believe they do—and they gave each other courage. That's the thing about pact mentality—"

"Bah." He cut her off. "Forget pact mentality. Why are so many teenagers getting pregnant? Is it Hollywood?"

"Maybe."

"*Maybe?* Open any of those magazines and there's a 'bump

alert.' A *bump alert*—what a pathetic phrase. A bump sits and does nothing. A baby does not. Do these girls understand the reality of being a parent? Popular culture gives them the wrong idea, and apparently we've done nothing to change that."

"Actually, we have," Susan cautioned. If he wanted to attack her parenting skills, fine; she could find fault with them herself, in light of what her own daughter had done. But attacking her as a school administrator was unfair. "Drugs, drinking, sex—we discuss them at every grade level, and we use what's happening in the news as an opening. We directly address these issues, Phil. The clinic nurse is always meeting with small groups to talk about things like safe sex and the pitfalls of early pregnancy."

He seemed not to hear. "So, was this a pact to imitate *celebrities*?"

"Don't I *wish*. That would give us something to talk about. But it isn't that in this case. These girls are close. They grew up supporting each other. They grew up seeing their mothers support each other. They decided that together they could do this."

"They're too young to make that decision."

"True. But we ask them to make other decisions. They drive; that involves making adult decisions. And these girls will be eighteen when their babies are born. At eighteen, they can serve in the army, carry guns, *kill* people."

"Bad analogy, Susan. A soldier acts out of necessity."

"But like soldiers, these girls adopted a group mentality. I'm not saying it's right, Phil. I'm just saying that's how it was. They were operating under a mind-set that made this doable."

"And that's what *I'm* saying," he shot back. "It's what they see on TV. Who is making it okay to be single and pregnant?"

There it was. Susan raised her chin. "I was single and pregnant."

"See, that's a problem." He waved a dismissive hand. "Another is the fathers. We need them to come forward. That would give it a semblance of morality."

"Talk about incendiary words," Susan said, vaguely offended. "Isn't *responsibility* a better one?"

"Call it what you want. I want the fathers to speak up."

"The girls don't want them involved."

"And the girls' families are okay with that?"

"No," Susan said, feeling personally attacked, but she hadn't gotten to where she was by cowering. Her mother was right; she did have a fuchsia heart. When she was provoked, her high color came out. "The girls' families are not okay with this. The girls' families are trying to decide what is the most *responsible* thing to do. Our girls made a pact. Part of the pact was that the fathers wouldn't be involved. No, I am not okay with it," she said with rising anger, "and I've told my daughter that, but would you have them drag those boys in front of us? Force them to be fathers, and you'll end up with teenage moms who are stuck in bad marriages and children who are resented from day one. I've been down this road, Phil. I could have married Lily's father, but it would have made for resentment. I don't want that for my daughter, or for her child."

"You condone it, then?" he asked in dismay.

"*No.* I'm *beside* myself. I'm just trying to make the best of a bad situation."

Phil was quiet, sitting back in his chair, studying her. Finally, he said, "I'm disappointed."

"So am I," she shot back fiercely. "I'm disappointed in Lily. I'm disappointed in Mary Kate and Jess. I'm disappointed in those boys for not using condoms *despite* what the girls might have said. And yes, Phil, I'm disappointed in myself, because a better mother might be able to read her child's mind, even when that child is seventeen. But if you're disappointed in me as principal, that's unfair. I've done a good job for you in the past two years, and there have been other crises. We've dealt with one student playing pharmacist in school, another hacking into his teacher's computer to steal exams. We've even had a *teacher* sending lewd e-mail to a coed. So this is a new challenge. I can handle it."

"You were an unwed mother at seventeen."

"And what about all I've achieved since then? Doesn't any of it count?"

He held up a conciliatory hand. "What you've done since is remarkable. I'm just telling you what people will see."

"Then we have to make them see something else."

"How."

Susan repeated what she had told Sunny and Kate. "If we get accurate information to the adult community, they can pass it on to students. I'll be happy to run a draft of the parent e-mail past you."

"Send an e-mail, and the *Gazette* will see it."

"You know the editor. Can you pull strings?"

Phil snorted. "To do what—hold him off? This is big news. The paper's out today, which means he has plenty of time to put a story together for next week's edition."

"Can you soft-pedal what he prints?"

"Possibly." Susan might have felt an inkling of relief if he hadn't added, "What about the school board?"

Her stomach clenched. "Well, they'll find out through Pam Perry," she said, realizing that she would have to handle that, too. "What if I ask her to set up a meeting so that I can tell them myself?"

"They'll skewer you."

Oh, they would, and several of the most ornery members would take pleasure in it. "But that's the best way to handle this, don't you think?"

THE SCHOOL BOARD ISSUE WAS A BIG ONE, BUT THAT wasn't why, as soon as Susan cleared the town hall steps, she called Pam. She wanted to tell her firsthand what was going on, not for political reasons, but because they were friends. Kate was right; Pam felt a special connection to Susan. But the connection went both ways. Pam had come from the same kind of constrictive home as Susan—they talked about it often, just the two of them—and while marriage to Tanner had helped, Pam hadn't yet found the self-confidence Susan had.

"Where are you now?" she asked when Pam answered.

"Tanner's office. Something's wrong. I hear it in your voice."

"Can I meet you there?"

"What is it, Susan?"

"I'm just leaving Town Hall. Give me five minutes?"

With nervous energy quickening her step, it took only three. The administrative offices of Perry & Cass were at the opposite end of the harbor, in a pristine house painted a seashore gray, with decks directly overlooking the pier and seagulls screeching in the cold. Like Phil's, Tanner's office was on the second floor, but that was where the similarity ended. The room was filled with rich mahogany, fine Berber, and the light that poured from a wall of windows. Pam had been sitting in that light, but dropped her knitting and rose the instant Susan appeared.

Tanner was on the phone, his back to the door, his tall, lanky frame stooped.

Grabbing her hand, Pam pulled her to the corner farthest from him. "Tell me."

"Have you talked with Abby?"

"Not since this morning. What *is* it?"

"Not good," Susan warned and told her about Jessica and Mary Kate.

Pam opened her mouth to speak, but no words came out.

"I wanted you to hear it from me. I don't blame Abby. It would have come out anyway. But now there's no hiding it."

"*Three* pregnant?" Pam asked in disbelief. "A *pact*? Jessica I can buy, but Mary Kate is as improbable as Lily. This is crazy. How could Abby not *tell* me?" Once started, the questions kept coming. "Who are the boys? You don't know or aren't telling? One has to be Jacob, but what about Lily? I didn't know she even had a boyfriend. And what does Sunny say? Omigod, she must be ready to strangle Jess. I would *kill* Abby if she did this."

Susan was hoping it wouldn't come to that, when Pam rushed on. "Why didn't you tell me sooner? Okay, I know you're in a bind being principal, but couldn't Kate or Sunny have called? We're friends. And we work together. Why am I always the last to know?"

"You're not. The only other parents who know may be ones whose kids heard the rumor. That's why I'm here. I wanted to tell you myself. I came as soon as I could."

Pam looked lost. "Why am I always left out of the loop?"

Susan tried to be sympathetic, but, bottom line, this wasn't about Pam. "We're dealing with our daughters. Trust me, we've barely talked with each other." She was thinking it was especially true with Sunny, when Tanner hung up the phone.

"Tanner," Pam said. "You have to hear Susan's news."

And so Susan repeated it. Grateful for small favors, she was glad that Pam was here at the office rather than at home alone. Tanner was a steadying force. Moreover, he was arguably more powerful in Zaganack than the mayor. If controlling the story was Susan's goal, he was an asset. He didn't panic. He was fair. He had led a privileged life, but he fully understood that. There was a kindness in him, a sense of charity.

Now, though, he was visibly disturbed. "A pregnancy pact. With Abby the messenger?"

"Inadvertently," Susan said.

Tanner looked at Pam. "Do we know that she isn't involved herself?"

"She isn't pregnant. She just had her period."

"That begs the question. If the plot was hatched last summer, she must have been aware of it. She was with the other girls every day, and she claims they're her closest friends. Talk with her, Pam," he ordered and eyed Susan. "This won't wear well in town."

"I'm not sure the girls realized that."

"Perry and Cass is about responsibility," he went on in his sensible way. "That's what makes the company work. Our employees know our name's on the line each time they seal up a package." He took a small breath, blew it out. "A pregnancy pact alone is bad, but involving three prominent girls?"

"The story will be contained," Susan assured him. "It won't hurt the company."

"What about PC Wool?" Pam asked her husband.

"It shouldn't be affected," he said, but he didn't sound convinced.

Susan was unsettled. "Beyond Zaganack, the people who buy our wool don't know the faces behind it. They'll have no way of knowing about this." When Tanner looked troubled, she said, "We're nipping the story in the bud by being up front here in town. That's the reason for my e-mail. Get it out quickly and move on." She faced Pam. "I want to talk with the school board. Can you set it up?"

"Absolutely," Pam said, as if the request were for almond bark from PC Sweets. "I'll get right on it. We'll hold an emergency meeting. When is best?"

"As soon as possible."

"I'll take care of it. How much should I tell them?"

"As little as possible," Susan said, unsure of what Pam would say. She loved a cause—poured herself into it quickly and fully. But her positions changed easily—which wasn't to say that Pam didn't feel loyalty to Susan, Kate, and Sunny, only that she was married to Tanner, and Tanner was worried about the company image. "I'd rather they hear it from me. Besides, with us being friends, you're in a delicate enough position."

"Actually," Pam said, "I'm not, since Abby isn't involved."

"ARE YOU?" PAM ASKED HER DAUGHTER A SHORT TIME later, after finding her in the school gym watching basketball practice.

"No, I am not," Abby said without taking her eyes from the court.

"Even though the girls are your best friends?"

"Were. Getting pregnant was dumb."

"Did you know they were making a pact?"

"No."

"You didn't hear them talking about it this summer?"

"No. They were friends before I ever came along. They don't tell me everything."

"But you were the one who got them those jobs."

Abby turned to her. "I was just the first hired. Lily was the one who made the initial contact, not me." She turned back to the court.

"You told me—"

"I didn't," the girl insisted, digging her hands deeper into the pockets of her jacket. "You assumed. You always assume things that aren't true—like my friendship with Lily, Mary Kate, and Jess. You want us to be BFFs, because you want their moms to be *your* BFFs, but wanting it doesn't make it happen."

"I do consider their moms my best friends," Pam said, though she was unsettled.

"Well, you're dreaming. Susan, Sunny, and Kate are a threesome, just like Lily, Mary Kate, and Jess. Why do you think they won't tell anyone who the fathers are? They don't want the boys to bust up their group."

Pam could empathize with her daughter's hurt. Hadn't she found her best friends at the barn, all knowing about the pact but none telling her? That said, she was certainly glad Abby had been left out. Getting pregnant at seventeen was totally irresponsible.

"Do you know the boys' names?" she asked.

"No."

"But you know Jacob fathered Mary Kate's baby?"

"Everyone knows that."

"What else does everyone know that maybe I don't?"

Abby stared at her. "Why does it matter? Why can't you just let it go?"

"Because I'm on the school board, which will be discussing this, so the more I know, the better. I'm also the only board member with children in the schools right now, and since you are best friends—*were* best friends with the girls involved, I can try and help work things out."

"Whatever I tell you, you'll tell the board."

"No. I won't. It'll just help me decide what to say."

Abby turned back to the court, grumbling, "I don't know anything more."

Pam studied her face. Not a happy one. She put an arm around her shoulders. "Well, I'm proud of you."

That seemed to upset the girl more. She whipped around a final time. "For *what*?"

"For separating from those girls. For *knowing better*."

Abby looked like she might cry—and Pam understood that, too. There was a trade-off to being on the fringe of a group. Not that Abby would want to hear that. She was only seventeen.

Chapter 12

SUSAN WAS UP LATE THURSDAY NIGHT CRAFTING AN e-mail to the faculty. After a final tweaking, she sent it out at dawn. She wanted her teachers to start the day with the facts—the nature of the pact, the names of the girls, the involvement of the school psychologist and the nurse.

The e-mail to parents was harder. It wasn't that the content was different, though she mentioned no names in this one. But with parents concerned on a more personal level than teachers, the stakes were higher. She wrote and rewrote in search of exactly the right tone. Then that e-mail was sent, too.

FOLLOWING A DIFFICULT DAY FILLED WITH QUESTIONS from all sides, she got home shortly after six. She wasn't surprised to find Lily; volleyball practice was over and Friday night plans not begun. Nor was she surprised that Lily had made dinner. She often did that when Susan ran late. She liked cooking.

What surprised Susan was her daughter's contrition, evident in the fresh flowers on the table, the crab and corn bisque, which was Susan's favorite but not Lily's, and the fact that Lily was waiting in the kitchen, not in her room phoning or texting.

Susan's cell rang. Ignoring it, she hung her jacket on a hook by the door, dropped her bag on the bench beneath it, and sat. "You've been busy."

Lily hovered near the table. "I just made a few stops after practice. Jess drove." The phone rang again. "Aren't you going to answer?"

"No. It's been ringing off the hook all day. Our land line will be starting soon."

The words were barely out when it did. Lily checked the caller ID panel. "Legere. Sara's mom?"

"Probably," Susan said with resignation. "I haven't heard from *her* yet." The woman was a royal pain. Everyone knew it. She decided not to answer.

"You sent out the e-mails," Lily deduced. "Was it bad?"

"Oh, the sending was fine. It's the replies that were bad."

"How bad is bad?"

Not rational or understanding, thought Susan—but then, since she hadn't mentioned the girls' names, some of the parents wouldn't have realized that Susan's own daughter was pregnant. "Do you really want to know?"

"Yes."

It suddenly struck Susan then that if Lily was old enough to be a mother, she was old enough for this. "There was disbelief. There was curiosity—lots of questions for which I do not have answers. And there was criticism. One mother called it a pathetic stunt. Another used the word *disgusting*. A father who obviously knew you were one of the girls said it was shameless that I couldn't control my own child."

Lily gave a half blink, clearly struggling to be strong. "They knew it was me?"

"Some did."

"Who called me shameless?"

Susan smiled sadly. "I was the one being called shameless, and I doubt it'll be the last time. This does reflect on me."

"It wasn't supposed to."

"How could it not? I'm your *mother.*"

The silence that followed was broken only by the soup bubbling on the stove. Lily turned off the gas. "I guess I didn't think through what you'd have to face."

"Oh, Lily. It isn't just me. You heard what Jacob did when he saw Mary Kate. This may kill their relationship, and what happens then to the father that Mary Kate assumed her baby would have? What do you think Jacob's weekend's going to be like? Or Adam's—at least I assume Adam was the one who fathered Jess's baby? And who fathered yours?"

Robbie, Lily mouthed.

Susan hadn't expected an answer. Startled, she sat straighter. "Robbie *Boone*? Are you *sure*?"

"Mom. I've been with one guy in my life. I think I know who the father is."

"But Robbie? He's—he's the boy next door."

"Not next door. Across the street."

The phone rang. They continued to ignore it.

Susan was having trouble picturing her daughter and Robbie together. "You've known him since you were six. He was your first trick-or-treat buddy. He taught you to ride a *bike*."

"Does that disqualify him?"

"No. I just didn't see the two of you that way." She grew guarded. "Does he know?"

"He suspects. But no one else does—and please, *please,* Mom, don't tell Kate or Sunny or—or least of all Dr. Correlli. How's he taking this?"

Susan might have asked more about Robbie if she knew where to begin, but she just said, "The superintendent is upset. He has a right to be."

"I'm sorry."

Susan couldn't stop thinking of Robbie. He was the youngest of three, which made his parents significantly older than Susan, but they had always been unfailingly kind. When she had bought the house twelve years before and, mortgaged to the hilt, had struggled with things like a burst water heater and hurricane damage to the roof, Robbie's father had directed her to men who helped for a nominal fee. To this day, after every snowstorm, Bill Boone was outside with his shovel, digging out what the town plow had piled at the end of her driveway.

Susan was thinking that Robbie had never been publicly paired with a girl and seemed as innocent as Lily, and that if Lily had truly seduced him, Susan might be on her own after the next storm, when there was another call, this one on her cell. "I'm not answering," she murmured, wondering how Robbie's parents might feel about their son fathering a child at seventeen. Livid, she feared. Both parents were affiliated with Percy State, his dad in the treasurer's office, his mom in the art history department. Talk about responsibility? They lived and breathed it.

When the cell rang a third time, Lily fished it from Susan's bag and glanced at the caller ID. Eyeing Susan apprehensively, she opened it and, mouthing *My dad,* handed it over.

Had it been anyone else, Susan would have passed it right back. But Rick was her consort. "Hey," she said softly.

"How's it going?"

She sighed, releasing a little tension. "You don't want to know."

"I do. I talked with Lily earlier. She said word is out about the pact."

"Only we're not supposed to use that word."

"Correlli? He's afraid of panic."

"Clearly."

"I take it this is all falling on your shoulders."

"If not now, soon," Susan said. Rising from the bench, she left the kitchen. "One girl, and people would blame her for being careless. Three girls makes it deliberate. People start off blaming the girls, but, after all, they are only girls." Just past the front door were the stairs leading to the second floor. She climbed three and sat against the banister. "If one of those girls has a mother who was pregnant and unmarried at seventeen herself—*and* who is in a position of responsibility for hundreds of impressionable teens—how easy is it to blame her?"

"You'll have allies. There must be others who had babies in their teens, and there are certainly other single parents out there. They'll identify. As for the rest, eventually they'll look at the good job you've done. Tell me, would you do anything different as principal now if this didn't involve girls you love?"

"No. But I'd probably be blaming the parents, too, so I can't entirely fault Correlli."

"He's blaming you?"

"Oh yeah." When Lily appeared, Susan turned away so that she wouldn't hear. "We had a pretty heated argument. I really do have good control, Rick, but when he attacked me, I had to defend myself. I mean, *really,* are these girls pregnant at seventeen just because I was?"

"Did Correlli suggest that?"

"He kept repeating, 'You were seventeen.' Like I set a bad example? No matter. I may have lost him as an ally."

"Give him time. You're his protégé, so the situation is personal right now. Are you feeling any better about the baby?"

"No," she confessed softly. "I'm not ready to bond. Is that an awful thing to say?"

"No. You're human. How are Sunny and Kate?"

Susan turned back. Lily needed to hear this. "Kate e-mailed before I left to say that Mary Kate is hysterical at the prospect of losing Jacob, and Dan is grilling Sunny over why she allowed me to send my e-mail to every parent in the school. But should I have sent it to senior parents only? Seniors and juniors but not sophomores? If the goal is to minimize rumor, what I did was right."

"What's happening with Abby and Pam?"

"Now, there's an interesting question. What's happening with Abby?" Susan asked Lily.

"We're not talking," the girl said. "She hasn't been much of a friend."

"Maybe she's just smart," Susan replied and said to Rick, "There's no way she'll keep trying to get pregnant now."

"She *was* pregnant," Lily cried.

"Excuse me?"

"Before *any* of us. It was right after we conceived that she lost it. And who helped her through that?"

Susan bowed her head and said into the phone, "Did you hear? Abby got pregnant first. How far along was she?" she asked Lily, who shrugged. "Does Pam know?"

"No, and please don't tell her. It's Abby's place to tell her mom."

"What about the boy?" Rick asked Susan. "Lily wouldn't tell me about him. Any ID yet?"

"Uh-huh."

There was a silence, then a wise, "But you can't tell me. She's right there."

"Yup."

"Please don't mention Robbie," Lily whispered.

"Did you hear his name?" Susan shook her own head in reply.

"Is he a decent guy, at least?" Rick asked.

"Very decent. It's actually a relief. Of course, I may not think so once he finds out."

"Want me back there?"

"No," she said, turning away from Lily again. "I can handle this. It isn't cholera, only scandal." She sputtered. "How pathetic is that? No communicable disease, no third world country, but it'll get dirty. My phone is just starting to ring."

"They love you in town."

"They did before this. I'm a good principal. I communicate with them, something they haven't had before. Do you think my predecessor would have opened up about a problem like I did today? No *way*. Wardell Dickinson would have taken himself off to a conference somewhere until the uproar died down. Of course, he couldn't have e-mailed parents, because he was computer illiterate. Technologically, our high school was behind every other one in the area. Now we're ahead. With one click, I was able to send out an e-mail that could directly impact my job. How ironic is that?"

There was a pause, then, "I think I should come."

"No," she said, quieting. "I'm just venting. You're the only one who goes way back with me."

"Speaking of which, my father called. Your dad's not well."

Susan's heart skipped a beat. "What does 'not well' mean?"

"'Feeling poorly' was how my father put it. He's in touch with a couple of people from back home. Your dad canceled his annual golf trip."

That didn't sound good. John Tate loved his golf nearly as much as he loved fishing.

"My mother would call me if it was really bad, wouldn't she?" Susan asked, but she didn't blame Rick for not responding. "I'd better call them."

IT TOOK SEVERAL HOURS FOR HER TO DRUM UP THE courage. First, she blamed the hour's time difference. Couldn't phone during dinner. Then she had to finish the row she was knitting, then the next. By way of penance, she answered several incoming calls—half expecting Robbie's parents to be calling in a furor. As it happened, most of the calls were from friends who expressed support, even when their voices held disappointment.

Finally, she dialed her parents. Her mother was always up late, but not her father, and it wouldn't do for the phone to wake him. He liked his sleep. At least, he used to. Susan really didn't know what either of her parents enjoyed now.

Ellen Tate picked up after a single ring, her voice fragile in a way that pricked Susan's heart. The woman was only fifty-nine, but sounded much older.

"It's me, Mom. Susan."

There was a pause, then a low "Yes."

How are you, Mom? I didn't wake you, did I? Were you watching TV? Knitting? It's getting cold here, what's it like there?

So many possible questions, ones that were conversational and caring, but Susan had been down this road many times, always trying to smooth out the contact, to pretend that their relationship was a typical one. After one answer too many that was either short or silent, she had come to rethink asking. Her questions only seemed to make Ellen tense.

So she got to the point. "I heard Dad wasn't well."

"Who told you that?"

"Rick. His dad told him. What's wrong?"

"Nothing much."

"It was enough to keep him from golfing."

"Oh, that," Ellen said offhandedly. "He just doesn't like to fly anymore."

"Not even for golf?"

"Flying tires him out." There was a tiny pause. "He tires easily."

"Has he seen a doctor?"

"Every year. Faithfully. But your father isn't young anymore. He'll be sixty-five in the spring."

Susan was well aware of that. She guessed that there would be a party, but was afraid to ask. She wouldn't want to know that she wouldn't be invited.

"Sixty-five is not old, Mom. Does Dr. Littlefield do blood tests and EKGs?"

"Of course he does," she said. "Our medical care is just fine."

"I know. But I worry."

"You shouldn't. You have your own life."

"He is my father."

"You haven't seen him in years."

There was an edge to her mother's voice that caught Susan the wrong way. "Is that my fault?" she asked quietly.

"Yes. Yes, it is."

"Well, I used to think so, but I'm not sure anymore. I was careless one night, and I happen to have an amazing daughter to show for it." *An amazing pregnant daughter,* she thought but didn't say. This conversation was less about Lily than Susan, and her fuchsia heart was beating fast. "Dad's pride was wounded. At what point does he realize that he's turning his back on his flesh and blood? I mean, what does Reverend Withers sermonize about every Sunday, if not forgiveness?"

Ellen didn't answer.

"Mom?"

"Reverend Withers retired six years ago. Reverend Baker took over, and she's a woman. Your father doesn't listen as closely as he used to."

Was that a subtle dig at her dad? If so, it would be a first. Ellen marched in lockstep with John, mainly because she adored him. And he adored her. He was home every day for lunch. Theirs was a very sweet romance that had lasted more than forty years, in part because they appeared to agree that John's way was the right way, the only way.

Adding insult to injury for Susan was her father's blindness toward his son. Jackson could do no wrong, even when he did—though, in fairness, his sins were petty. Then again, he had married a woman who had never acknowledged a note, a phone call, or a gift from Susan. In Susan's mind, that was a major sin. She wondered if Ellen, who did always write a note, would agree with that.

"I would like to have a relationship with you, Mom. We still have a lot in common."

"What, for example?"

Most immediately, a pregnant teenage daughter, but this was not the reason Susan had called. Or maybe, once past the excuse of her father's health, it was. She wished she could confide in Ellen, had truly ached for it at times. But Ellen's tone didn't invite that. And Susan couldn't bear a put-down on this.

What else did they have in common? Susan was thinking that they had different taste in books and food, and that Ellen had no *idea* what Susan's job was like, when, looking around, she spotted her yarn. "Knitting," she said, relieved to have found an answer. "What are you working on?"

"Why, a prayer shawl for the town clerk's mother," Ellen said on a lighter note. "She broke her hip two weeks ago, and she's doing well, but she'll be in rehab for a bit. I'm using a wonderfully soft alpaca that I picked up in Tulsa. It's beige."

Susan was familiar with the Tulsa store. It carried PC Wool—not that she would ever expect her mother to actually *buy* PC Wool. "I wish I'd known," she said. "We have alpaca. I'd have sent you some." Theirs was exquisitely soft, though not beige. Well, some colorways did have beige, but it would have been paired with celadon and orchid, navy or teal.

"I can afford to buy my own," Ellen said briskly. "Your father's income may have gone down, but that was because he voluntarily took a cut in his pension so that the town could avoid layoffs."

"I didn't mean—"

"Easterners tend to think they have the best restaurants, the best schools, the best doctors. They think anyone with any brains graduated from Harvard, but that is not true."

"I know that, Mom."

"Your father has done very well in his life, and that includes providing for his family. He's made arrangements for me. He's a good man that way, always concerned about me. We own this house, and our savings are safe in the bank. We live quite comfortably. I see no reason why that should change."

Susan was startled by the outburst. Reading into the words,

she worried that her father might not be around much longer—or that Ellen feared it. Susan wanted to ask, but couldn't form the words. Here would be something Ellen might share with a daughter and not a son. But not even in the best of times had Susan had the kind of relationship with her mother that she had with Lily.

She regretted that now, when they both had deep concerns. "I would like us to be able to talk on the phone without this tension."

Ellen was quiet for a minute, clearly regrouping. When she spoke again, her voice was calm. "Notes are fine."

"Not for me."

"Phoning puts me in an awkward position."

"With Dad."

"You've never tried to see it from his side, Susan. You decided early on that he was the villain. That was how you saw it, so that was how it was. Maybe if you'd approached him and apologized—"

"I *did*, Mom."

"Not in years."

"Because the older my daughter gets, the more wonderful she is. I won't apologize for having her. Besides, I've sent cards and gifts. Didn't Dad see that I was reaching out?"

"You never visited."

"I was never invited!" Susan cried, heartsick. "I was told to leave, remember? I was made to feel that I wasn't welcome."

"Your father gave you money to start a new life, and look where you are now."

Susan thought of the struggle it had been, through many months of loneliness and fear. She thought of the latest with Lily, and vowed that, even in this, Lily would have it easier than she had. And she thought of Ellen, who was missing so much, now times two.

"Oh, Mom," she said sadly. "I didn't call to argue. I just wanted to see how Dad was."

"He's fine," Ellen responded. "Thank you for calling."

"Will you tell him I'm thinking of him?" Susan asked. But there was no answer. With the formal thank-you, her mother had hung up.

Chapter 13

❧

SATURDAY MORNINGS WERE FOR DYEING YARN, AND if ever Susan needed a distraction, it was now. Wearing her wool jacket over an old shirt and paint-splotched jeans, she took her time entering the barn. The old boards sang of history, with the echo of hooves pawing the straw-strewn earth, a soft snort, the whisper of a whinny. No matter that the inner wood walls were new and insulated and the sounds strictly human, even mechanical when tape was being whipped around boxes of yarn, the original spirit remained.

Now, with the front stalls dim where computers and cartons stood idle, Susan headed toward the light at the back. Halfway there, she smelled fresh-brewed coffee, followed seconds later by the ageless odor of wet wool.

Kate was at a large tub filled with skeins soaking in water to open their pores. "I put these in last night," she said, repositioning them with a stick. "It was a good thing. I just got here five minutes ago."

Susan draped her jacket on the back of a chair. Her friend looked worn out. "Bad night?"

Kate shrugged and kept working.

After helping herself to coffee, Susan joined her at the tub, but Kate remained focused on the wool, either lost in thought or angry.

Fearing the latter and feeling the blame, Susan said, "I really am sorry, Kate. It was a choice between letting word dribble out on its own or setting the record straight with an e-mail. This way we're hit with the reaction all at once, and then it'll be done."

Kate smiled sadly. "Until our girls start to show. Until one of them goes into labor at school. Until the three of them share a bench at the harbor wearing their kids in BabyBjörns."

Susan rubbed her friend's arm. "Tell me about last night."

"Oh, Susie. Either it was my phone ringing or the girls running in to tell me who *else* had just called."

"People knew it was Mary Kate?"

"And Jess." A punishing look here. "Lily was the tip-off. By the way, you won't have to worry about imitators. The consensus is that the three of them are idiots."

"Your friends said that, too?"

"You mean, the people who called me?" Kate replied, giving the wool another stir. "I'm not sure they're friends. Funny how people come out of the woodwork when they want information." Her voice rose in imitation. "'Oh, Kate, it's been sooo long since we've talked, but did Mary Kate really *plan* to get pregnant, will she marry Jacob, and what does *Will* say about this?' It was horrible. Mary Kate is now angry at Jacob for being angry at her, and the tension is probably not good for the baby." She reached into the tub to separate two skeins. "She wanted to come with me this morning, and I told her no. I need time away. If that makes me a terrible mother, I'm a terrible mother." She looked around. "Do you have your colors?"

Susan produced her notebook. "Where's Sunny?"

"Not coming. She says she has too much to do."

It was an excuse. Sunny didn't want to be seen with Susan and Kate, whose daughters were her own daughter's cohorts. "Maybe I should call. She's having trouble with this."

"And we're not?"

"We aren't married to Dan." Easier to blame Sunny's absence on him than on not wanting to work with Susan and Kate. Saturday mornings were a ritual—a reward at the end of the week—an excuse to be with friends, reminiscent of Thursday nights at Susan's garage. When they were caught up in work, they could go on until Susan had to head to school for an afternoon game. When there was little work, a long cup of coffee sufficed. They knitted then, and if they weren't discussing the vagaries of a pattern, they discussed a book, a movie, even a town rumor.

It didn't feel right without Sunny. But that was only part of the problem.

"Has Pam called?" Susan asked.

"No. Haven't you heard from her?"

"Not since yesterday. She was supposed to get back to me about the school board." Not a comforting thought, that one. The unease Susan had felt leaving Tanner's office was as strong now as then.

Putting her cell on the worktable, she opened her notebook and crossed to the far wall, where shelves were neatly lined with bottles of powdered dye. She removed Scarlet, Sun, and Spruce. Liking her colors intense, she measured double the suggested amount into widemouthed jugs, added water to each to form a paste, and, after stirring, poured in enough water to make a gallon of stock solution. She would use this straight, diluted, or mixed for variations in hue. Taking a stack of measuring cups and a pair of rubber gloves from the supply shelf, she returned to the dye.

Behind her she heard trickling as Kate removed one skein at a time and squeezed each to remove water. Above the sound came a quiet "Jacob's parents called."

Susan looked back. Kate's expression said the news wasn't good.

"They're upset. I knew they would be. They say Mary Kate used Jacob." Hands filled with wet skeins, she swore softly. "I forgot to lay out the plastic."

Returning to the supply shelf herself, Susan wondered what Robbie's parents would think. Likely the same thing, she decided, which was why she tried not to even *look* at their house when she drove down the street and pulled into her driveway. She tore a length of wide plastic wrap from the spindle and flattened it on the table. Taking one skein from Kate, she arranged it in an oval.

Oh, yes, she was sorry that Sunny and Pam weren't there. But this part of PC Wool production was really up to Susan and Kate. Susan conceived the colors and worked out the formula, while Kate did the dyeing. The process had evolved from the early days in Susan's garage, growing more nuanced as they took courses and studied under experts. Though they had added implements like the skeining machine, the basic technique remained the same. Susan worked the dye, adding more or less and squeezing it through the fiber.

It wasn't an exact science. Much as Kate would take notes on dye proportions, the replication was never exact. But that was the beauty of hand-painted yarn. Each skein was unique.

Now, Susan filled a cup with eight ounces of Spruce stock and dipped in a paper towel to test the color. Even before comparing it to her notebook, she knew it was too cool. After adding a half cup of Sun, she did another test, but it was only after adding two more tablespoons that she was pleased.

Kate wrote down the measurements, then picked up where they had left off. "Jacob's parents are right. She did use him."

"They'll come around," Susan said. "They've always loved Mary Kate."

"They love her because Jacob loves her. If he stops, they stop. It isn't a visceral thing, like the way Will and I love her."

Susan considered the term *visceral*. "Do all parents love that way?"

"I think so. Don't you?" Kate asked in surprise.

"I used to. Now I'm not so sure." She told Kate about talking with her mother.

"They still love you," Kate assured her. "They just never got past the anger. When they sent you away, they stopped the clock. They never worked it out."

"Do you think I should go back—y'know, just show up one day and force the issue?"

"Now? No. You have enough on your plate. Get through this stuff with Lily. You didn't tell your mom about her, did you?"

Susan shook her head.

They fell silent. Wearing disposable gloves, Susan poured dye directly from the plastic cup onto the wool at three different spots in the oval, then studied the result. "More, I think," she said aloud. "This is my major color." She added more dye to deepen the saturation, then, while Kate turned the wool, applied dye to the underside. The dye didn't have to be perfectly even; one of the beauties of PC Wool was a fine subtlety in saturation. That said, there was nothing beautiful about a large patch of white in a colorway called Vernal Tide. Coral, yes. Pale green, yes. Even sand. But not white. A missed underside wouldn't do.

She shifted the wool to help it absorb the color, and

squeezed dye to the ends of each swath, and all the while, she was thinking about what Kate had said.

"Working out the anger, huh? Then the little squabbles I have with Lily have a purpose?"

Kate snorted. "I put the same question to Will. He says yes. The anger will fade. It takes time."

"I feel like I'm still paying my dues. Like this is another challenge that goes right back to my own pregnancy."

"That's ancient history."

"Then you don't blame me for what our girls did?"

"No. Only for being who you are now and having to make it public."

"I had no other choice, Kate. Please believe that. I'm suffering the fallout, too. Sunny and Pam may be angry, but I need your support."

Kate shot her a helpless look. "You have it. That's one of the reasons I'm so *pissed*. I need a scapegoat, and you'd be a perfect one, only you're my best friend. I was so proud of you when you got this position. Now I resent it."

"There's good and bad in every job. This is the bad."

"Right." She studied Susan's book, then the three stock solutions. "We need turquoise."

While she mixed it, Susan readied the yellow dye and began to apply it. When she had poured the most concentrated shade in two small spots, she stood back to look, spread it around a little, looked again, added a diluted patch.

"Incredible how you do that," Kate said. "Look how the two colors shimmer where they meet."

"Mm," Susan said, but her mind was on work. "I wish Phil were as understanding as you. He forwarded me a sample of the e-mails he received. People are blaming the school clinic for offering pregnancy tests, blaming me for establishing the clinic, blaming Phil for allowing me to do it."

"He must have sent only the bad ones."

"He says this is how people feel. So if I defend the clinic, and Phil points out that the school board had the final say in allowing the clinic, do you think the board will shoulder the blame? No way. They'll put it right back on me."

"Not just you. Me, too. Mothers always get hit—like our kids are extensions of our bodies. They'll blame Sunny, too."

But they wouldn't blame Pam, Susan realized. Taking a fresh plastic cup, she filled it halfway with Scarlet, added measured increments of Sun, then turquoise to get coral, but all the while, the issue of blame niggled at her. When she was satisfied with the shade, she set down the cup. "Did you know that Abby was pregnant?"

Kate eyed her in surprise. "I did not! *Was?*"

"She lost it. Pam doesn't know."

"We should tell her."

"Abby needs to do that," Susan said, because betraying Abby would hurt friendships all around. "But it raises an interesting point about who'd be blaming who if the world knew." She had *another* niggling thought. "If you were to guess—just a guess, since neither of our daughters has said—who do you think first suggested the pact?"

Kate didn't blink. "I have a hunch."

"Me, too."

They were thinking the same thing, with neither of them wanting to say it because it felt disloyal, when the front door opened. Susan thought she heard Kate murmur something like *Speak of the devil,* before Pam reached the back room. She wasn't coming to work, likely not even to have coffee when she knew they were working with dyes. She wore wool slacks, a silk blouse, and a lambswool jacket, all top-of-the-line PC designs. Her freshly styled hair shimmered with some of the same blond shades Susan hoped to capture on her yarn.

"Hey," Pam said, her eyes on Susan. "Tomorrow at noon?"

The school board. "Perfect," Susan said. "Thanks, Pam. I appreciate this."

Pam was studying the wool they were dyeing. "I like it. Where's Sunny?"

"Home, I think," Susan said, but Pam was already turning to leave.

"Aren't you staying?" Kate asked.

"Nah. I'm not dressed for it. Besides, you don't need me for this."

"Actually, I do," Susan said. "I want to copy the color of your hair."

"Cute."

"Stay for coffee, at least?" Kate said.

"Can't do," Pam called back without stopping. "We're driving down to Boston. Tanner promised me a shopping trip, and we have theater tickets, so we're making a night of it. We'll have to leave early if I want to get back for the meeting, but if I'm late, Susan, you'll understand?" She didn't wait for an answer.

They watched until she reached the door.

"Theater tickets? How lovely," Kate remarked. "You should have told her about Abby. That would give her something to discuss with Tanner over martinis at the Four Seasons."

But Susan was skating on thin ice. With the prospect of facing the school board extraordinarily daunting and Pam a questionable ally, she couldn't risk it.

THE BOARD MET IN A CONFERENCE ROOM AT THE TOWN hall. There was no harbor view here, only a glimpse of the church. It was an unassuming room, functionally appointed with a long table and fourteen spindle-back chairs. Narrower ladder-backs lined the walls to accommodate guests, and above them, compensating for the limited view, hung a collection of local seascapes.

Pam had not arrived when Hillary Dunn closed the door. Nor had Phil, though he hurried in seconds later. Taking one of the chairs that ringed the room, he stayed a comfortable distance from Susan. His message was clear; she was on her own.

Susan took a seat at the end of the table and thanked the six there for meeting on such short notice. She added a note of condolence to one of the men, who had just returned to town after his sister's funeral, and it wasn't mere gesture. Bald-headed Harold LaPierre was the library director. He was bookish and fair-minded, and while their paths never crossed socially, they had a good working relationship. Susan liked him. Aside from Hillary and Pam, he was her closest ally.

She began by distributing copies of the e-mail she had sent parents on Friday, trying not to be discouraged when several of the men quickly pushed the sheets aside. She explained her rationale for the mailing—that she wanted parents hearing directly from her about what had happened and what she was doing about it. She paused to invite reaction from board members. Getting none, she described the brainstorming she'd done with the nurse and the counselor, and the meetings they planned to hold on Monday with students. When she had finished, she paused again. No reaction this time, either.

"I'd like your feedback," she finally said. "My goal is to be direct. I don't want the grapevine turning this into something it isn't. Besides, tackling it head-on gives us an opportunity to discuss issues that are timely. National studies show that teenage pregnancy is on the rise."

"Is that s'posed to excuse these girls?" asked Duncan Haith, his Maine accent thick, his bushy white eyebrows pulled down. She knew him to be the curmudgeon of the group, but to start off this way was unnerving.

Refusing to show fear, she said, "Absolutely not. I'm just citing a trend and suggesting that the timing of this can be turned to good use. My biggest worry is copycat behavior. I'm meeting with the faculty early tomorrow. We'll coordinate student discussions throughout the day." She looked around, waited. "Are you . . . comfortable with this? I'm open to other ideas."

"But it's too late," Duncan complained, slapping the paper with the back of his hand. "You already told the world. That was not a good move." He shot Phil a look. "Did you approve this?"

Phil shrugged. "We couldn't sweep the problem under the rug."

"Why not?"

Phil gestured for Susan to go on.

"Rumors were already spreading," she said.

Duncan scowled. "So now, instead of a few people talking about it, everyone is? What's the point a' that?"

Not wanting to argue, Susan appealed to the others. Thankfully, Hillary Dunn came to her aid. Wife of the town meeting moderator and mother of three, she was originally from the Midwest, an outsider like Susan. "I see her point, Mr. Haith," she said now. "If people are going to talk, you want them to know the facts."

"But they didn't even get all the information," Duncan blustered. "This e-mail does not mention the names of the girls."

Susan suspected he knew the names, but she gave them anyway. If he wanted her to squirm, she would squirm. That was the easy part. The hard part was projecting command enough to make the board see her as the principal of the school, not the mother of one of the girls involved. She was wearing brown today—*fuchsia heart, be still!*—good solid earth tones, right down to her scarf.

"I didn't include names in the e-mail," she said respectfully, "because my priority is that the school community know what's happened, and that they know we're taking steps to make sure it doesn't happen again. The identity of the girls is secondary."

"Well, I'm sure you'd like that to be true," Carl Morgan remarked in a gravelly voice. He had headed the Perry & Cass accounting department before retiring and still prepared taxes for many Zaganackians. While he was known to be more reasonable than Duncan Haith, had it been April, he'd have been a bear. "We're talking about your daughter and her two closest friends, right?"

"Yes."

"No boys involved?"

Susan smiled politely. "Of course there were, but it's not my place to give out their names. We're focusing on the girls—in this case, on pact behavior."

"Bad word," muttered Thomas Zimmerman, a Realtor.

"Group behavior, then," Susan said.

"But explain it, please," Carl asked gruffly. "Why did they do this? You don't discuss that in your e-mail."

She hadn't felt it necessary there. Here she said, "They did it because they love children, and because, acting together, telling themselves that this was *their thing,* they were able to override what they'd been taught. That's what pact behavior is about."

"But why these girls?" Carl went on. "They're achievers."

"Maybe that's why," Susan reasoned. "Being achievers gave them the confidence to think they could pull this off."

Duncan sat forward. "So you'll confront this issue openly at school, and you'll keep your fingers crossed that your students listen, but what about these girls?"

"Oh, they'll be there."

"No." He laced his fingers. "I'm talking about punishment. Since you've gone public with this, don't we need a public response? They shouldn't get off scot-free."

Susan was startled. "They'll be living with the consequences of their behavior for the rest of their lives. But punishment? You mean, like detention? Community service?"

"I was thinking expulsion, or at the very least suspension."

"Expulsion would be illegal. And suspension? For getting pregnant?"

"Why not? My reading of the handbook says that the principal has the discretion to impose suspension. Or can't you do that he-ya because of your own involvement?"

Susan fought a rising anger. "Oh, I can do it, and I would, if it made sense. I've suspended students for bullying, for writing on the bathroom walls, for any number of infractions that involve harming someone or something, but there's nothing in the handbook that outlaws pregnancy. And who is the victim here? Their unborn babies? If that's the case, suspension is counterproductive. The idea is to let these girls finish their education so that they can make something of their lives. Wouldn't that be best for the babies?"

"But what's best for the rest of us?" Duncan asked, bushy brows raised. "We don't condone this kind of thing. Nathaniel Hawthorne had it right. They should wear a scarlet letter."

The remark was over the top. Susan couldn't let it go unanswered. "Nathaniel Hawthorne also came from Salem, which bowed to crowd hysteria and hanged innocent women." She tried to stay cool. "Singling girls out doesn't solve the problem. Communication does. That's why we're discussing this openly. We're putting the downside of teenage pregnancy front and center. We're giving parents reasons to carry on a dialogue with their kids."

"Like you did not?"

Susan took a tempering breath. "Oh, I did."

"Before or after your daughter became pregnant?"

"Mr. Haith," Hillary Dunn scolded softly, "you're being harsh."

He looked around innocently. "Are none of you as upset as me? Cripes, what was the point of her school clinic if not to prevent this?"

Susan glanced at Phil. Legs sprawled, arms crossed, he didn't meet her gaze.

Fine. She faced Duncan. "The goal of the clinic is to give students an alternative when they can't get help at home—and yes, it's for education. Unfortunately, what happened with my daughter wasn't for lack of education. All these girls knew what they were doing."

"So who is to blame?"

Susan couldn't answer.

"Isn't it a mother's job to know when her daughter's headed for trouble?" he asked.

Of course, it was a personal attack. But if Phil's forwarded e-mails were any indication, she'd have to get used to that.

Refusing to blink, she said, "My daughter and I talk all the time. But when a seventeen-year-old wants to hide something, she can be pretty good at it."

"So we just"—he tossed a hand—"chalk off parental responsibility because that parent may not *see* something? What about drug use?"

"With drugs, there are physical signs a parent can look for," Susan said, "but intent to become pregnant? If I'd seen any-thing—*guessed* anything—I'd have done my best to stop it. Believe me, Mr. Haith, I know what these girls are in for, and, yes, that's on a personal level. I also know how bad this looks for the town."

The door opened and Pam slipped into the room. On her way to a seat, she touched the shoulders of several fellow board members. Barely looking at Susan, she shrugged out of her coat and sat.

Susan imagined she didn't want to be part of the discussion. But Hillary Dunn promptly turned to her. "What is your husband's take on this?"

Seeming surprised to be called on so soon, Pam took a minute to organize her thoughts. When she spoke, she was poised. "He's upset. The company stands for responsibility. He feels these girls were irresponsible."

"Do you agree?"

"Totally."

Susan agreed, too. No damage there.

But Hillary didn't let Pam off the hook. "You're the only one of us who has a daughter the same age as these girls. Are you comfortable with what Ms. Tate is doing to keep their behavior from spreading?"

"For now? Yes."

"How does your daughter feel about what these girls did?"

Pam remained composed. "She's as shocked as we are."

"Have you heard from other parents?"

"Some. They're worried. But they appreciated Susan's e-mail."

A new voice came then. Neal Lombard headed the Chamber of Commerce. A pleasant-looking man with a benign moon face, he had four children. All were in their twenties, which meant that Susan hadn't taught any of them. Mention drugs, though, and teachers talked. More than one of the Lombard sons were known users. Had that made Neal more compassionate? Apparently not.

"What Mr. Haith is saying," he offered quietly, "is that an e-mail may not be enough. We ought to consider stronger steps to let people know we don't condone this behavior. I may be speaking out of turn here, because I wasn't a member of the board that voted on your appointment, Ms. Tate, but there's an argument to be made that you ought to take a leave of absence until this all quiets down."

Susan hadn't expected that. It took her breath away—but only for a second. "With due respect, that would be my last option."

"I was just thinking of what happened in Gloucester," the man said.

"So am I," Susan assured him, "but Gloucester was different. There was a spike in teen pregnancy and the principal called it a pact when there was none. He resigned under pressure for jumping to conclusions and creating hysteria. I'm not doing that. These girls did form a pact. We have to address it. Parents trust that I'll give them straight talk."

"Can you do that, with your daughter involved?"

"Absolutely."

"Look," Duncan chided, "it's a matter of credibility. I *was* here when your appointment was first raised, Ms. Tate, so I know your history. Back then, it was a selling point: unmarried mother defeats the odds. Now it's a drawback. Mr. Lombard may have a point."

"Is it a drawback?" she asked quietly. "I can be honest. I can tell students firsthand the downside of being a teenage mother."

"You're missing the point, Ms. Tate. What kind of role model are you? Your daughter is following in your footsteps. Is that what we want the rest of our students to do? Unless you think what you did was okay?"

Susan was offended. "You wouldn't ask that if you'd heard

some of the discussions I've had with my daughter this week, or last year, or the year before that. I don't approve of teenage pregnancies. That's one of the reasons I pushed for a school clinic—and, in fairness, we don't know the number of pregnancies the clinic has prevented."

"It didn't prevent three," said Neal Lombard, "one being your daughter's."

"Which puts me in a position of *greater* credibility with our kids. I can speak to them as one who's been there. I'd like to be given that chance."

Chapter 14

❦

"THEY WOULDN'T FIRE YOU," LILY SAID.

Susan wasn't so sure. Phil had been less than supportive at the meeting, and her job was in his hands. But his job was in the hands of the school board. If he felt that sentiment ran strongly against her, that if a second vote were taken, the board would vote to let her go, he would fire her first. Their friendship didn't go that far.

Nor, apparently, did Pam's, which was the one that really hurt. What was it she'd said when asked if she was pleased with how Susan was handling the situation? *For now, yes.* Not exactly a ringing endorsement. And when the meeting adjourned, she busied herself talking with members. As signs went, it didn't bode well. Susan's fears only deepened during the short drive home.

"Maybe not now," she told Lily, "but next week? Next month? There seems to be an obsession about who is to blame."

"Well, that's a no-brainer, since you weren't involved in the decision."

"Not a no-brainer at all." Susan reached for the teakettle. "Here's a basic lesson in Mothering 101, sweetheart. The buck stops here."

MONDAY MORNING, PRAYING THAT HER FACULTY would be less judgmental, Susan got to school in advance of the seven o'clock meeting. She set out coffee and dough-nuts in the hope of mustering good will, but most of her teachers dashed into the small amphitheater with seconds to spare.

Was she nervous? Not of leading the meeting. She had got-ten over that two years before, after realizing that her freckles mattered less than the professionalism she displayed. As long as she had an agenda, she was fine. And she certainly had an agenda today.

That said, she was nervous as hell. If she was fighting for her job, she needed the support of her faculty. All eyes were on her as she began.

"Thanks for coming so early. I met with the school board yesterday. We're going ahead with the plan to reach the entire student body. You've all read the e-mail I sent Friday. You should have also received the one I sent last night with the change in today's class schedule and bullet points for discus-sion." Lest some hadn't printed it out, she took a stack and passed it around. "The focus should be on the risk of teenage pregnancy and the danger of pacts. I've elaborated on both on page two." She gave a small smile. "I'm betting there are still questions. Please. Ask."

There were a few easy ones. *When are the girls due? Are all three keeping their babies? Will they be marrying the boys?* Susan gave succinct answers to each.

In the brief awkwardness that followed, Susan waited, then smiled. "Go ahead. Be blunt. I can take it."

"Do we give the names of the girls?" someone asked.

"Only if you feel it's necessary for the discussion," Susan replied. "Most everyone knows that my daughter is one of the girls. I'm close to the other two families and would have you protect them, but our first priority is protecting the rest of our students. If they ask, you tell."

"Will the girls be in class this week?"

"Yes."

"Won't that be hard for them?"

"Yes."

"What about the boys?"

Susan thought for a minute. "I'd downplay mention of them. Some of our students will know who they are."

"Do you?"

"I know one name. I'm sure you all know the same one."

"How do you feel about this?"

Susan was slow to speak as she waded through different levels of emotion. "I'm upset," she finally said, but it didn't seem enough. "As principal and a mother. These weren't accidental pregnancies. We don't want to glorify them." And still that didn't seem enough. "Some of you may be thinking that I'm taking a hard line because of my own past. I honestly don't think so. I'm not punishing these girls. I just want to discourage others from copying them."

"What if students ask about you?"

"I'll be going from class to class while you discuss this. They can ask me themselves."

. . .

SUSAN DID LITTLE ELSE OVER THE NEXT TWO DAYS. She talked with students in the classroom, the lunchroom, the halls, even the gym, answering their questions as honestly as she could. There were questions about her own experience, often relating to whether schools talked about birth control "back then," but most of the questions focused on the girls.

Same with the faculty. Talking with them before and after classes, she sensed that they agreed with what she was doing. She never got the slightest whiff, not even from Raymond Dunbar, that she wasn't a fit principal. Nor did parents suggest it. Their notes were overwhelmingly supportive, far more positive this week than the weekend before. They liked what she was doing. As she had hoped, open discussions in school were leading to discussions at home.

She answered every e-mail she received, working late each night. And all the while, as she scrolled through her inbox, she wondered if Robbie Boone's parents knew. Sooner or later, they would. They might e-mail or, worse, ambush her as she climbed from her car at the end of the day.

By Wednesday, though, she was starting to feel she was over the hump. Classes were back to normal, and though she continued to make herself accessible, students were more interested in the holiday basketball tournament that Zaganack hosted each year than they were in Lily, Mary Kate, and Jess.

Then came Thursday and the *Gazette*. There was no article; as promised, Phil had made his call. The paper's editorial was another matter.

> It's time to talk about family values. Zaganack has always taken the high moral road. Call us traditional, but we have the lowest divorce rate in the state, and violent crime here is rare. Our churches raise strong voices in this community, and we listen.

Now we learn about three girls who didn't. Three girls who are pregnant and happy about it. Three girls who have no plans to marry.

You might call this part of a national epidemic, an erosion of family values. But Zaganackians have a culture of responsibility that was supposed to protect us. Why did it fail?

These girls claim they acted alone. Did they? Do we blame the boys they were with, mere teenagers themselves? No. There are people who should have taught these girls right from wrong. Those people failed. They failed to teach. Failed to supervise. Failed to set an example.

Those people failed to understand that we can't redefine family values to suit our own needs.

What should the town do? We can't control what happens in individual families. But we can control what happens in our schools. We do have a say about who leads our children at this vulnerable time in their lives. Those children need the best possible role models.

One of the mothers of one of these girls holds a crucial position in our town. This is troublesome.

Zaganack needs to look long and hard at this problem.

"Phil," Susan breathed, reaching him on the phone minutes after finishing her third reading of the piece, "have you seen the *Gazette*?"

"Just did. This isn't good."

"Didn't you ask him not to do this?"

"I asked him to hold off on covering the story, and he did. There was no front page headline. There wasn't even a story inside. Just this editorial."

"Which is entirely one-sided. This isn't fair, Phil. I've made progress this week. If you want to talk about taking the 'high moral road,' I've done what you always like—turned this into a lesson for our students. Their parents overwhelmingly approve."

"Then this editorial will be a blip."

"A blip that every single person in town will see. Second to the front page headline, this is what people read. Have you heard from any of the board?"

"Zimmerman called me yesterday, but that was before this."

"This will not hurt property values," Susan declared, knowing Thomas Zimmerman's priorities only too well.

"I hope not."

"How can it? We're talking three girls in a town of eighteen thousand people."

"With a school principal who is the mother of one of those girls. See, that's the tricky part."

Susan didn't want to argue the point again. "So what do we do? The school is my first priority. I have to keep my focus here. You're higher up. Can you reach out to the broader community?"

He could write a letter to the editor. He could lobby on her behalf with the likes of Carl Morgan and Duncan Haith. As superintendent of schools, he had the ear of other community leaders.

"Tell you what," he said genially. "The Leadership Team isn't scheduled to meet for another week. I'll call everyone together tomorrow morning. You can answer their questions directly."

It wasn't quite what Susan had in mind. But she wasn't in a position to demand more.

SUNNY WAS ON THE PHONE IN HER TINY OFFICE AT the back of PC Home Goods, putting in an order with a loquacious candle supplier, when the paper arrived. While the man chatted on, she skimmed through to the editorial page.

The supplier rambled on, but she heard none of it, until there was a louder, "Mrs. Barros? Are you there?"

Sunny cleared her throat. "I am, Chad. I'm sorry. Something's come up. Can we finish this later?" She quickly hung up and, heart in her throat, reread the editorial. Then she picked up the phone and called her husband.

"Have you seen the *Gazette*?" she asked in a voice that shook.

"No. Sunny, I'm with someone here."

"Read the editorial."

"As soon as I can."

"*Soon*. Call me back." She hung up and waited. The digital clock on the shelf changed the half hour, then the hour, but the phone didn't ring. Soft bells jingled when the door of the store opened, but she had two saleswomen on the floor to handle customers. She couldn't face anyone who might have seen the *Gazette*.

When the clock registered another half hour, she pulled out her cell phone. She didn't want this call on the company line.

Her parents lived one time zone away, making it nine o'clock there, and even then her mother sounded groggy.

"If I've woken you, I am not sorry," Sunny began. "It isn't my fault if you and Dad watch old movies all night. And it isn't *my fault* that my daughter is pregnant. But that's what the paper suggests."

"What paper?"

"The local one—the *Gazette*—what other one would I care about? This paper reaches every person in town for *free,* so it's not like I can even unsubscribe. It isn't bad enough that my own daughter betrayed me or that my best friend Susan aired my dirty laundry in school all week, but now it's in print. I'll definitely sue the editor in chief for printing this."

"The Zaganack *Gazette?*" Delilah sounded distracted.

"You think this is funny, Mother? I do not. I had a good reputation before this, but now it's shot." She read aloud. " 'These girls claim they acted alone. But did they? Their mothers failed to teach. Failed to supervise. Failed to—' "

" 'Set an example,' " Delilah spoke with her. "Excuse me, Sunshine, but I do not see mention of mothers in this diatribe."

"Because I've only read you a tiny part."

"No, no. I have the whole thing on my screen right now, and I only see the word *mother* once."

"*People* is a euphemism for mothers. He's directing this at my friends and me."

"Mostly at Susan, but he doesn't mention her name either."

"Like anyone in town wouldn't guess? You don't seem to *understand*. I have trouble looking at my daughter, my husband has trouble looking at me, and wherever I go people stare. This is everything I've fought not to go through. Now we'll have to move."

"Rubbish," said Delilah.

"I'm not like you, Mother. You thrive on controversy. I find it Humiliating with a capital *H*."

"That's because you're Timid with a capital *T*. You have a fine daughter, who will do a fine job raising her child—and, for the record, your father and I weren't up last night watching old movies. He was up late tracking computer hackers, which is what he does for the government, which doesn't think we're anywhere *near* as embarrassing as you do."

Sunny knew that the government would think twice if her parents showed up for the annual White House Easter egg hunt dressed as rabbits. But she hadn't called to argue.

"Fine," she said. "But please, next time you talk with Jessica, do not encourage her. She did this for you."

"Wrong, Sunshine. She did it for you. When are you going to open your Eyes with a capital *E*?"

KATE WAS AT THE BARN WHEN ONE OF HER ASSISTANTS brought the *Gazette* in from the parking lot. She wouldn't normally read it here, but she knew it might have an article on the girls, and besides, there was a lull at work. Though she had started dyeing Vernal Tide, March Madness, and Spring Eclipse in each of five yarn weights—bulky, worsted, sport, fingering, and lace—Susan hadn't worked out the last two formulas. Nor had they gotten feedback from the others on the three they did have.

Saturdays had not been as productive as they needed to be. She and Susan were distracted and seemed to knit more than dye. Pam seemed totally disinterested and was clearly having second thoughts about giving PC Wool a push in the catalogue. And if Sunny was planning a special promotion at PC Home Goods, she hadn't mentioned it in days.

All of it was upsetting, but nowhere near as much as the public attention her daughter had garnered that week. Mary Kate claimed she was fine, but when Kate's friends asked about Jacob, she didn't know what to say. Her heart broke when she realized that the two of them might have permanently split. Oh, Jacob would take responsibility for the baby. He would support it once he could. He would negotiate an agreeable arrangement for visitation, even custody. But this wasn't an ideal way to bring a child into the world.

Slipping the *Gazette* from its plastic sleeve, she opened it on the worktable and skimmed through. She was starting to think they had dodged the bullet when she saw the editorial.

Her first thought was to call Susan. But Susan's phone would be ringing off the hook.

Her next thought was to call Sunny. But Sunny would be bouncing off the wall.

Her third thought was to call Will, but he was growing frustrated with Kate's anger, and what *she* needed was a target.

So she called Pam. "Have you seen the *Gazette*?"

"Just now. Tanner called."

"Was there no way he could stop this? His cousin is the publisher, and the publisher is George Abbott's *boss*."

"Tanner isn't involved in running the paper," Pam said coolly. "He didn't know this was coming. Besides, there's a problem with the website, so he's been preoccupied."

"A problem that affects PC Wool?" Kate asked. This was her livelihood.

"No."

That was a relief. With production falling behind schedule, the last thing they needed was a problem with sales. "So why did George Abbott write this? Do *you* think he represents the mainstream of public opinion?"

"How would I know, Kate? All I know is he's a good writer, and he puts the paper out with a limited staff. Ad revenues are down. He's having to do more himself than he used to."

"That explains it. He's overworked, so his judgment is poor. You do realize this is a total attack on Susan. There she is trying to salvage her credibility, and he undermines her with something like this? It goes two ways, y'know. She's a target because she's a public person, but because she's a public person—and, *yes,* working in a 'crucial position'—doesn't she deserve a little respect?"

"It's a thorny issue."

"Pam. You're supposed to be her friend. Do you not respect what she's done with her life?"

"Of course I do."

"Then *do* something," Kate urged. "She needs people like you speaking up for her. You're on the school board, and your name carries weight. Write a letter to the editor."

"That wouldn't help," Pam said. "George is a family friend. He'd take it personally."

"Whoa. You're afraid of hurting George's feelings? Which friendship means more to you—his or Susan's?"

"Susan's, but it isn't as simple as that."

Kate felt a flash of annoyance. "How's it complicated? Not only is Susan a *loyal* friend, but she's your business partner—speaking of which, Pam, we really have to meet Saturday. We need feedback from you and Sunny before we can finalize these colorways. I'm starting to think you don't care."

"I care."

"Do you care about Susan? This editorial hits her hard. How about showing her a little loyalty."

"Hey," Pam shot back. "You guys all knew about this. No one told *me* until the cat was out of the bag. Where's the loyalty there?"

"Come on, Pam. Do you know what an awful time we've had?"

"*I* didn't tell your girls to get pregnant," Pam said with just enough arrogance to goad Kate on, but hadn't she been looking to pick a fight?

"Fine. But if you want to place blame, what about Abby? She was with our girls all summer. She must have heard them planning this. That makes her an accomplice."

"Abby is not pregnant," Pam said.

"Not yet."

"I know my daughter."

"I thought I knew mine, too. Think about it, Pam. It could be that the only reason *you're* not in George Abbott's sights right now is a matter of luck."

PAM COULDN'T SHAKE WHAT KATE HAD SAID, ESPE-cially since Susan had said something similar a few weeks before. *Maybe you can talk with* your *daughter about not getting pregnant.* Pam told herself that they were just throwaway last lines. But it wasn't like Susan or Kate to use throwaway last lines. They weren't into empty small talk, the way so many Perry friends were. They were substantive.

Was this a warning, then? She wondered if they knew something she didn't.

Deciding she needed to see Abby, she left her a message saying she would pick her up after school, and she arrived early for a good spot at the curb. Closely watching the front door, she spotted her daughter the instant she came out—and, momentarily distracted, felt a helpless pride realizing that this striking young woman was hers. It wasn't only the blond hair and creamy skin. It wasn't even her father's height, though that certainly set her apart. More, it was the way she carried herself. She walked with the confidence of a Perry.

Pam had admired that carriage from the very first time she had met Tanner's family. She could carry it off herself when she tried. Her daughter didn't have to try. She was born with it.

Abby was with friends as she came down the stone steps, but not Lily, Mary Kate, or Jess. This was what Pam had wanted to see.

The girl spotted the Range Rover and crossed the grass. She didn't run, just walked with that calm Perry gait. Some called it arrogant. Pam called it classy.

"What's up?" Abby asked as she slid into the car.

"Cashmere. We're thinking of introducing it to the PC Wool line, but I need your opinion. You're my target audience."

"No way. Kids my age can't afford cashmere yarn."

"How do you know the cost?" Pam asked as she pulled away from the curb.

"Because I look online. Because you love cashmere and buy *me* cashmere, so now *I* love cashmere. But I do know it costs more."

"Would you knit it if PC Wool sold it?"

"In a heartbeat."

"Well, there you go," Pam said, feeling vindicated. "I found a woman up the coast who spins cashmere. I want to see the quality of her work, and I want your opinion."

Abby seemed content with that. "We're on a mission."

"We are. You didn't have anything else on this afternoon, did you?"

"No."

Pam didn't think so. Her daughter had been on the field hockey team with Lily, but the season was over, and Abby wasn't into volleyball. Pam had suggested she write for the school paper or join the yearbook staff, but Abby turned up her nose at both ideas.

"How was school?"

"Okay. Did you see the *Gazette*?"

"Did you?" Pam asked in surprise.

"You couldn't miss it. Everyone was passing it around. I mean, that editorial went after our principal. Poor Susan. How's she doing?"

"Good," Pam said, though she hadn't talked with her all week. They used to go to the gym together, but that hadn't happened in a while either. Susan was busy, and Pam was walking a fine line, not quite sure of the smartest position to take. "Susan's a survivor. How's Lily?"

"Good," Abby answered, echoing Pam's breezy tone, which made her wonder.

"Have you talked with her?"

"No, but I see her around. So, Mom, I was thinking maybe I'd go out for the Drama Club."

"You want to *act*?" Pam asked in surprise.

"I was thinking of set design."

"Don't the art classes handle that?"

"They need direction. Remember when we saw *Dirty Dancing* onstage? The set was amazing. Our productions don't come close."

"Yuh." Pam laughed. "One's professional, one isn't. One has millions to spend, one has nothing."

"Creativity doesn't have to break the bank. Isn't that what Dad always says? I'm creative. I've also seen more real theater than the other kids. I could be a liaison between the classes and the club—like you are with PC Wool." She looked sideways at Pam. "You're still doing that, aren't you?"

"I *am* PC Wool—well, a quarter of it. Why do you even ask?"

"You haven't been there on Saturdays." Her voice was cautious. "Is it hard for you after what I did?"

"No, no," Pam said. "I've just had other things to do. But I'm going this Saturday. We're finalizing the spring line." Her daughter was looking out the window. "What about you? Is it hard for you at school?"

"No way," Abby said a little too quickly. "I have other friends."

"But you were so close to the others." She took the ramp onto the highway. "I keep thinking about that, Abby. You were with them last summer when they hatched this idea. You must have heard them talking about it."

"No. They must've talked to each other at night."

"And they didn't mention it to you once? Not even hypothetically?"

"I told you," Abby stated crossly. "I am not in their inner circle."

"You came pretty close."

"So?"

"Nothing," Pam said quietly. She didn't want to argue. "I was just wondering. Do you wish you were pregnant, too?"

"Are you kidding? They're pariahs. They sit by themselves in the lunchroom."

"Maybe you should go over and break the ice."

"Oh yeah, and look what happened last time I did. Jess yelled at me for outing Lily, and now I've outed Mary Kate and Jess. I didn't mean to do that. It just happened. I was upset."

"Because they hadn't included you in their plans?"

Abby opened her mouth to answer, then glared at Pam. "You think I was."

Pam backpedaled. "No. I'm just curious, like everyone else. Were they talking about boys last summer?"

"We all talk about boys."

"Who was Lily talking about?" When Abby sent her a withering look, she didn't push. "Well, at least you're on the pill."

The girl didn't reply.

"Mary Kate was on the pill but stopped taking it," Pam said.

Abby turned the stare on her. "Mom. I am not pregnant. I

am not trying to get pregnant. For all I know, it wouldn't happen even if I did try."

"Why do you say that?"

"Look at *you.*"

"I had no trouble getting pregnant."

"But you were pregnant, like, six times and miscarried all of them except me. I mean, don't you think I *know* things like that are genetic—and anyway, your questions are really annoying. I've told you I didn't know. Isn't that enough?"

Pam was subdued. "I'm trying to be a good mother."

"By *bugging* me?"

"By talking." They were on the highway now, cruising at the speed limit. It required little concentration, allowing Pam to focus on what she should or should not say. The older Abby got, the trickier it was. "Mothers talk when they want to know what's happening in their daughters' lives. Maybe if the other mothers had done it, this wouldn't have happened."

"They talk."

"Not enough, I guess. But who am I to criticize them? If you had decided to get pregnant, I wouldn't have known."

Abby was quiet. Finally, sadly, she said, "Well, *I* think Susan's a good mother. You should give her a call. She's the best friend you have."

I could say the same about you and Lily, Pam might have replied if the sadness hadn't been contagious. She did miss seeing Susan. Susan was sensible and practical. When she set her mind to something, she did it. Same with the others, actually. Each of them dealt with challenges—Susan raising Lily alone, Kate managing five kids, Sunny living with Dan.

And here was Pam Perry, watching Regis and Kelly while everyone else went to work. She might make a phone call or two relating to school board business, might get dressed and meander to Tanner's office, might make another call or two from there.

Would anyone miss hearing her voice if she didn't call? Would anyone wonder where she was if she stayed in bed for the day?

Certainly not Susan, Sunny, or Kate, as long as Pam kept up her end of PC Wool. She just wished she knew how the pregnancies were going to play with the town. She didn't want to end up on the wrong side of public opinion.

Chapter 15

SUSAN COULDN'T ESCAPE THE *GAZETTE*. IT LAY IN THE faculty lounge, open to the editorial, for all to see. It was in the lunchroom, with students huddled behind it. When she stopped at the barn later that day, it was in the trash, but by the time she got home, it had risen again. Lily had it open and was rip-roaring mad.

"He's attacking you!" she cried before Susan had barely closed the door. "That's what this is all about. 'Erosion of family values'? He's angry because you're not married, and because you're the principal and you're twenty years younger than he is. He's *angry* because you didn't give his daughter A's."

Susan couldn't disagree. George Abbott had three daughters, the youngest of whom she had taught several years before being named principal. The girl was a mediocre student; George had been in to talk with Susan more than once about grades that he thought should have been higher. Understandably, given his job as editor in chief of the *Gazette,* he believed that his daughter should be a good writer—and Susan believed that she was. The girl's problem was attitude. And if that attitude produced a C, what could Susan do?

George hadn't voiced outrage when Susan was named principal. But he had written an editorial that spent an undue amount of time praising the runners-up for the job. It concluded, *Times have changed, and our schools need to keep pace. It's possible that the elevation of Ms. Tate will put us back in the forefront. But she is young and inexperienced. It remains to be seen whether she's up to the task.*

"And how dare he suggest that we don't value family?" Lily went on. "It's because I *do* that I'm having a baby."

Susan dropped her coat and bag. Quietly, she said, "Well now, you're doing exactly what he accuses you of—defining family values to suit yourself." Closing the paper as she passed—unable to bear having it open in her home—she went into the den.

Lily followed. "But who's saying his definition is the right one? Maybe there *is* more than one definition."

"Maybe," Susan said. Sinking to the sofa, she leaned back.

"Mom? Aren't you *angry*?"

"Right now, I'm exhausted. It's been that kind of week."

Lily looked momentarily stricken. "I'm sorry. I didn't know this would happen."

"Would it have changed anything if you had?"

"I'd have had second thoughts. I wouldn't knowingly cause you this . . . this . . ."

"Public humiliation?"

Lily was silent, then impassioned. "You have to do something. You have to fight this."

"What do you suggest?"

"For starters, talk with Dr. Correlli. I thought he was friends with George Abbott."

"For the record, Lily—just so you know—I did talk with

Dr. Correlli. He spoke with George Abbott last weekend and asked him not to do an article on this—and, in fairness, he didn't. He wrote a one-sided editorial instead. But there are many in town who agree with him."

"I'll bet there are many more who don't. You need to write a rebuttal."

"Not a good idea. I'm too involved."

"But he's attacking every single mother—every woman who works—every woman whose child does something *he* may not like!"

"Then it'll be up to those women to speak up. That's why we have Letters to the Editor."

"I'm going to write one. I'll say you had absolutely no part in this."

Susan shook her head. "You're missing the point. He believes that if I had been a proper mother, the thought of getting pregnant would never have crossed your mind."

"You mean, a proper mother raises a drone?"

"Try clone. He wanted that with his own daughters."

"Who never come back here to live. Do you realize that, Mom? They go off to college and never return. Wonder why that is."

They both knew, but the reminder didn't help Susan. Once again, she felt people were watching, talking, condemning. Like Hester Prynne, she felt branded.

She looked at Lily. "Do you feel that way, too—branded?" she asked, then realized she hadn't shared the original thought. "Do you feel like you're standing on a platform in the center of town, with a red letter on your chest and a baby in your arms?"

Lily laughed. "No, Mom." Her eyes widened. "Omigod, what if you were still teaching that book? Would that be awful!"

"Actually, not. If I were still a teacher, there wouldn't be such an uproar. It's because I'm the principal that George is so angry. We *do* have a say about who leads our children—they need the *best* possible role models. My being principal is a problem for him."

The girl sobered. "I am really, really sorry. I had no idea my being pregnant would cause you trouble. You're the best mother."

Susan put her head back again. "Tell me more."

"You *are* a role model. I wouldn't be who I am today if it weren't for you."

"Isn't that what George is saying? Look where you are. Seventeen, pregnant, unmarried." She stared at her daughter. "What does Robbie have to say about all of this?"

"Nothing."

"Is he still suspicious?"

Lily gave a one-shouldered shrug. "He asks. I tell him he's wrong, but I don't think he believes me. He's like everyone else, wondering who the father is, and no one else has come forward. Doesn't say much about guys who want to be with me, does it?"

Susan was startled. "Are you *disappointed*?"

"Not disappointed. Just . . . well, who *wouldn't* want guys fighting over her?"

"Lily. That's insane. This isn't about a date to the prom."

"Anyway," the girl went on, "since there are no other suspects, Robbie thinks it's him. The weird thing is, no one else suspects him. I mean, he and I have been friends so long that when people see us talking, they don't think anything of it."

"Are you planning to tell him?"

"Eventually."

"Before the baby is born?"

"Maybe." Her face brightened. Sitting down beside Susan,

she took her hand. "Know what the baby's doing now? She's the size of a baseball, and she's moving her arms and legs. She can even suck her thumb. Isn't that weird?"

Weird was one word for it, Susan mused. She was trying to think up another word, when Lily said quietly, "I really want this baby, Mom, and not because of sharing something with my two best friends, not even so we can have a bigger family. This baby is me. She has my genes. What I do impacts her. If I have a Coke, she gets a sugar high and wiggles all over the place."

"Do you feel movement?" Susan asked in surprise.

"Not yet, but I know it's happening, and I know she's looking more like a person. I can't wait to see her. The sonogram's the week after next. Think she'll look like me? Or like *you*? What if she's blinking her eyes? What if she's sucking her thumb?"

"What if she has a penis?" Susan asked.

"She won't," Lily said with the confidence of a seventeen-year-old. "She'll be perfect."

SUSAN WAS THINKING OF PERFECTION SEVERAL HOURS later, wondering if it was ever possible to achieve, since people defined it so differently, when she heard a noise near Lily's room. She listened for a minute, wondering if something was wrong. Slipping out of bed, she crossed the hall.

The butterfly nightlight cast its glow on two bodies—and for an instant, Susan panicked. She did not want to find Robbie Boone here, absolutely did not.

But the heads that rose had long hair. "Jess?" she whispered, crossing to the bed.

"I had to leave," Jessica said quietly. "Mom and Dad were arguing again. This was the only place I could come."

"Does your mother know you're here?"

"She won't care. She can't stand the sight of me."

"That is absolutely not true. She's upset, and doesn't know how to deal."

Jessica made a sound. "That's because Martha Stewart doesn't cover family crises."

Susan sat on the tiny strip of bed that was free. "Unfair, Jess. She's trying to understand you; you have to try to understand her."

"We are just so different."

"You're really not. I know you both too well. You share the same goals. You'll just take different paths getting there."

"*Totally*. So what I'm doing is *fine*."

"Excuse me," Susan cautioned, lest there be any misunderstanding. "Pregnancy at seventeen is not a shared goal. Happiness is. Success is."

"But at least you can talk about those things. My mother can't."

"This has been a shock."

"For you, too, but you're sitting here with us. Can I move in? Just 'til my baby's born?" She was serious.

Flashing back to her own experience, Susan was, too. "No. You need to be at home."

"My parents may get divorced because of me."

"They won't. They just need to work through this." Susan had to talk to Sunny. "Stay here for tonight," she said as she stood. "I'll let your mom know. But you're back home tomorrow. Right?"

SUNNY WAS SUBDUED. "SHE RACED OUT OF HERE. I TOLD Dan she'd be going to your house, but he doesn't trust what I say. I don't know what to do, Susan. We're okay, until she walks in the room."

"Is he siding with her?"

"No. He's as upset as I am that she's pregnant. But he thinks I'm handling it wrong. I'm starting to think he's bought into the bad-mother hype."

"No, Sunny," Susan said, because she did know Dan. "If he's coming down hard on you, it's because he feels helpless."

"And I don't? Want to take my daughter in for the next few months?" she asked, echoing her daughter's request.

"N-O, *no*. It's enough having to deal with my own. And Jess needs to be with you. Please, Sunny," she begged, "don't make the same mistake my parents did."

SUSAN DIDN'T BLAME HER PARENTS FOR HER PREG- nancy, simply for making it harder than it had to be. She might have worried that she was doing the same with Lily, if morning hadn't come so fast.

The Leadership Team included the superintendent and the town's six principals, and met monthly to discuss the issues at hand. There were always a few. Susan had always found her fellow principals to be thoughtful and fair-minded. But she had never before been the subject of their discussion.

The meeting was set for eleven. In advance, Phil forwarded copies of the e-mail Susan had sent to her faculty and parents, along with a note explaining that he wanted to know what they were hearing in the wake of the *Gazette* editorial.

Usually with this group, discussion was brisk. One of the middle school principals, in particular, shot from the hip, but he didn't this time. It was an elementary school principal who finally, hesitantly, spoke.

"I've had lots of questions. Many of my parents hadn't known about this until the paper came out. I tell them that Susan is a great principal." She slid Susan an apologetic look. "They want to know more."

Susan said nothing. This was Phil's meeting.

"What more?" he asked.

"They want to know how three girls could have done this."

"They're concerned about the pact, then," Phil said. "That's fair enough. We have information to give them on that. Susan will forward it."

No one spoke. The discomfort was tangible.

Finally, another of the elementary school principals said, "It's more than the pact. It's that Susan's daughter is one of the girls. My parents don't like that."

The more pensive of the middle school principals weighed in. "Mine are upset, too. Their own children are hitting puberty. Some are way past it and going to the high school next year. They don't want their kids getting ideas." She looked helplessly at Susan. "I'm sorry. This isn't what you want to hear."

No. But she wasn't surprised.

Phil addressed the other middle school principal. "You're quiet, Paul. No calls from your ranks?"

Paul shrugged. "I can ignore some, like from the parent who's on probation for shoplifting or the one whose kids go home to an empty house most days of the week. But there are some calls from parents I admire. They're talking about morals."

"They read the *Gazette,*" Phil said.

"It isn't just that. They know how young Susan is and that she's single. They're doing the math."

Susan had expected this, too. She girded herself for more questions on it, but there were none.

"So the response is overwhelmingly negative," Phil concluded. "Okay. How do we deal with it?"

No one replied.

"It's all about information," he said, and talked about what Susan had done to open discussion at the high school, and what he felt was appropriate at each of the lower grade levels. He didn't consult Susan, though there were times he might have. Nor did the other principals interrupt.

Susan listened quietly, trying to maintain her dignity, though she was dying inside.

When the meeting ended and the others left, she stayed where she was. Phil was sitting back, an elbow on the arm of the chair, a fist to his chin. He was brooding, staring at the desk, then at her.

Finally, he dropped his hand. "I don't know what to say."

"Neither do I," Susan managed. "I expected this. But I have to tell you. When I stand back and look at the situation, I'm amazed. Three girls got pregnant, but this is a referendum on moms."

"Not moms, plural. One mom."

Right, she thought—because it all went way back to what had happened seventeen years before. "But I had a handle on this, Phil," she said. "Everyone at school responded so well to what we did. I had good will on my side. How can one opinion piece change things so fast?"

"It gave people permission to question."

"Fine. Question me as a mom. But I'm a good principal. Isn't that worth something?"

"You can't separate the two."

"Sure you can. Come on, Phil. If I was a Perry, I wouldn't be getting this criticism."

"If you were a Perry, you'd have a husband, and your kids

would be younger than Lily. When a Perry gets pregnant at seventeen, she aborts it before anyone's the wiser."

Something about the way he said it gave Susan pause. "What?"

Phil seemed to realize he'd spoken out of turn. He waved a hand. "Oh, one of those daughters a while back. But the fact is that you did have Lily at seventeen. How did your father handle it?"

"My father chose the town over me. I was banished. End of story."

The silence that followed was as foreboding as any. Phil was brooding again, refusing to look at her now. Suddenly she was back at the school board meeting, sensing that her career was up for grabs.

"No, Phil," she said softly. "Don't suggest it."

He sighed, raised his eyes. "Not even a leave of absence?"

"I can't. This job means the world to me."

"Only until the smoke clears?"

"It would be an admission of guilt, when I've done nothing wrong."

She waited, but Phil was silent.

"Why would I take a leave?" she asked.

"Because certain members of the board have asked for it. I've had calls since the meeting."

"How many?" There were seven members. Four would make it a majority vote.

"Three. They don't know where this is headed and feel that the town might be better cutting its losses."

"Losses?" Susan cried. "Excuse me. What have they lost?" When he began to hedge, she said, "Their innocence? Their world reputation? Their self-respect?"

"Mock it if you want, but this is a traditional town."

"Yes," she said, then paraphrased the editorial, "with the

lowest divorce rate in the state and zero violent crime. But we do have MaryAnne and Laura raising their twin daughters over on Oak Street, and we do have a town meeting moderator who attends AA meetings every night."

"They don't generate publicity."

This was true. Susan was over a barrel. "Are you telling me to take a leave?" If he was ordering her to do it, actually putting her on suspension, she wouldn't have much choice.

He sat straighter. "No. I'm just suggesting that you might want to consider it."

"I have. I want to stay. There's too much work still to do."

He raised a hand that said, *Fine. Your choice. You stay.*

But there was no victory in it for Susan. On the way back to school, she wondered if she had simply delayed the inevitable.

Chapter 16

SUSAN WAS THE LAST ONE TO ARRIVE AT THE BARN
Saturday morning. She had overslept after another uneasy
night, and might have been sleeping still if Kate hadn't called.

"I'm so sorry," she said as she hurried to the back. The other
three were nursing coffee, together for the first time, really, in
over a month. The sight of it did her heart good. For the
briefest time, life was normal again.

She took the chair beside Pam and squeezed her hand. "I've
missed us. Oh, wow," she exclaimed, standing again to study
samples of the three colorways that she and Kate had worked
out. "These look amazing, Kate. What do you guys think?"

In a measured tone that Susan guessed had more to do with
her life these days than yarn, Sunny said, "I like them. Vernal
Tide and Spring Eclipse are soothing. They're a nice contrast
to March Madness."

"Which isn't as soothing." Susan had embellished on it since
its inception in her attic, raising the temperature of the yellows
and greens that lay amid gray and white. Clearly, her own

mood had come into play here, strong strokes of color against a calm field. "Too much?"

Sunny studied the sample. "I don't think so."

Susan repeated the question in a look at Pam, who said, "They're good. When will you do the last two?"

"Today. Kate needs time to dye enough skeins for photos to meet the catalogue deadline. Should we go ahead and book the photographer?"

"Actually," Pam said, "I think we should photograph finished items this year, rather than unknit skeins."

Kate looked startled. "We've never done that."

"Other knitting catalogues do it."

This was true—and heartening to Susan. "Is it what Cliff wants?" she asked. Clifton Perry was Pam's brother-in-law, and the catalogue was his domain. A staunch voice for the dignity of Perry & Cass, he was an unlikely ally, given Susan's notoriety.

"Well, he hasn't exactly said it," Pam hedged. "But he knows I have a feel for marketing, so he listens to me. Once he sees the layout, he won't turn it down."

"Does he even know about this yet?" Susan asked softly.

"No. I'm going out on a limb for you guys," she said with a hint of anger. "It's a good move, don't you think?"

Susan didn't like the "going out on a limb" part, but at least it was a positive plan, so she nodded. "Definitely." She turned to Kate. "Can we get samples knit in time?"

Kate was doubtful. "It'll be a challenge, with Christmas so close, and me having to spend every minute dyeing yarn. I'd have my girls do small items, like socks or a hat, only this is a bad time for them in school."

Same with Lily, Susan knew. Besides, Lily was working on something else that would likely take priority. Susan didn't want to *think* about that project, much less mention it to the others. "I'd have time to knit a scarf, but that's it. Could you do a shawl, Pam?"

"Possibly, but Kate's right. Christmas is close. What about our freelancers?" PC Wool had a stable of women who knit for trunk shows and magazines.

"That might work," Kate said. "I have enough of them, and they'll want the money for the holiday, but I'll have to pick patterns ASAP. I was planning to see our designer in January. I could push that up. How many items do you want for the spread?"

"One for each colorway," Pam said, "preferably in different weights."

"That'd be a lot of work for nothing if Cliff opts for the old tried-and-true."

"A lot of work for nothing if he nixes PC Wool *entirely,*" Sunny muttered.

But Susan had to be hopeful. "Maybe what Pam's trying to say is that if Cliff sees a more impressive finished product, he'll forget what's happening here."

"Speaking of which," Pam told her, "I did talk with George. We had dinner with him last night. I said you were a fabulous principal and that he was wrong to suggest otherwise."

"Will he print a retraction?" Susan asked, though she knew the answer.

So did Pam. "He's prickly, not an easy guy to reason with."

"Then his job suits him," Sunny said. "He can sit in his office and write unfair things without having to run them past anyone else." To Susan, she added, "You did not tell Lily to get pregnant."

"But I didn't prevent it, so maybe I am to blame," Susan said. She was still trying to make sense out of the public turn-around, wondering if *she* was the one who didn't get it. "Lily is my child. At what age does a child become responsible for her own acts?"

"By law in the state of Maine, eighteen," Sunny shot back, echoing what Susan suspected had come from Dan.

"Then I am responsible." Acknowledging that brought Susan to the topic she really wanted to discuss with these friends. "So am I a bad mother?"

"If you're a bad mother, we all are," Kate mused. "What does it take to be a good one?"

This was what Susan had been thinking as she had lain awake last night. There was no single answer, but for current purposes, one did stand out. "Vigilance. A good mother watches her kids closely."

"We *do*."

"Apparently, not closely enough," Susan went on, mocking her detractors. "In order to have prevented these pregnancies, a mother would have to eavesdrop on her daughter's conversations, monitor her texts, hack into Facebook."

"A neurotic mother does that," Kate said. "I refuse to. A good mother trusts."

"After she teaches right and wrong," Susan added, because teaching was her thing. "But it's like riding a bike. At some point a parent has to let go, even if it means the child falls."

"Training wheels," Sunny trumpeted. "They add structure. They help when the mom can't be there to hold on."

Pam smirked. "You can't keep training wheels on forever."

"I know that, Pam. We're talking metaphorically. I've built training wheels into my kids' lives. Our home has structure. They know where snacks are when they come in from school. There's a chalkboard by the kitchen phone for messages. We have dinner at seven, and we start with grace. These are comforting things, things to fall back on. I am there for them."

"You're not there," Pam argued. "You're at work."

"Right down the street, a two-minute drive, one phone call away. And what about you? You're not sitting around the house all day. Does Abby know where you are every second?"

"No, but she can always reach me."

"But you don't work. Do you think that's good for Abby to see? I mean, what if she marries someone who isn't as rich as Tanner? What if she *needs* to work? She'll have no role model."

Pam smiled a little snidely. "But she's seen you all. She'll do fine. Besides, I'm on the school board. *And* I raise money for charity. Being civic-minded is important, too."

Sunny's face reddened. "You agree with George Abbott. You think women who work aren't as good mothers as women who don't."

"I never said that."

"Come on, guys," Susan cut in. "Don't fight."

"It isn't a fight," Pam insisted. "It's a discussion. I may not have a career like you all, and I am constantly made to feel guilty about that, but I *am* there every day when my child gets home from school."

"And that makes you a good mother?" Sunny asked in dismay. "You *do* agree with George."

"Sunny," Susan breathed, frustrated.

But Pam put a hand on her arm. "It's okay. If she wants to attack me, she can. Deep in her heart she knows." She gathered her things.

"Knows *what*?" Sunny cried.

"That training wheels are rigid," Pam said as she stood and picked up her coat. "Kids rebel against rigidity. I keep a good house, Sunny. I take care of my daughter. So maybe we have dinner at six one night and seven another, and maybe I'm in Portland when Abby gets an asthma attack, but I'm back in an hour. Don't confuse scaffolding with love." She had her coat on.

"Don't leave," Susan cried.

"Are you saying I don't love my children?" Sunny asked.

"I'm not helping," Pam told Susan. "You three have more to discuss than I do."

"Oh, really?" Sunny cried.

"But you're part of this," Kate told Pam.

"Am I? I'll call you, Susan," she said as she set off.

With a frightened look at the others, Susan ran after her. "Wait, Pam. I'm sorry if Sunny offended you. We're all super-sensitive right now."

"And I'm not?" Pam asked without stopping. "Honestly? I have a stake here. My reputation's on the line. I've become known in the family for PC Wool, and now my brother-in-law may dump it from the catalogue."

"Were his kids perfect?" All three were grown, but the stories lingered. "His daughter got divorced eleven months after a huge white wedding. Does he ever blame himself or his wife?"

"Of course not. Corey was a difficult child all along."

Susan had a sudden thought. "She's the one who got the abortion?"

Pam stopped with one hand on the door. "Where did you hear that?"

"It doesn't matter. But if it's true, shouldn't Cliff be a little more compassionate?"

"Cliff is a Perry," Pam said with a sigh. "I have to go."

Susan let her leave. Only after watching the Range Rover head out of the lot, did she return to the others.

"She is *impossible*," Sunny cried as soon as she was within earshot.

"So were you," Susan said. "Ease up, Sunny. This is hard on

all of us, but if we don't try to understand what the other is feeling, we're lost."

"She basically said I didn't love my children."

"No. She simply said she loved hers. She was defending herself."

"As well she should. Did I tell her how involved her own daughter *really* was? That would have been the *honest* thing to do, but I kept my mouth shut. That took restraint."

"She'll find out about Abby," Susan said, pouring herself coffee. "Abby will tell her."

"When? Five years from now? A lot of good it'll do then. Pam Perry needs to be taken down a peg *now*. She needs to make sure that PC Wool stays alive."

Susan returned to the table. "Exactly, which is why fighting doesn't help. Pam's heart's in the right place. That was the whole point about ratcheting up our coverage in the catalogue. She wants this to work."

"And I don't?" Sunny asked. "PC Wool is a growing part of the department I manage. If something happens to it, my department sees a loss."

Kate waved a hand. "Whoa. This is my *entire* livelihood. If something happens to PC Wool, I'm out of work! Susan's right. You have to ease up, Sunny. We need Pam on our side."

Sunny stared at her, then rose and grabbed her coat. "Pam's right. You don't need me here."

"Sunny—"

"Oh *please*—"

"No, no," Sunny insisted, pushing her arms into the sleeves. "I'm better off at home imposing rigid rules on my family. She wouldn't have said any of that if she'd grown up the way I did. We were on our own—no rules at all—parents who totally resisted them." She finished buttoning her coat. "I do believe in structure. Children need to know what their parents expect. And still sometimes they break the rules. I'm trying to cope."

"You have to *listen,*" Susan said. "My parents wouldn't. That's what I was trying to say Thursday night. My way or the highway—that was my dad's credo, and look where it got us."

But Sunny was past hearing. "My daughter and I aren't talking, my husband and I aren't talking, and I'm trying to hold things together. I'm just doing my best. Isn't that what a good mother does?"

"Yes," Susan cried, but Sunny kept going, and Susan didn't follow this time. She was too discouraged. Turning back to Kate, she waited only until the front door closed, then echoed Sunny's words. "I'm just doing my best. Aren't we all?"

WAS HER BEST ENOUGH? SUSAN USED TO THINK SO— used to believe she had done the best job in the world with Lily. Now, with critics all around, she was second-guessing herself.

She thought she was a good principal. In her mind, openness set the right tone. But maybe she should be more punitive in her approach.

She thought she was a good friend, but she had let Pam, then Sunny, walk out the door. Maybe she should have been more insistent that they stay and work things out.

Hell, she didn't even know if the last two colors she and Kate had formulated were any good—and now Pam and Sunny were angry, the catalogue issue was unresolved, and the survival of PC Wool itself was in doubt.

And finally, here was Lily, home at six on Saturday evening, joining Susan in the den to complain of heartburn—a perfect opportunity for Susan to coddle her daughter, who might, just might not have bargained for what she got. But the best Susan could do was to offer to reheat pizza left over from dinner earlier that week.

Lily's sigh said it all. Dismally, the girl looked out the front window—then ducked and croaked, "Omigod. Robbie and his parents. *Omigod.*"

Susan froze. "Here? Now?"

"Coming up our walk," the girl whispered as the bell rang. "Don't answer. Do not answer."

Susan didn't want to. She wasn't any more ready for a confrontation than Lily, but what choice did she have? "They must have been waiting for you to get home. They know we're here. The car's in the driveway and the lights are on." Besides, hiding would only postpone the inevitable. Robbie must have said something to his parents.

Bracing herself for yet more flagellation, she opened the door. Bill and Annette Boone stood there, with Robbie slightly behind. The boy looked nervous and his parents awkward, maybe even guilty. It occurred to her that they didn't know who had seduced whom.

"I think we need to talk," said Bill.

Stepping back, Susan gestured them inside. Lily was leaning against the archway to the den, hands in her pockets, arms pressed to her sides as if to contain her panic. She was barely looked at by the senior Boones when Susan shepherded them to the couch. Taking his cue from Lily, Robbie stood against the opposite arch.

"Would you like something to drink?" Susan asked his parents.

"I'd take a double scotch straight up if I thought it would help," Bill said.

His wife looked at him. "Is this amusing?" Then at Robbie. "Is anything about this amusing?"

Bill cleared his throat and addressed Susan. "Our son tells us he's the father of Lily's baby. I take it you figured that's why we're here, so she must have told you, but we'd like to hear it from her."

All eyes turned on Lily, who looked cornered.

Say it, Susan instructed silently. *They have a right to hear it. You cannot lie.*

After what seemed an eternity, the girl nodded.

"How can we know for sure?" Annette asked.

"You can't," replied Lily in low voice.

"She certainly can," Susan argued. She didn't like Annette's tone, but Lily's wasn't much better. "When I asked the same question," she told the Boones, "my daughter was offended. She told me she would know, because she's only been with one boy in her life. I believe her."

"If she was my daughter, I'd believe her, too. That doesn't mean it's so."

"Mom. It *is*," Robbie said.

His father held up a hand and said softly, "Please, Annette. We agreed we would do this. I know you want proof, but we can't do a paternity test until after the baby is born, and in the meanwhile, there's a good chance this young girl is carrying our grandchild." He looked at Susan again. "We're prepared to help."

Hadn't her father said something like that? And he hadn't stopped there. *We're prepared to help you get set up, but you won't do it here.* Susan refused to have her daughter exposed to that.

"We're all set," Susan said. "No help needed."

"Babies are expensive."

"We'll manage."

"I'll be glad to marry Lily," Robbie offered.

"*Robbie,*" his mother protested.

"I will," he insisted with a naïveté Susan might have found endearing if she hadn't been down that road before.

"Lily's father said much the same thing to me." Susan looked at Lily. "Do you want to get married?"

"No *way*. Married at seventeen is stupid!"

Like motherhood at seventeen, Susan was thinking, when Annette said, "It would only make a bad situation ten times worse."

That hit Susan the wrong way. "For the record," she said, "Robbie could do far worse. Lily will be a great mother. I just don't want her rushing into marriage."

"Good to know," Annette remarked. "And while we're being honest, I'd prefer it if you didn't send the school an update about this."

That, too, hit Susan wrong. "With due respect, Robbie isn't my major concern right now. No one will hear his name from me. Lily?"

Lily puffed out a breath and held up a hand, *No.*

"I'm not ashamed," Robbie told his parents in a voice far bolder than his expression. "Lily is the coolest person in school. If people ask me, I'm telling."

"Do not do that, Robbie," Lily ordered, her hand now on her middle.

"Why not? Are *you* ashamed?"

"*No,* but this isn't about you. This baby is *mine.*"

"It's half mine," Robbie argued.

Susan quickly stood. "Excuse me," she said in a voice that trembled, "I can't deal with a custody battle right now. This argument is better saved until after the baby is born. I suspect your parents agree."

"Completely," Annette said, on her feet as well.

Susan moved toward the door. The meeting was over. She

wanted these people out of her house. "Thank you, Robbie. It was kind of you to come." She opened the door.

Annette left without a word. After a quick look at Lily, Robbie followed. Only Bill paused and said quietly, "The offer of help stands."

"Thanks, Bill. But really, we're fine." The instant he cleared the threshold, Susan closed the door and, feeling the kind of wildness that comes from one trauma too many, looked at Lily. "Nightmare! Robbie wants to take credit. Like he has a job and can provide child support? Like he had a *say* in this? And *Annette's* angry—like I'm *not*? Does she not get it that my *job* is at risk?" She clutched the top of her head. "I'm . . . I'm . . ." She didn't know what to say.

"I'm sorry," Lily said meekly. "I never imagined it would spread like this. I *never* thought your job would be affected."

Susan was about to cry, *You're a smart girl, how could you not?* when the phone rang. "Don't answer. I can't talk."

But Lily had gone into the den to see the caller ID. "It's Dad."

Susan's panic waned. She held out a hand for the phone. Lily brought it, punching in the call as she handed it over.

"Hey," Susan said with a sigh.

"Hey," Rick said back but without his usual punch. "What are you doin'?"

"Leaning against the front door in a mild panic because the parents of *The Boy* just came over. What's wrong?" Something was. She could hear it in his voice.

"Is Lily with you?"

The fact that he didn't ask about The Boy frightened her all the more. "What is it, Rick?"

"Bad news, Susie. Your dad died."

Susan felt a blow to her gut. It was a minute before she could ask, "When?"

"This morning. My father just called me. It was a massive heart attack."

Knees shaking, she slid to the floor.

"Mom?" Lily asked in alarm.

"Dad," Susan managed to say, then whispered, "Omigod."

"They're having the wake at the house. The funeral is Tuesday."

"Omigod," Susan whispered again. The details sailed past her. Stricken, she saw the larger picture—her father dead, no closure, no reconciliation *ever*—and though she hadn't realized she wanted that, the sadness of it tore at her heart.

Dropping the phone, she covered her face and began to cry.

SHE HAD TO GO, OF COURSE. SHE KNEW IT THE INSTANT her tears dried. She didn't know what kind of reception she would get, didn't really care. She needed to say goodbye to her father.

Within an hour of Rick's call, she booked two tickets home. Lily, who had been hovering, frightened by Susan's tears, was staring at the screen. "Two? You want me there?"

"Yes," Susan said. This was another thing she knew. Her relationship with her father was lost. All the what-ifs—what if she had reached out, called him more, even gone home—were pointless now. There was no going back. But going ahead? She didn't want to make the same mistake twice. "You're part of me. He needs to meet you."

"But he's dead, and I'm pregnant."

Susan looked at her. "So?"

"And I've never met your mother."

Feeling an odd calm, Susan smiled. "My brother's kids call her Nana. You can call her that, too."

"But I don't *know* her," Lily cried. Her eyes were filled with terror—but they were still the same hazel eyes that Susan's father and her brother had. "I don't know Jackson or his wife or his kids," the girl cried. "And I'm *pregnant*."

Susan took her hand. That fact was nowhere near as upsetting as her father being dead. Maybe she was simply getting used to it. Or maybe, by comparison, nothing her family could dole out at home would be as bad as the last week had been. The thought of leaving Zaganack for a few days appealed to her. It would mean missing a play put on by the Drama Club—but thinking of school gave her a thought.

"You have that fabulous little skirt you bought for the Zaganotes, and a black sweater that hides a multitude of sins. No one'll ever know."

Lily wasn't amused. "What if someone there has seen the *Gazette*?"

"Who there would read the *Gazette*?"

"What if someone asks?"

"Why would anyone ask?"

Lily took her hand back and tucked both under her arms. She seemed horrified. "Are you looking *forward* to this?"

"Not to my father's funeral," Susan said quietly, eyes filling again as she said it. "But to fighting, yes. Weren't you the one who wanted to fight—against the Zaganotes for voting you out, against the editorial in the *Gazette*? Maybe I need to start by going home."

She thought of what Kate had said. *They still love you. They just never got past the anger. When they sent you away, they stopped the clock.* Maybe it was time to start it again.

"I haven't seen my mother since I was pregnant," Susan said determinedly. "I want her to meet my child."

Chapter 17

❧

KATE'S HEART WENT OUT TO SUSAN. TO HAVE SO MUCH
happen at once was unfair. "I'm *so* sorry," she said. "You sensed
something when you talked to your mom. But the timing
couldn't be worse."

"Actually, it's okay. You were right; the clock stopped. I do
need to go back. Maybe I'm running away from what's happening here, but this also feels like unfinished business. If
things are better there, great. If not, well, Lily will understand
what I've been talking about all these years. It will be a learning experience for her."

"Like working as a mother's helper last summer was?" Kate
asked dryly.

Susan made a quiet sound. "*That* one backfired."

"Slightly."

"This could, too." Susan sighed. "If nothing else, Lily will
see a different part of the country."

Suddenly Kate had the best idea. "Why don't I come? I

could give you moral support. You wouldn't be quite so out-numbered."

"You're sweet, Kate. But no. I have to deal. Besides, you can't leave your family."

"And I wouldn't love to run away with you? Hey, I could leave Mary Kate in charge. Let her get a taste of what's in store."

WHEN KATE CALLED SUNNY, SHE WAS STILL SMARTING from the fiasco at the barn, thinking that Susan and Kate might have stood up for her more. Hearing the news, though, she forgot all that.

"Omigod. Poor *Susan*."

"She's taking Lily there," Kate said. "I told her I'd go with her, but she wouldn't hear of it."

"I'll go," Sunny offered. "I'd love to get out of town."

"That's what I said. Sad that it would be for this reason."

Susan's father's death, PC Wool, Jessica, Dan—Sunny wasn't feeling good about any of it. Then she thought of her own father and felt even worse. She admired Susan for having courage to face the enemy. Forget visiting; Sunny refused to *call* her parents now, she was that humiliated by her mother's put-down. And there was Susan, going back home after being disowned. It was a sobering thought.

"Is there anything we can do while she's gone?" she asked Kate.

"Keep PC Wool moving. That means I keep dyeing, while you push ahead with the promo for the spring line."

"Like how?"

"Like adding finished items to your current display."

"I already have some."

"Add more. Photograph them. If Pam's going to get Cliff to sign on to an enhanced catalogue spread, let's give him a taste of what he'll get."

"What good will it do if Pam lets us down and there's no coverage at all?"

"Pam will come around. I'll call her. I have to tell her about Susan's father anyway."

Sunny was happy to let her make the call. She had no desire to tangle with Pam again. Besides, with Dan downstairs watching old episodes of *Law and Order,* Darcy upstairs watching a Harry Potter movie, and Jessica somewhere or other out of the house, she was feeling sorry for herself. When she felt sorry for herself, she went for ice cream.

PAM HAD COOKED DINNER FOR EIGHT THIS SATURDAY night, but as she often did when the Celtics were on, she took orders for dessert and drove with whoever wasn't watching to pick it up at PC Scoops. This night, she had two other wives with her. If not for that, she might have backed out of the store when she saw Sunny. But she was stuck, opening the door before she could think of a diversion, and, within seconds, was face-to-face with the woman, who looked none too happy to see her, either.

"Did Kate call you?" Sunny asked awkwardly.

Pam shook her head.

"Susan's father died this morning. She's going back home."

"Oh my." Even beyond the death was the going home part. Susan hadn't been back since before Lily's birth. "She's such a good person," Pam said, believing it in that instant, despite what Zaganack thought. Then she remembered her manners. "Sunny, you know Joanne Farmer and Annie McHale, don't you?"

After quiet greetings, Sunny left. Pam ordered from her list, but her thoughts were on Susan. Once home, after handing out the various sundaes and shakes, she excused herself and went upstairs. As soon as Susan answered the phone, she said, "Sunny told me about your father. I am sorry, Susan. You must be stunned."

"At first. Now I'm just sad. The chance to make this right is lost forever. So please, Pam. Do not let that happen with us. The scene this morning really bothered me."

Pam hadn't called to talk about that, but since Susan had raised it, she couldn't resist. "Sunny can be a bitch."

"So can you."

"She overreacted."

"She's feeling vulnerable. We're all questioning the way we've raised our kids."

"And I'm not? My daughter betrayed her friends. That bothers me." A *lot* about Abby bothered her right now. There was more to the story than she was telling. If Pam faulted Susan, Kate, and Sunny for not knowing what their daughters were doing, how could she not fault herself? For the betrayal alone, Pam felt incredible guilt.

"But Abby isn't pregnant and Jess is," Susan said. "And I'm not sure I'd call Sunny's home rigid, just organized. You know where that comes from."

Pam did, but she was still annoyed. "She needs to relax."

"We all do. Friends are my family, Pam. I need you guys."

Pam wanted that. In the privacy of her bedroom, she could admit it. Downstairs? That was harder. There had been talk about Susan during dinner. It hadn't been flattering.

"Anyway, Sunny says you're going home. I admire you for that." Pam wasn't exactly estranged from her family; she talked with her mother often. But her family couldn't keep up with the Perrys. They lived by their own rules in a modest house in a modest neighborhood in a different state. The wedding had been here in Zaganack, in the backyard of Tanner's parents' estate, and Pam had spent hours making her family presentable. In the years since, she had kept them at arm's length. She was a snob, though not without guilt.

"Is Lily going with you?" she asked Susan.

"Not happily. She's terrified. But I can't leave her here."

"She could stay with me," Pam offered, then caught herself. "But she probably wouldn't want to after what Abby did, but I miss their being together. I wish they could still be friends."

"Would Tanner agree?" Susan asked.

No. He would be mortified if Lily showed up on their doorstep while Susan was gone. Even Abby might not be ready for that—not that it wouldn't be a good lesson. The idiocy of the pregnancy pact notwithstanding, Abby shouldn't have betrayed her friends. She claimed she had known nothing about it last summer, but Pam wasn't convinced—and she couldn't share her doubts with Tanner. Town sentiment was running too strongly against the Tates.

She must have been a little too slow in replying, because Susan said softly, "It's fine. Lily needs to be with me anyway. It's her grandfather who died. She has to pay her respects."

Pam nodded, feeling awkward. "Is there anything I can do while you're gone?"

"I'm okay, I think. Evan Brewer will cover for me at school."

"You should have an assistant principal."

"Tell that to the board. They were the ones who eliminated the position."

"It was a budget decision," Pam said. "They did it at all the schools. Besides, Evan headed a private school before coming here. He has administrative experience."

"How convenient is that," Susan remarked.

It was a minute before Pam followed. "That isn't what I meant. No one is moving into your office while you're back home burying your father. Have you talked with Phil?"

"Uh-huh. He said it was a bad time to leave."

"It is." All the assurances in the world were worthless if Phil decided that Evan had done a fabulous job, even for the few days Susan was gone. If it came to that, what could Pam do?

"I didn't plan this," Susan said.

"I know. There's no good time for a death."

"Will you tell the school board that?"

LILY WAS ASLEEP WHEN THE PHONE RANG AND, REACH-ing for it, was too groggy to be cautious. "Hello?"

There was a silence, then Robbie's deep voice. "Your light's still on. I thought you'd be awake."

She had fallen asleep on her back. Again. Now she rolled to her left side, the one the books said allowed the best blood flow for the baby, and rubbed the spot where her ponytail had dug into her scalp. "I was knitting. I didn't realize I'd fallen asleep."

"Are you okay?"

No. As details of the evening seeped back, she realized she was not. "My grandfather died."

There was a pause, then a startled, "The grandfather you've never met?"

"Yeah. Mom and I are flying to Oklahoma tomorrow."

"That's heavy. You should have said something when we were there."

"We didn't get the call until after you left, and anyway, after so many things go wrong you just get numb." She hesitated. "That wasn't a fun scene tonight. Your mom didn't look at me once."

"Be grateful. Not looking is better than glaring, which is what she does each time she sees me."

"This baby wasn't your doing."

"You said it was."

"You know what I mean. Having sex wasn't your *idea*—but you didn't tell your parents that, did you." It wasn't a question.

"I don't want them hating you."

"You shouldn't have told them at all," Lily said. This baby was supposed to belong to her and her mother. As bad as it was that the whole town knew, the Boones knowing made it worse. She was losing control. She hadn't counted on this.

"I meant what I said," Robbie declared. "I'll marry you."

"I'm not getting married."

"Then at least let's date."

"So everyone at school will guess? Robbie, this baby isn't about its father. I said that the first time you called."

"But you picked me. You could have been with any guy at school."

"No," she said and might have elaborated, only she was growing emotional again. It happened last time she talked with Robbie, too. Then she had blamed it on hormones. This time she blamed it on the prospect of flying to Oklahoma tomorrow to meet the family from hell.

"Maybe I should go with you," he said. "He was my baby's great-grandfather."

Lily was beside herself. "Robbie. Listen to me. This is not your baby. It's *mine*."

"You admitted I'm the father."

"Biologically, but that's it. Tell anyone at school, and I'll deny it."

There was a pause, then a wounded, "Is there something wrong with me?"

"No! It's *me*. Robbie. *My baby*."

"You're going to need help."

"I have my mother."

"I have money."

"You do not."

"I do. My mother's father left some to each of us."

"She'd never let you use it on me."

"Not on you. On my baby."

"Omigod. I can just imagine it. Your mother would *never* forgive me then." It was unfair, Lily realized.. Annette Boone had always been warm and friendly before this.

Robbie must have been thinking the same thing, because he said, "She's not like that. She just didn't think this would happen. If she acts angry at you, it's because she's disappointed in me. This isn't what she planned."

Shades of Susan, Lily thought. "Why is it," she cried, "that our lives have to follow our parents' plans? Why do I have to go halfway across the country to meet a side of the family that effectively disowned me because my mother didn't follow *their* plans?"

Robbie left enough of a silence to give the question merit, then asked, "How long will you be gone?"

"Could be one day, if they kick us out. Could be three if they don't."

"Are you nervous?"

"*Terrified.* I mean, like, they're going to look at me like I'm the devil—and they don't even know I'm pregnant!"

"Will you tell them?"

"I might. That'd *really* give them something to talk about." But she hoped it wouldn't come to that. Her mother would be crushed, and Susan was already bearing the brunt of this pregnancy. Lily regretted that.

"Can I call you while you're there?"

"Sure," she said, thinking she might need all the help she could get.

"Will you call me if anything happens?"

"Sure." It was going to be an interesting trip.

"What if someone asks me straight out if the baby's mine?"

Lily closed her eyes. "Think of your mom. She doesn't want this getting out. And think of me." She sighed. "All I wanted was a baby. How did this get so messed up?"

Chapter 18

IT WAS A LONG TRIP. AFTER DRIVING TO PORTLAND, they flew to Philadelphia, then Chicago, then Tulsa, where Susan rented a car and drove an hour. There was a tiny inn in the center of her town, still open all these years later, according to the Internet, but if they had stayed there, news of their arrival would be all over the place before Susan could make it to the house. Her nightmare scenario had her being barred from entering.

Playing it safe, she had booked a room at a Comfort Inn two towns over. By the time they checked in, it was eleven at night. Lily had napped during parts of the trip, curled in her seat on the airplane with her history book on her lap and her head on Susan's shoulder, so childlike that it was hard to remember she was pregnant. So Susan didn't. She turned the clock back six months and took comfort from her daughter's closeness during those moments when she wasn't obsessing over changes to the school handbook, a draft of which was on her laptop, over thought of Evan back home, over anticipation of her mother's reaction to seeing her.

Too keyed up to sleep, Susan knitted to unwind. She had taken a skein of the sport weight wool that Kate had just dyed and was making a cowl for the catalogue spread. The pattern looked complex but was not, which made it a good project both for her now and for customers later.

There was no e-mail, though her BlackBerry had plenty of bars. Evan Brewer had filled in for her a time or two when she'd been at conferences. Politically, she couldn't have asked anyone else to cover. He had age and experience.

But he was ambitious. Not hearing from him made her nervous. Finally, she was tired enough to let that go, too.

They slept soundly, took their time getting dressed, and read the paper over breakfast in a coffee shop. Refusing to think about Evan or even her mother, Susan drove slowly, studying the landscape she hadn't seen in so long. The day was brightly overcast; she wore dark glasses to break the glare.

"Very flat," Lily remarked. "Not as green as home."

Much of that was seasonal, Susan knew. "We've been spoiled by evergreens. Out here, there are more oaks. Once spring comes and they leaf out, it will be beautiful. There's hickory farther east and pine to the south. Over there by the river, those are cottonwoods." They, too, were bare and bowing to the wind. "I'd forgotten about the wind. It's a prairie staple in winter." Indeed, it buffeted the car as she drove.

She pointed to a pretty sign that marked the town line. "That's new." A minute later, they were passing farmhouses. "Those've been here forever. Farmers used to focus on cattle and wheat, but they've branched out. Poultry is huge."

A few miles more, and the houses were closer together. They were small and single-storied, folk-style homes with additions tacked on at the back or the side. As they approached the center of town, the style didn't change, only the extent of improvements. Here there were stone fronts and two-car garages.

Turning, Susan drove down a side street to show Lily her high school. And the house where a friend had lived. And Rick's house.

Back in the center of town, she pointed out the drugstore, the feed store, the dress shop owned by her mother's good friend. The window display was surprisingly chic. A new owner?

She was slowing to admire what looked to be a newly built library when Lily said a quiet, "Mom. We agreed we'd get there early. It's after ten."

Yes. They had agreed on early. The wake ran from eleven to six, and given the prominence of Susan's father, there would be crowds. She wanted to get there before the rest did.

Picking up speed, she drove the few blocks to her parents' street and, with growing anxiety, passed more of those single-storied homes, now of brick, until she reached the one with the gabled front, the one in which she had grown up.

Parking, she turned off the engine. There were already four cars in the driveway, though she had no way of knowing to whom they belonged. Her parents had always loved Chevys, but seventeen years later, who knew what they drove?

"The porch is new," she told Lily. "And the basketball net. That must be for Jack's son."

"Thomas," Lily droned. "Age ten. Big brother of Emily, who is eight, and Ava, who is five. The mom is Lauren, who never sends thank-yous."

The last thing Susan needed just then was lip—and, oh boy, *there* was an expression from the past. *I don't want lip,* her father used to say, mostly to Jack.

"Aunt Lauren and Uncle Jackson," Susan corrected.

"This is really weird."

Susan didn't comment, simply watched another car pull in front of her and park. A couple emerged from either door. "LeRoy and Martha Barnes. LeRoy played poker with your grandfather. Martha loves to bake." Sure enough, foil-covered plates were emerging from the backseat. Straightening to adjust her load, Martha glimpsed Susan. She stared a moment too long.

"Foiled," Lily whispered dramatically.

"This isn't funny."

"I know, Mom, but these are only people, and they have very little to do with who you are. You have a life. You own a house that's nicer than this one. You have great friends and a great job. Let that lady stare."

She was right, of course. By the time Susan had given Lily's hand an appreciative squeeze, Martha Barnes was heading into the house with her husband in tow.

Susan took a deep breath. "Let's go." Heart pounding, she slid out of the car, pocketed the keys, and, holding Lily's hand, went up the walk. Once inside, she heard voices coming from the kitchen, but her eyes quickly went to the living room. She saw no people, just a large coffin. It was open, as she had known it would be. John Tate was as close to royalty as this town got. His minions would want to see him one last time.

So did Susan, which was why she'd come all this way. But suddenly she couldn't move. "I don't know if I can do this," she whispered brokenly.

Lily linked their arms tightly. "You can," she whispered back. "You're a survivor, Mom. This is a piece of cake compared to some of the things you've done."

It wasn't, but having Lily there was a help.

Removing her dark glasses, Susan approached the coffin. Her father looked amazingly well—dark hair thinner than it had been when she'd left, but skin attractively tanned. He was a handsome man.

What to tell him? Susan couldn't think of a thing. Wrapping an arm around Lily's waist, she drew her closer to the coffin. He would know who the girl was.

"Is this how he looked?" Lily whispered.

"Yes. Always in a suit. He said it added dignity to the job of mayor. He took great pride in that."

Lily reached out, but inches shy of touching his hand, she pulled back. Susan completed the gesture herself. Her father never had the roughened skin of a cattle farmer, but his hands were strong. Even now, fingers linked lifelessly over his middle, they had that commanding quality.

Not once, though, had he raised a hand to Susan. There had been many sweet times between father and daughter, but they were forgotten when Susan was sent away. Remembering them now, she felt a searing pain. So much was lost.

Her eyes filled with tears, which was why she didn't notice a nearby movement until Lily's elbow tightened around hers. At the foot of the coffin stood Ellen Tate. She looked smaller than Susan remembered, though not as much in height as in an odd inner quality. Her eyes were filled with exhaustion and grief, but not surprise—no, not that. She gripped the edge of the coffin, seemingly for support, but Susan imagined a certain possessiveness and, caught trespassing, released her father's hand.

"Mom," she said softly.

Ellen just stared at her.

"I couldn't not come," Susan explained. "He was my father."

Ellen said nothing.

"I wanted Lily to see him. This is the only chance she'll have."

Ellen's eyes skittered to Lily—reluctantly, even involuntarily, Susan thought. Of course, Ellen had seen pictures of the girl. Susan had sent plenty over the years, and though there had never been any acknowledgment, she had to believe her parents had looked at them.

"Lily, this is your grandmother."

"Hi," Lily said in a small voice. There was no "Nana," but Susan couldn't fault Lily on that. Nothing about Ellen right now was warm and fuzzy—or welcoming, for that matter.

Susan might have been angry, if she hadn't been juggling so many other emotions. She had seen newspaper snaps of her parents at events here in town, but it wasn't the same as real life.

"You're looking well, Mom." Exhaustion and grief aside, she actually did. Her hair, Susan's sandy shade laced with silver, was stylishly cut to the chin. She wore a black sweater and slacks not entirely unlike the ones Susan wore, and though she was a bit too thin, she held herself well. She was only fifty-nine. Had her face not been drawn, she would have looked younger than that.

Ellen still made no response. From the archway, though, came a grating, "What the hell?"

It was Jackson, four years older than Susan, a head taller, and scowling darkly. "What are you doing here?" he asked, coming to stand beside Ellen, her protector now that John was gone. As preordained, he had taken over as mayor when his father decided not to run again. Susan had followed that in the paper as well.

Now she was angry. Her mother not welcoming her was one thing. But Jack? He had basked in his father's love. It wouldn't have hurt him to show a little compassion to Susan, who had not.

Granted, they had never been close. Jack had always been the heir apparent and way too arrogant for Susan's taste.

Through the trauma of her final weeks here, he hadn't offered a word of support, though in his own twenty-one years, he had broken every rule except impregnating a girl. And now he was head of the house? How pathetic was that?

She raised her chin. "I've come for Dad's funeral."

"He would not want you here."

"How do you know? Did you ask?"

"I didn't have to," he said smugly. "I was here. I saw what he did when he was alive. He didn't ask for you even when his health started to fail."

Ellen shot him a glance, but if it was a warning, she let it go and looked at Susan again.

Susan was on her own and uncowed. "Thanks for telling me that, Jack. I might not have known."

"I'm Lily," came a surprisingly strong voice from her side.

Jack spared the girl a brief glance before returning to Susan. "I want you to leave."

Lily replied before Susan could. "We just got here, and we had to spend all of yesterday traveling to do it. Mom left town at a time that was really, really bad for her, that's how much she wanted to be here. And I've never been to Oklahoma before."

She wasn't entirely on her own, Susan realized with a glimmer of pride.

Jack stared at the girl. "Then I'm sorry the trip will be so short. You'd be better off back in school anyway."

"Actually, I wouldn't," Lily said, and Susan did nothing to stop her. "I brought books with me and can get my assignments online. That was one of the first things Mom did when she became principal. You know that's her job, don't you?" Jack didn't answer. "She's the youngest person ever to hold the position, and she's the best. I mean, like, everyone loves her— the kids, the parents."

"Then it won't be hard for her to turn around and go back," Jack said.

"No," Lily argued calmly. "You don't understand. She's good at what she does because she cares, and that's why she's here. I know all about you. You're married to Lauren, my cousins are Thomas, Emily, and Ava, and you live in a big yellow house in town that was owned by the Farrows when my mom lived here. See, even with none of you giving her an ounce of encouragement, she taught *me* to care."

"But she didn't teach you not to talk back."

"I'm not talking back. We're having a discussion."

"What about respect for your elders?"

"When they earn it," Lily said.

Susan nearly clapped. Had it not been for the coffin and Ellen, she would have been enjoying herself. Jack had met his match.

So he turned on Susan. "You think she's cute, but wait. That kind of lip causes trouble. She must inherit waywardness from you."

"Either that or sensibility," Susan said. "And for the record, I wouldn't call what she said cute. I'd call it true."

He sighed. "Okay. Look. It's been a trying few days here, so let's cut to the chase. You want money."

That took Susan by surprise. "Excuse me?"

"But why would he leave you any? You weren't a part of his life."

"*Excuse* me." Susan was indignant. "I'm his *daughter*—but the *fact* is that money never crossed my mind. He paid me to leave town, and I haven't asked for a nickel since, and, believe me, there were times when I could have used it. But I have money enough of my own now. I have a wonderful daughter. I have friends. There's not a lot I'm wanting except maybe some closure with my mother. I'm wondering what she would say if you weren't standing guard."

Jack turned to Ellen, who murmured, "I'll be in the kitchen," and left.

Pleased, he faced Susan again. "There's your answer, I believe." Before she could say anything more, he followed his mother.

SUSAN REFUSED TO LEAVE, IF FOR NO OTHER REASON than to annoy Jack. She introduced herself to people who might have forgotten her, introduced Lily to some who wanted to forget them both. And when the issue of money came up again, this time from Jack's wife, Lauren, Susan was cool. "It isn't about money."

"Jack said you'd claim that," Lauren argued, her nasal voice a perpetual whine, "but if that isn't it, why are you back? You've never come before."

"I never felt welcome." Nor did she now. When she walked into the kitchen to replenish a plate of cookies, talk stopped. Old family friends watched her every move, not a one asking about Zaganack or Susan's work.

"Y'know," Lauren confided, "I probably shouldn't say this, but there really isn't much money. Well, there may be a small bequest, but most of what's left is going to Ellen." She seemed to wake up. "That's why you're here? To get in good with *Ellen*?"

Susan felt no fondness for Lauren Tate. For all the gifts she had sent that had gone unacknowledged, she said, "The only ones obsessed with money are you and Jack. It makes me wonder whether you have that bequest already spent and are terrified you'll lose some of it to me."

"Why! No!"

Susan took her arm. "Please, Lauren, listen to me. I don't want money from anyone here. If someone offered it, I'd donate it to the church."

Lauren just pulled her arm free and walked off in a huff.

AND SO IT WENT, NOT A HAPPY DAY. BUT DESPITE Lily's pleading looks, Susan stayed. She had let herself be driven away once. When she left this time, it would be her choice.

She chose to leave at eight, after dinner and dessert were done, the coffee urn was washed and set up for the next day, and Jack and his family were gone. Only a few of Ellen's friends remained when Susan finally ushered Lily to the car. The girl was silent until they pulled away from the house, when all she had swallowed came back up.

"Okay, Mom. I understand that my cousins have never met me before, but for a *five*-year-old not to warm to *me* means that there's been some serious brainwashing. Every time I tried to talk with them, they ran away. I did *not* try to talk with my uncle Jackson, nor did he try to talk to me, probably because he was too busy talking for your mother. He acts like she doesn't have a brain. Why does she put up with it?"

Susan could only rationalize. "It's how she's always been. My father made all the decisions."

"That's sad."

"It works for some women."

"*I* couldn't live like that." Lily's profile was tense against the diner lights as they passed back through the center of town.

"Nor could I," Susan said, "but that doesn't mean it's wrong."

"But she's your *mother*. Doesn't she realize what it took for you to come here? Doesn't she have *any* feelings?"

"She's tired right now, probably numb."

Lily persisted. "But aren't you *hurt*?"

Looking back on the day, Susan tried to decide how she felt. From the moment she decided to return, she had been dreading the confrontation, but it could have been worse. Silence was better than name-calling. "Hurt? After all these years, I'm immune. But I did hope that there'd be something warmer. So I'm disappointed."

"Disappointed that your mother wouldn't talk to you? I'd be *furious*."

"My mother was never a big talker."

"But you're her daughter, whom she hasn't seen in years!"

"She just lost her husband."

"Fine," Lily granted, "but that is *not* how a good mother behaves—and see, that's what I mean, Mom. I may be only seventeen, but I know this. A good mother is sensitive to what her child is feeling."

Susan had a striking thought. In a shame-filled voice, she said, "By that standard, I've failed."

"Are you kidding? You taught me this. You totally understood what I was feeling when the Zaganotes voted me out, and when Robbie's parents came over? You knew then, too. We were absolutely on the same page."

"Not about the baby."

Lily took a quick breath but said nothing.

Susan tried to explain. "It's hard sometimes. I do understand what you're feeling, but my own feelings get in the way."

They were silent. On the outskirts of town, now, the car sliced through the dark with only the headlights to mark the road.

"At least you're telling me that," Lily finally said. Her voice lowered. "Do you still not want the baby?"

"I want the baby," Susan said.

"You don't sound convinced."

"I'm working on that."

BACK AT THE HOTEL, SUSAN'S BLACKBERRY WAS DING-ing with e-mail sent during the day but only just arriving. There must have been a connectivity problem at her parents' house—how ironic was that?

She read condolence notes from Kate and Sunny, and a brief e-mail from Pam saying she had been in touch with the school board. More urgently, there were notes from Evan Brewer. Three disciplinary problems had arisen, one involving a boy accused of cheating. Susan's heart sank when she read that one. Michael Murray had recurring problems; she'd been working closely with the family. Evan complained that Susan's assistant wouldn't give him access to the boy's full file.

Susan kept certain reports under lock and key—namely, those that contained sensitive information from parent confer-ences—and the Murray file was one. Husband and wife were struggling to hold their marriage together. The home situation was occasionally violent.

As reluctant as Susan was to give Evan access to that file, she felt he had to see the full picture. So she instructed Rebecca to show him what she had, but asked Evan not to act on the case. She would be at school Thursday morning. It could wait.

Well after sending the e-mail, though, she was bothered. She wasn't convinced Evan truly needed the file. She was still the principal; her word should have been enough. And yes, she was being hypersensitive, but it had been that kind of day.

Trying to relax, Susan began to knit. It helped clear her

mind of Zaganack, but not of Lily. The girl had fallen asleep after changing into pajamas, at which time Susan had noted a definite bulge. The image stuck with her.

In time, though, another image took its place. Her father's face. In this instance, the clock was not so much ticking as turned back. Good memories were returning—of being five and going with her father to Oklahoma City, of riding beside him in an open convertible for the Fourth of July parade when she was nine, of being hugged at eleven when she had tripped over Jack's outstretched leg and broken her arm.

Revisiting these memories, she found John's death all the more tragic. It was as if she was losing her father all over again.

THE FUNERAL WAS SET FOR NOON SO THAT TOWNSFOLK who worked could attend during their lunch hour. In reality, though, much of the town was closed for the day, which meant that there were more people than ever at the house when Susan and Lily arrived. Some were actually friendly. Most left the living room, though, when the hearse pulled up outside to take John to the cemetery.

Susan waited, keeping her distance, while her mother stood by the coffin for a final goodbye before it was closed. Pallbearers carried it to the hearse. Ellen and the Jackson Tates followed in a black limousine.

Lost in the long line of cars, by the time Susan and Lily reached the cemetery, the crowds were twenty deep. Buttoning her coat to the throat and triple-wrapping her scarf, Susan told herself that standing in back was for the best. But the mass of humanity did nothing to cut the wind, which blew brutally cold across the bare land, and she couldn't shake the feeling that the crowd was intentionally keeping her away.

Listening to hymns sung by the church choir's soprano,

Susan choked up at the intense sense of loss. She didn't realize she was trembling until Lily wrapped both arms around her. And then there was another arm. Through tears, she looked up at Rick. He kissed her forehead.

The wind wasn't as bothersome then. With Rick's warmth on her left and Lily's on her right, she listened to the prayers and the eulogies. By the time the soprano sang again, Susan was feeling loved, at least.

They didn't see her mother leave. Ellen would have been flanked by Jack and his family, anyway, and Susan was focused forward, working her way through the departing crowd toward the grave. Refusing to remember the bad now, only the good—how *many* times had her father succumbed to her pleading and reread *Amelia Bedelia*—she watched while two grave diggers shoveled dirt over the coffin, watched closely, making sure they were doing it right, until there was no mahogany left to see.

Finally, she took a shuddering breath. She held Lily for a minute, but it was only when she turned to Rick with clear eyes now that she saw the man who stood not far from his shoulder.

She gasped and, teary again, reached for him. She had seen Big Rick several times over the years, but always on the West Coast. Knowing that he was here for the first time in nearly as long as it had been for her, she began to weep.

"Thank you for coming," she finally managed. She had said the words dozens of times at the house, but truly felt them now.

"I wasn't sure I should," Big Rick said, and this close he was big indeed. If Rick was six-four, his dad had to be six-six.

"I insisted," Rick said. "He needed to be here. We were shooting to arrive yesterday but had to spend the night in Chicago. You doin' okay?"

Susan nodded. "Lily's been great."

Big Rick gave Lily a kiss. "It's been too long," he said. If he knew she was pregnant, he didn't let on, and once back at the house, Susan understood why. When he had expressed qualms about returning, he hadn't been kidding. He was awkward seeing these people again, and though old friends greeted him with smiles, he remained visibly ill at ease. Susan was about to ask Rick about that, when she noticed Ellen looking straight at his dad.

Quietly, Big Rick excused himself and worked his way through the crowd. He stood for a minute before Ellen, then gave her a gentle hug, and where Ellen had been dry-eyed moments before, now her shoulders shook and her hand clutched his sweater. Confused, Susan looked at Rick.

He smiled crookedly. "I didn't guess either."

"Guess what?"

"That there was more to his leaving than just us."

Susan was too astonished to follow. "*What* more?"

Rick steered her away from the crowd. "I'm at his house, thinking he's coming back here with me, and he starts to balk. He says John wouldn't like it. When I ask why, he explains. Apparently, he and Ellen had a special attachment."

"Special attachment?"

"Were sweet on each other."

"Had an *affair*?"

"No, they just liked each other a lot. Your father thought it was more, though, and while he was railin' on about me, he lit into my dad. 'Chip off the old block. Can't get the one for you, so your boy takes the other. Apple doesn't fall far from the tree.'"

"That's awful!"

"Which—the accusation or the affection?"

"The *accusation*. Did your mother think there was something between them?"

"No. She knew my father loved her. Maybe it was a macho thing on John's part, because everyone else knew Ellen loved her husband. I don't know why he'd be insecure."

Nor did Susan. "Your father moved away because of that?"

"It was part of the picture."

Susan looked across the room. Ellen was talking with Big Rick now, only as animated—no more, no less—than she had been with other friends from out of town. When several local people recognized Big Rick and approached, she disappeared.

"Where's Lily?" Rick asked, looking around.

"Walking around, I guess. She's feeling a little lost."

"Does anyone know?"

"No. Does your dad?"

"No. I'm guessing this hasn't been a fun trip for her."

Susan shot him a rueful look. "She was hoping something good would happen."

LILY HAD BEEN TOO CAUTIOUS TO EXPLORE THE HOUSE the day before. She felt she was being watched and didn't want to be caught snooping.

This afternoon was different. She knew there were three rooms in the side wing and wanted to see which one had been her mother's. The first door she opened was to her grandparents' room, dominated by a four-poster double bed piled high with coats. The next door opened to a full bathroom, larger than the lav off the kitchen, and the one after that to a boy's room that she guessed, from the banners and trophies, had barely changed since Jackson lived there. The room at the end of the hall had to be Susan's.

Only it hadn't been a bedroom for years, to judge from the worn sofa cushions, stuffed bookshelves, and overflowing baskets of yarn. This was a sitting room, and, right now, perhaps escaping the crowd for a few minutes, it held her grandmother. She was knitting.

Lily hated the way Ellen had treated her mother, and would have liked to speak up in defense of Susan, much as she had done to Jack. But this woman was older. And she was her grandmother. Hadn't Lily always wanted to meet her?

Ellen didn't see her at first, and Lily didn't quite know what to do. Then the woman looked up, and Lily refused to run. The fact that Ellen seemed stunned gave her strength.

Ellen blinked first. Her eyes fell to her work. So did Lily's. Here was something to discuss.

"What are you making?" Lily asked from the door.

"A sock."

"Do you like making socks?"

"Yes."

"Have you made a lot?"

"I have."

Lily was challenged. Ellen might not be much of a talker, but there had to be a way to get her to say more than two words. "You're using circulars. Why don't you use DPNs?"

Ellen seemed surprised by the question. But her voice remained quiet. "I'm hemmed in by DPNs. Two circulars feel more open." She stopped, then started again. "Lots of ladders with DPNs. I don't get them with circulars."

"Have you ever tried Magic Loop?"

Ellen reached into her bag and pulled out the second sock. It was being worked on one very long circular needle. Magic Loop.

Lily smiled. They did have this in common. "Which do you prefer?"

"I'm more comfortable with two circulars." Ellen paused. "I take it you knit, too."

"Absolutely. My best friends' moms are my mom's partners. We all knit. Are those for you?"

Ellen fingered the socks and nodded. "Winter's coming on. The warmth will be good."

"Are they merino?"

"With a touch of alpaca and silk."

But not PC Wool. Lily knew that from the color, which was neutral, perhaps practical, but bland. "They look soft."

Ellen held out one of the socks.

Pleased by the invitation, Lily approached. Opening her hand, she cradled the sock to examine the pattern. It had elements of lace and was more complicated than anything Lily had made. Lace was the rage, but only for knitters who had the time and the skill. "You knit beautifully."

Ellen nodded her thanks.

"I understand why my mother is so good."

"Oh, she didn't get it from me. Whatever I made when my children were young was purely functional."

"When did you start making things like this?"

"Just recently."

"Nana?" It was Jack's daughter, eight-year-old Emily, looking warily from Ellen to Lily. "Daddy's looking for you. He's worried. Are you all right?"

Ellen tucked both socks in the bag. With a soft, "I'm coming," she pushed herself up.

The moment was lost. Lily didn't know what she'd been looking for, but felt a quick resentment. Having stepped back the instant her cousin appeared, she preceded Ellen to the door. The girl, Emily, watched her with the same dislike she had shown earlier, when Lily had tried to get her to talk. *What grade are you in? Do you play sports? Do you like Hannah Montana?* Third, no, and yes. Unspoken, but definitely there in the girl's eyes, was a defiant, Want to make something of it look?

The child was rude, inhospitable to someone who had traveled halfway across the country—and who was her first cousin!

Vowing that her own daughter would never be like that, Lily came to within a foot of the girl and bent swiftly. *"Boo!"*

The girl jumped.

That was the extent of Lily's satisfaction. She never found her grandmother alone again, and they didn't stay late at the house, which was just fine. Lily hated casseroles. They had dinner at a steak place, and though Lily wasn't eating red meat, the salad greens were fresh and the company of her parents and Big Rick far preferable to the people at the house.

Back at the hotel, Lily closed the door to their room and said, "Want me to bunk with Grampa tonight?"

Her mother looked at her, startled. "What?"

"Dad can sleep here." When Susan drew back, Lily smiled. "I know you guys sleep together. It's nothing to be ashamed of. You're grown-up, responsible adults, and if you haven't gotten pregnant all these years, I assume one of you takes precautions."

"Where did this come from?"

"Haven't you told me that sex between grown-up, responsible individuals is beautiful?"

"What makes you think . . ."

"Doors, Mom. Closed. You don't close your door when it's just us at home, and I know you're not closing it to keep him out. Besides, there's that creak in the floor you say always gives you advance word when I'm coming in. Well, it gives me advance word, too."

Susan looked upset. "How long have you known?"

"A couple of years. It's okay. He's my dad. If you're going to be with someone, I'd rather it be him. So. Should I take my pillow next door?"

Susan stared at her. Then, for the first time since Lily had said she was pregnant, she gave her a spontaneous hug. "Absolutely not. Rick snores."

LILY DIDN'T KNOW WHETHER HER BABY WAS RESPOND-ing to the hug or the sheer relief of heading home. But when they were sitting in the plane, waiting to back away from the jetport, she felt a flutter.

"Oh wow," she whispered with a hand on the spot and eyes on her mother. "Something moved."

Susan looked frightened. "Moved?"

"I just felt it." She pushed her seatbelt a little lower, but there was no repeat motion.

"A cramp?"

"The *baby.*" She turned on her phone and before Susan could argue, said, "Mary Kate and Jess need to know." She texted the news and shut down the phone. By then, the plane was rattling enough on its way to takeoff that if the baby moved again, she wouldn't have felt it. They were late landing in Chicago and had to run to make their connection, so she was breathing too hard to feel it then. Nor did she notice anything while they were in Philadelphia, waiting to board the flight to Portland.

"Do you think something's wrong?" she asked when they were in their own car, leaving Portland for Zaganack, and still the baby was quiet.

"No," Susan assured her. "You're not even four months along. It's early to be feeling the baby move."

"I wasn't imagining it."

"It may not have been the baby, only your body doing a little inner twitch."

Lily was beginning to think Susan was right when, back

home in bed, the feeling came again. The sensation was so small that she might have missed it if she hadn't been waiting.

She smiled in the dark. She didn't rush to tell her mother this time, didn't even text Mary Kate or Jess, both of whom said it was too early, too.

But Lily knew what she felt.

Chapter 19

❧

SUSAN TRIED TO BE EXCITED, BUT SHE SERIOUSLY doubted Lily had actually felt the baby, and she had more pressing worries. Evan Brewer had gone ahead and imposed a three-day suspension on Michael Murray, which meant that the boy would miss even more school, just what Susan didn't want. She learned of Evan's action while they were waiting to leave Chicago, and though she e-mailed him to express dismay, e-mailed Phil, e-mailed Michael's parents, it was done.

That weighed on her.

Likewise her mother's parting words the evening before. They had never had a good chance to talk, and suddenly it was time to leave. "Thank you for coming," Ellen had said, as if Susan were no different from a dozen other guests.

But she didn't regret going. It was the right thing to do. Being with Rick and his father had been a solace; the four of them were a little family independent of the Tates. And she did feel closer to Lily.

Still, Zaganack was her real world. She had hoped that, in her absence, the uproar caused by the pregnancies would have died. Instead, here was Evan.

Evan Brewer was forty-nine. He had resigned as headmaster at a private school when they wanted him to commit to a major building campaign. He didn't like raising money, he explained at length when Susan interviewed him, and she could commiserate. She didn't like fund-raising; fortunately, her job required little of it.

To his credit, Evan was an excellent teacher. He had a command of his subject and presented it with an authority that made students sit up and listen. It was the way he conducted himself at faculty meetings and approached parents that made her uneasy. He was full of himself, she decided. And he wanted her job.

He was five minutes late for their meeting Thursday morning. She sensed it was deliberate, because when he finally arrived, he neither apologized nor even expressed condolences on her father's death, simply launched into a defense of his action on the Murray boy.

"He blatantly disregarded the rules. I don't know whether he thought the holiday would have people looking the other way, but he's been caught cheating three times this year alone. Where I come from, three strikes and you're out."

Susan was bristling well before he stopped. "Not here," she said. "He's a senior, Evan. A suspension on his record now raises a red flag for college admissions officers. This is a bright boy who is struggling to keep up with even brighter older siblings and parents he desperately wants to please."

Evan arched a brow. "By *cheating*?"

"He cheats when he thinks he's failing," Susan explained as she shouldn't have had to with a man of Evan's experience, "but we're working with him. He and his parents are in counseling. Surely, you read that in his file."

"I did, but the case for leniency just wasn't there. I had to make a decision."

"I asked you not to. You knew I'd be back today."

"When a child pummels another child, he goes into time-out now—not tomorrow or next week."

"This isn't a case of bullying," Susan argued. "When Michael cheats, he hurts no one but himself."

"He hurts the morale of the school."

"Which has never been higher. Disciplinary problems are down since I took over, and it's because we're looking beyond the infraction to the cause. That's my policy, Evan. If you're not comfortable with it, this may not be the right school for you." He had exploited her absence. She couldn't see it any other way.

But he didn't back down. "I talked this over with Phil Correlli. He agreed."

"You should have talked it over with me. This is my school."

Evan's expression said he didn't like that either, and, glancing at his watch, he claimed he had a student conference. But even after he left, Susan fumed. She knew that Michael Murray would survive, but she disapproved of Evan's action as a matter of principle. If a student was suspended, what did he learn by sitting at home? Conversely, if his punishment was, say, to tutor illiterate adults and, in the process he realized his own gift, a greater good was achieved.

At least, that was her opinion. And it *was* her school.

And she had chosen not to punish the three girls who had formed a pact to become pregnant.

.   .   .

IT WAS MID-MORNING WHEN THE *GAZETTE* ARRIVED. There was no scathing editorial this week, actually a pleasant one about the holiday spirit that Evan Brewer should have read before suspending a boy with psychological problems. But the page opposite the editorial was a horror. This week, too, George Abbott had held off on running a story on the pact, but he made up for it with negative letters on the subject. They practically filled the page.

Susan called Kate. "Anonymous? *Anonymous?* Since when does the *Gazette* print anonymous letters?"

"Since our daughters got pregnant and George became the arbiter of moral judgment," Kate replied in a shaky voice.

"But there's no credibility if letters aren't signed!"

"The positive ones are signed."

"All two of them," said Susan. "But twenty negative and two positive? If this honestly represents the sentiment of the town, I might as well throw in the towel."

"Don't you dare! The only thing this page represents is George Abbott's attempt to impose his views on the rest of us."

"And succeeding."

"We don't know that."

No. They didn't. Rick might; he had good instincts on things like this. But Susan decided not to call. He had been a saint coming to the funeral—John Tate hadn't been particularly nice to him, either—but he was in Ecuador now, doing a piece on oil pollution. And this was her mess.

SHE HAD JUST PUT DOWN THE PAPER WHEN SUNNY called. "I don't understand it," she cried, sounding close to tears. "They're fixated on us! Did *we* tell our girls to get pregnant?" She began reading. "'Not all mothers are like this. Don't these mothers set rules? What are these mothers thinking?' I give up. What *am* I thinking? I'm trying to hear what you said, Susan. I'm trying not to make the mistake your parents made. But all this makes it hard."

"Not all the letters are about mothers," Susan mused. "Two don't mention the word at all."

"Those two talk about the breakdown of values. That's code for Bad Mothers. They're referring to us."

"With that talk about the school clinic encouraging sexual promiscuity? No, Sunny, they're referring to me."

SUSAN CALLED PHIL, WHO, TO HIS CREDIT, DID ASK about the funeral. "I'm sorry you have to come back to this," he said with what sounded like genuine regret. "George must not have known why you were gone."

"Either that or he did," Susan said. "I'm sorry to be cynical, but I don't think it would have made a difference. This has become George's crusade."

"Bah. People take what he says with a grain of salt."

"Not according to those letters. To read today's *Gazette*, you'd think the whole town agrees. Honestly, Phil? I'm shocked. I always thought Zaganack was an understanding place."

"It is. But three pregnancies frighten people. They wonder if their daughter's next."

"So they attack me? Does that make them safe?"

"They think it does."

"Because I haven't suspended the girls?" she asked, but calmly now. With Phil determining her future, she had to take a page from Evan Brewer's book and project authority. "Because I support a school clinic that gives condoms to boys who would otherwise have sex without protection? Because I believe in constructive punishment—which brings us to

Michael Murray. You know I've been working with his family. Evan says you okayed the suspension."

"You weren't there. Something had to be done."

"I was gone for three days, and I wasn't playing golf. I've worked so hard with that boy."

"Maybe you need to take a different approach."

Susan was startled. It was a minute before she managed to ask, "You agree with him, then?"

"I don't know. I'm trying to keep an open mind."

An open mind about whom—Michael Murray? Evan Brewer? Susan Tate? Not knowing which, she was silent.

Phil sighed. "See, I would rather George had not printed those letters, but he did. Now I want to think it's over. The naysayers have had their day."

"Then you think this is just a blip in the scheme of things?"

"I think," he cautioned, "that if you're still adamant against taking a leave, you'll have to be proactive. Call Pam Perry, and get her to lobby on your behalf, because if the school board insists I take action, I'll act."

PAM WAS COOL, THOUGH WHETHER FROM DISTRAC- tion or frustration, Susan didn't know. "I'm already doing what I can. I talked with several of the men. I explained why you were away. I said your father's death was unexpected. They have to be thinking George is kicking you while you're down."

"Would you tell them that?" Susan asked, afraid to leave it to chance. "Spell it out?"

"Bad idea," her friend warned. "I'm the youngest member of the board. I'm the *newest* member. I can't tell them what to think. No, they'll get it on their own."

"Duncan Haith? Carl Morgan? I'm worried, Pam. This is one more week with just one side of the story in the paper."

"Maybe you could write a rebuttal."

"And give credence to George Abbott's accusations? Maybe you could."

"No. Not with my position in town."

She could if she wanted to. But she didn't. Hurt, Susan asked, "Do you think these letters represent the town's feelings?"

Pam was silent a few seconds too long. "I don't know."

"Do you agree with what they're saying? Am I less of a mother for what Lily did?"

"No, but I can't control public sentiment."

"What about Tanner? When he talks, people listen."

"I can't involve Tanner."

"You know what this job means to me, Pam."

"Hey," her friend said lightly, "I don't imagine anything will happen because of the letters. You just have to hang in there a little longer. School break starts next Wednesday. By the time the holidays are over, everyone will have forgotten about this."

Susan didn't think so. She wasn't sure Pam believed it either, but clearly she didn't want to do anything more. That cut deeply on a personal level. On a professional one, it made Susan very, very nervous.

IT WAS ALL SHE COULD DO TO GET HERSELF TO GO TO the basketball tournament that afternoon. She would much rather have stayed holed up nursing her wounds. But her concept of a principal entailed being a leader in good times and bad, which meant showing up to root for the home team, even when *she* was the biggest underdog around.

In hindsight, she was glad that she did. Sporting events were a good place to talk with parents. Some came over to express condolences on her father's death, others to discuss the

Gazette. The latter were dismayed by the letters and supportive of Susan's position.

Then came Allison Monroe. She reported that she had over-
heard Evan Brewer in the faculty lounge that morning making arguments for why his approach to discipline was the best.
Furious, Susan pulled out her BlackBerry and sent him a note.
My office. Seven A.M. tomorrow.

ON FRIDAY, TOO, HE WAS FIVE MINUTES LATE, AND
then he walked in with coffee from Starbucks—only one cup,
clearly for him. Not that Susan wanted coffee. But if she
sensed she had done something her boss didn't like, *she* would
have brought a peace offering. Not Evan Brewer.

Acting the mature professional with Phil was important,
but Evan wasn't Phil. And Susan was pissed. "Are you bad-
mouthing me in the faculty lounge?" she asked with little pre-
amble.

He gave her an odd smile. "Am I what?"

"Bad-mouthing me. You were discussing Michael's case
with other teachers."

"Who said this?"

"That's not the point. Your discussing it is a violation of
Michael's privacy—*and* totally unprofessional. You were basically saying that your way of disciplining Michael is better than
mine."

"No, Susan. It was a philosophical discussion."

"With you taking the opposite position from the one that
your boss takes?" *Really* pissed, she said, "Would you have
appreciated your faculty second-guessing your decisions when
you were the headmaster?"

"I'm sure they did. A head can't control what his faculty
does. But in this case, I was only trying to help."

"Help how?"

He shrugged. "This may be the last thing you want to hear right now . . . but there's been a lot of talk about the lack of discipline here. I presented my argument in a way that suggested you *do* consider all possibilities. In that sense, I was standing up for you." He arched an arrogant brow. "Look at it this way. I'm older and have more experience. My being more visible isn't a bad thing."

Susan could not have disagreed more. "You aren't principal here, Evan. Assistant principal isn't even part of your title. It's bad enough that I asked you not to act on Michael's case and you went ahead and did it. But now to talk up the issue behind my back?"

He made a dismissive sound. "They were already talking. I wasn't saying anything they didn't want to hear."

"You think so? For the record," she said quietly, "I was hired because the parents here wanted a different approach to running this school. I've had no problem with the faculty." Legitimately puzzled, she frowned. "I don't understand, Evan. I hire and fire my staff, which means that your job is in my hands. Doesn't that worry you?"

He stood up, even though she hadn't ended the interview. "Hey, I was just trying to help."

"Please don't."

SUSAN WAS ITCHING TO VENT WHEN SHE REACHED the barn Saturday morning, but something stopped her. It might have been the power of this place imposing its own kind of calm. Or the fact that Sunny and Pam were no-shows. Or the lure of spending the entire day dyeing wool, which, once they finished the last of the formulas, was what she and Kate did. Kate had staff to help get PC Wool out in quantity. But like knitting itself, dyeing was therapeutic.

They didn't talk much. Susan couldn't bear to speculate on what it meant for Sunny and Pam to be sitting this out, she was tired of thinking about the *Gazette,* and when Kate asked if she had talked with her mother since returning, she just shook her head.

They did discuss wool. That was acceptable.

Babies were not. But two little grandbabies must have been with them in spirit, because the colorway Susan and Kate worked up first was Robin At Dawn, which contained reds, browns, pinks, and blues—far more of the last two than Susan had expected, though hers was the hand that poured the dye. And even then, when Kate made a comment about Monday being the big day, Susan didn't follow.

"Lily's sonogram," Kate prompted. "Mary Kate and Jess are all fired up about it. They're still betting it's a girl. What do you think?"

"I think," Susan began but faltered. She had so much else on her mind besides a baby. "I think I'm still not ready. Are you?"

"No. I'm glad Lily's first."

They worked on a bit before, anguished, Susan stopped. "I used to fantasize about inviting my parents to Lily's wedding. She'd be marrying a great guy; they'd be an absolutely beautiful couple. And then when kids came, and I could tell my parents that they were going to be *great*-grandparents—wow, that would have been something. Now Dad's gone, Mom's not talking to me, Lily is doing exactly what they wouldn't want, and my job is on the line. How awful is that?"

Chapter 20

SUSAN BEGAN MONDAY WITH MIXED FEELINGS. ON
one hand, she was not looking forward to the sonogram. Sonograms made babies real. She wanted Lily's to stay abstract for a
while longer, at least until she got the rest of her own life
straightened out.

But she loved Lily, and since Lily was beside herself with
excitement, Susan couldn't help but catch some of her mood.
In Lily's mind, it was like the first day of kindergarten or the
night before Christmas. The hospital where she had her
appointment was a thirty-minute drive from Zaganack, and
she chatted the whole way.

"They take pictures during the sonogram, did you know
that, Mom? We get to take them home—and I *know* she'll
look Martian, but she's four and a half inches long now. I'm
going to frame the pictures. I mean, I am going to take pictures
constantly once this baby's born, but these will be the very first.
You waited to learn the sex."

"Lots of parents still choose to wait."

"Not me. I want to know for sure. Actually, they may not be able to tell me today. It depends on the baby's position. Thank goodness I'm this far along." She crinkled her nose. "I wouldn't like having the sonogram done transvaginally—I mean, I'd be okay with it, but transabdominal is more comfortable, and I think they can see more this way because they can move the probe more to get a better view. Doesn't that make sense, Mom? I mean, it'll be *so* much easier when the baby gets bigger. Mary Kate wanted to come, but I told her no. This time's just for you and me. That's how it should be, don't you think?"

You should be twenty-five and married, and your husband should be the one driving you, Susan thought. But she was coming to accept that these things weren't to be. The baby was something else. Bracing for the reality of it, she was feeling flutters in her own stomach when the sonogram began. Lily lay on a table with the small swell of her abdomen exposed. The technician squirted a gel, spread it with the transducer, and images soon appeared on the screen. Reaching for Susan's hand, Lily drew her close to the head of the table, but the images were hard to decipher. The technician was patient, explaining what she saw, and suddenly Lily gasped.

"Omigod. Look, Mom!"

Susan felt the same amazement. Even in a grainy image, the blotch on the screen had become a baby. Moving her probe, the tech was able to show them its profile—eyes, nose, mouth—primitive but distinct—and familiar, though Susan would have been hard-pressed to say which one feature was Lily's. The tech took a picture, adjusted her equipment, and pointed out arms and legs. But the second Susan knew she was lost was when she saw the pulsing point of a beating heart.

This was why she hadn't wanted to hear the heartbeat

before; a heartbeat meant life. She remembered the first time she'd heard it when she was carrying Lily. It had been the moment Susan truly realized she was a mother.

And now? In an instant, Susan's perspective changed. It was no longer about her teenage daughter being pregnant. Now it was about her daughter's child—her own grandchild—a very real human being. Susan felt pure awe.

The technician fiddled with the transducer, moved it higher, then to the left. She made a puzzled sound, to which Lily asked a worried, "Can you not see the sex?"

The woman repositioned the transducer. Susan kept her eyes on the monitor but saw nothing recognizable.

"You sure you want to know?" the woman asked, and when Lily cried an excited yes, she said, "See this?" She pointed to the screen. Susan squinted. "If I were to guess, I'd say you have a little boy in here."

A little boy. Not what Lily wanted. Susan looked at her daughter, and yes, those were tears in the girl's eyes, a brief "Oh" of disappointment—then a brilliant smile.

"A boy," she said, testing the word. "That's okay, that's okay. Mary Kate will die. She wanted a boy until Jess and I bugged her so much she changed her mind. So much for having another generation of girls."

If the remarks registered with the technician, she didn't comment. She was moving the transducer again, first one way, pressing a little, then another, and all the while her eyes were on the screen. She was looking for something.

"What do you see?" Susan finally asked.

"I'm not sure."

Lily picked up on Susan's concern. "Is something wrong?"

"I'm just trying to get another view," the tech said, but her voice was hesitant.

"You're not sure it's a boy?"

Susan didn't think it was that. Her gut told her that the tech saw something else. "What is it?" she asked.

Setting the transducer aside, the woman gave them a quick smile. "It's likely just me. My eye isn't trained well enough. Let me get the radiologist. He'll know."

As soon as the woman was gone, Lily turned large eyes on Susan. "She's worried, but how can something be wrong? I mean, I'm young, I'm healthy, I feel great."

Susan held her hand. "Everything's probably fine, but the reason they do these sonograms is to detect even the smallest little thing."

"Like what?"

"You'd know that more than me, sweetie. You're the one who's done all this research."

"Down syndrome. But there are serious calculations involved, and she wasn't doing any, so maybe she saw something structural, but everything that was supposed to be there was there, wasn't it?"

"Absolutely," Susan said. "I'm sure it's nothing."

"What if it isn't?"

"If it isn't, we'll deal."

The technician returned with the radiologist, who introduced himself, then said calmly, "Let's take a look," and picked up the transducer. Susan studied the monitor, trying to decipher something, but all she could identify was that little heart beating what she thought was a totally normal beat.

Finally, the radiologist pointed at the screen. "This is the baby's chest. I see the intestines," he moved the tip of a pencil, "and the kidneys, but they look to be outside the abdominal cavity."

Lily's hand started to tremble. Holding it tighter, Susan asked, "What does that mean?"

He moved the transducer again, but Susan couldn't see anything this time either. When he paused, he didn't look relieved. "This isn't uncommon. It happens once in about every twenty-five hundred births. We call it a congenital diaphragmatic hernia."

"Please explain," Susan said, knowing Lily would ask if she'd been able to speak.

"The diaphragm is a muscle between the abdominal cavity and the chest. It forms at the eight-week point, but occasionally it has a hole. When that happens, organs that would normally be in the abdominal cavity are not."

"His organs are *outside* his body?" Lily wailed.

"No. They're inside. They're just in the chest cavity, not the abdomen."

"What does *that* mean?"

"It means that there's less room for the lungs to form, so one or both may not fully develop."

"My baby will *die*?"

"No. There are different severities of CDH, and even for the most severe, the survival rate is continually getting better. But I don't know for sure that this is CDH. We'll know more in a few weeks."

"Weeks?" If there was a problem, Susan wanted to *act*.

The doctor remained calm. "The baby's in no immediate danger. Right now, it breathes through the placenta. Typically, we monitor the fetus to confirm its condition and see if it worsens."

Lily started to cry.

Holding her, Susan said, "We need to know more. If the baby does have this, how is it treated?"

"Surgery after birth. Depending on the severity as the fetus grows, prenatal surgery is even an option." He spoke to Lily now. "Like I said, your baby is in no imminent danger. We'll send the sonogram to your OB." He checked the file. "She'll take it from there."

AS SOON AS THEY REACHED THE CAR, SUSAN CALLED Dr. Brant, who suggested they come in on the way home. Lily was silent, pale, and frightened. The best Susan could do during the drive was to try to reassure her.

"Don't assume the worst, sweetie. The danger of early tests is that they can be wrong. It may be nothing."

But Dr. Brant was concerned enough after talking with the radiologist to refer Lily to a high-risk obstetrician. The first appointment they could get was for the next morning, which meant a long night of worry. Mary Kate and Jess slept over, and Lily had told enough other friends she was having the sonogram that the phone wasn't quiet for long. When Lily couldn't bear talking about it anymore, the two other girls helped. *Lily's sleeping. Everything's great. It's a boy!*

Long after the girls turned off the lights, Susan was Googling *congenital diaphragmatic hernia,* reading different accounts, alternately encouraged and discouraged. It was a case of a little information being dangerous, especially once her imagination kicked in. And she didn't know that the baby had this at all.

That was why she didn't call Rick. She had never called when Lily got a rash as a baby, not until the doctor knew what it was. If it turned out to be a heat rash, she didn't call him at all. That was what she wanted this scare to be—like a heat rash, gone by morning.

JANE LABREIA, THE NEW DOCTOR, WAS YOUNGER THAN Eileen Brant and had trained at Mass General. A small woman with short blond hair and a quiet manner, she was wonderful with Lily, for which Susan loved her. They had an instant rapport.

After examining Lily and studying the sonogram, she said, "I agree with the diagnosis. What I see in these pictures is consistent with CDH, but there isn't much we can do right now. At week twenty, we'll do a level three ultrasound, which is a more in-depth version of what you had yesterday. If the diagnosis stands, it will tell us whether the baby's condition is getting worse. If we need an even better picture, we'll do an MRI." Turning to Lily, she explained, "When a fetus has CDH, we worry first about the lungs being too small to sustain breathing, and second about the heart. Right now, your baby's heart sounds strong and perfectly normal. We want to keep it that way."

"How do you do that?" Lily asked in a weak voice.

"By monitoring it. If we hear stress and see the CDH worsening, we have choices."

"What choices?"

"We can do nothing and let nature take its course. Or we can operate."

Let nature take its course. Susan knew that meant letting the baby die at birth, but of course there was another option. The pregnancy could be terminated now.

Mercifully, Lily had glommed on to the doctor's last option. "You'd operate before the baby's born?"

"We would. There are new, minimally invasive procedures. The results have been stunning."

"But there's a risk."

"Any surgery involves risk, but that's what pediatric specialists are for."

"My baby could still die."

"The chances of that are less likely today than they were five years ago. You should have a strong, healthy baby."

Lily looked like she wanted to believe her but couldn't quite.

"Really," the doctor insisted gently and said, "I recommend amniocentesis. The more information we have, the better. If we rule out other possible problems, we can concentrate on the CDH. Amnio entails a small risk, though, so perhaps you'd like to think about it."

Susan knew that the doctor's request wasn't an idle one. More than one of the articles she had read mentioned that a fetus with CDH often had other abnormalities.

With Lily bewildered and silent, Susan said, "How soon can it be done?"

LILY WAS GRIEF-STRICKEN. THE PLAN HAD BEEN TO get pregnant, breeze through nine months like she'd breezed through AP bio, and pop out a healthy baby. Other people had physical problems, but not her, because her mother hadn't. Weren't these things hereditary?

But the doctor was telling them they had to wait and see, her baby may or may not need surgery, may or may not be normal, may or may not *live*—and her mother had gone ahead and scheduled a test Lily did not want to take.

She let Susan hold her hand until they left the building, but her resentment was building. Stopping halfway to the parking lot, she snatched her hand free and turned on Susan. "How could you *agree* to that, Mom? Amniocentesis can lead to *miscarriage,* which would be *fine* with you—you don't *want* this baby—but I do, and I *don't* want amniocentesis." When Susan reached for her, she stepped back. "This is *my* baby. I *told* you that. *I* make the decisions."

"There's a reason why the doctor wants it, Lily."

"To rule out other problems, but what other problems could

there be? Isn't this one bad enough?" Internal organs in the wrong place? It was freaking her out. "I don't *want* amniocentesis. How could you schedule it without asking me? I was sitting right there!"

"Lily. I looked at you. You had a chance to speak but didn't."

"I *couldn't.* I was too upset. Don't you think this is a shock, Mom?"

"Absolutely," Susan said with annoying calm, pulling her aside for another family to pass, "but you're still my child, and I made the best decision I could. Amniocentesis will tell us something."

That was what frightened Lily. Her voice shook. "What if it tells us my baby is really sick?" Her eyes filled with tears. "I read online, too, Mom. What if it has other, really awful things wrong with it? What'll I do then?" Suddenly sobbing, she let Susan hold her. She was terrified.

Even when she stopped crying, her mother didn't let go. In a calm voice that Lily hated but desperately needed to hear, Susan said, "We'll deal, sweetie. We'll deal."

Lily wanted to believe her. But she wasn't a child, she was *having* a child. She had to be realistic. "What if it's so awful that my baby won't be able to live?"

Smiling gently, her mother brushed tears from her cheeks. "Let's take it one step at a time. If you don't want the amnio, we'll cancel it."

That put the burden on her. Which was what Lily wanted. Except that her mother had really, really good judgment. "You think we should do it."

"Yes. The risk is less at your age. It'll be even less if we use someone who does amnio all the time. Good news will definitely make the waiting easier."

"What if it's bad news?"

"We'll deal."

"You keep saying that, but it could mean *anything*," Lily said, tearing up again. "Not in a million *years* could I terminate this pregnancy. This is my child. I don't care what's wrong with him. Miracles happen, don't they?"

"They do—but why are you expecting the worst? We have *never* lived like pessimists."

"We've never faced something like this. Why did this *happen*? What did I do *wrong*? Was it deciding to have a baby without telling the father? Without telling *you*? I mean, people my age have babies all the time, and they're healthy. Was it sports? I was playing field hockey while his diaphragm was forming. Maybe I ran too hard, or fell and the impact tore something."

Even before she finished speaking, Susan was shaking her head. "I don't think that's how it happens."

"Then how *did* it?" Lily asked. She needed an explanation.

"It was a quirk of nature."

"Survival of the fittest? But why isn't *my* baby the fittest?"

"It may *be*."

"My baby was supposed to be perfect!"

"Your baby *is*."

A MOTHER HAD TO BE STRONG FOR HER CHILD, WHICH was why Susan still didn't call Rick. She knew that if she heard his voice, she would lose it.

But she had to do something and returning to school wasn't it. Rather, she hit the highway for Portland and, determined to raise Lily's spirits, ushered her to their favorite Old Port restaurant. Lily claimed she wasn't hungry, but when Susan reminded her that the baby needed feeding more than ever, she downed corn chowder and a chicken sandwich. Afterward, they went shopping, and here Lily was cautious.

"We don't know what'll happen," she said, looking at the price tag of the jeans Susan held.

"We do," Susan replied with confidence and led her to a fitting room. Two hours, three stores, and a fortune later, Lily had a maternity wardrobe befitting the luckiest pregnant teen. Susan knew that clothes weren't the answer, but they helped. Lily's spirits were better—though she still didn't call Mary Kate or Jess. This development set her apart. Her phone remained off in her pocket. Exhausted, she slept through the drive home.

Having been awake with her much of the night before, Susan was exhausted, too. But she had to catch up on some calls during the drive. This was the second day in a row that she was missing school. The timing couldn't have been worse.

Susan did what she could from the car to reschedule appointments she had missed, and then, back home, she followed Lily's lead and ignored the phone. Together, they made room in the closet for Lily's new things, and when Lily picked up the sweater she'd been making for a daughter, they talked knitting.

When Lily asked what she should knit for a boy, Susan said boys needed sweaters, too, and when Lily turned up her nose at designs involving trains or trucks, Susan suggested cables. They spent a while looking at patterns online.

Were they in denial? Absolutely. But the alternative was worse.

After dinner, Susan sent Lily off to study. *Life doesn't stop. You have exams in January. Yes, it does matter, even if you're going to Percy State. You can't let your grades slide.*

Lily went upstairs, leaving Susan to think about college,

which might have to be postponed if the baby was sick. PC KidsCare couldn't take a sick child, and, besides, Lily wouldn't want to leave the baby there if he had special needs. Mention of special needs sparked a new round of worries. Susan's health insurance was good, but was it good enough? Special education in Zaganack was good, but, again, was it good enough? And what did she know of Jane LaBreia, beyond an impressive wall of diplomas? And hospitals? The local one didn't have an NICU, which was a must for CDH babies. Most of them had surgery at birth—and Lily would have a cesarean herself, which meant a longer recovery.

By the time Susan drove back to school for the Christmas concert, she had worked herself into a panic. Had it not been for the likes of Evan Brewer, George Abbott, and Duncan Haith, she might have stayed home, but making a public appearance seemed crucial. She chatted, she smiled, she moved through the crowd, and made it through three-quarters of the program before slipping out. While she shivered in the cold waiting for her car to heat up, her panic returned.

That was when she called Rick, and while she thought *she* would be the one to lose it, he was. *Why didn't you call me yesterday? I'm her father! Do not treat this casually, Susan. It's a serious problem.* The barrage of questions that followed were more detailed than she could answer, and she grew more upset—the upshot of which was that Rick grew more calm. *No sweat, honey,* he finally said. *I'll get the answers. This is my specialty.*

She listened. She believed. She was actually feeling better by the time she got home, which was when she called Kate.

Chapter 21

KATE WAS STILL STRUGGLING WITH THE IDEA THAT
Mary Kate would be stuck at Percy State, that car seats and
diapers would be back, that there would be another mouth to
feed at a time when her sons were still eating everything in
sight. The house was supposed to feel bigger as children
moved out. She and Will were supposed to finally have *we*
time.

But her self-pity came to a halt with Susan's call. She listened with growing horror before finally saying, "I was *sure*
it'd be a false alarm." When Susan told her about the amnio,
she was quick to agree. "You're doing the right thing. The
more info you have, the better. What can I do to help?"

"Call Sunny and Pam? They need to know, but I don't have
it in me to phone."

Kate wasn't sure if she did either, but she said, "Consider it
done."

. . .

SUNNY WAS LYING IN BED READING *MARTHA STEWART Living*. Home décor magazines were a must for her work; they gave her ideas, often determining what she ordered for the store. But there were personal reasons as well. She loved changing the look of a room with a single item—loved plotting how to make her own home look like the site of A-list events. Right now, the house was dressed for Christmas, but that would change soon. There was nothing worse than a balsam fir whose time had come and gone.

Actually, she modified that thought, one thing *was* worse. Nurseries. Whenever she flipped a page and saw plans for a nursery, she flipped the page again. She refused to make any nursery in the house. She wasn't giving up the guest bedroom, where Dan's parents occasionally stayed, or the den, where she could watch *her* TV programs. If Jessica wanted a baby, she could keep it in her own room. Period. Cap *P*.

Actually, Sunny was thinking of setting the girl up in an apartment in town. It didn't have to be big, didn't have to cost much. It certainly wouldn't be the kind of exile Susan's parents had imposed. They would see each other. Just not all the time.

The phone rang. Dropping the magazine, she picked up to hear Kate conveying the news about Lily.

"Poor *Susan*," she wailed. "To have this on top of everything else? *Nightmare*. Is there a chance Lily will lose the baby?"

"A lot depends on how bad the CDH gets."

"And what the amnio turns up," Sunny realized with growing horror. "Can you imagine going through all this and then having the baby die?" And Sunny was worried about being *embarrassed*? Realizing that, she felt suddenly shallow, self-absorbed—*petty*. "What can I do to help?"

"Call Pam."

Petty was one thing, masochistic another. "Anything but that. Pam hasn't called me, and besides, I have a better idea. I'll cook. Susan shouldn't have to think about dinner while she's going through this. I'll organize a group of people, and we'll rotate. My bake sale friends would love to help out."

"Too soon," Kate cautioned, "but hold the thought. Let's see where this goes."

PAM HAD FALLEN ASLEEP ON THE BEDROOM CHAISE, but woke up fast when the phone rang. Grabbing it, she hurried out to the hall so that she wouldn't disturb Tanner and, even then, she spoke in a hushed voice.

"Susan?"

"It's Kate. I told Susan I'd call. She's beat."

Pam had been hoping Susan would call herself; it was about needing to know they were still friends. She wanted to distance herself from the three pregnancies, not from Susan, but it was a tricky dance. She feared she was missing the steps.

When Kate gave her the message, though, she could understand why Susan hadn't called. "How awful," she said. "So they just have to *wait*?"

"Pretty much. They'll do the amnio Monday, and they'll put a rush on getting the results, but with this hitting at the holidays, there may be a delay."

"Some Christmas for Susan and Lily. They're spending it with you, aren't they?"

"I was counting on it, but Susan's talking about staying home."

"Just the two of them? Not a good idea. They'll only brood. We're having Christmas dinner at my mother-in-law's house, or I'd invite them to join us. Not that Susan would want to," she added. "It could be awkward."

"Awkward for her or for you?" Kate asked.

"I'll forget you said that."

"No, Pam. Here's the thing. Right now, Susan needs support. You're either with her or not."

"Oh, Kate," Pam tried to explain, "it isn't about me. It's about being a Perry. There are expectations."

"Change them. Tanner didn't marry an airhead. He married a woman who has ideas and maybe a few loyalties of her own. Stand up for them."

"I *do*. Some subjects are just more sensitive."

"Hey, I know you hate it that our girls are pregnant, but did you ever think that maybe there was a time last summer when Abby wanted to be, too? If that had happened, you'd be singing a different tune."

"I'm not singing any tune," Pam said quickly, fearing Kate might be right and hurrying past the thought. "I'm not happy about what's happened any more than you are. I don't like that the school board is turning on Susan. I don't like that her job's in danger. I don't like that people are criticizing her as a mother, because if she's a bad one, so am I. I can't get Abby to talk, but I know she's unhappy. She misses being with your kids—and I miss being with you—but you're putting me right in the middle."

"No," Kate reasoned. "You've done that yourself. You see this great divide between being a Perry and being with us, but why do you have to choose? Why can't you tell Tanner how you feel? Why can't you tell Abby what you feel? I mean, you are on the *school board*, Pam. That gives you power."

"My name got me there." She hated to say it. But it was the truth.

"Fine," Kate cried, "but you *are* there, so you can say what you want. Do you agree with the old men on the board?"

"No."

"Tell them that."

Pam sighed. Quietly, she said, "I may, but right now, what can I do for Susan?"

"Get off the fence!"

Get off the phone, Pam told herself instead. "Okay, Kate. I hear you. Thanks for calling. I'll talk with Susan myself. Bye."

She hung up before Kate could say another word, but the silence mocked her. Needing to break it, she went down the hall into Abby's wing. A sliver of light under the door said the girl was still up. With a little knock, Pam turned the knob.

The first thing she saw was a blond ponytail. It swung when Abby glanced up from her desk.

Approaching, Pam leaned over her shoulder. "Spanish test?"

"After vacation. I was bored. It seemed like a good thing to do now."

Pam could identify with that. How often did she knit for lack of anything better to do?

"Have you heard anything?" Abby asked cautiously.

"Kate just called." Pam related the news.

Abby went pale. "Are they sure?"

"She's having more tests to monitor the extent of the condition."

"How can things like that happen?"

"They just do."

"But to Lily? She's the kindest person in the world."

Pam tucked a strand of hair behind her daughter's ear. "You miss her."

Abby didn't answer.

"Talk to me, please. I keep worrying that you'd have loved to be pregnant along with her."

"It wouldn't have been bad," her daughter said and stared, daring her to be scandalized.

Tanner's wife would have been, but, at that moment, she was Abby's mother, and very upset.

Abby looked away.

"Give her a call," Pam suggested. "I bet she'd love to hear from you."

Abby shrugged. "What would I say?"

"That you're sorry to hear about the baby. That doctors do amazing things. That if there's anything you can do to help, she should let you know."

"How could I possibly help?"

Pam searched for ideas. She had thought loyalty came naturally to Abby, until her daughter had outed her friends. But charity was a virtue, too. "Offer to drive her to school."

"She's pregnant, and I'm a Perry. You don't want me driving her to school."

"This problem with the baby changes things. It gives you an excuse to reach out."

"Dad wouldn't be happy."

"He wouldn't mind."

"Like he wouldn't mind if you spend all day Saturday at the barn? Be honest, Mom. He wants you to distance yourself from Susan. He thinks things are going to get worse."

Pam couldn't argue with that, but Kate's words were still fresh in her ear. *Get off the fence!* This might be a roundabout way. "Think about Lily. She could use your support."

"Well, maybe I'm a little angry at her, too. I mean, it was so easy for her to get pregnant—so maybe she deserves this."

"You just said she was the kindest person in the world."

"She *is*. But she's pregnant and I'm not. So what do I have in common with Lily?"

"School. Friends."

"I'm leaving for college in August. She's staying here."

"You can't IM or text? You won't be back every vacation?

You will, Abby. You'll be back, and someday you'll have a baby of your own—"

"How do you know that?" Abby cried shrilly. "Maybe I won't! Maybe I'll have some kind of fabulous career and be so busy that I absolutely won't have *time* for any of that. Don't plan things for me, Mom. If you're waiting to be busy with a grandchild, don't."

Startled by the outburst, Pam managed a meek, "I'm not waiting."

Abby stared at her mother for another minute before turning back to her book with the whip of her ponytail, effectively shutting her out.

"I CAN'T GO TO SCHOOL," LILY SAID THE NEXT MORN-ing when, hearing no sound, Susan went into her room.

"Why not?" Susan asked, though the answer didn't surprise her at all.

"I'm giving the baby a rest."

"Like the baby is the one taking notes in class?"

"Come on, Mom. It's only a half day anyway."

"That makes it perfect, then. Easy day, light exercise, no stress." When doubt remained in Lily's eyes, Susan sat and traced the heart of the girl's face. "I thought we put the field hockey theory to rest yesterday, but if not, please listen to me, sweetheart. Nothing you do"—she punctuated the words with her hands—"will hurt the baby. The doctor said you should do what you normally do. She said you need to be moving around."

"I feel safer here. And I know my baby. He needs a rest."

"That's you, Lily. You need a rest. And you'll get one starting at noon. But you've already missed two days of school this week."

"Exactly, so what's half a day more?"

"Call it practice. Moms have to do things they don't feel like doing. You're scared, but you can't lie in bed for the next five months."

"It may not go that long," Lily warned, looking frightened.

"Upbeat, sweetie. Moms have to be upbeat."

"You mean, say things they know aren't true, just to cheer up their kids?"

Susan made a wry sound. "That would be a lie. This isn't. It's easy to imagine the worst, but why do we have to do that? CDH is treatable—and we don't even know he *has* it. Here's the thing. When you're up and moving, your little boy feels like he's in a warm little swing. It's soothing, don't you think? Besides, Mary Kate and Jess need to see that you're okay. They e-mailed me last night to ask how you were. You made a pact to do this together, sweetie. You have to answer their texts."

LILY WASN'T SURE IF HER MOTHER WAS BEING SARcastic. After having been so angry over the pact—so angry over Lily's pregnancy itself—Susan seemed to have accepted both. Lily didn't know if the turnaround would last, but she did go to school, and not only to see Mary Kate and Jess. She had an agenda.

First, she sought out the volleyball coach and resigned from the team. "I know it's still okay to play," she said, "but if something bad happens to the baby, I'll always wonder."

Second, she went looking for Jacob Senter. Pulling him out of the hall crowds between classes, she said, "You're going to med school. I need a second opinion." She explained what the tests showed. "I know my baby will need treatment, but how will the treatment affect him? Will he be normal? Will he be able to play like other kids? Will this problem cause other ones as he gets older?"

Jacob looked alarmed. "Uh . . . jeez, Lily, I . . . I don't know. I'm not in med school yet. I'm not even in college. I was wait-listed at Duke. Did Mary Kate tell you?"

Lily gasped. "No. Does she know?" Realizing it was a loaded question, she rushed on. "You'll get in in April. You're too smart not to. And you *do* understand medical terms. Maybe you could Google *CDH* and give me your take?"

"I have to spend Christmas vacation writing college apps."

"I have to spend it worrying about test results. This is life or death, Jacob."

Cautiously, he asked, "Is it that serious?"

"Surgery on an infant? I'd say."

"Does this happen often? Is it, like, more common in moms your age?"

"You mean, is Mary Kate at risk? No. The odds would be totally against that." Lily took his arm. "But every pregnancy involves risk. You need to start talking to Mary Kate. She's stressed without you. That could hurt your baby."

"She didn't ask if I wanted to be a dad, Lily. She didn't tell me what she was planning. Did she think I'd just go along? I mean, this changes everything!"

Lily was sober. "Right. I want my baby born perfect, but it may not be. So now I have to do things I don't want to do, because that's a mother's job. Isn't it a father's job, too?"

The bell rang before Jacob could answer, and they had to run in opposite directions to make it to class. But Lily was barely back in the hall after U.S. gov when Robbie came along-side.

"What's wrong with the baby?" he asked.

Jacob must have blabbed. But Lily wasn't sure how much to say. Telling Jacob to talk with Mary Kate was one thing; they'd been together forever. Not Lily and Robbie.

"The baby's okay," she offered tentatively.

"Sami Phelps says there's a problem with its insides."

Lily stopped walking. "Sami?"

"She heard you tell the volleyball coach that you couldn't play anymore. What's wrong?"

Lily might have asked what was wrong with Sami that she couldn't keep her mouth shut, except it was her own fault. She should have been more careful when she had talked with the coach. She supposed that if word would be spreading about this now, Robbie was the one person who really did have a right to know.

As they walked, she explained. He asked who her doctor was and when the next test was scheduled, but when he asked if he could go along, she refused. Robbie was the boy across the street who just happened to have fathered her child the one time they'd been together. Now that she was pregnant, she had no idea what their relationship was supposed to be.

Chapter 22

SUSAN WOKE ON CHRISTMAS MORNING WONDERING THE
same thing about her mother. They hadn't talked since the
funeral, and barely then. But Christmas was Christmas, and
Ellen was alone. Though Susan had sent a gift, she wanted to call.

But first, there was hot French toast, the traditional holiday
breakfast she and Lily shared, then their own little ritual of
gifts—small things for each other, collected one per month
through the year, along with the complete set of rosewood
knitting needles for which Lily had been not-so-subtly pining
and the antique oak spinning wheel Susan had craved as an
inspiration to learn how to spin.

Lily didn't mention the baby, though Susan saw her touching her stomach from time to time, communicating with her
child in a way it would feel, looking soulful and mature. Susan
would have done anything to give her back a piece of her
childhood for Christmas. But the best she could do was try to
cheer her up.

"Have you thought of a name?" she asked.

Lily looked surprised by the question—coming from Susan, who hadn't wanted this baby to be real. "Chloe."

Susan smiled. "Try again."

"I haven't thought of boys' names."

"You will." She added a soft, "He'll be here with us next year. Won't that be something?"

It would be something, she realized. Her first Christmas away from home had been lonely. Same with the second and third. Then Lily grew, and Susan made friends, and Christmas at Kate's came to be. And still Susan dreamed of the day when she and Lily would have more.

Next year they might.

"HI, MOM, IT'S SUSAN. MERRY CHRISTMAS."

"Merry Christmas to you," Ellen said with her usual reserve.

"How are you doing?"

"I'm fine. I went to church last night."

"You did?" Historically, her parents went in the afternoon. "Good for you. Will you be going to Jack's later?"

"Yes. For lunch. At one, I believe."

"That should be nice."

"And you?"

Had the question been specific, Susan might have shared some of what was happening. But Ellen didn't want details. Her tone was more polite than interested.

So Susan said, "We'll be at my friend Kate's. I've told you about Kate. She's our head dyer. By the way, did you get the package I sent?" It held yarn, packed in project bags that were all the rage—though Susan had been careful to choose ones in the most muted colors. No fuchsia heart in Ellen. Hot pink wouldn't do.

"Yes," her mother said. "Thank you. I have to finish what I'm working on before I start something else, though."

"I know. I just thought you'd like to see our newest yarns. They won't go on sale for another few months."

"You said that in your note. They're very pretty."

Very pretty. Susan took the compliment as the best Ellen could give. "We're rushing out samples to shoot for the catalogue. You're the best knitter I know. Want to make a scarf?"

"Oh, well, I'm not quite finished with the other."

"Okay. Maybe another time." Susan paused, but there were no questions about Lily, Susan's work, or even vacation plans, any of which might have offered an opening to share the news. Finally, Susan just said, "So, I'll let you go, Mom. Have a good time at Jack's."

"Thank you, Susan. Bye."

DESPITE YEARS OF UNSATISFYING COMMUNICATION, Susan always hoped for more. This time she had hoped that with no one in the background monitoring Ellen's end of the conversation, there might be a change—had hoped that if, deep down inside, Ellen did love her daughter, there would be some small display of interest in Susan or Lily. After all, Ellen was alone, perhaps lonely, and surely more attuned to mortality than she had been in the past.

And Susan was as needy as she had ever been. She would have liked to share what was happening with Lily, so that her mother would put on a bright face for *her*. Indeed, the one person whose approval might counter the disapproval of the town was Ellen Tate. A word of encouragement from Ellen would go a long way.

That said, Susan was actually feeling heartened. The *Gazette*'s Christmas Eve edition was skimpy, with only a handful of letters to the editor and none about the pact. Zaganackians, bless their souls, were in holiday mode.

She and Lily went ahead and had Christmas dinner with Kate's family, all of whom did a masterful job of ignoring the upcoming amnio, and on Saturday, to distract themselves, Susan took Lily to the barn.

Kate wasn't there. She and her family had piled into the car for a last-minute trip to New York City, and though Kate invited them to come along, Susan declined. She wasn't in the mood to share a hotel room with a crowd, and besides, it had started to snow.

Which was lucky for Sunny and Dan, who had taken the kids skiing.

And lucky for Pam and Tanner, who had taken theirs to Hilton Head.

But driving to New York in a nor'easter, with a daughter whose pregnancy might be troubled, was not Susan's idea of fun. Besides, she had promised Lily a rest, when, in fact, she needed one herself.

So they had the barn to themselves—at least, that was the plan. Ignoring the wail of the wind, they dyed wool for pure fun, playing with wild combinations of colors, and tested out a new yarn winder that a vendor had sent. They were getting ready to bundle up and go for lunch when the barn door opened and, in a snowy burst, Rick appeared.

Susan wasn't entirely surprised. He usually came unannounced, never quite knowing when breaking news would hijack his plans. His arrival today, though, with so much hanging over their heads, was a gift.

It was actually only the first of several. He brought lunch, which they ate there at the barn, and afterward he followed them during the slow drive home in the snow. Once in the house, he set up the Blu-ray player he had bought them for Christmas along with a boxful of movies, a popcorn maker, and bags of kernels.

As diversions went, he was a huge help.

ON MONDAY MORNING, RICK INSISTED ON DRIVING. Having done his homework, he agreed with Susan's decision to have the amnio. Moreover, since he knew everything about the test itself, as well as the doctor involved, he could answer a lot of Lily's questions.

Susan could have managed without him—a good mother rose to the occasion—but with the worry shared, the load was less.

That said, she was the one who held Lily's hand through the procedure. She wouldn't have had it any other way.

Back home after the procedure, Lily settled in on the sofa. Two hours of rest, the doctor had advised, but with a foot of snow outside, a stack of good movies inside, and Rick eagerly waiting on his two women, there was little for Lily to do anyway. They watched movies; they played Scrabble; they kept an eye out for cramping, contractions, or fever, but Lily weathered the amnio well.

By the next morning, that particular fear was gone.

There were still the results to await and, of course, Susan's fate, but with school closed and the streets deserted, she could almost imagine that the attacks on her were over—that, like during a flu epidemic, snow cleared the air. She worked for a while on the midyear report she had to present to the school board in January, refusing to consider that the job might not be hers by then, and Rick worked beside her, a novel distraction.

When she closed her laptop, he closed his and suggested

they drive to Boston. Since he rarely stayed for more than two or three days, it was a gift Susan couldn't refuse. In no time, he booked a hotel suite, made several nights' worth of dinner reservations, and, knowing that Susan and Lily adored the ballet, bought tickets to *The Nutcracker*. Once in Boston, they found so much else to do that they stayed until New Year's morning. They were packing to check out when Susan called her mother again.

"It's Susan. Happy New Year, Mom."

There was a cordial "And to you."

"How are you doing?"

"I'm fine. I went to the Cummings' for dinner last night."

"You did?" It was an annual New Year's Eve event, but Susan hadn't been sure Ellen would go so soon after John's death. "I'm glad. Did they have a big crowd?"

"Not this year. I wouldn't have gone if they had. I don't love crowds."

"But they're all friends."

"Too many people," Ellen said and was quiet for a moment, before abruptly asking, "Is Rick with you?"

"Yes. Why do you ask?"

"Big Rick called. He said Rick was visiting him and left. Something about seeing Lily."

Susan caught Rick's eye. *Does your dad know about Lily?* she mouthed. Rick shook his head. "He's been here since Saturday," she told Ellen and might have comfortably segued into Lily's news, except that there was nothing comfortable about Lily's news. Telling Ellen would be testing a relationship that was shaky at best. She had no idea how her mother would react.

So she simply said, "We've had a great time."

"That's nice."

"Big Rick was sweet to call you."

"It was a short call. He's feeling bad that he didn't see your father before he died. He asked what I was doing with your father's fishing gear. He'd like to buy it."

"Do you have other plans for it?"

"No. But I can't think about disposing of things. It's too soon."

"I understand. It is. You must miss Dad."

"He was a good husband."

Susan wanted to add he was a good father, but couldn't get the words out. He had loved her once, but not when it really counted. As for being communicative, even in the best of times, they had never been confidants.

Was being a good father altogether different from being a good mother? The world would say yes, which meant that the bar was higher for mothers. That didn't seem fair.

"Well," Susan said. "I guess that's it for the holidays. If you ever feel like getting away, we have a spare room. I'd love you to come."

There was a pause, then a sharp, "Is that because your father can't?"

Susan refused to be baited. "No, Mom. I invited both of you soon after I bought the house, but you said Dad wouldn't fly east. I repeated the invitation several times. This is just once more."

"Well," Ellen said, more measured again, "I'm not yet ready to think of going places. But thank you. I'll keep the invitation in mind. Bye, Susan."

AS THEY HEADED HOME LATER THAT DAY, SUSAN HAD a hollow feeling. She blamed it first on her mother—*would it have been so difficult for her to say she would come?*—but by the time they hit the New Hampshire border, the hollowness was a knot. Returning to Zaganack meant returning to everything she had been trying to forget. Now it rushed back. They still had the weekend, but she couldn't shake the idea that this was the calm before the storm. By Monday, the town would be up and running again, Susan would be back at school, Rick would be gone, Lily would be waiting for the test results. This little break would be done.

SUSAN CREPT DOWN THE HALL THAT NIGHT, CARE-fully avoiding the floorboards that creaked, but she wanted to lie with Rick. They had been good—nothing prior to going to Boston, and at the hotel, he had used the foldout in the living room, while Susan shared the bedroom with Lily. But if he was leaving, she wanted this first.

He was reading. With a finger to her lips, she quietly closed the door, tiptoed to the bed, and pulled her nightgown over her head. Naked, she knelt over him, but she left the light on. Too often they made love in the dark. This time she wanted to see the way his sable hair was messed, the way his cheeks grew red under his tan. She wanted to see his hands on her, wanted to see his face when, rearing back, he found his release.

Afterward, she lay in his arms. The light was out now, heightening other senses. Being naked with Rick was her chocolate after a diet of veggies. She was savoring every last bite.

The thought made her smile.

"What?" he asked.

"You're my splurge."

"Good. I was thinking I'd stick around for a few days."

Startled, she rose on an elbow to see his face. "You don't usually."

"I don't usually have a child in crisis."

"There's really nothing to do. We're just waiting."

"I can wait, too," he said, adding soberly, "What'll we do if there are other abnormalities?"

"She won't hear of abortion."

"What if the baby doesn't have a prayer in hell of living?"

She rested her cheek on his chest and whispered, "I don't know."

"To carry it to term and then lose it within hours of its birth would be devastating."

"I know."

"She'll need our advice. What would yours be?"

Susan wanted to say she couldn't go there. Only she had been doing just that in unbidden moments since the first sonogram. "I saw the heartbeat."

"You agree with her, then."

"I don't know." How to explain her feelings, when they were so complex? "Being pregnant right now is not what I wanted for Lily. I wouldn't have minded if she miscarried spontaneously. If that makes me a horrible mother, I'm a horrible mother, but my first thought was for the well-being of my own child. Seeing that heartbeat? That's something else. If it were earlier in the pregnancy, I might say we should terminate it. But she's almost halfway through. I don't know if I could tell her to do that. I don't know if it would be the best thing for her. She's come this far. She's bonded with this child. She may need to see it through, and if she has to deal with sorrow, she will."

Rick was quiet.

"What would you tell her?" Susan asked.

He took a breath. "I don't know. I haven't seen the heartbeat."

"Stick around and you will," Susan warned, then added, "But how can you stay? The network calls you constantly."

"They're spoiled. Maybe I have to unspoil them."

"What does your contract say?"

"That I'm a free agent in two months. They haven't made an offer yet. Money's an issue. I make more than most. They can hire two twenty-somethings for what they pay me."

"But you have a following. They won't want you to leave. They'll renew your contract."

"They may change the terms. Am I prepared to take less money for more work? With a child starting college?"

Susan was wistful. "She's made it easy for you there. Percy State costs less than the Ivy League. But if you blow them off, where would you go? Another network?"

"I could. I could also write. You said it yourself. I have a following. I've been places in the last few years that would make for great books."

"But you love traveling."

"I'd travel. Just not as much." He moved his legs. "Your feet are cold."

She might have laughed and said something about usually sleeping in socks, but she only murmured, "You can't stay in Zaganack. I might get used to leaning on you, and that'd be bad because you will leave, sooner or later. It's in your blood."

"How do you know?"

"Look at your *life*, Rick."

"I am. I'm thinking I have a helluva lot of frequent flyer miles and nowhere to go. Susie, why are you picking a fight?"

"I'm being realistic."

"I could rent somewhere in town if you don't want me living here. I could even buy a little house of my own."

"In Zaganack? I wouldn't do that, if I were you. If my job falls through, I may have to leave."

He was quiet. "You don't want me here."

"I do," she said. "That's the problem. I'm trying to protect myself. And what about Lily? If she gets used to having you here and you go, she'll be devastated."

Again he was quiet. Then, "I'm going to be a grandfather."

Susan heard the awe in his voice and rode with it. "What do you want to be called? Gramps? Papa Rick? Your dad is Grampa, so you can't use that."

"Why not? He'll be Great-Grampa. Wonder what he'll have to say about that."

"When'll you tell him?"

"When we know more."

Susan crept back down the hall soon after that. She said she wanted to be in her own room if Lily needed her, but it was all part of the dependency thing. She could get used to sleeping with Rick. Even now, her bed felt cold.

She reached for socks. They were ones she had knit of a PC Wool colorway from two years ago—Bobcat Ridge, done in shades of gray, white, and gold. Thinking of PC Wool made her think of the catalogue shots that were overdue, which made her think of Pam, which made her think of the school board—not the nicest of thoughts, but paling in comparison to the prospect of a baby born ill.

RICK'S PRESENCE DIDN'T ELIMINATE THE WORRY, but he was a distraction for Lily, which was a help. Susan called the doctor's office twice a day, even over the weekend, but there was nothing.

Nor was there any news on Monday morning. In fact, quiet seemed to be the order of the day in general, when school resumed. She greeted students, none of whom mentioned Lily, the pact, or the *Gazette*. She was able to make headway on her midyear report, as well as on the staff evaluations she had to do before hiring for fall. For that little while, she felt she was the good principal, the good mother, and even the good friend, because when news came midday Monday that the oldest living Cass had died, the first thing she did was to call Pam.

They didn't talk for long. Pam was distracted by what sounded like a newsroom on her end. But Susan imagined she appreciated the call.

Chapter 23

THE PASSING OF A CASS WENT BEYOND ZAGANACK.
The story broke online and was covered on the evening news
and in newspapers nationwide. Funeral plans were extensive,
allowing for attendance both by Zaganackians and by members of the national business community who had known and
admired Henry Cass. The governor and one of Maine's sena-
tors planned to attend.

It was a sorrowful occasion. But Susan wasn't sorry for the
preoccupation of the town. Coming on the heels of the holiday
breather, this was another event that deflected attention from
Susan's issues with the board.

With the town shut down on Wednesday for the funeral,
there was no school, which was why Susan was home when
she got the amnio results. She had gone upstairs alone to call
the doctor, thinking to spare Lily another roller-coaster
moment. When she was done, she pressed the phone to her
chest, closed her eyes in a tiny prayer, and ran down the stairs.

Lily was in the den. She had a chem text open on her lap, but she was knitting. When she saw Susan, the peace on her face turned to fear.

Susan burst into a smile. "The baby is fine!" She took Lily's face in her hands. "No genetic disorder, no chromosome abnormality, no neural tube defect. He is perfect."

Lily closed her eyes and let out a long, grateful sigh.

Hearing a quieter version of that, Susan looked back at Rick, who stood under the archway looking relieved.

"But he still has CDH?" Lily asked.

Susan would have given anything to deny it, but denial wouldn't make things easier. "Yes. The sonogram next week will tell us more—but this is big, sweetheart. Ruling out these other things makes what we have to face absolutely *doable*." Susan kissed her forehead. "This is a *huge* relief. *Definitely* cause for hope."

LIKEWISE WAS THURSDAY'S *GAZETTE*, WHICH WAS A cover-to-cover eulogy for Henry Cass. There were histories of his role in the store, lengthy stories of his life, full-page memorials sponsored by Perry & Cass departments and other business interests for miles around. There were three full pages of letters to the editor, every one of them a tribute to the man.

Susan didn't read each in detail. She had been at the funeral and heard the praise, and while these letters were lovely, she was simply pleased to have faded from view herself.

THAT CHANGED ON FRIDAY NIGHT. WITH RICK AT THE house, Susan worked late at school. She had just arrived home and was hanging up her coat when the front doorbell rang. Shooting a puzzled look at Rick and Lily, who were together at the stove, she went to answer it.

The man outside was thirtyish and wore a down parka and jeans. "Susan?" he asked in a friendly enough way, his breath white in the frosty air.

She gave him a curious smile. "Do I know you?"

"I'm Jonathan Hicks. I'm with NBC. We were in town covering the Cass funeral. I understand you're the principal of the high school. Do you think we could talk?"

Susan was uneasy. "I can't tell you much about Henry Cass. I didn't know him personally."

"We're doing a bigger piece on the town. Zaganack is unique in the way it combines business with tourism. How long have you lived here?"

Looking beyond him, she saw a van at the curb. It had the call letters of the Portland affiliate on its side and a satellite dish on the top. She was *very* uneasy. "Not as long as most. If you're doing a piece on the town, there are others who can tell you more."

"They sent me to you," he began, then abruptly stopped.

Rick had approached. "What did you say your name was?" he asked the reporter.

"Jon Hicks." He seemed puzzled. "Man, do you look like—" He swore under his breath. "Damn. You beat me. But you don't do local feed. Last I saw footage of you, you were in . . . in *Botswana*."

"Close enough," Rick said, confirming his identity. "What're you after?"

"Same thing you are."

Rick smiled. "I doubt that. Who sent you here?"

"The guy who heads the Chamber of Commerce. He said

Susan was a good example of Gen X and that she had an inter-esting story to tell."

Susan bet the head of the Chamber of Commerce had said a lot more. Neal Lombard was the school board member who had suggested she take a leave.

"What story?" she asked.

"A pregnancy pact."

Not knowing what to say, much less how to react, she was relieved when Rick took over. "There's no story."

"Then why are you here?"

"Susan is family."

"*Your* family? The guy didn't tell me *that*."

"No. So you know who I am, but I don't know you. Are you out of Portland?"

"New York. Assistant producer."

"Ahh. Bloodhound sniffing out stories. Got a card?" In an instant, he was studying it. "Well, Jon Hicks, you're barking up the wrong tree. For one thing, this town's about Perry and Cass. For another, I know your boss, and if he gets wind that you're harassing my family, he won't be happy."

The producer took a step back. "Hey, man, no harassment."

"Good," Rick said with a smile. "Keep it that way. Hey, my girl and I just made dinner. I'd invite you to stay, only we don't have extra. We'll talk shop another time, okay?" He put a hand high on the doorframe, watching Jonathan leave. Only when the van pulled away did he ease Susan back inside.

That was when reality hit. "The national press?" she cried. "What *next*?"

"It was inevitable."

"I thought the *Gazette* was bad, but if this is on network TV, we're in trouble. A pregnancy pact is hot stuff. If he runs his story, Zaganack will be inundated with media from all over the country. I'll lose my job—I mean, I'll *have* to step aside or the kids will suffer. The whole *town* will suffer."

"Who is Neal Lombard?" Rick asked calmly.

Susan folded her arms. "He came on the school board right before Pam. He has four troubled sons, and he's covering up his own sense of inadequacy by pointing the finger at people like me. He must have been upset when the *Gazette* left me alone this week. We had the media in town, and he couldn't resist slipping them word. He's killing two birds with one stone—ruining me and creating publicity for the town. The Chamber wants tour buses here. Neal doesn't care what brings them."

"It's okay, Susie. I can pull strings. If Jon Hicks goes ahead with a piece on this town, he won't mention you."

"He may mention you. You told him you were family." Not many people in town knew that. Susan had always been miserly with the information. Lily, too. Rick was their secret.

He scratched the back of his head. "Okay. Well, I had a choice. Either I had a solid personal reason for being here, or he was going to think he had fallen into a *really* big story, in which case he'd call in reinforcements and stake out the place."

"What if Neal Lombard calls someone else?"

"Talk to Pam. See what she can do."

PAM WASN'T THRILLED TO BE ASKED TO HELP. "I don't know Neal very well."

"Tanner does. A word from him would go a long way toward shutting up the press."

"Oh, Susan, with the funeral and all . . ."

"The funeral is over," Susan argued. If Pam was a friend, she would do this. "Henry was long retired from the day-to-day running of Perry and Cass, so it's not like there'll be a corporate change in command. The company's had good press in the last few days. This would be bad press. Does Tanner want that?"

"No. Okay. Let me talk with him."

BUT EITHER SHE DIDN'T OR TANNER CHOSE NOT TO act, or it was simply too late, because Susan was returning from visiting a Spanish II class on Monday morning when a young woman fell into step. "Ms. Tate? I'm Melissa Randolph, *People* magazine. I wonder if we could talk."

Susan died a little inside. "About what?"

"Teen pregnancy." The woman was in her early twenties. Wearing dark tights, a pencil skirt, and heels that stilted her walk, she wasn't as intimidating as Jonathan Hicks with his satellite van. That made it easier for Susan to stay calm.

"Sure. Follow me." She continued on to her office, thinking the whole way about what Rick would do. When they were seated, she asked, "Melissa Randoph? Is that correct? What do you do for the magazine?"

"I'm a reporter," the woman said and, as if to prove it, pulled out a dog-eared notebook and prepared to take notes.

"Were you here for the Cass funeral?" Susan asked.

"No. I just arrived."

"Specifically to do a story on teen pregnancies?"

"Actually, the story is on mothers—the whose-fault-is-it kind of thing. We're running a story in this week's issue, but we just heard about your situation and wanted to rush it in. Our focus is on average middle-class mothers. We have one in Chicago whose son is into identity theft, and one in Tucson whose DUI daughter killed a friend. Both mothers are being skewered, even though they're hardworking and well-liked. You're in the same boat."

"I am?" Susan asked, mildly annoyed. She didn't consider her daughter, Mary Kate, or Jess in the league of a thief or a drunk. "Where did you hear that?"

"The local paper."

Susan frowned. "Do your production people read the Zaganack *Gazette*?"

"We got a tip."

"Ahhh," Susan said. "That wouldn't by chance be the local Chamber of Commerce trying to drum up a little more attention for the town? And you fell for it?"

The reporter squirmed. "We've talked with teachers and students. We know that three girls are pregnant. Of the moms involved, you're the most visible."

"There's been a spike in teen pregnancies all over the country," Susan said. "I'd guess that we're at the low end of the spectrum."

"But the three in question formed a pact. That's a headline. And you were pregnant at seventeen yourself."

Susan refused to react. "I'm a school principal. I worry about pact behavior as it affects other students. If a pact leads to violence, it's troubling."

"You don't consider a *pregnancy* pact troubling?"

Susan sat back. "Any teen pregnancy is troubling."

"Especially when it involves your own daughter, I would think."

"I'm sorry. I won't talk about specific cases."

"I understand that as principal you have to say that. But I really want to talk with you as a mother. Would you be more comfortable if we talked in your home?"

Susan gave her a sympathetic smile. "This really is a private matter. My first priorities are my daughter and my school. I don't aspire to being nationally recognized."

There was a pause. "That's a 'no comment,' then?"

"Oh, it's a comment," Susan said, perhaps pedantically, but

she was suddenly livid. "My comment is, my first priorities are my daughter and my school. I don't aspire to being nationally recognized." She looked at her watch and stood. "I have a class to teach. I need time to review my notes."

Looking skeptical, the reporter rose, too. "Since when does a principal teach?"

"Since budget cuts discourage hiring subs when a regular teacher is sick." She opened the door. "I'm sorry I can't help you. I'm sure your piece will be just fine focusing on those other two women." She waited until the reporter left, then closed the door and grabbed the phone. Rick was working at home. Her hand shook punching in the number.

"*People* magazine," she said. "Just here. Neal must have called them, too. How scary is that?"

"What did you say?" Rick asked quietly.

"That I wouldn't talk. But she says she's already talked with faculty and students. Was she bluffing? There are teachers— *like* Evan Brewer—who would love to cut me down, and kids I've disciplined who'd spill their guts in a second. She could write her story without ever quoting me, and the piece will be totally skewed, like the editorial in the *Gazette*. I could talk with her and set things straight. But then Phil would be on top of me for talking with her, and the school board would say I was hurting the town."

"Did she have a photographer with her?"

"I didn't see one. But I wasn't looking. Now I have to teach a class. Do I dare leave my office?"

"You have to. You have a job. Go do it, while I make a few calls."

RICK SPENT MOST OF THE DAY TRYING TO PLUG THE leak, but it had spread too far. The media was hungry for headlines, and the juicier the better. That meant the Zaganack story took on hyperbolic twists. The pact grew to twelve; the girls were the leaders of the senior class; Susan advocated teen pregnancy.

By day's end, she had received calls from two other magazines and *Inside Edition,* not to mention multiple messages from Sunny and Kate.

"Do *not* talk," she advised Kate, who sounded frazzled.

"They called me at the barn and again at home. They're obsessed with our friendship and the idea of our daughters forming a pact. How do they know where I live? This is *such* a violation."

Sunny was furious. "Dan talked with the last one and threatened to sue for harassment. Of course, he doesn't have a case, because what's one phone call, but how did this get out, Susan, who *told* these people to *call*?"

Susan figured that Neal Lombard might have lit the match, but that others were fanning the flames. She kept hoping nothing would come of the calls, but that night, *Inside Edition* did a piece on high school pacts, with its reporter live on the steps of Susan's school citing the three Zaganack girls as the latest example.

The media inquiries continued into Tuesday and Wednesday, but, at some point, Susan tuned them out. On top of her usual work, she had a parent coffee to host, a grant application to file, and two drunk students and a bully to deal with— which wasn't to say she wasn't aware of the buzz around school. People were talking about Lily, about Susan, about the press.

Phil was decidedly unhappy.

That said, the buzz might have been in her own head. It was all well and good to try to stem a scandal, to fearfully surf the Web and assess the damage. But Lily's next sonogram was coming on fast, bringing with it a worry that drove the others from her mind.

SUSAN BLESSED RICK NOW. PULLING OUT ALL STOPS, he found the hospital with the most up-to-date machine and booked the most highly recommended and experienced radiologist to do the sonogram.

Early Thursday morning, they headed back to Boston. Forbidden to pee, Lily was uncomfortable, but she didn't complain. She was doing what had to be done, though she looked fearful and very much seventeen. Susan kept reminding her that amnio had ruled out complications, making CDH a simple problem. But the machine was a more sophisticated one, sensitive enough to pick up the slightest abnormality, and the doctor—a woman—was somber. Susan was intimidated, and she was thirty-five. She could only imagine what Lily felt.

Rick stayed with them, asking the doctor to back up here, explain this, repeat that, with an insistence Susan might not have had, vacillating as she was between fascination with the baby's features and dismay at the extent of the problem.

An hour later, Lily was squeezed in for an MRI, and an hour after that, for consultation with the surgeon with whom Rick had connected prior to the trip. This surgeon, too, came highly recommended. He was a specialist in treating congenital diaphragmatic hernia.

He had already talked with the radiologist who had done the sonogram and was able to compare today's pictures with those taken three weeks before. Sitting beside Lily and Susan, he showed her the changes.

"With the mildest cases of CDH, the condition remains steady," the man explained gently, "but you can see the difference three weeks has made. We use mathematical formulas to describe the degree of herniation, but I'd rather talk here in lay terms. Look at the two pictures. Look at the lungs. See how the one on the left is smaller than the one on the right in this newest shot?"

"It's *teeny*," Lily cried out in dismay.

"Definitely smaller, because look here, the intestines, the liver, the kidneys are crowding it out. This kind of adverse movement in three weeks suggests a momentum that will prevent lung development and eventually affect the heart. Even if this child makes it to term, he won't have the means to survive outside the womb. Some parents believe that if that happens, it was meant to be." He looked beyond Lily to Susan and Rick.

It was the moment of truth, Susan knew. If they didn't want this baby, now was the time to speak up. But the only thing she felt was that this child was part of her child, that it was already familiar to her, and that if she ever fought for anything in her life, it should be for this.

In that instant, she was fully committed. "We want this baby to live."

He smiled and looked at Lily, who nodded in agreement. "Then we operate. This kind of case excites me, because we're catching it early. Correcting the abnormality now maximizes the baby's chances."

Susan put an encouraging arm around Lily, who, sounding very mature, asked for details of the operation.

In clear terms, the doctor explained. "We make two tiny incisions, one in your belly and one in your uterus, and we insert a tiny telescope into your baby's mouth." When Lily made a sound, he squeezed her hand. "Not at all hard for the baby. Don't forget, he doesn't use that mouth for anything much yet. We put the telescope into his trachea and leave a tiny balloon behind, blown up just enough to obstruct the windpipe."

"Obstruct?" Lily asked in alarm.

The doctor smiled. "The baby doesn't need that windpipe until the moment he's born, but a funny thing happens when we block it. The lung starts to grow," he said. "As the lung grows, it pushes those wayward internal organs back out of the chest cavity and away from the heart." Again, he looked at Susan and Rick. "It's remarkable, really."

"How do you get the balloon out of his windpipe?" Lily asked, calmer again.

"Very simply. We do the beginnings of a cesarean section, lift the baby's head out of the uterus while the umbilical cord is still attached to the placenta and doing the breathing for him. Then we reach into his mouth and pull out the balloon. We cut the cord, and your son is born."

Lily was momentarily rapt. "And he'll be okay? This fixes the problem?"

"There's never a guarantee. But we've had remarkable success. Once we've blocked the windpipe, the organs grow normally. Minor surgery soon after birth closes the hole in the diaphragm."

"What does minor surgery mean?"

"Low risk. We have it down to a science."

"Will he have a scar?"

"A small one, but it'll look smaller the bigger he gets. Babies grow; scars don't."

Susan wasn't bothered by scars, if the result was survival. "Will Lily be able to carry to term?" she asked.

"I've had some cases where we've taken the baby at thirty-eight weeks, which is considered full term. More likely, we'd take him a little earlier. In order to know when, we'll be monitoring him closely after the procedure. We'll start with a weekly sonogram; then, if all is going well, we'll space them out. We want to watch that little lung grow."

"Will all my babies have this?" Lily asked.

"Your boy only has CDH. If there were other abnormalities, I'd be more cautious, but with just CDH? Chances of a repeat are slim."

LILY WAS NUMB AS THEY HEADED HOME. CRUISING the highway between states, she knitted in the backseat. It was the only thing she could do that brought comfort. Last summer seemed an eon away and the person she had been then pathetically naïve.

At least now she believed her baby had a chance. She hadn't loved the radiologist, but the surgeon was nice, and if Rick said he was good, he was good. She wasn't even as frightened by the pictures. Driving down this morning, she had expected worse—even that her baby was dead. It wasn't until she saw the heart beating strongly on the screen earlier that she truly believed he was still alive.

She was the mom, which meant she had the final say on what they did for her baby. But having her parents in her corner meant a lot. Her mother had said they would deal. And so they would.

Lily accepted that her little boy had this problem and that they could fix it. The surgery was scheduled, along with tests to monitor the fetus during the next two weeks. As for weekly trips to Boston, no sweat. She could knit.

Missing school worried her a little. Now that other friends were hearing from colleges, she sometimes thought about Wesleyan and Williams, both of which she loved. Briefly, she had considered applying even if she was pregnant. Her scores were good enough. For all she knew, the schools would like having a student who was different.

But it would be too difficult, too far from home, too distant from Mary Kate and Jess. Especially now.

Percy State was definitely the way to go. But even there, if she missed too much school this spring, she might have to defer. Not that she loved being at school right now. There was constant whispering—mostly speculation about her mother's job, which, of course, wouldn't be happening if Lily wasn't pregnant.

"What're you thinking?" Susan asked, looking back between the seats.

Lily considered lying, but her mother always knew. She set down her knitting. "I'm thinking I've screwed up your life. What if *People* writes an awful article?"

Susan considered that. "I'll just have to turn the other cheek."

Lily had to learn to do that, too. But it was hard when she passed Zaganotes in the hall or saw Abby. And Robbie? She didn't think turning the other cheek would work with him, but she didn't know what would.

"I can't tell Robbie what happened today," she said.

"Why not? He already knows there's a problem."

"But he doesn't have to know I need surgery. Didn't the doctor say the baby would be fine?"

"Robbie can handle the truth."

"I'm not worried about Robbie. I'm worried about *me*. He'll ask questions, like what caused this, and, okay, maybe it wasn't field hockey. But it happened in my body."

"Hey," Rick called back. "You didn't cause this."

"Listen to your father," Susan said. "What happened isn't your fault."

"Fine." Lily didn't want to argue about whose fault it was. "But there's another thing, Mom. The more I tell Robbie, the more he'll want to be around. He's taking this all very seriously."

"As well he should," Rick put in.

"But the more involved he is, the more involved he'll *be*. I like Robbie's genes, but I'm not marrying him."

"How can you know that now?" Rick asked.

"Because she's smart," Susan told him. "Because she has too much else on her plate."

"But maybe he is the right guy. I'm not saying they should get married now, but why rule him out just because they're seventeen? High school sweethearts marry all the time."

"When they're old enough to know the relationship is right."

"How can they know, if they don't give the relationship a chance?"

Susan looked back at Lily. "There are relationships, and there are relationships. I'm talking about the biological one. Robbie is the baby's father. You have to keep him in the loop."

"But if they bond, he'll never leave."

"Of course he will. He's a shoo-in for acceptance at Brown. His parents will see that he goes."

Lily wasn't so sure. "He just applied to Bates. His parents don't even know. Bates is an hour away. He could be in Zaganack all the time."

"That would be good," Rick remarked.

"It would be *awful*," Lily argued. "He would be totally in the way."

"Of what?"

"My life. My family. My friends."

Rick caught her eye in the rearview mirror. "And there isn't room for him? You liked him enough to want him as the father of your baby. Now you want him to leave town?"

"It worked for you guys."

She got them with that one. There was a brief silence.

"It did not—" Rick began, but Susan cut in.

"Our situation was different. Rick was five years older than me. He had already left town."

"But you didn't drag him back or follow him to the ends of the earth," Lily said. "I mean, you guys have been together more in the last few weeks than *ever*. Am I right?"

Again, a silence.

Susan looked at Rick, then back at Lily. "How does this apply to you and Robbie?"

"There are parallels," Lily insisted. "You guys don't argue. Like, I have never heard you disagree. You have your own lives, and there's a definite division of labor when it comes to parenting me. You don't get in each other's hair, and that's good."

"Maybe it isn't," Rick said.

"No, Dad. I've thought about this a lot." Her outburst before Thanksgiving still embarrassed her. "There were times when I wanted you here, but maybe that wouldn't have been the best thing. Maybe the reason you have such a great relationship with Mom is because you don't live together."

"Am I that hard to be with?" Susan asked.

"Maybe Dad is, but that's not my point. What if I include Robbie in everything just to see where the relationship will go, and then it doesn't work out? Our son will suffer. It's hard with him living right here. We'll be in each other's faces. I really think," she concluded, "that the best way is to set limits from the start. There'll be less tension."

"And less support," Rick said. "Less help."

"I have you guys. I have my friends."

"That's not the same as having the baby's dad."

"No one's asking you to marry him," Susan put in.

"But you could," Rick added. "Down the road."

"I don't need to get married," Lily put in. "Mom didn't."

"But what if you want to?" he asked.

"She's only *seventeen*," Susan cried.

There was another silence.

Then Rick warned, "You're giving her the wrong message, Susie."

"Me? How?"

"Marriage is not always bad. My parents were married more than forty years. Same with yours."

"They were married first, *then* had kids. When kids come first and force a marriage, it can be bad."

"No one's talking about force. I'm just saying that their having a child together lends itself to giving the relationship a chance. If it works out, *great*."

Okay, Lily thought. *Let's talk about something else.*

"But she's right," Susan said. "We didn't."

"Whose fault was that? I wanted to get married."

"You did not. You were just doing what you thought was the right thing."

Enough, Lily would have cried if anyone had been listening to her. But Rick was totally focused on Susan.

"How do you know that?" he asked. "How do you know I wasn't totally in love with you?"

"You have never said those words."

"Because *you* made it clear you didn't want to *hear* them. You sent me away."

"You had a *job*—"

"*Stop!*" Lily shrieked. "I'm sorry I raised it, it's no big thing—Robbie's a good guy. I don't know why I brought it up, except I don't *know* how to handle him, and I've never had surgery before, and my life is out of control, and it wasn't *supposed* to be like this!"

SUSAN COULD IDENTIFY WITH THAT. EVEN HOURS later, she was shaken. She had never argued with Rick before, and while she wanted to be angry—wanted to be *furious* that he was contradicting her in front of Lily—she couldn't. Because she wasn't sure he was wrong.

Chapter 24

PEOPLE REACHED MAILBOXES ON FRIDAY. THE STORY was written by three correspondents, not just Melissa Randolph, so that while Susan wasn't quoted, others in town had provided enough information to fill an entire page. The good news was that the story was at the end of the issue. The bad news was that the word *pact* grabbed the reader first, making it hard not to want to finish the piece. Moreover—in Susan's mind, at least—pulling up the rear after the mothers of the drunk and the thief, she came across less as a besieged innocent than as a woman who was guilty as hell—and a lousy mom, to boot.

Add lousy principal to that. Or so Phil implied. He faulted her for allowing reporters into the school, and pointed out that he had been called but refused to talk. When he suggested that her ability to do her job was compromised, she listed all she had done that week. And when he again raised the idea of taking a leave, she repeated the argument she had made in November when word of Lily's pregnancy first leaked out—

that her dealing firsthand with students and parents was the best way to go.

She held an emergency faculty meeting that afternoon to alert her staff, which was uniformly supportive.

Evan Brewer had a prior commitment and didn't attend.

SUSAN WENT TO BED EARLY THAT NIGHT. SHE WAS lying awake in the dark when Rick slipped in and sat beside her. He was fully dressed.

"This has taken a toll," he said softly.

"It's cumulative. I feel weak."

"Angry."

"That, too. I can't sue *People,* because they didn't print anything false or defamatory. I can't strangle these three girls, because I love them too much. I can't fire Phil, because he's my boss." She paused and reached for his hand. "And I can't fault you for what you said. You may be right. I may be giving Lily the wrong message. I may have given her the wrong one all along. I thought I was teaching her to be strong and self-sufficient. I thought I was teaching her responsibility—that she was in charge of her own life."

"You have. You've produced an incredibly strong, independent, responsible young woman."

"Who's afraid of being hurt, like I was," Susan admitted and waited for his reaction.

He was quiet for a time, studying their hands. "You had reason. We rely on our parents for unconditional love. Yours took theirs back. So you built a wall. I'd have done the same."

"That doesn't make it right. Walls are isolating. The thing is, we have such good friends here that we don't *feel* isolated."

"Maybe that's all you need," he said. Before she could

respond, he stretched out on the quilt with his forehead to her cheek and her hand near his heart.

There was so much to say that she didn't know where to begin, and she was suddenly too filled with emotion to speak. So she slept.

KATE WOKE UP AT TWO. SHE MIGHT HAVE HEARD ONE of the boys coming home from a date, but there were no footsteps on the stairs. Slipping out of bed, she checked the window. The driveway was full of parked cars, everyone in for the night.

Arms around her waist, she stared out at the dark for a bit. When she began to feel chilled, she thought of returning to Will. But other thoughts—*new* thoughts—had come to her mind.

Taking her robe from a hook on the back of her door, she went down to the kitchen and brewed a cup of tea. Setting the mug on the table, she settled sideways on the bench and tucked her feet under her robe.

Five minutes passed—or was it ten? The microwave clock had died six months before. But she heard footsteps in the room over her head and knew Will was coming.

"Hey," he whispered moments later. He was a big, gentle guy in a frayed T-shirt and boxer shorts. "You okay?"

"Maybe."

Will didn't normally sit on the bench, preferring the openness of a chair. But with surprising grace, he folded himself there now and tucked Kate's feet under his thighs. "Why am I guessing you're not thinking about *People*?"

Chin on her knees, she smiled. "I wish I was. *People* is irrelevant. It stays for a week, then gets thrown in the trash. It's the important stuff that stays."

"Like babies."

"Like moms and the things they say. I've said things I wish I could take back. I haven't been the best mother in the world."

He made a dismissive sound. "You're too hard on yourself."

"Maybe. But it's how I feel. I'm not happy Mary Kate's pregnant, but I'm not about to give the baby back. I know how to roll with the punches. And Mary Kate's baby is healthy. We're very lucky." More so than Susan. Lily's situation had shaken her. It put things in a new light. "Her little guy's in rough shape."

"They'll fix him up."

"We hope."

"Heeey. Weren't we always positive when you were pregnant? Jason was breech, and they delivered him fine. The twins were a month early."

"This is different," said Kate. "Google CDH, and the picture you get is serious. If they decided on surgery, that baby has to be pretty bad. The prognosis may be good, but it's scary. What if this was Mary Kate's baby? I'd be sick." She looked around her kitchen. "We need a new microwave. The oven struggles to light, and the fridge is on its last legs. All petty. Just like me. And they're going after *Susan* for being a bad mom?"

A movement at the door drew her eye. Mary Kate was a waif, standing there in her nightgown. While Kate loved all her children, this one was still her baby. There was something to be said for that.

She patted the bench, and seconds later, her baby was there. "Did we wake you?"

The girl gave a quick headshake. "I keep thinking about how things go wrong. I don't know what happened, Mom. Last summer everything sounded so easy, and now all this?"

"No day at the beach."

"If I'd imagined the *half* of it, I might not have gone ahead."

It was a life lesson, Kate realized, but in what? Kate often acted on impulse without thinking things through. Was Mary Kate all that different?

Thinking that her own hair, loose for the night, was every bit as wild as her daughter's, she touched the small mound of Mary Kate's belly. "Still, it's my grandson in here." They had just learned it was a boy.

Mary Kate covered her hand. "A little Jacob." She teared up. Kate guessed she was missing Jacob badly—a sad life lesson there. "What if my baby has problems?"

"Your sonogram was perfect," Kate said. "We had them look closely."

"Okay, but what if he's an impossible baby?"

"We'll have to make sure he isn't."

"How?"

"By giving him care and understanding. By letting his uncles earn their keep by playing ball with him in the yard. By giving him love."

"Love isn't enough when there's a physical problem."

"When it's all you have, it's enough." Will's hand was warm on her leg.

Mary Kate studied them. Finally, with hopeful innocence, she asked, "You're really okay with this?"

Kate decided that she really was. Life wasn't about a crowded kitchen or bedrooms crammed with beds. In pleasing her own baby, Kate felt the kind of satisfaction she hadn't since Mary Kate had broken the news. Pulling her daughter close, she held on tightly.

SUNNY HADN'T SLEPT WELL FOR WEEKS, BUT THE last two nights were the worst. She wanted to blame it on the media. Talk about public humiliation? As punishment went for her sins, this was harsh.

Not so harsh, though, as what was happening with Lily's baby. When she awoke in the dark now, she thought about this. Birth defects were always sobering, but when they happened to someone you knew? She wasn't sure whom she felt most sorry for—Susan, Lily, or the baby.

As she tossed restlessly, her thoughts drifted back to Jessica. The girl was shaken, no longer as smug as she had been when proudly announcing her pregnancy. She was less quick to talk, less glib when she did, and, notably, less critical of Sunny. Approaching the end of her fourth month, she had her own sonogram next week. Suddenly, she was brooding over a list of possible problems, previously ignored.

Just punishment for having blithely become pregnant? Sunny had thought it for a while. But she was increasingly concerned about her daughter. Lately, Jessica was looking pale and drawn. And Sunny felt bad.

Shortly before dawn, she gave up on sleep and went down to the kitchen. Deciding that a special breakfast was the way to go, she began mixing batter for Belgian waffles. Both girls loved them; Sunny usually saved them for holidays. But Jessica needed fattening.

Pulling the waffle iron from her small-appliance bin, Sunny put it on the counter, fished a huller from her gadget drawer, and was heading to the refrigerator for strawberries when there was a knock at the door. There, to her horror, his nose pressed against the glass above the café curtain, was her father.

"Omigod," she whispered. "Not them, not *now.*"

But, of course, she couldn't ignore that face—or the fuzz of a hat to its right that would mark the top of her mother's head. When she didn't react quickly enough, one of them rang the bell. Twice.

Sunny opened the door in a flash. "Do you know what *time* it is? It's barely seven, and it's Saturday morning. My family is *sleeping.* And anyway, how did you *get* here at this hour?" They lived twelve hours away by car. Usually, Sunny thought that was far enough, but not this time.

"We drove all night," said Samson and gave her a peck on the cheek.

Delilah followed with a two-cheek peck. "Hello, Sunshine. I can't tell you how psyched we were to see your light on. Your French press makes *the* best coffee." She looked around.

But Sunny hadn't gotten to coffee yet. "If you'd called to let me know you were coming, I'd have had it on."

Her mother dismissed that with a short sputter. "If we'd called first, you'd have said you were going away for the weekend. I'm actually surprised you didn't. After the article in *People,* I'd have thought you'd run off somewhere to hide."

"Ah, yes," Sunny said, recalling their last discussion. "Timid, with a capital *T.*" She raised her chin. "No, Mother. You're wrong. We're here."

Delilah smiled and dropped her coat on a chair. "Well, so are we." She rubbed her hands together and spotted the iron. "I love waffles."

"That was quite some article, Sunshine," said Samson, who had taken a banana from the basket and was peeling it. "You should have warned us." He tossed the peel in the sink, uncaring that it straddled the faucet. "We were wallowing in oblivion when the calls started to come."

"What calls?" Sunny asked, fearing for an instant that *People* would run a prequel that included Samson and Delilah, in which case Sunny *would* run off somewhere.

"Friends," Delilah said with a chiding look, then glanced at the hall door and broke into a grin. "Well, hello, Darcy. Did we wake you up? Come give us a hug." She opened her arms.

Darcy, who had never been as enamored of her grandparents as Jessica, was cautiously complying when Jessica appeared.

"Hey," the girl said from the door. "I didn't know you guys were coming."

Delilah's eyes lit up. "Nor did we until dinner last night, but after going back and forth about all of the *ink* you folks have generated here, we knew we had to help."

"Help?" Sunny asked. "How?"

Her mother was suddenly looking smug, so much like Jessica that Sunny felt a tiny jolt.

"We think Jessica should come live with us," Delilah announced, "at least until after the baby is born. That way she'll be out of the limelight your friend Susan is generating."

Not so long ago, Sunny might have accepted. Now she was just amused. "Why would I let my daughter live with you?"

"It would be easier."

"Easier?"

"Well, you clearly don't want her here."

"Who said that?"

"Sunshine. Please. We all know that this pregnancy upsets you."

So does a physical abnormality, Sunny mused, but Susan wasn't asking Lily to abort her baby. "Y'know, Mother, I really am not as small-minded as you think. I can handle things."

Samson wandered out of the kitchen, leaving Delilah to her skepticism. "But pregnancy? Think about it, Sunshine. All those people staring at you? Talking behind your back? Wouldn't it be better if we just took Jessica home with us?"

Sunny didn't miss the ridicule and should have been hurt. But another emotion had come into play. The world could fault her for being angry enough to want to banish her daughter from their home. But Lily's problems and Susan's remarkably responsible response had been a wake-up call for Sunny. Thinking of Jessica now, she felt protective. Protective and possessive—this was the kind of mother she wanted to be.

Jessica hadn't moved toward her grandmother. Sunny took courage from that. *Wouldn't it be better if we just took Jessica home with us?* Delilah had asked. "Actually, no," Sunny answered. "I want my daughter with me."

"Why don't you discuss it with Dan?"

But here was another emotional shift. For nearly twenty years, Sunny's husband had held her responsible for having a mother like Delilah. But he had to move on, and she had to give him a push. "I don't need to discuss it with Dan," she said, never as sure of anything as she was of this.

Delilah looked hurt. "Do you hate us that much?"

"No, Mother," Sunny scolded, feeling an odd affection. "I've never hated you. This has nothing to do with who you are, but with who I am. I'm Jessica's mother." She moved closer to the girl. "I want my daughter here."

"She doesn't embarrass you?"

Inching closer still, Sunny said, "No. I need her with me. She has friends who need her here, too."

Jessica leaned into her just enough to say she agreed.

"But we traveled all this way to get her," Delilah argued and looked around. "Samson? *Samson? Where are you?*"

Samson was asleep on the living room sofa. He still had his coat on, but he had kicked off his boots. Not that, just then, Sunny cared. There were other things that mattered. Besides, she had the Bentley of vacuums in her broom closet right down the hall.

BY LATE SATURDAY, SUSAN'S LITTLE HOUSE WAS FULL. Kate and Will were there with Mary Kate and one of the twins; Sunny and Dan had driven over with Jess and Darcy. Sunny was cooking up a storm in the kitchen, and if she was occasionally frustrated not finding a little something she wanted—*No lemon zester? Every kitchen needs a lemon zester!*—Susan forgave her.

Likewise the mess in the bathroom, where Kate and five girls were playing with Kool-Aid—Great Bluedini, Blue Raspberry, Ice Blue Island Twist. The point was to dye skeins of yarn suitable for boys, and if Jess learned she was having a girl, they would repeat the exercise using Pink Lemonade.

The tub was a mess, which might have bothered Sunny if she hadn't known to steer clear. For Susan, it was a vote of confidence, friends saying that Lily's baby would be fine.

Buoyed, she was returning to the kitchen when the phone rang. "I'm being pressured," Phil said, his voice tense. "You have to help me here. The school board wants to see you Wednesday night at six. Can you make it?"

"Of course," Susan said. What choice did she have?

ACTUALLY, THERE WAS ONE. SHE THOUGHT ABOUT IT long and hard through dinner in her busy house, but it wasn't until they were having coffee and dessert in the living room, kids mostly on the floor with the seating space full, that Rick said a soft, "You're only half with us. What're you thinking?"

She met his gaze. "Maybe I should resign."

"You're not serious."

"The board's going to ask me to. Phil might have, if he hadn't felt so bad about the baby, but if the board does it first, he's off the hook. Maybe I should keep my dignity and volunteer to leave."

The room had grown gradually quiet.

"Did you just say what I thought you said?" Kate asked,

pausing with her elbows up, midway through tacking a handful of curls to the back of her head.

Susan didn't deny it. "There are times when I feel like I'm swimming upstream."

Kate pushed the knitting needle into her hair. "No. Absolutely not. Do not resign."

"I'm tired," Susan said. "There's part of me that would love to go back to teaching. The English department has an opening for fall. I could hire me before I resign."

"And let Evan Brewer take over? *No.*"

Susan had considered that, too. "Evan is too obvious. Phil knows he would use my job as a stepping-stone to his. Besides, there's plenty of time to do an outside search for a replacement."

"*No.*" This from Sunny.

"For the sake of the kids," Susan argued. "This media stuff isn't good for them."

"Are you kidding? They *love* it."

"We love it," piped up Darcy, whose innocence made Susan smile, albeit sadly.

"It's a distraction. I'm imposing my own problems on the students. That makes me a not-so-great principal."

"Wrong," said Lily with a ringing echo from Jess.

But Susan wasn't so sure. "I thought I was a good principal. I thought I was a good mother—"

"You *are.*"

"Maybe good, but not good enough. If I'm going to be fired, I should resign now and spare us all the agony." She turned to Rick.

Lips compressed, he shook his head. "Not a good message," he whispered.

"About dignity?" she cried. "What message should I send?"

"That you fight for what you want."

"That you believe in yourself," Kate picked up.

"That there's more than one way of doing things," Sunny put in and turned to her husband. "Can they fire her for this? Actually, don't answer. She can't resign."

If Dan had a reply, he chose not to give it. Same with Will.

"Resign now," Kate said, "and you'll be letting down every mother in town. You'll be admitting blame for having done nothing wrong. Know that phrase 'Don't go near the fire if you can't take the heat?' That's what they'll say. You'll be setting the women's movement back years."

"Totally," declared Mary Kate, but Lily's were the words that struck home.

"I remember when you were in school, Mom. Maybe I was three, maybe four, but when I woke up at night, you'd be studying. If I was sick, you worked in my room. You didn't have to tell me how much it meant to you to get a good job. I could see it. So now I'll be doing the same thing you did, only it'll be easier for me because of you. People will accept me more because of you. It's my future, and you're paving the way. If you turn back now, it'll be like pulling the yarn at the tail of a sweater and unraveling the whole thing. You've worked too hard for that. Don't? Please?"

Chapter 25

THE CAMPAIGN DIDN'T END SATURDAY NIGHT. KATE and Sunny kept calling to keep Susan on track, and while the one call she really wanted was from Pam, she had to settle for Dan, who followed up with a visit on Sunday to study her contract.

His legal opinion? "They can't dismiss you. You haven't violated anything in your contract, and this contract runs for another year. Correlli may choose not to renew it then, but if they try to fire you now, you can sue."

Susan wouldn't sue. Lawsuits were often messy, expensive, and public. It would be bad for her and bad for the town. She still believed resignation might be the compassionate alternative.

Rick disagreed. Once the school week began, he e-mailed from home. *A good principal loves her students. She finishes what she begins. A good principal doesn't let outside forces erode her work.* And Lily joined up with her dad. *A good mother fights. A good mother wants her daughter to have choices.*

How fair was that? Not fair at all, but as the school board meeting neared, Susan held the words close.

SHE REFUSED TO WEAR BLACK. BLACK MIGHT BE professional, but it was the color of death. Her father had died; her grandson might die; her professional dreams might be shot to smithereens. But she was a color person, and, while moderation was in order, she couldn't squelch her personality. On that score, she and Rick had strategized. She wouldn't be confrontational; quiet dignity was better. If board members wanted to vent, she would hear them out, but she wouldn't be stepped on.

She decided on blue—navy slacks with a lighter, bolder sweater and scarf. She covered her freckles with makeup, and nixed hoop earrings for studs. Granted, the studs were bright red, but they were small—a gift from Lily at her last birthday, and precious for that.

All seven members were present when she arrived at the town hall. Creatures of habit, they sat in their usual places. Pam had laughed about this once, though she, too, was in her usual place now. Likewise, Phil occupied a chair by the wall.

Though the room was quiet, an air of tension suggested there had already been talk. Eyes touched hers only briefly. Susan caught Pam's—*please, help me out*—before Pam turned to the chairwoman.

"You know why we've asked you to come," Hillary began.

"I'm not entirely sure," Susan confessed. "I know you're upset by the media—"

"Upset is an understatement," one of the men said.

"We're *appalled*."

"That may be so, Mr. Morgan," scolded Hillary, sounding weary, "but we live in the twenty-first century. I don't like the media being here, either, but this is how things work nowa-days."

"Are you saying I'm old?" Carl asked in his gravelly voice. "If that's so, then old is good. We didn't have these kinds of crises when my children were in school."

"We should have acted sooner," someone else said.

"*Dr. Correlli* should have acted soon-ah," corrected Duncan Haith.

There, in a nutshell, was Susan's problem. Phil's reluctance to force her out was likely what had brought this meeting about. If a majority of the board shared Duncan's frustration, Phil would have no choice but to fire her. Letting her hear the board's anger firsthand would absolve him of guilt.

To his credit, Phil said, "We have acted. Within the school, things are under control. We weren't the ones who invited the press."

Carl's bushy brows rose. "No?"

"They came for Henry's funeral," Pam said. "They were supposed to leave after that."

"Someone tipped them off."

"Who?"

When several members eyed Susan, she was startled. "I'm the *last* person who would want reporters around."

"Then who would?" Carl asked.

Here was her first challenge. "I was told it was the head of the Chamber of Commerce."

"Who said that?" Neal Lombard asked, his moon face benign.

"The producer from NBC who showed up at my door. We were able to kill that story, but someone must have called other media."

"That producer lied," Neal stated quietly.

The members returned to Susan, who knew enough not to call Neal a liar.

Duncan used the standoff to say, "Well, you did get the NBC story killed. Did the fellow you're living with handle that?"

Susan smiled curiously. This was the second challenge. "That fellow's my daughter's father. We've had a medical emergency with Lily and her baby. He's here to help."

"Living with you."

Hillary sighed. "Duncan. His being there makes sense. These aren't the dark ages."

"Now *that*," the man said, "is the attitude that gets us in trouble. I believe in marriage"—he held up a gnarled hand—"but fine, not everyone does. Susan Tate could live with a gorilla, for all I care, if she weren't principal of our high school."

All eyes turned to Susan, who remembered Dan's legal opinion. "Please explain your concern. Am I not carrying out my job?" She directed her appeal to Pam, who was in the unique position of having a child in the high school. *Tell them,* she begged.

But Carl Morgan spoke first. "The issue is morals. It's been one offense after another."

Susan couldn't be still. There was no morals clause in her contract. "I don't see the offenses. I'm successfully doing the job I was hired to do."

"You weren't here when a troubled student cheated for the third time," Neal volunteered. The fact that he knew about Michael Murray spoke of Evan Brewer's loose tongue.

"My father died," she said. "My contract allows five days off for a death. I took three."

"But now there's a problem with your daughter's baby,"

Duncan said kindly. "Wouldn't you be better off staying home to take care of her? Isn't that what a good mother would do?"

Susan was one step ahead. "I considered it, but my daughter's doctor vetoed the idea. He wants Lily at school and says my hovering would be counterproductive. He wants her living normally. She has exams. He wants her to take them."

"If you wanted to take time off, Evan Brewer could fill in," offered Neal, clearly retaliating for Susan having named him the snitch. "He has experience heading a school."

"You and Evan are old friends," Pam pointed out.

"Like you and Susan," Neal said with a smile.

"That's why I haven't spoken out."

Neal either didn't get the message or ignored it. "But this would be a practical fix. Evan is already in place."

When the board members turned to Susan, she looked at Phil. Naming a successor, whether interim or permanent, was his job.

"Evan doesn't share our philosophy," he said. He sounded begrudging, but Susan didn't care. At least he had told the truth.

"He headed a school," Neal pointed out.

Phil dismissed Evan with a wave. "If he hadn't resigned, he would have been fired. My concern isn't Evan. It's our students."

"Correct," said one.

And another, "It's a grave concern."

"That's why Ms. Tate is here," said a third.

Susan waited for more. When it didn't come, she murmured, "So the purpose of this meeting is . . . ?"

"To convince us you ought to stay," Hillary said. "Perhaps you'd share your latest thoughts on how to best help our students at this time."

"My thoughts come from the faculty," Susan replied. "They

say what we're already doing is working. Our kids are discussing the issues. They're understanding them and moving on."

"That's not the sense of the town," said Duncan.

"Didn't you read the *Gazette*?"

"Bet you thought you had more friends than that," Neal gloated.

Susan didn't respond. She was grateful when Pam said, "Most of those letters were unsigned."

"But they were not in support of Susan," Thomas Zimmerman remarked.

Harold LaPierre, the library director, had been sitting quietly with his hands folded. The overhead lights reflected on his bare scalp, spotlighting him when he spoke. "For all we know, they were written by the same person."

"There's a cynical view."

"Can't rule it out," Harold said.

Duncan grunted. "Well, we have to do somethin'. You all know it, but won't say it, so I will. There's two choices. Ms. Tate can take a leave. Or she can be dismissed."

Susan had feared it would come to this. "Please tell me the grounds."

There was a silence among the board. She guessed they were caught up by the word *grounds*. Finally, pushing up his glasses, the Realtor said, "Would you sue us if we demand your resignation?"

"I haven't thought that far, Mr. Zimmerman. I love my job, and I do it well. I do not want to resign."

"What if we pay you full salary to take a leave until the end of the school year?" rasped Carl Morgan.

"It's not about money," she said. "It's about the kids."

"What about the sentiment of the town? Our citizens want you gone."

"Do they?" she asked respectfully. "I agree with Mr. LaPierre. I'm not convinced that what we see in the *Gazette* is a fair representation of town sentiment."

Pam spoke with sudden enthusiasm. "That's an easy problem to solve. What if we held an open meeting of the board? Parents could tell us directly what they think."

"AN OPEN MEETING IS THE PERFECT SOLUTION," PAM told Tanner and Abby over dinner. "We were at a stalemate. As soon as I made the suggestion, everyone leaped at it. I mean, I was dying, not knowing what to say. I could feel Susan looking at me, wanting me to stick up for her, and I really wanted to do that, but how could I? I mean, this whole thing just *looks* so bad!"

"That sometimes determines it," Tanner murmured around a piece of flank steak.

"Determines what?" Abby asked. Sullen, she hadn't touched her food.

Tanner finished chewing. "The outcome. If the town thinks something's bad, it's bad."

"Susan doesn't see that," Pam complained, adding more mashed potato to her husband's plate, knowing he could eat all that and more without gaining a pound. "She was polite, but she didn't give an inch. She kept saying she was doing her job."

"Isn't she?" Abby asked, watchful now.

"Technically, yes. But what's happened here goes beyond her job."

"It shouldn't," the girl said.

"That's the way it is. You aren't eating, Ab. Is the meat too well done?"

"It's fine. I'm just upset."

Pam, on the other hand, was relieved. "An open meeting

will be better for Susan." To Tanner, she said, "We really need to get new blood on the board. How can someone like me speak up, when I'm overpowered by men twice my age. They have no idea what's going on in the schools."

"They've given a lot to the town," Tanner advised. "You can't just turn around and kick them out."

"I understand that. But if they faced opposition, they might decide to retire. The key is getting some of our parents to run. There are a few who'd be good. I'll talk with them."

"About Susan?" Abby asked.

"About running for school board. Convincing those men of anything new is like hitting a brick wall."

"Did you try? Susan's your friend. You should be defending her."

"I have to be impartial."

"No, you don't," Abby said sharply. "You have to be loyal. She's your friend and business partner, and she's done nothing wrong."

"It isn't as simple as that," Tanner put in, but Abby wasn't done with Pam. She seemed to be picking up steam.

"Did you tell those men they were wrong, Mom? Did you tell them Susan isn't responsible for things she didn't do?"

"But she is responsible," Tanner said. "That's what it means to hold a position of authority."

Pam didn't think Abby heard her father, the look on her face was so intense. "She's your friend, Mom. You told me to reach out to Lily, but you're not reaching out to Susan. Maybe if you come right out and publicly say you're on Susan's side, this wouldn't be so bad. You're a Perry. Doesn't that put you in a position of authority, too?"

"This is *my* fault?" Pam asked in dismay.

"No. It's not," came Tanner's quiet voice. "It's the fault of three girls who made a really dumb decision."

Abby was suddenly woeful. "It wasn't all their fault."

"What do you mean?" her father asked.

Given the look of misery on her daughter's face, Pam's heart sank. She knew the answer. There had been one too many hints from Susan, Sunny, and Kate, and one too many doubts of her own.

"It was my idea," Abby said.

"What was?" Tanner asked.

"Getting pregnant," Pam answered with chagrin. "Oh, Abby. How many times did I ask? You denied it again and again."

The girl had tears in her eyes. "I didn't think it would get to this. But now Lily has a baby that is sick, and you all are saying Susan is a bad mother. She didn't have anything to do with Lily getting pregnant. It was *my idea*."

Pam tried to see Tanner's reaction, but his eyes were fixed on Abby. "What are you talking about?"

"*I was pregnant,*" she wailed. "It was Michael's, and it was an accident."

"*You* were pregnant?" He glanced at Pam. "Did you know this?"

Stunned, she could only shake her head.

"No one knew, Dad. I didn't even tell Lily, Mary Kate, and Jess, that's how lousy a friend I was. I just said it would be totally awesome if we all had babies together, and they bought it. Only they got pregnant, and then I miscarried—"

"When? Did you know about this, Pam? What doctor didn't tell us?"

"*No doctor,*" Abby cried. "I tested positive for six weeks, then had this really heavy disgusting period, and the tests after that showed negative."

Pam knew about disgusting periods. She remembered a pain that went beyond the physical, felt it even now.

But Abby was hurrying on. "I tried again and *kept* trying, but I'm not pregnant. *Something's wrong with me.*"

Tanner looked bewildered. "You kept trying? This doesn't make sense."

"Not to you! You don't have to worry about friends. I do!"

"You do not. You're a Perry."

"Like that guarantees happiness?" the girl asked, pushing back from the table and rising to her full Perry height. "Like it guarantees I'll grow old with three friends I love? Like it guarantees I'll *ever* be able to have a baby? You don't understand. These things matter!" She ran from the room.

Tanner stared after her before turning to Pam. He looked dazed. "I don't understand. I asked you to talk with her."

Pam stood with her arms circling her middle. She was torn apart inside, hearing *something's wrong with me* and wanting to go to Abby, but needing to pacify Tanner first. "I asked. She denied. What more could I do?"

"You should have known."

Pam was slow in answering. She kept hearing Tanner tell Abby that she was a Perry, but now Pam wondered who *she* was. Arguably, she had more in common with Susan, Sunny, and Kate than with her husband's family. When she was at the barn, she wasn't just a Perry. She was someone who contributed.

These friends made her a better person. She wondered if that was the appeal.

If so, she had let them down. "They have every right to hate me."

"Who?"

"Susan, Sunny, and Kate. They knew Abby was involved. But they were too loyal to say anything."

"Loyal, or cowardly?"

"Loyal, Tanner," Pam said, offended. "Loyal to me, loyal to

Abby—and now, I need to be there for Susan when she needs help."

He retreated. "Fine. But even if Abby suggested the pact to the others, she didn't hold a gun to their heads."

"But she was *part of it*. If things had gone as planned, the pact would have involved four girls, and the press would be at *our* door. Are we any less guilty than Susan?"

"Susan's the principal of the high school."

"And you're the CEO of Perry and Cass."

"It's different. I'm a man. You're the mother. You should have known."

He was wrong. She didn't often think it. But right now he was dead wrong, a Perry through and through.

She was not. Suddenly that didn't seem so bad.

"I should have known?" she asked softly. "Like Susan should have known what Lily was planning? It doesn't work that way."

"Abby's a good girl."

"So are Lily, Mary Kate, and Jess. And Susan is the best mother I know."

"She's still the principal."

"And you're still a Perry," Pam said, irritated. "That means more responsibility, and right now it means helping someone who's being made to pay for the . . . the *priggishness* of this town."

Tanner was silent, then curious. "Do you really think that?"

"I do," she said, realizing it was true. "Susan's being scapegoated. And that's wrong. You have to put your support behind her."

"I can't."

"Why not? Because Perrys don't get dirty? Is it all about appearance? What about going out on a limb for a friend when you know it's the *right thing to do*?" His silence goaded her on. "Think about it, Tanner. There but for the grace of God go I. Don't you find that humbling?" She certainly did.

Tanner had risen. He rubbed the back of his neck, then said, "I can't announce to the world that my daughter caused this fiasco. It's bad enough that I know it."

Pam nodded angrily. "It's not the first time a Perry's been knocked up." He winced at the phrase, but she didn't care. "You ought to be grateful. In Abby's case, the problem solved itself, so we're in the clear. Your job's not on the line. But Susan's is. You need to help."

He shook his head. "Not my place."

Pam disagreed. "It is *totally* your place. If this isn't a case that cries out for responsibility, I don't know what is. If not for this, what *do* you stand for?" she cried in dismay and went upstairs to Abby.

ABBY WAS TALL, BUT HER ROOM WAS MUCH TALLER, making her seem small and vulnerable as she sat cross-legged on the window seat. Her eyes were wet with tears.

Settling beside her, Pam took her hand. "Talk to me, Abby."

"I'm a terrible person."

"Me, too. So talk to me."

Abby must have been brimming with a need for catharsis, because the words came in a rush. "I didn't plan to get pregnant, I swear I didn't. I knew it would be the worst thing for a Perry, because they *do* expect more from us, and you'd both have *hated* me for it. I thought about getting an abortion, but I didn't know where to start looking, and I realized that if *that* got out, it'd be even *worse*. So then I thought it wouldn't be so bad if there was a good reason I was pregnant. So I suggested the pact to the others, and they bought it, and for a little while, it was really neat. I mean, I could be a good mother. I would *love* to focus on a baby. But this has been so bad, Mom. Look at what's happening to Susan. And to Lily's baby? Who'd have imagined that? If I could do it over again, I wouldn't have suggested a pact—and I would never have outed my friends. But now the joke's on me. What if I never have a baby?"

Pam said the only things she could. "I had you, didn't I?" Then, "You'll have your baby." Then, "Maybe this just isn't the right time."

"But I wanted to do it with them."

"That is not a reason to have a child at this age. For now, you can give them support."

"Will you?"

"Yes." Pam hadn't thought it through, but it wasn't rocket science. Tanner could do what he wanted, but so could she. "I'll lobby for Susan. I'll get everyone who loves her to the meeting. You could do the same with the kids. Have them talk to their parents."

"Like my word matters? Everyone knows we're on the outs."

"Tell them Susan's the best principal they've ever had. Tell them they need to keep it that way." Pam paused, heart aching. Knowing of Abby's involvement, she felt more responsible. "You could also tell Lily you're rooting for her baby."

"She wouldn't listen," Abby murmured, pulling up her knees. She still looked miserable, but at least she wasn't crying. "They hate me now."

Pam thought of Susan, Sunny, and Kate. "They probably hate me, too."

"I loved being with them."

"Me, too." The need to belong—the basis of pact behavior—was wrong in this case, but Pam understood its power.

"Why don't we fit in?" Abby asked.

"Maybe because we haven't been . . . relevant," said Pam.

"We have to make ourselves relevant." She had an idea. "Like with knitting. I'll pull strings to get an awesome catalogue promotion, and if your uncle Cliff balks, I'll threaten to shut down PC Wool."

Abby looked up. "You wouldn't shut it down."

"Not, but I'd threaten to if he doesn't give me the space I want, and we both know how profitable PC Wool is. So," Pam said, "we have to make sure we have enough finished samples. Kate will tell me what's already done, but you and I can knit more. Susan suggested I make a shawl. I can do that. You can knit gloves. Gloves are very in."

"I can't knit gloves. I've never knitted gloves."

"You've done socks."

"No one sees mistakes in socks. They see every last one in gloves."

"Then you'll have to make sure there are none." Pam had another idea. "Cashmere," she breathed reverently. "The woman we visited was good, and she has stock. What if Kate could dye up a batch really fast? Would you do a pair of gloves then?"

Abby looked tempted. "Cashmere? I could try."

"Trying isn't good enough. We both have to *do* it. We could make a pact, the two of us. No more trying. Just doing. What do you think?"

Chapter 26

❦

PAM HAD ALWAYS CONSIDERED TANNER A LEADER, but now wondered if his leadership skills were limited to Perry & Cass. She knew he liked Susan, but he was avoiding helping her. Disillusioned, Pam refused to discuss it further, which meant that they weren't talking, which meant she had more energy to talk with friends.

Defiant? Oh, yes. For the first time in her married life, she was bucking the tide. That made success very important to her.

She set herself to the task first thing Thursday morning, and it was an awakening. Everyone she called thought Susan was a good principal, but the editorial in the *Gazette* had many on the defensive. *I talk with my kids. I watch them. I know what they're doing.* The implication was that Susan did not, and that to side with her was to side with a bad mother.

So Pam fine-tuned her approach, and, in doing so, discovered her own strength. Lady of leisure that some accused her of being, she often had coffee or lunch with other parents and therefore knew them better than, say, Kate or Sunny might. This allowed her to make her calls more pointed.

Okay, Lisa, remember the rough patch you went through with Trevor? You thought he was on drugs. He kept denying it, but you weren't sure you believed him. He got through it, but in hindsight, what do you think? Was he experimenting? You asked all the right questions. And so did Susan. Is she any different a mom from any of us?

Hey, Debbie, you have a daughter. She didn't want to look like a nerd, so she refused to study. Who talked her through it? Don't you owe Susan something for that?

Zaganackians were complacent. It was up to her to rile them up.

KATE DIDN'T HAVE A BUSINESS DEGREE, BUT SHE DID have common sense. Since PC Wool was her livelihood, she kept a list of her customers. She had never used it for anything personal before, and did feel a moment's qualm. She was, after all, one of the town's bad moms.

But was she any worse than others whose kids hadn't always followed the rules? Was her daughter any less good a person because the rule she broke had created a life? Who would be affected by it, beyond Mary Kate and her family? No Mello was asking for handouts. They would take care of their own.

Resentful of those who would judge, Kate worked up a head of steam, then e-mailed every Zaganackian who had ever placed an order for PC Wool. She worded it like a party invitation. *Knitters love knitters. Come support our own Susan Tate by rallying around her at the high school auditorium on Wednesday evening. It starts at 7. See you then.*

There was nothing subtle about the message. She guessed

that if her bosses at Perry & Cass knew she was using the list, they would not be happy. But she wasn't happy with Tanner Perry.

Besides, would he ever know? She seriously doubted it. His nose was stuck up too high for him to see what the town wanted. Even Pam was defying him now. That alone was reason for Kate to join in.

LEFT TO HER OWN DEVICES, SUNNY MIGHT HAVE stayed under the radar. Her own daughter was pregnant, and while she and Jessica were on the same page now, the girl's condition wasn't something Sunny wanted to flaunt.

Then she got Kate's e-mail and, soon after, a customer mentioned talking with Pam. If Kate could speak up, so could she. And Pam? Pam embodied Respectability with a capital *R*.

Increasingly the idea of standing up for Susan held merit. Wasn't it one step removed from standing up for herself? She had stood up to her mother with amazing success. No one had ever said respectability required invisibility.

So she began talking with customers who either knew Susan or had kids in the schools. *You're a mother, just like Susan. Have your children never disobeyed you? Does that make you less good a mother?* And then, even more shamelessly, *You'll want to be supportive. This is a rough time for Susan. You know about the baby, don't you?*

The more she talked, the bolder she grew—because people were actually listening. Rather than being a liability, her own daughter's pregnancy seemed to give her legitimacy. *I know what I'm talking about* was the message.

It was definitely Empowering.

. . .

SUSAN WASN'T AS PLUCKY. SHE WAS WORRIED ABOUT Lily, worried about the baby, worried about her job. As grateful, even touched, as she was when she learned what Pam, Kate, and Sunny were doing, she was still frustrated. She had always been her own best champion. Now she was in an awkward position.

She decided that an e-mail to the parents was the way to go. But begging them to sing her praises wasn't her usual style.

"Maybe it should be," Rick said that evening. "If you don't toot your own horn, who will?"

"My friends. Lily's friends. They're all into it. An e-mail from me is something else, not to mention that I can just hear the guys on the school board. 'She's using her position to coerce parents to support her. They'll show up out of fear that if they don't, she'll take it out on their kids.' I'd be using my position to help myself."

"It's done all the time."

"Not by me."

"Then let's pick words you can live with," he suggested, and together they drafted a message alerting parents to the upcoming meeting: *My earlier e-mail has kept you abreast of what we're doing in school to help our students deal with the current crisis. In light of the recent media coverage, the school board has decided to hold an open meeting to give you a chance to weigh in on the debate. If you'd like to give us an update on how your child is doing and tell us if you're satisfied with the steps we've taken, please plan to attend.*

She gave date, time, and place, and sent it out Thursday night, knowing that she was taking a risk. If her guess was wrong and the letters in the *Gazette* were representative of town sentiment, she was toast.

· · ·

SUSAN HADN'T RUN THE E-MAIL PAST PHIL. WHEN HE showed up at her office Friday morning looking like he'd lost his best friend, she wondered if that had been a tactical error. He sank into a chair, his legs sprawled. For a split second, she feared he had lost *his* job.

She wasn't far off. "You have to help me here, Susan," he began, sounding as weary as he looked. "I'm under pressure. The school board wants you out."

"The *whole* board?" Susan asked in alarm. Surely not Pam. Or Hillary, or Henry.

"No. But a majority. You know the ones."

"*Before* next week's meeting?"

"They don't want that meeting. They don't believe the parents should decide. They think what happens in our schools should be determined by the people in charge."

Susan was incensed. "Like George Abbott and the *Gazette*? Like those anonymous citizens whose letters he printed?"

"I understand why you're bitter. You haven't gotten a fair shake. I do believe you've done a great job."

"Tell them that, Phil. Fight for me."

He sighed defeatedly. "Neal Lombard called. Your e-mail didn't go over well. One of the parents told Evan, who told Neal, who told Tom, Duncan, and Carl. That's four of them who want you fired, and they want me to do it. If I say no, that's four of them who'll vote to fire *me*. I'm fifty-eight, Susan. I can't start looking for a new job now. So I can fire you, and you can sue me for wrongful dismissal, in which case my career's hurt anyway. Or you can resign."

"Because my daughter is pregnant," Susan said in disbelief. "If those men found my e-mail threatening, they must be afraid of the crowds it'll draw."

He sighed again. "It doesn't matter. I just need you to resign."

She actually felt for him. A friend, he had given her career a major boost. But weren't they *both* being railroaded? "I can't, Phil."

"Sure you can," he coaxed. "You're young. There are lots of communities looking for a good high school principal. You'll find another job."

"That's not the issue." She was thinking of Lily now. *It's my future, Mom. You're paving the way.* "I can't resign. Not before that meeting. If it turns out the parents disapprove of me and the job I've done, you'll have my resignation by the end of the evening. That's the best I can do."

IT WASN'T GOOD ENOUGH FOR THOSE SCHOOL BOARD members whose bluff she had called. They didn't fire Phil; not yet. They simply went to Plan B, which entailed moving the open board meeting from Wednesday to Thursday.

Pam was furious. Having declared her allegiance to Susan, she argued forcefully with the board in a conference call Friday afternoon.

"Thursday night is impossible," she said. "Susan will be in Boston for Lily's surgery."

"Ms. Tate doesn't have to be there," one of the men said.

"Of course she does. This is a referendum on her."

"Let her change her plans."

"Would you have her postpone critical surgery—you all, who are obsessed with her being a good mother? Why not hold the meeting the week after next?"

"It has to be next week. We've waited too long. Unless you want Correlli fired first."

Pam did not. Once they fired Phil, they would fire Susan, and if Neal Lombard had his way, they would elevate Evan Brewer. Even with Hillary and Harold on Pam's side, the opposition would win.

"Hillary, this is blackmail," she complained.

"Yes," Hillary said. "Threats are counterproductive, Mr. Morgan. What about holding the meeting Tuesday night?"

Pam could live with that. She could get a phone tree telling people of the change.

"Bad night," said Tom Zimmerman. "Rotary Club meeting."

"Thursday is worse," Pam argued. "Perry and Cass is holding its biannual staff meeting, which means half of our parents will be *there*. Besides, they're using the auditorium."

"Why can't we hold our meeting where we usually do?" Tom asked.

"In Town Hall? That's *way* too small."

"We've held open meetings there before."

"This one involves too many people. There has to be a better place." But the middle schools didn't have their own auditoriums, the elementary schools only had gymnasiums, and the churches were all small and tight.

"We could use the Perry and Cass warehouse," Duncan Haith said with a dry chuckle.

Pam ignored him. "Tell you what. I'll agree to Town Hall as long as we have mikes and speakers in every room there. That's the kind of crowd that'll come out for Susan Tate."

"Isn't *that* a threat?" asked Neal Lombard.

"No, sir," Pam replied. "It's a promise. You all are playing a game that isn't in the best interest of our kids. I have a child in the school. Same with most of the parents who'll be at this meeting. Either you give them a say now, or they'll have theirs when your terms expire next year."

SUSAN BARELY WINCED WHEN PAM CALLED TO TELL her the meeting would be held Thursday night. It was just one more blow. And there was nothing to consider.

"Lily has to be at the hospital at six Friday morning, and she needs to sleep Thursday night. That means checking into the hotel by nine, so I'll miss the meeting. You'll have to represent me, Pam."

As she hung up the phone, the last shred of her complacency dissolved. She had to notify parents of the change, and she was angry enough to be blunt. *Important correction,* she wrote in the subject line of her e-mail, and in the body, *Next week's open meeting of the school board will be held on Thursday at Town Hall. I will not be there, but will be in Boston for my daughter's surgery. For those of you who don't know, Lily's baby has a congenital problem that has to be repaired if the child is to live. Since I'm unable to attend this crucial meeting, I'm counting on you all to be there in my place.*

GIVEN A UNIFYING CAUSE, SUSAN, KATE, SUNNY, AND Pam were all at the barn on Saturday morning. If dissension lingered, it was hard to spot. Not that there was loud laughter, as there used to be in Susan's garage. Their purpose wasn't funny at all.

They plotted ways to notify nonparents about the upcoming meeting. They created a theme for the PC Wool promotion. They talked about Lily's surgery, Mary Kate's heartburn, and the baby girl Jessica had just learned she was having. They talked about Abby.

By then, they were knitting.

LILY WAS KNITTING AS WELL. SHE HAD SLEPT LATE and, with Susan at the barn, had gone out for breakfast with Rick. They ran errands on the way home—town dump, drugstore, supermarket—and made a brief stop at the pier, but the January wind off the water was cold. Leaving the seagulls to guard the boats, they returned home and settled down in front of a fire in the den.

When there was a knock at the door, Lily put down her knitting. Most people rang the bell. Only friends knocked.

Robbie stood there. Having run across the street without a coat, he slipped quickly inside. "Hey," he said with a smile. "How're you feeling?"

"I'm good."

"I like your shirt." It was a form-fitting knit from the Portland cache. "You don't look very pregnant."

"I'm not very pregnant," Lily said, running a hand over her belly. The bulge was still small. "But I will be soon."

"Uh, that's why I'm here," he said soberly. "I want to be at the hospital next Friday, and don't tell me not to come, because I'll go anyway. I have a stake in this. It's my baby, too."

Lily thought quickly. "What if I just have my mom call you as soon as the surgery's done? That'll save you the trip."

"I want to be there."

"Just to stand around and wait?"

"It's my baby, too."

Lily didn't remind him that he'd had no say in its creation. It was time to move on. "The thing is," she said, "I'll be looking *awful*."

"I don't care how you look."

"I mean, it'll be embarrassing to have anyone see me all sweaty and pale."

"You won't be in labor."

"I know. But having someone other than my parents around will be stressful."

"I'll be invisible. I just want to be there. My dad said he'd drive me down."

"Why don't you drive down with us?" Rick suggested from behind Lily.

"Dad—"

"We have room in the car."

"But what if I want to lie down?" Lily asked.

"You can put your legs on my lap," Robbie said in a bolder voice, clearly encouraged.

"What if I just don't *want* you there?"

"Give me a good reason, and I won't go."

She tried to come up with one. But all she could think of was her parents arguing about Susan keeping Rick at arm's length and Lily saying she had wanted him closer. Now she was having a boy, who, if he made it through this surgery, would do boy things, for which a dad would be good.

"I can't," she wailed softly.

Robbie smiled. "Thought not." He high-fived Rick, opened the door, and headed out—only to deftly pivot to avoid hitting Abby, who had her knuckles raised to knock.

Abby was the last person Lily expected to see, but old habits died hard. Pulling her inside by the sleeve of her parka, she shut the door and turned to Rick. "That high five was too familiar. Did you guys plan this?"

"I swear, we did not," Rick said. "I was just as surprised as you to see him—not that I'm disappointed. He should be there."

"That's *my* decision to make."

"You did make it."

She supposed she had. In a way. Feeling cornered, she turned to Abby, who looked so uncharacteristically unsure that Lily couldn't bear to ask why she had come—at least, not with Rick standing there. Oh yeah, she wanted him around, just not all the time. Fathers didn't need to know everything.

Still holding Abby's sleeve, she led her up to her room and closed the door. "There. He can't hear."

"It's okay if he does," Abby said. She didn't look quite so tall. "I mean, anyone with a brain knows I should be shot."

Lily wanted to say it wasn't true. Only it was.

Sagging, Abby said, "If I hadn't been pregnant last summer, I probably wouldn't have suggested the pact, and if I hadn't done that, you wouldn't be pregnant. If you weren't pregnant, your mom wouldn't be in trouble, your baby wouldn't be in trouble, our friendship wouldn't be shot. I'm sorry about the baby, Lily. Do you think he'll be okay?"

Lily touched the spot where he was. "The doctor says so."

"You've never had surgery before. Are you scared?"

"Mostly for the baby."

Looking stricken, Abby dug her hands in her pockets. "I want to say I know. Only I don't. I wish I was pregnant, too, Lily. It would have been nice to have something important like that. My mother says there'll be a better time. She's really fighting for your mom, by the way. I've never seen her as determined. Actually," she added, "I've never seen her angry at my dad before."

"I'm sorry."

"Not your fault, absolutely not your fault. Besides, someone has to take on the school board. You should hear her on the phone with those guys. I mean, she is awesome."

Lily smiled. "I'll bet she is."

"I've been talking with everyone I know. They're all going to the meeting." Her voice cracked. "I really am sorry all this happened. If I could change everything, I would. Is there anything I can do? Anything you need?"

Not from you, Lily might have said if she were a different kind of person. But she had always liked Abby before, and really didn't want their friendship to be shot. If she was giving Robbie a chance, shouldn't she give Abby one, too?

Suddenly she had a brilliant idea. It was perfect, actually. "I need moral support. Want to drive to Boston with us next week?"

Chapter 27

༺◆༻

DUSK HAD FALLEN HOURS BEFORE, BUT SUSAN DIDN'T
have to check her watch to know the time. If it hadn't meant a
late night for Lily, she would have waited to leave Zaganack
until after the meeting. Though only part of her future would
be determined there, it was an important part—and, in truth,
she had no idea whether the turnout would be pro or con. The
campaigning might backfire if recipients felt they were being
strong-armed—because however you looked at it, the issues
were incendiary. PREGNANCY PACT. PRINCIPAL'S
DAUGHTER. BAD MOTHER.

People liked Susan; she truly believed that. But this wasn't a
simple matter of like or dislike. The debate involved parenting
styles, politics, even professional considerations, if allies were
lost to the Perry & Cass meeting across town.

"Packed," said Abby, reading a text message. She was on
Lily's left, her face lit by the glow of her phone. "The boardroom, the hall, Dr. Correlli's office. The *stairs*."

"Good turnout," said Rick, eyes leaving the highway only to shoot Susan an encouraging look.

She didn't reply. Packed meant nothing if the crowd believed she was a disgrace.

From behind, Lily said, "How do they decide who sits in the boardroom?"

"First come, first served," Abby explained, "but they have monitors to call on people in the other rooms. Mom insisted on that."

"She's a trooper," Susan said. "Her skipping the Perry and Cass meeting was an issue. Families usually attend."

"Your dad's upset she chose Town Hall?" Lily asked Abby.

"Not Dad. His cousin Rodney, who publishes the *Gazette*. He is angry at Mom for supporting Susan. *His* guy took the other side, so he feels personally insulted."

"How does your father feel?"

"I don't know," Abby said, but her eyes were on the phone. "This is from Stephie, who's inside the boardroom. Mrs. Dunn is saying that the meeting is about leadership. She says they're split about who should head the high school."

"Then it is a referendum on you, Mom," Lily said.

"We knew it was," Susan acknowledged, glancing back. Lily was gnawing her cuticle. She was nervous about the surgery, but she seemed to like having Abby there. Same, actually, with Robbie, who, for the sake of extra legroom, sat behind Susan. She'd had mixed feelings about his coming, but liked the way Lily was being supported.

"Here we go," said Abby. "The first speaker is Sue Meader."

Rick glanced questioningly at Susan. "Friend," she told him. "We've worked on projects together. She has five kids. She's totally sympathetic."

"She calls you masterful," Abby reported as the text appeared.

"So does my dad," Robbie put in. "He says you've done a great job handling all this."

"Does your mother agree?" Lily asked.

"Not yet," he said in a way that implied she would in time.

Susan hoped so. Things would be awkward once the baby was born if Annette Boone was still angry at Lily.

"John Hendricks," announced Abby, then added a low, "Disappointed."

"Disappointed in *what*?" Lily cried. "That his kids never made headlines? I mean, like, they are *huge* losers."

"He has a right to his opinion," Susan said.

"It's biased."

"That's what Mary Webber is arguing," Abby reported.

"And how will they decide this anyway?" Lily asked. "Take a vote? A show of hands at the end of the night? Thumbs up or thumbs down for Susan Tate?"

Susan smiled wryly. "Ideally, there will be so many yeas that the nays will shut their mouths and go away."

"Anne Williams," Abby called out. "Praising you, Susan. And Mom's saying to tell you women outnumber men two to one."

That was good, Susan thought. "Women may be more apt to support another woman." She paused. "Unless they're lousy moms and want to look good by making me look worse. Or unless the prevailing sentiment is against me, in which case they may jump on the bandwagon."

"Isn't that pact behavior?" Lily asked.

"More likely *pack* behavior," Rick called back. "They just follow the leader and go in a group."

"How is that different from a pact?"

"A pact is premeditated. The group agrees to it, and it usually involves something that's socially, morally, or legally forbidden. The group gives individual members the courage to act."

"Absolutely," said Abby. "People come together to support something they'd never support by themselves. Take Lily's singing group. Their vote was premeditated. They talked about doing it. They gave each other the courage to act. That was a pact. People we know make pacts every day."

Susan thought they were onto something, when Lily asked, "So why was it okay for them to do it and not okay for us?"

"Because yours involved pregnancy, and you're underage. That's unacceptable around here."

"Uh-oh," warned Abby in a back-to-the-meeting voice. "Emily Pettee. Bad."

No surprise there, Susan thought.

"Why are people so hung up about mothering?" Lily asked.

"Because it's the most elemental job in the world."

"I'll be a good mother."

"I know you will, sweetheart."

"Caroline Moony," Abby read. "Raves."

And so it went. Abby gave them a running commentary on who said what, and they didn't need a pencil to keep score. For every voice saying Susan's e-mail had opened a dialogue, another said the dialogue was a distraction. For every voice saying Susan was the kind of mother the school needed, another was critical. It was too close to call, no landslide at all.

Susan feared she had miscalculated. She was thinking that if there was as much negative feeling as this, she did need to resign, when Lily said, "She's calling on the wrong people. I mean, if women outnumber men, there should be more women talking, right? And what about everyone at Perry and Cass? Your fans must be there. Was that meeting mandatory?" she asked Abby, but Abby was watching her phone.

"Listen to this," the girl said. "J.C. is out in the hall. She says the people there are upset. They're all Susan's people." Her thumbs flew. "I'm telling Mom. Someone stacked the deck.

They must have paid nays to come early to fill up the board-room."

"Would they do that?" Lily asked.

"Absolutely. Mom says the men are ruthless."

It was their last hurrah, Susan knew. They hadn't wanted her to be principal in the first place.

"Mr. Lombard," Abby announced. "He was just recognized by the chair. Who is he?"

"Chamber of Commerce," Susan said worriedly. "What's he saying?"

There was a flurry of texting. "He wants to hear from a faculty member."

Susan could guess which one. Pulling out her own phone, she passed it to Lily. "Who else is in that audience?"

"Taylor."

"Text her. Tell her to call my number. I want to hear this."

A minute later they had Evan Brewer on speakerphone. His voice was dim; Lily raised the volume. The quality wasn't great, but they could hear the words. ". . . is my superior," he was saying. "I respect what she's trying to do."

Neal's voice came then. "Is it what you did when you were head of school?"

"No. Her style differs from mine."

"As an administrator."

"And a parent. I set rules. My kids knew the penalty for breaking them. Would I have done the same thing as Ms. Tate? I don't know. My kids never made pacts."

"Low blow," Rick murmured.

"Lie," Susan said. "They uncovered a drug ring at his school. If that isn't a pact, tell me what is."

"Mom's furious," Abby related. "She's calling Dad."

But Evan continued. "Ms. Tate isn't alone. Parents today are more lax. Mothers are juggling lots of balls. Inevitably, one or two fall."

"*Low* blow," Rick muttered.

"Get that man away from the mike," Susan cried.

"Dad's phone is off," Abby reported at the same time that they heard a disturbance in the boardroom. It was a minute before they realized what was happening. "They're going after Mom for *texting*?" Abby asked in disbelief just as one voice rose above the drone.

"That is one of the problems we have!"

"Duncan Haith," Susan said, recognizing the voice.

"There's no respect, no decorum," he charged. "And when parents are the ones doing this, it's no wonder their children misbehave. We didn't have any of it in *my* day."

"Didn't you?" came a different voice, very Maine, very genteel. "Maybe we need to talk about that."

"Omigod," Abby whispered loudly. "It's my *dad*."

The murmurs from the phone suggested that others in the boardroom were as surprised as Abby. And Susan? She was nervous. Tanner had come from an important meeting of his own, but to hurt or help?

The background hum died. She imagined him standing at the foot of the long table, tall and lanky, his face unlined, his confidence clear.

"What's he doing?" Abby asked.

"I'm confused," Tanner began, sounding hesitant indeed. "This whole situation raises questions." He paused.

"Where's he *going*?" Abby whispered.

"I can't answer them, and this bothers me. I like answers. But the questions we've been asking around here are making me think about some things I hadn't considered."

"What is he *saying*?" Abby cried.

Susan shushed her gently.

"I always assumed I was a good parent," Tanner said. "Who of us doesn't? We do the best we can, and sometimes it works, sometimes it doesn't." When he paused for a breath, the room remained still. "When it doesn't, do we suddenly become a bad parent?"

"With due respect, Mr. Perry," came Carl Morgan's gravelly voice, "*we* are not the principal of the high school."

"No. But we're CEOs of businesses, retired CFOs of the same, and the head of the Chamber of Commerce. We're members of the school board. We make decisions that affect a whole town of children."

"What are you saying?"

Tanner was slow to respond, and still the room remained silent. "I'm not saying anything," he finally went on. "I can't, because, as I said, I don't know the answers. So I'm asking. Are any of us perfect? Have we never made mistakes? Have we never had the experience of doing everything right and still having something go wrong?"

Duncan Haith spoke up, his own accent thicker than Tanner's. "All good general questions, Mr. Perry, but let's be specific. This woman knew the pitfalls of having a baby at seventeen, and still she let her daughter do it."

"You *didn't*—" Lily began to protest, but Susan held up a silencing hand.

"And you, Mr. Haith?" Tanner asked gently. "If you knew the pitfalls of divorce, why would you let your daughter do it? Or you, Mr. Lombard? If you knew the pitfalls of drugs, how did two of your sons end up in rehab? Or you, Mr. Morgan? If you knew the pitfalls of estate planning, why is your wife's will being contested in court?"

"Whoa!" exclaimed Abby over the applause in the room.

"*Yesss,*" Lily cried.

Robbie whistled.

"That is a personal attack," Carl Morgan charged.

"So is yours," Tanner replied with uncharacteristic passion. "People in glass houses shouldn't throw stones."

"I," Carl stated, "don't live in a glass house."

"Then you're one of the few, Mr. Morgan. The rest of us aren't so perfect. We see some things and miss others. We try to be good parents, but who's to say that the next pact won't involve a child of ours?"

Neal Lombard's voice rose. "You can't be objective. Susan Tate is a family friend."

Tanner's voice turned thoughtful. "True. I know Susan. I know all the mothers involved, and I know the girls. They're good girls who made a bad choice. Have none of our kids made bad choices? So do we ostracize them? Or do we offer a hand in help. They won't shame this community unless *we* invite the shame to exist."

There was silence, then a burst from Carl. "Your father must be rolling over in his grave. Responsibility was his credo."

"It's mine, too," Tanner argued. "Anyone who knows me knows that. But if I'm a responsible person, I have to think responsibly. And when I do, I realize this discussion has grown too personal. The school board shouldn't be deciding who is or is not a good mother. This discussion should be limited to whether Ms. Tate is a good principal. I believe she is. Thank you. That's all I have to say."

THE MEETING ADJOURNED SOON AFTER. BETWEEN excited calls and texts, the car buzzed as loudly as the boardroom had when Tanner finished speaking.

Pam phoned Susan. "He came through," she said with what sounded like utter relief.

But Susan knew better. "You were the one who got him thinking, Pam, and you got people to the meeting to hear him."

"The *best* was the look on Neal's face. I wish you'd been here to see it."

But she wasn't, and the reason why seemed to hit her at the same time as it did her friend. "We're rooting for you," Pam said quietly.

AS THEY LEFT THE HIGHWAY FOR THE CITY STREETS, Susan needed all the help she could get. The pace here was light years removed from the pace in Zaganack. She was so not a city person, and thinking of the reason they'd come? Sobering.

Their hotel was adjacent to the hospital. They took two rooms, one for girls, one for guys. Had Robbie not come, Susan would have stayed with Rick. She was nervous, and he was steady.

But she had to settle for a hug.

IT WAS BEFORE DAWN WHEN THE WAKE-UP CALL came. With the surgery scheduled for eight, Lily had to check in before seven. Susan had fully expected to walk her over alone, but none of the others wanted to be left behind.

For several minutes, they sat in the waiting room with other patients and their families. The occasional newspaper rustled; if there was talk, it was a murmur.

When the nurse who came for Lily waved Susan along, she went gratefully. Lily was frightened, her face pale, her eyes worried as each new person entered her cubicle. Susan held

Lily's hand, whispered encouraging thoughts, answered questions asked of Lily when the girl was too tongue-tied to reply.

The doctor stopped by, as did the anesthesiologist, who inserted an IV for the medication that would sedate Lily during the procedure. She was wide awake, though, when they came to fetch her.

Leaning over, Susan tucked a last strand of hair into her cap. "They say once the medication starts you won't remember much, but I want you to tell me everything you do. Your son will want to know the details." She drew a heart in the outline of Lily's face. "He has an amazingly good mother."

Lily gave her a hug so tight that it hurt inside. Choked up, Susan watched them wheel the girl off.

So she was already feeling emotional when she returned to the waiting room. Between this day's surgery, last night's meeting, and all the days and nights of worry that had come before, her composure was nil. That may have explained why, when she approached Rick and saw the man and woman with him, she turned away.

Rick was quickly at her elbow, guiding her down the hall until she stopped, stared at him, and asked weakly, "What was that?"

"My dad and your mom."

"How?"

"I told Dad on Wednesday. I never dreamed he'd show up, much less with Ellen. I'm as surprised as you are."

"She knows?"

"Looks it."

"Did she want to come? Or did he force her?"

"Maybe a little of both. All I know is she looked terrified walking in here just now."

Susan was terrified herself. "I haven't had a decent conversation with her in years. What am I supposed to say now? I saw her last month and didn't tell her Lily was pregnant. I've talked with her on the phone since, and didn't tell her. Do I apologize? Do I try to explain? What am I supposed to *do* with her?"

"Nothing," Rick said. "My dad brought Ellen, so she's his responsibility. Your only responsibility is Lily."

That sounded all well and good. But Ellen was her *mother*.

Of all the times Susan would have died for her mother's support, this wasn't one. She didn't want Ellen making her feel like a lousy mother—didn't want to spend *one second* wondering what Ellen thought about Lily's pregnancy. And as for Ellen's relationship with Big Rick, Susan could not have cared less.

Rick took her hand. "C'mon. Let's go get coffee. They won't be starting the surgery for a while. It'll be close to an hour before we hear anything."

THEY WENT TO THE COFFEE SHOP AND SPLIT A doughnut, wandered through the lobby, explored the gift shop. When they ran out of places to go, Rick took her back upstairs.

Susan was prepared to see her mother this time. Still, she felt a jolt opening that door and meeting Ellen's eyes. The woman looked well—hair more silver than not, but stylishly combed, black slacks, peach sweater. The fact that she looked frightened was some consolation to Susan, who was frightened herself.

But she was, after all, a big girl now.

So she kissed Big Rick's cheek and took the chair beside Ellen. "Thank you for coming," she said softly. "Lily will be touched."

Ellen nodded. After a minute, she murmured, "I had no idea."

That Lily was pregnant? That the baby had problems? That Susan had nearly lost her job? "Some things are hard to discuss," Susan said. "Did you fly up with Big Rick?"

Again Ellen nodded. "I'm no traveler. He dragged me along."

An unwilling companion, then? Or just a poor choice of words? It struck Susan that her mother might not know what to say to her, either.

"You must have landed last night." It was a safe remark, but barely spoken when a man in scrubs approached, then went on past and into the hall. After a worried glance at the clock, Susan caught Rick's eye.

"Too soon," he said softly.

She sat back, hugging her middle, and thought of Lily and the baby. She didn't try to talk to her mother. Rick was right; her focus should be on Lily. Needing to relax, she took out her knitting.

A few minutes later, Ellen did the same. She wasn't working with PC Wool, but with a glitzy novelty yarn.

"What're you making?" Susan asked.

"A scarf for Jack's Emily. She chose the yarn."

The mention of the girl's name rubbed Susan the wrong way. "Emily. Ahhh. Darling child." Instantly remorseful, she remarked on the yarn, "It's pretty."

"No, it isn't," Ellen murmured. "It's tacky. And no pleasure to knit."

"Why are you making it, then?"

"Because she asked."

"You never made a scarf for me."

"You never asked."

"Maybe I was afraid I'd be refused." Setting down her knitting, she rubbed her forehead. Her voice was a whisper, for Ellen's ears alone. "This is unreal. My pregnant daughter is on the operating table while doctors try to save her baby, and I'm arguing with my mother, whom I have seen once in nearly eighteen years and *never* east of the Mississippi. This is blowing my mind."

Ellen continued to knit her tacky yarn.

Susan glanced at the clock, then at Rick. "Do you think something's wrong?"

"No. We're just impatient."

Try superstitious. Susan was starting to wonder if her job had been spared to cushion the blow of losing the baby. Or losing Lily.

Desperate for comfort, she returned to her very beautiful, very artistic, very original PC Wool scarf.

"That's very pretty," her mother said. "It's one of the new colors, isn't it?"

"Yes. Robin At Dawn. We want to photograph finished pieces for the catalogue. I told you about that."

"Yes," Ellen said. Susan had knit another row, before her mother asked, "Are those short rows?"

"Yes."

"Interesting design."

Susan passed her mother the pattern, but continued to knit. She focused on the stitches, focused on the rhythm, focused on turning at the gap. When Ellen returned the pattern, Susan tucked it back in her bag and kept on knitting. Knitting was familiar at a time when everything around her was strange.

At the ninety-minute point, she caught Rick's eye. Setting his laptop aside, he checked with the nurse, but returned moments later with no news. "They're still in the OR."

"Why so long?"

"They may have started late."

"What if they found something they didn't expect?"

Rick touched a finger to her mouth. "They won't," he said and returned to his seat.

THE GOOD NEWS WAS THAT BETWEEN IMAGINING possible complications—oh yes, the Web had given her every last one—and praying, Susan didn't dwell on her mother's unexpected presence. The bad news was that it was two hours before the doctor emerged. By that time, she was frantic.

But he was fully at ease. "All's well," he told her. "Your daughter was frightened, so we spent a little while calming her. We gave her a tour of the OR and showed her the balloon we'd be inserting. She'll remember that part and be stronger for it. As for her little guy, his heart is beating good as gold. He'll do fine."

A LITTLE WHILE LATER, SUSAN WAS ALLOWED BACK TO wait with Lily until they could transfer her to a room. She would be staying overnight in the hospital for monitoring, though the fetal monitor was only part of it. If they discovered any kind of amniotic leak, Lily would be on bed rest for the remainder of the pregnancy.

The girl was sleeping off the sedative in little cat naps. Susan waited until she was more awake before telling her that Big Rick was there.

Her eyes lit. "He came all this way for me?"

"He did. And he isn't alone. He brought your grandmother."

Lily didn't respond at first. Then she frowned. "*Your* mother?" When Susan nodded, she cried weakly, "She knows I'm pregnant?"

"Yup. Big Rick told her."

"Is she angry?"

"She doesn't look it. She looks like she's not sure she's welcome here."

"Is she?"

"Of course. She's my mother."

"What do I *say* to her?"

Susan couldn't answer that. "You're asking the wrong person. I just wanted you to know so you won't be as shocked as I was."

LILY HANDLED ELLEN WITH APLOMB. BUT ELLEN wasn't her mother. Mother-daughter relationships had to be the most complex in the world, while grandmother-granddaughter ones were more forgiving, Susan decided. As wary as Lily had been of Ellen in Oklahoma, she was all smiles now. Relief surely played a part; with the surgery successfully done, Lily would have embraced Scrooge.

Abby, who held no past grudges and seemed honored to be part of an historic meeting, treated Ellen like a special guest. Susan might have resented it, if she hadn't been so grateful to have her mother occupied. And reinforcements arrived late that afternoon in the form of Kate, Sunny, and Pam, who had driven up on impulse.

Through it all, neither the baby nor Lily appeared any the worse for wear.

SUSAN DIDN'T ASK WHERE ELLEN WAS STAYING, BUT with Kate, Sunny, and Pam overnighting as well, there was a crowd in the coffee shop for breakfast the next morning and later in Lily's hospital room. Lily was sore at the points of incision, but there continued to be no other problems, and she was eager to be home.

By mid-afternoon, they were on the road, two SUVs loaded with people, flowers, and balloons. Susan kept looking back at Lily, who smiled every time. She kept thinking about the baby, whom she had seen on a sonogram again that morning and who was adorable, balloon and all. She kept thinking about Rick, who had watched that screen with the same vulnerable look as Lily—kept thinking about the follow-up tests and the doctor's appointments, but with optimism now—kept thinking about her school, her students.

And Ellen? She let that one ride.

A GENTLE SNOW BEGAN TO FALL SHORTLY AFTER they crossed into Maine, and though it remained light as they drove up the coast—the Penobscots had known what they were talking about when they named the town for its moderate weather—it accumulated enough to cover the January dirt. With night falling before six, they saw lights as they entered Zaganack. Main Street was largely Perry & Cass crimson, with the harbor lights more blue. Between the masts of diehard fishermen, festive colors outlining restaurants, and clusters of seagulls overnighting on the town dock, it was so picturesque, that if Susan hadn't already forgiven the town for doubting about her, she would have now.

And that was before they approached her little house, which was spattered with color well beyond sea green and teal. A rainbow of balloons was tied to the mailbox, a large WELCOME HOME SUSAN AND LILY banner hung between windows. More balloons flanked the door, a navy-and-yellow bouquet for Lily, a fuchsia one for Susan, and on the steps were a mound of foil-covered bundles, food from friends, left to chill in the snow.

Two cars sat out front, disgorging a gaggle of girls the instant they turned into the driveway.

If Susan had wanted her mother to see that she and Lily had a rich life with friends who loved them, she couldn't have asked for a better homecoming.

Chapter 28

SUSAN SETTLED LILY IN THE DEN. WHEN RICK DISAP-
peared soon after, she found him upstairs packing his things.

"What are you doing?" she asked in alarm.

He shifted socks from drawer to duffel. "I'll stay at the inn
in town with my dad. You need the bed."

"I don't," Susan argued. "Ellen can stay at the inn."

"She's your mother. She's come a long way, and she should
stay here." He opened the next drawer.

"Don't leave me alone with her." He smiled chidingly, but
she was serious. He was a buffer—between her and the town,
the media, and now Ellen. "I want you to stay. You can sleep in
my room."

His smile turned wry. "Now there's an interesting proposi-
tion. What was it, less than two days ago that you dodged the
morals bullet?" Dropping shirts in the duffel, suddenly
unsmiling, he straightened. "We need a bigger house."

"We?"

"You and me. It's time, don't you think?"

"For what?"

He put his hands on his hips. "*Us*. Let's pool resources. Get a bigger house. Maybe even get married."

Married? *Married*? "You don't want to get married."

"How do you know?"

"You love your freedom."

He stared at her. "I think you love yours more."

"Not true. I just don't want to be hurt."

"Me, neither, which is probably why I've never said the m-word before. Only this is ridiculous." His eyes softened. "Hell, Susie, I've always loved you."

Her heart tripped. They had never used the l-word either. Oh, she had said it to friends over the years, as in *Rick is a love,* or *I just love Rick,* but never aloud and face-to-face. "You loved me even when you were twenty-two?" she asked skeptically, because the declaration was too neat. One intimate summer; that was it. They had been young and unformed, certainly different from the adults they were today.

"Smitten," he said without blinking. "There was never a doubt. Do you not love me?"

She barely had to think. "Of course I love you."

"So what's the problem?"

Susan tried to think of one. Yes, love was a given, she realized. She and Rick got along too well for it not to be. Formalizing their relationship was something else. Somewhere around the time she left home, pregnant with Lily, she had crossed marriage off her list of dreams. She had her daughter; that was enough.

"See?" he argued. "You always push me away."

"No. You always leave."

"And you let me go, like I'm not worth keeping."

"Are you *kidding*?" she cried. "Why do you think I've never looked at anyone else? No one ever came *close*."

"Okay," he said, amending the charge, "then you let me go like *you're* not worth keeping. Is that your father's legacy? That you aren't good enough to keep?"

Susan thought of recent weeks, when everything she had worked so hard to achieve had been questioned. Yes, this was what she brought from the past, and it haunted her still. She was a good educator. She was a good mother. But good enough? "I'm flawed."

He made a frustrated sound. "We're *all* flawed. So we can either be flawed separately or together. There's your choice."

"It's not that simple."

"It is. None of us is perfect. God knows I'm not, or I would have pushed this issue a long time ago."

She studied his handsome face. He had lost some of his tan to the New England winter, and his hair was longer than usual, but his eyes were as blue, his voice as rich. She couldn't imagine his not having shared that with people all over the world. Marriage meant giving it up.

"You wouldn't have," she said.

"You're right. Because I got a rush being in war zones or running alongside trucks bringing rice to the starving poor. My high was being recognized, *adulated,* which makes my point. I am totally flawed. So we make mistakes. So we're sometimes slow to see them. Slow doesn't mean never."

"But what if I can't be a good wife?"

"What if I can't be a good husband? C'mon, hon. We'll do our best."

She rubbed her forehead. "This is a big step."

He came closer. Framing her face with his hands, his mesmerizing blue eyes steady, he asked so gently that her heart melted, "What scares you most?"

"You," she whispered. "Me. Change. I'm used to controlling my life."

Slipping his fingers into her hair, he lifted her face and gave her one of those kisses that tasted of longing, the kind of kiss that made her mindless, the kind she remembered most when he was gone.

Clutching his wrists, she drew back. "Oh-ho, no. That will not work. This has to be a rational discussion."

"About control," he conceded. "Would it be so awful to share it?"

Terrifying, she thought. *I'd be hurt.*

Granted, Rick had never hurt her. What he promised, he gave. But then, she had never asked for much.

You let me go, he said, and he was right. *Like you're not worth keeping,* he said. Right again. But how does one get rid of old baggage?

She felt the loss of his warmth when he stepped back. "Lots to think about," he said and returned to his packing.

SUSAN COULDN'T THINK ABOUT MUCH ELSE, WHAT with a houseful of friends who were happy to wait on Lily, cook dinner, and occupy Ellen. Once Rick left, she took refuge in his room. It always smelled woodsy when he was around. She breathed it in for a bit before reluctantly stripping the bed.

She had just unfolded fresh sheets when her mother appeared and went to the far side of the bed. Catching a fitted corner, Ellen stretched it over the mattress. "It's good of you to have me here." She smoothed the sheet with a hand.

"I wouldn't have you any other place."

"I'm displacing Rick."

Who wanted a bigger house. Who wanted *marriage.* "That's okay." Susan needed to think. She whipped the top sheet out over the bed. "How long will you and Big Rick stay?"

Ellen brought the sheet down on her side. "I can't speak for him. We're just friends who happen to share a granddaughter." Susan was thinking that Ellen was finally out from under her husband's thumb and could do whatever she wanted with any man, when Ellen added, "He can either drop me off in Oklahoma on his way back west. Or I can stay. I don't want to put you out."

"I invited you."

"I'll only stay as long as I can help."

Help? Susan eyed her blankly.

Ellen spoke quickly. "The doctor wants Lily off her feet for a few days, and you have to get back to work. And they want to keep checking on the baby, so Lily will have to go for tests. And once he's born he'll need extra care."

The implication was that she might stay awhile. Rick. *And* Ellen? And a *baby*? If change was an issue, this was a triple whammy, and that was totally apart from the history Susan had with her mother. Tension? Disapproval? Rejection? Did she want it? *Need* it?

"I could fly back and forth," Ellen said, sounding defensive. "I have the money."

"You hate flying."

"I can do it."

"You don't really want to."

"How do *you* know?" She softened. "Not that you need me here. You have Rick. You have friends."

"I need you here," Susan said. It was a knee-jerk reaction— but not. The only way to deal with old baggage was to open it up and sort through. How else to know what to keep and what to toss?

"There are hard feelings."

"I always wanted us to be closer."

"You must hate me for what I did," Ellen insisted, seeming determined to confront the issue.

"It was a long time ago," Susan said, not wanting the confrontation just then, but her mother wouldn't let it go.

"You can't have forgotten."

"Okay. I still try to understand the why of it."

"Aha. You do have hard feelings."

Pushed far enough, Susan cried, "How could I not? You threw me away. I was young and scared, and you banished me for something I didn't even know I'd done until it was too late. Do you think I *planned* to get pregnant? My daughter *did* plan her pregnancy, and when I found out, I was furious. So I did what you did. I shut her out. If I have hard feelings toward you right now, it's because you set a bad example."

Ellen seemed taken aback by the outburst.

Telling herself her mother had asked for it, Susan continued. "So how *do* you feel about Lily being pregnant?"

Ellen swallowed. "Not as bad as I'd have felt if your father were still alive." It was quite an admission. Susan was trying to process it, when her mother went on. "I'm sorry she's pregnant. I'm sorry about this scare with the baby. I'm sorry these things happen."

"But they do. And you need to be okay with it. Because, honestly, Mom, much as I want you to be part of my life, it won't work if you don't accept my daughter. I don't want history repeating itself."

"It can't. I wasn't a good mother. You are."

Of all the open sores, this one went deepest. Needing encouragement from the voice that mattered most, Susan asked, "What makes you say that?"

"I saw you with Lily back home. I see you with her here. There's a connection between you. You like each other."

"I love her. She's my daughter."

"It's more. You're friends."

"I let her get pregnant."

"Like I let you get pregnant?" Ellen smiled sadly. "I was a bad mother, but not because of that. I didn't stand up for my child. I didn't speak up to your father."

"That was your relationship with him."

"It was wrong. He was wrong." Her eyes held Susan's, daring her to disagree.

Unable to, Susan bent over to tuck in the sheet. "I survived."

Ellen tucked in her side. "Without my help."

"I forgive you."

"Maybe you shouldn't. I don't know my own granddaughter. What kind of person does that make me?"

"It's circumstances."

"No. It's choices. I made bad ones." She paused. "Lily seems like a very nice person."

"She is," Susan said. "So are her friends. If she had to be involved in a pact, I'm glad it's with this group." She drew up the comforter.

Ellen did the same on her side. "Isn't a pact just a group of people who bow to peer pressure?"

Remembering the discussion in the car Thursday night, Susan said, "Sometimes."

"Then my friends and I formed a pact against you."

Susan straightened. "I'm okay with it, Mom. Really. Let's try and forget all that."

"Hard to do back home. All the memories." Ellen frowned for a minute. "I met a young woman on the plane. She asked about my knitting, and we got to talking. She said she didn't have the patience to knit. I told her she had it backwards, that knitting *gave* me patience. She said her grandmother says the same thing, and that maybe she'll feel that way when she gets old."

"You're not old," Susan said, because fifty-nine wasn't old and Ellen looked good. She was stylish and trim. If there were wrinkles on her face, they were faint.

"Not in years," she replied. "In mind-set. But I keep hearing that word—*old*—and not wanting to be. Old is stiff, unable to bend. Funny, I'm okay when I knit. When I make a mistake, I rip back to where I botched it, even if that means ripping out hours of work to get it right. Why can't I do that in life?"

"It's a luxury we don't often have."

"I have it now," Ellen said with a direct look. "I want to know Lily. And I want to know her baby."

Still afraid of being hurt, Susan made light of it. "Oh, a baby is a total blob. You don't want to be changing diapers."

"There you go again, telling me what I want. Y'know, Susan, you're just like your father. 'I know what you want,' he always said. But he didn't, and it got so I didn't either. We both assumed he knew best. But maybe he didn't. Maybe he needed to ask once in a while. Maybe he needed to listen. But he's not here anymore, so it's too late. And maybe I wouldn't have had the courage to say it to him, anyway. But I'll say it to you. You need to listen."

Susan had never had an open discussion with Ellen— certainly not about mistakes—but her mother kept talking. "You invited me, so I'm here. I got on that plane. I could do it again. I don't have to be entertained, y'know. But I could help. I could be a good mother."

Listening, Susan heard her say *mother*. Not grandmother. Not great-grandmother. Mother. And suddenly the old baggage was wide open, lots of bad stuff, but one big thing she knew she wanted to keep. It brought a lump to her throat, along with the dire need to hug and be hugged.

But she didn't have a physical relationship with Ellen, never had.

So she simply nodded, swallowed, and said a soft, "I'd like that."

THE NEED TO HUG AND BE HUGGED LINGERED. BACK in her own room later that night, Susan thought of calling Rick, but hesitated. Something else came back to her from the discussion in the car Thursday night. Mothering was elemental. It was life's first relationship, the one from which everything else sprang.

Ellen. Susan. Lily.

Light-footed on the creaking floorboards, she crossed the hall to her daughter's room. In the faint glow of the butterfly nightlight, Lily was still just a blip under the quilt. Lily and her baby. Not as bizarre a thought as it had once been.

The girl stirred, but it was a minute before she realized Susan was there. Scooting back, she opened the quilt.

As soon as Susan was underneath, Lily snuggled against her. She was quiet, breathing evenly. Susan was beginning to think she had fallen back to sleep, when there was a whispered, "Awesome."

"What?" Susan whispered back.

"Your mom. She's different from the way she was in December."

Place played a part, Susan knew. So did time, no funeral now. And mind-set, Ellen's own word. She had chosen to visit.

"She's evolving," Susan whispered against the top of Lily's head.

"Awesome."

"Would you be okay if she stays a little while?"

"Totally."

"Rick, too?"

"Mmm."

"He asked me to marry him."

Lily went very still. "Really?"

"Yes."

She scrambled up. "Omigod." She threw her arms around Susan's neck. "That is *awesome*."

"Y'think?"

"Don't you?"

The idea was growing on her. "Actually, yes."

"*Omigod*. Wait'll I tell the others. They'll *die*." She sat up. "My baby did this. He brought us together. How poetic is *that*? So. When'll you do it?"

Susan tucked Lily's hair behind her ears, leaving her thumbs to trace the familiar heart. "I don't know. I haven't accepted yet."

"Mom. You won't find a better man than him."

Susan didn't need a man at all. But maybe Lily would. Besides, there was a difference between need and want. Rick's being here had been wonderful during a very hard time. He didn't seem bored hanging around. And when there was a baby for him to play with, how *exciting* would that be?

"Life is a work in progress," she finally said. "For me. For your grandmother. She wants to know you and your baby."

Lily hung her wrists over Susan's shoulder. Their noses were inches apart. "He's going to be okay. I know that, Mom. With so many people pulling for him, how could he not?"

"People pull for him because they love *you*. You're a kind person."

"Because you are. I mean, how lucky am I? So many babies have worse problems."

Susan nodded. She had to be doing something right if her daughter realized that.

Lily settled against her again. "Mom?"

"What, sweetie?"

"I still can't call her Nana."

"Give it time."

"I think it's neat she came because of the baby."

"She wants to make up for what she missed."

"Because she messed it up the first time? What if I do? What if I make mistakes, too?"

You'll rip it and reknit, Susan thought, remembering what her mother had said. "You'll try again."

"Will you love me anyway?"

"Always."

Lily's breathing steadied, warm against her throat. "You're a good mother," she whispered.

"I try."

Epilogue

❧

"WHAT DO YOU THINK?" SUSAN ASKED, STANDING back for a better view. She was with Kate, Sunny, and Pam in the attic of the old Victorian that was her new home.

She had married Rick at the end of May, but they didn't find the house until July. Rick wanted a stone front, Susan five bedrooms and a studio, and it went without saying that a lawn with an abundance of grass and trees was a must. This house had barely gone on the market when they grabbed it. Sited on an acre of land, it was closer to the center of town and twice as large as Susan's old one, and though it needed work, Rick was game. Directing the renovations, he kept a crew of locals moving quickly, so that by mid-September, new heating, plumbing, and electrical systems were in place. As soon as the hardwood floors were sanded and sealed, they moved in.

From its steep gabled roofs and wraparound porches, to its deep bay windows and staircase nooks, there was plenty to paint. *You pick the colors, that's your thing,* Rick said, but, given the freedom, Susan was reserved. In deference to him—and to the fact that, though she simply couldn't choose the pale blues and yellows of neighboring homes, marriage was about compromise—she had the shingles painted a light teal and the trim a crisp white. Both looked stunning against the brilliant fall leaves, at their peak now, this first week in October.

She had been more adventurous with the inside colors, going deeper in some rooms, wilder in others. Then came the attic, its newly installed skylights shaded by the crown of a hundred-year-old oak. At the back, under rafters painted sky blue with clouds, was a playroom. At the front was her studio. It was fuchsia.

This was what Susan studied now. "Too much?" she asked the others.

"Actually not," Kate decided.

"It's very you," Sunny said.

Pam had her hands on her hips, which were otherwise lost under a paint-spattered shirt. "You deserve this, Susan. You were so disciplined downstairs."

"Excuse me. Our bedroom is burgundy. Rick says he loves it, but is he just being kind? I have to keep reminding myself that it isn't only me anymore."

"It was never only you. It was Lily, too."

"But this house is half Rick's."

Kate guffawed. "The man is so in love with you, he'd let you paint the place *neon green,* if that was what you wanted."

Susan smiled. She had been in denial for so long that the reality of Rick continued to amaze her.

"Come on, Susan," Sunny teased softly. "Admit it. You love being married."

Susan sighed. "I do. It was a long time coming. Maybe I grew up enough."

"Maybe he did, too," Pam remarked.

Kate refastened her hair, one strand of which now matched

the wall. "He was cute, living with you all those weeks, like he was going to prove that it'd work before he popped the question."

"I'm not sure it was deliberate," Susan mused. "It just crept up on both of us. Our living together definitely helped when the obvious finally hit. Still, things are different when you're married. It's final. When we get in each other's way, we have to deal. It's not like he'll be leaving in a day or two, like he always did before. I mean, obviously, he still travels," she drawled with a quick look at her watch. Rick had been on special assignment in London and was due back momentarily. Though he had been gone for only three days, she was impatient to see him. Thinking about that, she cried, "I've grown totally dependent. How pathetic is that?"

"Dependent doesn't have to be bad."

"It's scary," Susan insisted.

"For what it's worth," said Kate, "he's grown just as dependent on you. It's sweet to see."

"Well, that raises a whole other issue. I have a partner now, so my life is easier. Lily's is harder."

"Not your doing," Sunny reminded her.

"No, but it's hard to watch. I swear, Rick and I discuss this every single day when our instinct would be to just pitch in and do. Lily has to learn to care for her son without assuming we'll always be there. But I have so much more help now than I ever did that I feel guilty."

"Really." This from Kate. "There are times when I stand in my bedroom listening to the baby cry. I want to go to him, but—same thing—I know it wouldn't be good for Mary Kate. She has to do this herself."

"Isn't she?" Pam asked.

"Actually, she is. She has more strength than I'd have

expected—an awful thing to say about my own child, but taking care of a baby is *challenging*. Will and I are still struggling with the equipment, and we've done it five times before."

"That's why you're struggling. You didn't think you'd be doing it again."

Kate lit up. "But Willie is the best thing to come along since . . . since Mary Kate. My boys are obsessed with him. I swear, they'll stick around even after they graduate, just to grow up with that child."

"If they stick around, it's a tribute to you," Susan said, to which Kate gave a wry smile.

"Some tributes I can do without. I still wish Mary Kate had started college, but she isn't ready, I understand that. She'll start in January, and even then she's going to have trouble leaving the baby in day care. So here's another thing I feel guilty about. I ought to offer to take him for a day or two. I know she'd be happier if he were with me. But I work. I need to work. I *want* to work. I suppose that what I earn will offset the cost of day care; still, I worry about it."

"At least Jacob's helping," Sunny reminded her. "Adam is long gone. He won't be coming back much."

"Has he admitted he was the one?" Susan asked.

"No. He never will."

"Do you know that he is?"

"Jessica says so, and his parents are so quick to walk the other way when I come near, that I think they know it, too."

"How can they not be curious?"

"What kind of people would deny their own grandson?"

Sunny held up a *let's not go there* hand. "Dan periodically suggests taking him to court to force a paternity test, but to what good? I agree with Jessica on this. If Adam wants no part of the baby, we're better off without him. Besides, do I want •

him butting into our lives? N-O. Adam isn't the nice guy Robbie is. You're lucky, Susan. Robbie's there just enough, gone just enough."

"Is Lily warming to him?" Kate asked.

"She likes him a lot. She always did. And now? She's impressed with how good he is with Noah and how well he handles his mother—who, by the way, *is* curious. She and Bill drop over once a week. But does Lily want to marry Robbie? Not yet. They both have a lot of growing to do." She shot Pam a sheepish look. "I'm sorry. We always seem to be talking about this."

Good sport that she had become, Pam listened graciously, and though she wasn't clamoring to babysit, she went out of her way to help out with PC Wool when baby emergencies cropped up. Moreover, with Abby at college and Tanner accepting that his wife had a right to a life, she had become the face of PC Wool at trade shows. At the same time, her voice on the school board continued to grow. Two of the men, Morgan and Lombard, had decided not to run again, so she was recruiting replacements, and the initiative was self-perpetuating. The more she spoke up, the more people listened, and the stronger she grew. It was about self-confidence. She didn't work as hard now at being tight with Susan, Sunny, and Kate—the upshot of which was that she more naturally fit in.

"Hey, it's okay," she said now. "I'm glad it's you guys and not me."

"What's the latest from Abby?" Kate asked. "Will they let her dump her lousy roommate?"

"No, but she's found someone to live with second semester, and she loves her classes. Fall break is next weekend. I can't wait to have her home."

Susan was looking forward to seeing her. Not that she

didn't feel a quick twinge. Abby was doing what she had wanted Lily to do.

But dreams of the past were fading, those wistful moments few and far between. Lily was an attentive, capable mother, and the baby—well, the baby was a miracle. At five months, he was becoming a smiler, remarkable for an infant who had survived a life-threatening condition. His temperament had been sweet from that first little cry in the delivery room, moments after the balloon had been removed from his trachea, as if he was simply grateful to be alive.

Susan couldn't picture life without him. But then, her own life had changed so much that it was hard making comparisons to the past, period.

For one thing, her job was secure now in ways it had never been before. The town knew the worst and had stuck with her. She had proven herself under fire.

For another, there was Rick. A rock, he had remained calm through Lily's labor and Noah's surgery, and he willingly changed diapers when Lily truly needed the sleep. Likewise, he did his share of work around the house—not that he was perfect. Susan was still training him to wipe out the bathroom sink after he shaved, to take dirty towels to the laundry room, and even—*Yes, Rick, that basket is full!*—put the wash in himself. But if she had to be dependent on anyone, Rick was a good choice.

And then there was Susan's mom, the non-traveler who now shuttled between Oklahoma and Maine like a pro. Jack had charged Susan with making unfair demands of her, and though Ellen hadn't argued, she didn't change a thing. She seemed content in Zaganack, smiling more than Susan ever remembered her doing. She liked Susan's friends, and, now that Lily was fully recovered from childbirth and able to take care of Noah, Ellen had taken to being at the PC Wool barn with Kate. Timid about doing the actual dyeing, she busied herself with other chores at the oak table in the back. Kate and company had come to look forward to her visits.

So, surprisingly, had Susan, though she found it easier to think of Ellen as a friend. The mother part was shadowed by the past, and with their relationship comfortable now, neither wanted to rock the boat. When sensitive issues popped up, Ellen steered them back to the present. And maybe she was right, Susan decided. Motherhood was about picking up and moving ahead. It was about trying to do better, rather than being paralyzed by what couldn't be changed.

She and Ellen were enjoying life and each other. Wasn't that the important thing?

LILY WAS THINKING ALONG SIMILAR LINES AS SHE sat at the harbor with Mary Kate and Jess. Lulled by the fall breeze off the ocean and the sough of waves against the pier, all three babies were asleep. Neither the cry of the gulls nor the clang of moorings had woken them. It was a rare moment.

"I think we lucked out," Lily said, rocking Noah's carriage with her foot. "Our moms adore these kids."

"What's not to adore?" Mary Kate asked.

"Crying," remarked Jess. Addison Hope Barros spit up all the time. She had just been diagnosed with reflux.

"It'll be better once the medicine kicks in," Lily said in encouragement, "and besides, she'll outgrow this. Your mom knows that. She isn't asking you to go live with Delilah."

In the hope that holding Addie upright would keep her food down, Jess had her in a carrier on her chest. Peering down, she adjusted her hat. "Delilah wouldn't be good with illness. My mom is. She's right on top of the medicine thing. She keeps lists."

"Are you being sarcastic?" Mary Kate asked.

"I am not. She's been awesome. I mean, if there's a problem, I look up and there she is with whatever I need."

That made Lily's point. "She's adapted. They all have."

"So have we," Mary Kate said quietly.

Lily knew she was thinking about college. How not to, when friends there were constantly sending them excited messages?

Well, not constantly. The texting had slowed. Lily had to adapt to that, too. "No more word from Jacob?"

"Not in four days. I guess that's okay. He knows I'll tell him if there's a problem."

"Doesn't he want to know what Willie's doing?" Jess asked.

Mary Kate shot her a wry look. "Eating, sleeping, pooping? I mean, that's pathetic, but it's what being four months old is about. I get a smile from him once in a while, and he's precious when he coos. I could watch him sleep for hours. Jacob wants him to play. Think about it. Right now, these babies are pretty boring."

"I don't have time to think about it," Jess remarked. "I'm too busy cleaning spit-up."

As she could do only with these two, Lily said, "I do think about it. I think about what I was doing this time last year. I mean, I wouldn't change a thing. But, boy, is life different— and in good ways even aside from Noah," she said, because Susan taught her to look at the positive first. "I have a new house. I have a dad. I have *grandparents*."

Mary Kate's eyes went wide. "Are Ellen and Big Rick dating?"

"Not officially. But she likes it when he comes."

"Like you like it when Robbie comes?" Jess teased.

"I like it," Lily informed her, "because I think it's good for the baby. Robbie enjoys him."

"Is he still texting so much?"

"Oh, yeah." His messages came multiple times each day, and he had been home twice since classes started. He really was so cute with Noah, and since Noah meant everything to Lily, she would start thinking Robbie had potential. Then he'd return to school and annoy her by starting to text again. "Every few hours I get a blow-by-blow of college life. Like I can identify."

"With all-nighters?" Mary Kate asked in a high voice. "I can identify with that. Of course, *they* sleep until ten the next morning. When was the last time we did that? I did sleep for four straight hours last night. That's a record."

Lily's record was five, making Noah the best sleeper of the three. With his organs now neatly tucked where they should be, he seemed to be eating to make up for lost time. Maybe that was why he slept well. But then, he was an easygoing guy. Jess's Addie was higher strung. To Lily's knowledge, she was still screaming for food at the three-hour mark. Of course, she was only fourteen weeks to Noah's twenty.

A wail came from her now. Jess jumped up, adjusted the pacifier, and, swearing softly, began a frenetic swaying.

"You can't do that, Jess," Mary Kate warned.

"Swear?"

"Get tense. She senses it. You have to relax."

"That's easy for you to say. You don't have to worry whether your baby is getting enough food." But she did slow the swaying to a calmer pace. "It's like she's always hungry. I'm not sure the new formula is doing a thing."

Lily wondered if breast milk would have been better, but Jess had stopped nursing after three weeks when the baby couldn't seem to get enough. They would never know whether reflux, not lack of food, had caused the crying. Or whether it was Jess's nervousness. Or just Addie's personality.

But Lily agreed with Mary Kate. Jess had to relax. "If this formula doesn't help," she said, "you'll try another, and then another, and before you know it, she'll be past this stage."

"I guess," Jess said, swaying more tiredly now. "It's probably a good thing Adam isn't around. He'd hate this. Did I honestly think he'd be a good father?"

"We never asked ourselves that. We didn't want them involved raising our kids. Adam has good genes. That's what counts." Or so they had said. But Lily liked seeing Robbie with Noah. She liked seeing Rick with him, too. And Big Rick. And Ellen. Not to mention the fact that when someone else played with the baby, she got a break. Even with six hours of sleep, she couldn't believe how tired she was. She had no sooner changed him than he pooped, had no sooner washed his clothes than more were dirty. The work never ended.

"I feel guilty complaining," Jess said. "Addie didn't ask for this. There are times when I'm cleaning her up and she gives me this really apologetic look, like she's saying, 'I'm sorry, Mommy. I didn't mean it. I won't do it again,' and I feel so bad. I do have a lot going for me. Darcy can't get enough of Addie. Dad takes her for walks. And Mom, she's loosened up a lot. Sometimes I think that the less neurotic she is, the more I am—like it's drained out of her and into me."

"You aren't neurotic," Lily said. "You worry, is all."

They were silent for a bit, resting there by the pier. Finally Mary Kate cleared her throat. "Have we decided what to do when Abby is home this weekend? She wants us at her house."

"Not just us," Jess said. "She's invited everyone who'll be home. What'll we have to say to them?"

"We can listen," Lily offered. "They love to talk."

"So do I. Will they ask about my life?"

"No. But Abby really wants us there. She'll be disappointed if we don't go."

There was another silence, then from Mary Kate a cautious "We could bring the babies."

Lily shook her head at the same time that Jess said a firm "No."

"What if we went for just an hour and asked our moms to babysit?" Mary Kate tried.

Lily knew why Mary Kate wanted to go. "Will Jacob be there?"

"I don't know, I haven't asked," she said, "but it'd only be for an hour. I mean"—she looked from Lily to Jess—"okay, so we hate to ask. Our parents have not been begging us to let them babysit. As far as they're concerned, giving up a social life was part of the pact." Her voice grew more meek. "But maybe they'd do it just this once?"

Lily didn't answer. She was wondering how her mother had managed with no one, ever, to help. In that instant, it struck her that getting pregnant was the easy part. Giving birth wasn't bad either, what with a room full of people pitching in. The hard part was what came after—taking care of a baby three-sixty-five twenty-four-seven.

Her mother had done it alone. That was scary. Lily didn't know what she would do if she didn't have Susan around.

Seeming to read her mind, or perhaps just ready for a shot of mom-support herself, Jess said, "I think we should start back. Addie'll be wanting to eat."

Minutes later, each lost in thought as they crossed Main Street, they were startled by the honk of a horn. It was Rachel Bishop, back from Vassar. Slowing, she waved excitedly, pointed to the babies, and gave a thumbs-up, then accelerated again and was gone.

In her wake, all was still. Two carriages, one BabyBjörn, and three young mothers walked on.

. . .

SUSAN HAD DECIDED THAT IF THE BABY'S HALF OF the attic had a cloud-strewn sky, her half needed grass. They were in the process of adding windblown blades to the lower walls when Susan glanced at her watch. Setting her brush aside, she stood and went to the window—and there he was, pulling into the driveway.

Heart pounding, she trotted down two flights of stairs and outside, feeling an excitement she wouldn't have expected. She had known Rick most of her life, had been with him sexually more than half of that, but with commitment, their roles were redefined. Marriage said that he wasn't going away, that he would be part of her life forever, that he loved her. It gave her *license* to be excited.

He was grinning when he climbed from the car and, arms opening, scooped her up—and here was another change. Public Display of Affection was totally okay. When it was done, she took his hand and dragged him up those two flights of stairs.

"Whoa," he said when the fuchsia hit him.

"You hate it?" Susan asked worriedly, but he was already looking past Susan's part to the sky with its billowy white clouds.

"That I love," he said, eyes sparkling with hellos to Kate, Sunny, and Pam.

"But you hate the fuchsia."

He grinned crookedly. "As long as I'm not the one working here, the fuchsia is great."

"It'll be better when the grass is done. I may even add some giant sunflowers."

"Add whatever you want. It's your space. We can always

hang a curtain to pull if it bothers me when I'm playing trains with the boy," he teased, then said quietly, "No carriage on the porch. Where'd they go?"

"The pier. They'll be back any minute."

He went to the window and had barely glanced toward the harbor end of the street when he said, "There," and was off like a shot.

Taking his place at the window, Susan watched him stride down the front walk and turn onto the sidewalk as the caravan of girls and their babies appeared.

"He is adorable," said Kate from her elbow.

From her shoulder, Pam said, "So excited, like it's his own child."

"It is," Susan murmured, thinking of Lily, because Rick hugged her first. Leaving a hand on her arm, he kissed each of the other girls, then leaned down to see Noah.

"The pièce de résistance," Sunny whispered in appreciation.

As they watched, Rick reached in and picked up the baby and, cradling him with admirable ease, guided the girls up the walk.

"Blown off for a five-month-old," Pam announced.

But Susan only smiled. She couldn't ask to see anything better. Sharing was precious.

She was a mother. She had learned this.

Acknowledgments

Deepest thanks to Nancy Shulman, Debbie Smith, and Dianne List for sharing their expertise on yarn, medicine, and school, respectively. If I've strayed from reality on any of these subjects, please understand that I've taken literary license—and forgive me for it.

My thanks, also, to Amy Berkower, Phyllis Grann, and Lucy Davis, each of whom helped, in her own special way, to make possible the book you now hold.

As always, I thank my family, without whose love I'd be lost.

Readers' Guide

The questions and topics that follow are designed to enhance your book club's discussion of Barbara Delinsky's *Not My Daughter*. We hope they will enrich your experience of this compelling novel. For special reading group features, visit the author's website at www.barbaradelinsky.com.

Introduction

No writer captures the tender rewards and unique challenges of family life better than Barbara Delinsky. Raising provocative questions about motherhood, *Not My Daughter* marks new heights of captivating storytelling for Delinsky. In the novel's opening pages, high school principal Susan Tate confronts a devastating secret. Her seventeen-year-old daughter, Lily, has revealed that she is expecting a baby—and that this is not an accidental pregnancy. Susan soon learns that some of

Lily's friends are pregnant, too: they've made a pact to become moms in high school, intentionally having unprotected sex. Naïve but determined, they yearn to raise their babies on their own, and to keep the fathers away for as long as possible. For Susan, the news threatens to destroy her career. Once a teen mom herself, she has launched high-profile campaigns to educate students about preventing unwanted pregnancy. Then Lily makes a frightening discovery about the baby she is carrying, and she and Susan begin to see their futures in a new way. Gripping and heartwarming, *Not* My *Daughter* will keep you enthralled on every page.

Questions and Topics for Discussion

1. What do the novel's opening pages tell you about Susan's relationship with her daughter? What advantages and disadvantages did Susan experience as a single parent? Would you have married Rick at age eighteen if you had been in her situation?

2. How does Susan's life compare to the lives of the other moms in the book: Kate, Sunny, and Pam? What do their daughters (Lily, Mary Kate, Jess, and Abby) have in common? Are there any similarities between the way the mothers interact and the girls' circle of friendship?

3. How did you react when Abby revealed why she had wanted to form a motherhood pact with her friends? What longings were they each hoping to satisfy by becoming pregnant? Were they seeking unconditional love, or rebellion against their parents, or something else altogether? How did their motivations change throughout the novel?

4. Though *Not My Daughter* is entirely a work of fiction, in the summer of 2008 media coverage erupted over a group of teenage girls in Gloucester, Massachusetts, who were alleged to have made a pact to become pregnant and raise their babies together. What does this say about the way our idea of motherhood has changed over generations? Do pregnancy and parenting mean something different to modern women, compared to our grandmothers' generation?

5. Jess's extended family is full of interesting contradictions. How was she shaped by Samson and Delilah, and by the ongoing friction between them and Sunny? Is Sunny right to think of Martha and Hank as "Normal with a capital *N*"? How does Jess define "normal," based on her family life?

6. The girls have unrealistic ideas about how much it costs to raise a child. Already living on a tight budget, Will and Kate are especially upset by the financial implications of Mary Kate's news. How does money affect parenting? Who are the best parents in the novel?

7. How did Rick and Susan's relationship change over time? Is Lily the only reason they stayed connected, or were there other constants that gave them an emotional attachment into adulthood?

8. How would you have responded to Lily if she had been your daughter? Would you have wanted her to have the baby? If so, would you have wanted her to give up the child for adoption? Would you offer to raise your children's children?

9. How is Lily transformed by the unsettling news of her fetus's CDH? Was she prepared for the ultimate parenting job

of managing a crisis and responding to events that are beyond her control?

10. Why does Lily resist Robbie? Is there a difference between girls' and boys' responsibilities when a teen pregnancy occurs? Should fully adult dads have more rights than teenage ones?

11. PC Wool represents a dream fulfilled for Susan. What do the colors, the creativity, and the camaraderie mean to her? If Perry & Cass is a metaphor for family, what kind of family is it? How was Abby affected by her parents' wealth, and the Perry legacy?

12. Discuss the relationship between Susan and her brother, Jackson. Why do he and Ellen have so much animosity toward her? How does Lily feel about family after she attends her grandfather's funeral? How does Susan's understanding of her mother change with the revelation that Big Rick and Ellen were once very close?

13. How did you respond to George Abbott's editorial in the Zaganack *Gazette*? Was Susan in any way responsible for Lily's pregnancy? Who is responsible for preventing teen pregnancy: schools? parents? the media? someone else? On some level, was Lily trying to embarrass her mother by letting history repeat itself?

14. Discuss the novel's title and the way it captures some parents' belief that their children are immune from peer pressure. How much do you trust your children? How much did your parents trust you?

15. How did the epilogue compare to the ending you had predicted? What did all children in the novel (adults and infants alike) teach their mothers?

16. What truths about the gifts of motherhood are illustrated in *Not My Daughter,* and in other novels by Barbara Delinsky? What is special about the way she portrays the bonds between parents and their children?

An excerpt from the forthcoming

ESCAPE

by Barbara Delinsky

Available from Doubleday

Chapter 1

⚜

HAVE YOU EVER WOKEN UP IN A COLD SWEAT, THINK-ing that you've taken a wrong turn and are stuck in a life you don't want? Did you ever consider hitting the brakes, backing up, and heading elsewhere?

How about disappearing—leaving family, friends, even a spouse—ditching everything you've known and starting over again. Reinventing yourself. Rediscovering yourself. Maybe, just maybe returning to an old lover. Have you ever dreamed about this?

No. Me, neither. No dream, no plan.

It was just another Friday. I awoke at 6:10 to the blare of the radio, and hit the button to silence it. I didn't need talk of politics to knot up my stomach, when the thought of going to work did that all on its own. It didn't help that my husband, already long gone, texted me at 6:15, knowing I'd have my BlackBerry with me in the bathroom.

Can't make dinner tonight. Sorry.

I was stunned. The dinner in question, which had been on

our calendar for weeks, involved senior partners at my firm. It was important that James be there with me.

OMG, I typed. *Why not?*

I received his reply seconds before stepping into the shower. *Gotta work late*, he said, and how could I argue? We were both lawyers, seven years out of law school. We had talked about working our tails off now to pay our dues, and I had been in total agreement at first. Lately, though, we saw little of each other, and it was getting worse. When I pointed this out to James, he got a helpless look in his eyes, like, *what could he do?*

I tried to relax under the hot spray, but I kept arguing aloud that there were things we could do if we wanted to be together—that love should trump work—that we had to make changes before we had kids, or what was the point—that my coyote dreams had begun when I started getting letters from Jude Bell, and though I stuffed those letters under the bed and out of sight, a tiny part of me knew they were there.

I had barely left the shower when my BlackBerry dinged again. No surprise. My boss, Walter Burbridge, always emailed at 6:30.

Client wants an update, he wrote. *Can you do it by ten?*

Here's a little background. I used to be an idealist. Starting law school, I had dreamed of defending innocent people against corporate wrongdoing and, by graduation, was itching to be involved in an honest-to-goodness class action lawsuit. Now I am. Only I'm the bad guy. The case on which I work involves a company that produces bottled water that was tainted enough to cause irreparable harm to a frightening number of people. The company has agreed to compensate the victims. My job is to determine how many, how sick, and how little we can get away with doling out, and I don't work alone. We are fifty lawyers, each with a cubicle, computer, and headset. I'm one of five supervisors, any of whom could have compiled an update, but because Walter likes women, he comes to me.

I'm thirty-two, stand five-six, weigh one-twenty. I spin sometimes, but mostly power walk and do yoga, so I'm in shape. My hair is auburn and long, my eyes brown, my skin clear.

We gave them an update Monday, I typed with my thumbs.

Get it to me by ten, he shot back.

Could I refuse? Of course not. I was grateful to have a job at a time when many of my law school friends were wandering the streets looking for work. I was looking, too, but there was nothing to be had, which meant that arguing with the partner-in-charge of a job I *did* have was not a wise thing to do.

Besides, I mused as I slipped on my watch, if I was to put together an update by ten, I had to make tracks.

My BlackBerry didn't cooperate. I was hurrying to finish my makeup when it began making noise. The wife of one of James's partners wanted the name of a pet sitter. I didn't have a pet, but could certainly ask a friend who did. Thinking that I would have had a dog or cat in a minute if our lifestyle allowed it, I was zipping on a pair of black slacks when another email arrived. *Why won't sharks attack lawyers?* said the subject line, and I instantly clicked DELETE. Lynn Fallon had been in my study group our first year in law school. She now worked with a small firm in Kansas, surely having a kinder, gentler experience than those of us in New York, and she loved lawyer jokes. I did not. I was feeling bad enough about what I did. Besides, when Lynn sent a joke, it went to dozens of people, and I didn't do group email.

Nor did I do anything but blue blouses, I realized in dismay as I stood at the closet. Blue blouses were professional, my lawyer side argued, but I was bored looking at them. Closing my eyes, I chose a blouse—any blouse—and was doing buttons when the BB dinged again.

Okay, Emily, wrote my sister. *You booked the restaurant, but you haven't done music, photography, or flowers. Why are you dragging your heels?*

Kelly, it is 7 am, I wrote back and tossed the BlackBerry on the bed. I turned on the radio, heard the word 'terrorism,' and turned it back off. I was brushing my hair back into a wide barrette when my sister's reply arrived.

Right, and in two minutes I have to get the kids dressed and fed, then do the same for me so I can get to work, which is why I'm counting on you for this. What's the problem?

This party is over the top, I typed back.

We agreed. You do the work, I pay.

Mom doesn't want this, I argued, but my sister was relentless.

Mom will love it. She only turns sixty once. I need help with this, Emily. I can't hear myself think when I get home from work. If you had kids you'd know.

It was a low blow. Kelly knew we were trying. She knew we had undergone tests and were doing the intensive-sex-at-ovulation routine. She didn't know that I'd gotten my period again this month, but I couldn't bear to write the words, and then—*ding, ding, ding*—my inbox began filling. It was 7:10. I had to get to work. Burying the BlackBerry in the depths of my purse so that I wouldn't hear the noise, I grabbed my coat and took off.

We lived in Gramercy Park in a condo we could barely afford, and though we didn't have a key to the park itself, we had passed Julia Roberts on the street a time or two. I saw nothing today—no Julia, no pretty brownstones, no promising June day—as I hurried to Fifth Avenue, sprinting the last half block to catch the bus as it pulled up at the curb.

I was at my desk at 7:45, and I wasn't the first. A low drone of voices already hovered over the cubicles. I awoke my computer and logged in, then logged in twice more at different levels of database security. Waiting for the final one, I checked my BlackBerry.

Are you going to yoga? asked the paralegal who worked two floors below me and hated going to yoga alone. I would be happy going alone, since it meant less chatter and more relaxation, which was the whole point of yoga. But if I had to go home to change before the firm dinner, yoga was out. *Not tonight*, I typed.

Colly wants Vegas, wrote a book group friend. Colleen Parker was getting married in September and, though I had only known her for the two years I'd been in the group, she had asked me to be a bridesmaid. I would be one of a dozen paying three hundred dollars each to wear matching dresses. And now a bachelorette party in Vegas? I was thinking the whole thing was tacky, when I spotted the next note.

Hey, Emily, wrote Ryan Mcfee. Ryan worked one cubicle down, two over. *Won't be in today. Have the flu. Don't want to spread it around.*

This should have been important. It meant one man-day of lost work. But what was one more or less in a huge cubicle room?

Logged in now, I set to gathering Walter's information. It was 7:50. By 8:25, I had a tally of the calls we'd received from last weekend's newspaper ads—and I could understand why our client was worried. The number of claimants was mounting fast. Each had been rated on a ten-point scale by the lawyer taking the call, with tens being the most severely affected and ones being the least. There were also zeroes; these were the easiest to handle. When callers tried to cash in on a settlement with proof neither of harm nor of having ever purchased the product, they stood out.

The others were the ones over which I agonized.

But statistics were impersonal and, in that, relatively painless. I updated the figures on how many follow-ups we had done since Monday, with a numerical breakdown and brief summaries of the claims. At 8:55, I emailed the spreadsheet to Walter, logged in the time I'd spent making it, shot a look at my watch and dashed downstairs for breakfast. Though I passed colleagues in the elevator, being competitors in the game of billable hours, we did little more than nod.

Going from the 35th floor to the ground and up again took time, so it wasn't until 9:10 that I was back at my desk with a donut and coffee. By then, the cubicles were filled, the tap of computer keys louder and the drone of voices more dense. I had barely washed down a bite of donut when the phone began to blink. Hooking the earpiece over my head, I logged in on my time sheet, pulled up a clear screen on my computer and clicked into the call.

"Lane Lavash," I answered as was protocol with calls coming in on the toll-free lines listed in our ads. "May I help you?"

There was silence, then a timid, "I don't know. I got this number from the paper."

Frauds were confident. This woman sounded young and unsure. "Which paper?" I asked gently.

"The, uh, the *Telegram*. In Portland. Maine."

"Do you live in Portland?" I readied my fingers to enter this information.

"No. I was there with my brother last weekend and saw the ad. I live in Massachusetts."

I dropped my hands. Massachusetts was prime Eagle River distribution area. We'd received calls from as far away as Oregon, from people who had been vacationing in New England during the time the tainted water was on sale. Strict documentation of travel was required for these claims, well before we looked at documentation of physical harm.

I cupped my hands in my lap. "Do you have cause for a claim against Eagle River?"

Her voice remained hesitant. "My husband says no. He says that these things just happen."

"What things?"

"Miscarriages."

I hung my head. This was not what I wanted to hear, but the din of voices around me said that if not this woman, someone else would be getting pieces of the Eagle River settlement. Miscarriage was definitely one of the "harms" on our list.

"Have you had one?" I asked.

"Two."

I entered that in the form on my screen, and, when the words didn't appear, retyped them, but the form remained blank. Knowing that I wouldn't forget this, and not wanting to lose the momentum of the call, I asked, "Recently?"

"The first one was a year-and-a-half ago."

My heart sank. "Had you been drinking Eagle River water?" Of course, she had.

"Yes."

"Can you document that?" I asked in a kind voice, though I felt cold and mean.

"Y'mean, like, do I have a receipt? See, that's one of the reasons my husband didn't want me to call. I pay cash, and I don't *have* receipts. My husband says I should've made a connection between the water and the miscarriage back then, but, like, bottled water is always safe, right? Besides, we were just married and there was other stuff going on, and I figured I was miscarrying because it wasn't the right time for me to be pregnant." Her voice shrank. "Now it is, only they say there's something wrong with the baby."

My mind filled with static. I tried to remember the company

line. "The Eagle River recall was eighteen months ago. The water has been clean since then. It wouldn't harm your baby."

I heard a meek half-cry. "The thing is, we try to buy in bulk because it's cheaper that way. So we had a couple of twenty-fours in the basement and kind of forgot about them. Then I got pregnant, and my husband lost his job, and money was really tight, so I saw the water and thought I was doing good by using what we had instead of buying fresh. I didn't know about the recall."

"It was in all the newspapers."

I don't read newspapers, the ensuing silence said. "Newspapers cost money."

"So does bottled water."

"But the water from the tap tastes so *bad*. We thought of putting a filter on, but that costs more than the bottled water, and it's not like we own this place."

"Maybe your tap water is tainted," I said, playing to script. "Have you asked your landlord to test it?"

"No, because my husband drinks it, and he's healthy. I'm the only one with the problem, and I only drink bottled water. I noticed your newspaper ad, because I always drink Eagle River." Her voice was a whispered wail. "They say the baby won't be right, and my husband wants to get rid of it, and I have to make a decision, and I don't know what to do. This *sucks*."

It did suck. *All* of it.

"I don't know what to do," she repeated, and I realized she wanted my advice, but how could I give that? I was the enemy, an agent for the company whose product had caused a deformity in her child. She should have been yelling at me, calling me the most cold-hearted person in the world. Some of them did. There had been the man whose seamstress wife had developed tremors in her hands and was permanently disabled. Or the woman whose husband had died—and yes, he had a pre-existing medical condition, but he would have lived longer if he hadn't drunk tainted water.

The names they called me weren't pretty, and though I told myself not to take it personally, I did. Thinking that this job *definitely* sucked, I swiveled sideways and lowered my eyes. "I'm Emily. What's your name?"

"Layla," she said. I didn't try to enter it on my form. Nor did I ask for a last name. This had become a personal discussion.

"Have you talked with your doctor about options?"

"There are only two," she said, sounding frightened. I guessed her to be in her early twenties. "My mother says I shouldn't kill my baby. She says God chose me to protect an imperfect child, but she isn't the one who'll be paying medical bills or maybe losing a husband because of it." *Losing a husband* . . . not on the formal list of "harms" but a plausible side effect, one that had to resonate with any married woman in this room.

Or maybe not. We didn't talk about this—didn't talk about much of anything, because we were being paid by the hour to do our work, and time sheets would only allow for a lapse or two. What I was doing now was against the rules. I was supposed to stick to business and limit the time of each call. But Layla was talking quickly, going on about the bills that were piling up, and I couldn't cut her off. Somewhere in the middle of it, she said, "You're a good person, I can tell by your voice, so my husband was wrong when he said I'd be talking to a robot. He also said we'd have to sign away our lives if we got money for this. Would we?"

I was stuck on *good person*, echoing so loudly through my fraudulent soul that I had to consciously refocus at the end. "No, Layla. You'd have to sign a release saying that you won't further sue Eagle River, its parent company or distributors, but that's it."

She was silent for a beat. "Are you married?"

"Yes."

"With kids?"

"Some day." I was on the clock, but I couldn't return to the claim form.

"I'm desperate for them," Layla said in her very young voice. "I mean, you work for a law firm. I work in a hardware store. Kids would give my life meaning, y'know?"

"Absolutely," I replied just as a sharp voice broke in.

"What's happening here, Emily," Walter asked. "No one's working."

I swiveled toward him, then rose from my chair enough to see over the cubicle tops. Sure enough, our team stood in scattered clusters, most looking now at Walter and me.

"Computers are down," called one. "Forms are frozen."

Walter eyed me. "Did you report this?"

I pushed my mouthpiece away. "I hadn't realized there was a problem. I'm working with a claimant." Adjusting the mouthpiece, I returned to Layla. "There's a technical glitch here. Can I call you back in a few?"

"You won't," she said, defeated. "And anyway, I don't know if I should do this."

"You should," I advised, confident that Walter wouldn't know what I was saying.

She gave me her number. I wrote it on a Post-It and ended the call.

"He should what?" Walter asked.

"Wait half an hour before going out, so that I can call her back." I buzzed our technology department.

"Are you *encouraging* people to file claims?" Walter asked.

"No. I'm listening. She's in pain. She needs someone to hear what she's saying."

"Your job is to document everyone who calls and tell them

what medical forms we'll need if they want a piece of the pie. That's it, Emily. You're not being paid to be a shrink."

"I'm trying to sort through claims so that we know which are legit and which aren't. This is one way to do it." When I heard a familiar voice in my headset, I said, "Hey, Todd, it's Emily. We're having trouble up here."

"Already on it." He clicked off.

I relayed the message to Walter, who wasn't mollified. "How long 'til we're running again?"

It was 9:40. I figured we'd lost ten minutes, fifteen max. "Todd is fast."

Walter leaned closer. A natty dresser, he never looked ruffled. The only things that ever gave him away were his gray eyes and his voice. Those eyes were rocky now, the voice low and taut. "I'm under pressure, Emily. We were named to manage this settlement only after I personally assured the judge that we could do it quickly and economically. I can't afford to have my lawyers wasting time holding hands. I'm counting on you to set an example; this is important for your career. Get the facts. That's it." With a warning look, he left.

I should have been chastised, but all I could think was that if anyone was wasting time, it was the people who called us hoping for help. They wouldn't get what they deserved; the system was designed to minimize reward. Besides, how did you price out a damaged baby, a ruined life?

I was telling myself not to be discouraged—to keep avoiding wine and caffeine and always wash my prenatal vitamins down with *good* water—when a crescendoing hum came, spreading from cubicle to cubicle as the computers returned to life. I should have been relieved, but, to my horror, my eyes filled with tears. Needing a distraction, even something as frivolous as Vegas talk from Colly's friends, I turned when my

BlackBerry dinged. It was James. Maybe coming tonight? I wondered with a quick burst of hope.

Just got a brilliant idea, he wrote and, for a final minute, still, I believed. *The dinner Sunday night?* That was *his* firm dinner. *I want you to do it up big—new dress, hair, nails, the works. I have to work tomorrow anyway.* That would be Saturday, the one day we usually managed a few hours together. *A couple of favors? Pick up my navy suit and my shirts. And my prescription. And get cash for the week. Thanks, babe. You're the best.*

I scrolled on, thinking there had to be more, because if that was all, I would be livid.

But that was it. *Thanks, babe. You're the best.*

Keyboards clicked, voices hummed, electronics dinged, jangled, and chimed, and still, as I stared at the words, I heard James's voice. *I want you to do it up big—new dress, hair, nails, the works.* Like I needed his permission for this?

Suddenly it all backed up in my throat like too much bad food—bad marriage, bad work, bad family, friends, feelings— and I couldn't swallow. Needing air, I grabbed my purse and, as an afterthought, the Post-It with Layla's name and number.

Tessa Reid was as close as I came to having a friend in the firm, which was as sad a statement as any. We never socialized outside work. I did know that she had two kids and two school loans, and that she shared my revulsion for what we did. I saw it in her eyes when she arrived at work, the same look of dread reflected in my own mirror each day.

She lived three cubicles to the right of mine. Ducking in there now, I touched her shoulder. Her earpiece was active, her hands typing. One look at my face, and she put her caller on hold.

"Do me a huge favor, Tessa?" I whispered, not for privacy because, Lord knew, my voice wouldn't carry over the background din, but because that was all the air I could find. I pressed the Post-It to her desk. "Call this claimant for me? We were talking when the system went down. She's valid." I was banking on that, perhaps with a last gasp of idealism. For sure, though, Tessa was the only one in the room whom I could trust to find out.

She was studying me in concern. "What's wrong?"

"I need air. Do this for me?"

"Of course. Where are you going?"

"Out," I whispered and left.

A gaggle of clicks, dings, and murmurs followed me, lingering like smog even when the elevator closed. I made the descent in a back corner, eyes downcast, arms hugging my waist. Given the noise in my head, if anyone had spoken, I mightn't have heard, which was just as well. What could I have said if, say, Walter Burbridge had stepped in? *Where are you going?* I don't know. *When'll you be back?* I don't know. *What's wrong with you?* I don't know.

The last would have been a lie, but how to explain what I was feeling when the tentacles were all tangled up? I might have said that it went beyond work, that it covered my entire life, that it had been building for months and had nothing to do with impulse. Only it did. Survival was an impulse. I had repressed it for so long that it was weak, but it must have been beating somewhere in me, because when the elevator opened, I walked out.

Even at 9:57, Fifth Avenue buzzed. Though I had never minded before, now the sound grated. I turned right for the bus and stood for an excruciating minute in traffic exhaust, before giving up and fleeing on foot, but pedestrian traffic was heavy, too. I walked quickly, dodging others, dashing to make it over the cross street before a light changed. When I accidentally jostled a woman, I turned with an apology, but she had continued on without looking back.

I had loved the crowds when I first came here. They made me feel part of something big and important. Now I felt part of nothing. If I wasn't at work, others would be. If I bumped into people, they walked on.

So that's what I did—just walked on, block after block. I passed a hot dog stand but smelled only exhaust fumes from a bus. My watch read 10:21, then 10:34, then 10:50. If my legs grew tired, I didn't notice. The choking feeling had passed, but I felt little relief. My thoughts were in turmoil, barely touched by the blare of a horn or the rattle of the tailgate of a truck at the curb.

Nearing our neighborhood, I stopped for my husband's suit and shirts, and picked up his prescription, then entered the tiny branch office of our bank. The teller knew me. But this was New York. If she wondered why I cashed more money than usual, she didn't ask.

The bank clock stood at 11:02 when I hit the air again. Three minutes later, I turned down the street where we lived and, for a hysterical second, wondered which brownstone was ours. Through my disenchanted eyes, they all looked the same. But no; one had a brown door, another a gray one; and there was my windowbox, in which primrose and sweet peas were struggling to survive.

Running up the steps, I let myself in, emptied my arms just inside, and dashed straight up the next flight and into the bedroom. I pulled my bag from the closet floor, but paused only when I set it on the bed. What to bring? That depended on where I was going, and I didn't have a clue.

ALSO BY BARBARA DELINSKY

FAMILY TREE

For as long as she can remember, Dana Clarke has longed for the stability of home and family. Now she has married a man she adores, whose heritage can be traced back to the *Mayflower*, and she is about to give birth to their first child. But what should be the happiest day of her life becomes the day her world falls apart. Her daughter is born beautiful and healthy, and, in addition, unmistakably African-American in appearance. Dana's determination to discover the truth about her baby's heritage becomes a shocking, poignant journey.

Fiction

THE SECRET BETWEEN US

Deborah Monroe and her daughter, Grace, are driving home from a party when their car hits a man running in the dark. Grace was at the wheel, but Deborah sends her home before the police arrive, determined to shoulder the blame for the accident. Her decision then turns into a deception that takes on a life of its own and threatens the special bond between mother and daughter. *The Secret Between Us* is an unforgettable story about making bad choices for the right reasons and the terrible consequences of a lie gone wrong.

Fiction

WHILE MY SISTER SLEEPS

Molly and Robin Snow are sisters in the prime of life. So when Molly receives the news that Robin has suffered a massive heart attack, the news couldn't be more shocking. At the hospital, the Snow family receives a grim prognosis: Robin may never regain consciousness. Feelings of guilt and jealousy flare up as Robin's family struggles to cope. It's up to Molly to make the tough decisions, and she soon makes discoveries that shatter some of her most cherished beliefs about the sister she thought she knew.

Fiction

ANCHOR BOOKS
Available wherever books are sold.
www.randomhouse.com